MW01199804

THE BILLIONAIRE

Edited by Beth of VB Edits
Cover illustration by Chloe Quinn at quinnasaurus.com
Cover design by The Book Brander
Dedication art by @jacqueillustrates
www.oliviahayle.com

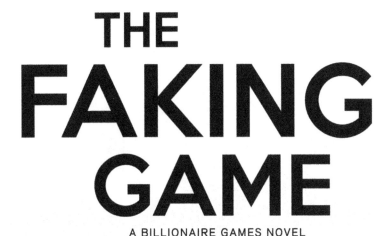

THE
FAKING
GAME

A BILLIONAIRE GAMES NOVEL

OLIVIA HAYLE

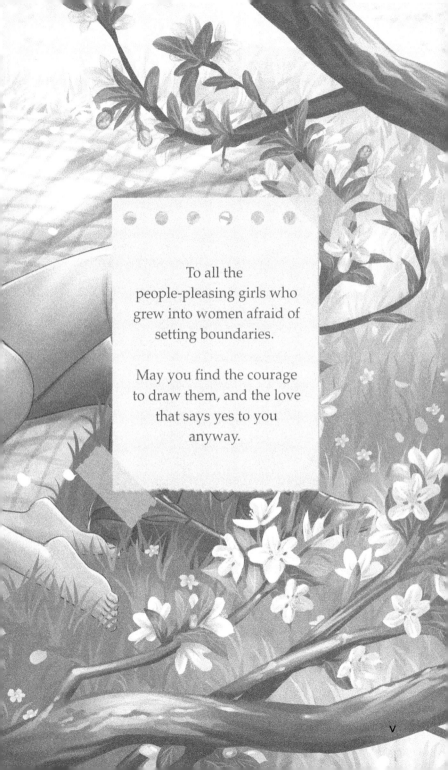

To all the
people-pleasing girls who
grew into women afraid of
setting boundaries.

May you find the courage
to draw them, and the love
that says yes to you
anyway.

CHAPTER 1
NORA

The best part about going to a nightclub is when you finally get to leave.

I've been inside the heart-pounding place for less than an hour, and it's still been thirty minutes too long. Pulsing neon lights slice through the darkness, painting the writhing bodies in rainbows of color. I can barely hear Poppy talk beside me.

I texted her yesterday after I finished unpacking in my New York rental and asked if she wanted to meet up. We met through modeling, and maybe we could be friends. I've wanted some here in my new city.

This is where she wanted to go. The VIP booth in an upscale club with seven other model friends.

"...right? Wouldn't that be so much fun?" she screams into my ear.

I nod and smile, like I understood what she said. I hoped for dinner tonight, maybe drinks. A place where we could actually talk. Another woman, blonde and the tallest of the group, leans across the table. "Another round?" she shouts, holding up an empty champagne bottle.

The others cheer, and a friendly androgynous model I've worked with a few times holds an empty glass up high. Also in the booth are two men who seem to be paying for all of it. They're probably in their thirties or forties, with flashy credit cards and arrogant smiles.

I don't really know their names. Chad and... Dean, I think. Or something. The short one with the spiky haircut screamed it into my ear earlier, his hand on my low back.

I smiled and wriggled away.

Poppy grabs my arm, pulling me close. "Isn't this amazing?" she gushes. "I'm so glad you're back in the city!"

"Yeah, I'm glad to be back!" I tell her.

She smiles and turns back to listen to something Dean says. Or Chad.

Poppy is nice. Or so I always thought when we were shot together for campaigns or walked the same fashion shows. That's why I reached out again. It felt like we'd had fun together; real fun. Not the fake kind of fun when people want to get close to me for my last name.

I glance at my watch. It's only been eight minutes since I last checked. Way too soon to suggest an after-party somewhere quieter. I have hours of this left if I choose to stay. I should stay, really. See if I can make friends here.

Poppy leans in closer and looks down at my wrist. "Is that an Artemis?" she half-screams.

"Yeah," I say with a nod.

Her fingers brush the platinum watch. It's the brand my family has produced for almost a century. It even has a tiny Swiss flag inlaid on the back to show that production remains in the valley my grandfather was born in.

"Wow. You must have, like, your pick of all of them." Her fingers drift off my wrist, and she grins again. "Will you be modeling any of your family's brands this season?"

I shrug. "Some of them, yeah, but I'm not really here to model."

"What?"

I lean in closer. "I'm not back in the city for modeling!"

Her perfectly plucked eyebrows shoot up. "Then why are you here?"

"I'm designing my own fashion line," I say. I'll take part in the Fashion Showcase a few months from now, competing alongside twelve other anonymous designers.

Her expression shifts, a mix of surprise and something else I can't quite read. "Oh, wow. That's... different. Why don't you wanna model anymore?" She leans in closer. "You could be a top model, you know. With your connections."

I reach for my near-empty glass. "I like modeling, I do, but I want to try something else."

Poppy nods, but I can tell she's not really listening anymore. She turns back to the others and shifts her shoulders in tune with the music. Damn it. Modeling is still her job, even if I hate it. Maybe I shouldn't have said anything.

Next time I'll try harder.

I drain the last of my drink. The table is stuffed far back in the corner of the VIP section, under a dark ceiling and in full view of everyone on the dance floor. I need to move for a bit.

I push off the couch and head over to the bar.

Maybe I'll use the restroom too.

Maybe I'll just leave and go back to my new apartment.

I'm a few steps shy of the bar when I feel the hand on my lower back again. Shit. It's Chad or Dean. He's leaning close. So close, in fact, that I can smell the mixture of cologne and sweat.

"Hey," he says in my ear. His breath washes over my skin, and I shudder. Ugh. "Where are you sneaking off to?"

Maybe other women find this charming. Maybe it's wrong that I can't. I twist, and his hand falls off my body. "Just getting more to drink."

His eyes are glazed. Has he taken something? How does Poppy know these guys? "I'll buy you a drink!" He's screaming, but the words barely reach me over the pounding music.

He leans in closer, his hand now searching again. It lands on my hip. "What was your name again?"

"Eléanore!" I scream.

He grins. "I love that name! It's actually my favorite name."

God help me. "Really?" Why is the line for the bar moving so slowly? I try to take a step away, but he follows along, like we're dancing.

"You're a model too, right?"

"Yes. But I don't model a lot anymore." Or that's the goal, even if it's hard to say no when my modeling agent calls. She works for my family's company, and for my older brother, and it seems like they want me to be the face of something all the time.

He nods, two quick dips that make it seem like he didn't really hear a word I said. "Yeah, yeah. You know what, it's loud in here. I live close by! In Tribeca!"

Shit. I hate when guys do this, and I'm already finding the words to say no. Blame it on a headache. I have plans. There's a water leak in my apartment... I want to stay here. Turning guys down is the one thing I'm really, really good at.

It's all I've ever done.

He leans in even closer, and oh *god*. There are people behind me, around me, and then him. Blocking me in.

Clubbing used to be fun, once. Now it's filled with cramped VIP spaces and expectations.

"Back off." The words are deep, audible over the sound of the speakers. A man has pushed his way between me and Chad, his broad shoulder half hiding the other man from view.

My stomach drops. I recognize that voice.

"I'm sorry!" Chad yells. "Is she with you?"

The man turns and looks down at me. I haven't seen him in almost six months. I've tried not to think of him, the way I always do, this man my brother calls his best friend. He has a legacy that rivals my own. He was once the famed Calloway heir, but after his father died, he took over all of it.

The estates, the company, the power.

West looks at me with narrowed eyes. His dark brows are pulled down low, that scar cutting through the one on the left. I've always wondered how he got it.

"Yes. She is," he says. "And she's leaving."

Chad melts away. Disappears back into the crowd in a way that West can't, not with his height and build.

"What are you doing here?" I ask him, even if I know. If I suspect.

He leans closer. Right. *The music.* I stand on my tiptoes, getting closer to him than I ever have before. "What are you doing here? Did Rafe send you?"

"He didn't have to," West says in a clipped voice. "Come. We're leaving."

"I don't want to leave," I say. Even if my feet ache, I'm tired, and I can't wait to get some fresh air. There's only one reason he's here. Rafe *did* send him to babysit me.

West's hand closes around my elbow. "We're leaving," he says, and the crowd I battled with only moments ago parts for him. Lets us through. I follow him, and damn it, each step that leads us to the door allows me to breathe a bit easier.

We emerge out onto the busy New York street. People are lining up to enter the club, and we pass them all, straight to the large black vehicle idling at the curb.

"What were you *thinking*?" West's voice is frustrated as he releases my elbow. "You didn't bring the security I assigned."

"I don't want guards following me around."

His handsome face hardens, turns into an angry mask. I wrap my arms around myself. It's late April, but the evening air is not nearly warm enough for the thin dress I'm in. It's one of my newest designs.

"Why not?" he demands. "They reported to me an hour ago, saying that you left using the back door of your apartment building without informing them of where you were going."

"It's none of their business, and it's *definitely* none of yours."

"It is mine. Your brother made it mine." His eyes narrow. "And *you* made it mine when you moved to New York."

"I'm here to work, not to be monitored." I left that behind in Europe.

West stills. It's a scary stillness, his whiskey-colored eyes narrowing. Judging from his suit, he was probably out somewhere when he got the call about me. Did I interrupt him? Ruin his evening?

"Correct me if I'm wrong," he says, "which I won't be, but you've been receiving threats for the last four months. Letters, texts, messages and, most recently, photos that make it *very* clear that someone is stalking you. Rafe organized a private security detail for you back in Paris. Now that you're here, the task has fallen to me. And yet you *thought* it was a good idea"—he leans in closer—"to go to a club in the middle of the night without protection?"

"I was surrounded by people. I was in public the whole time."

"Yes. Strangers."

"I can take care of myself," I say.

He laughs. It's a short, humorless sound. "Clearly. That's why I had to rescue you from that drunk idiot pawing at you."

"I didn't ask for your help," I snap. "Those security guards should not report to you directly."

"Of course they should. I'm the one who's been asked to take care of you."

"I may be Rafe's little sister, but I'm not a child."

His jaw clenches. "No, you're not. Not anymore. You need to take this seriously."

"I just wanted a normal night out," I say, and how dare

he? I am taking this seriously. I've been taking it seriously every single day since the weird messages started. But I'm in a new city and hoping so badly that I've left all of that behind. I just wanted to make a friend.

The wind picks up, lifting my brown hair.

West's gaze drops to where goose bumps race across my arms. His face sets in even harder lines, and he shrugs off his suit jacket. "Here," he says, draping it over my shoulders.

"Thank you." I hate that it's warm. I hate that it smells good even more.

He nods toward the car. "Let's go. I'm taking you home."

I hesitate, clutching his jacket tighter around me. "I can get a cab. You don't have to—"

West sighs. "Get in the car."

"*Fine*." I step past him, my heart beating fast. I can't handle conflict. Never have. But he has always seemed to bring it out in me. I get snappier around him than I do with anyone else.

I slide into the back seat of the sleek black SUV. West moves like there's gravity to him, rearranging the world around him with every stride. Shifting my own course for the night.

He's always been larger than life.

His last name is a household name in this country, not to mention many others. One of the classics from the Gilded Age. The Astors. The Vanderbilts. And the Calloways. One of the few whose company is still intact and their manor family-owned.

He's the heir to a legacy too large to contemplate. I bet the arrogance is part of it. Handed down from father to son in the Calloway line. Rulers of their own little kingdoms.

"Don't do that again," he says in the darkness of the car. I close my eyes and rest my head against the headrest. His voice is deep and soothing.

But he's saying things I've heard so many times.

Do this. Do that. Stand here. Say this.

Be a good girl. Be a good sister. Take care of your younger siblings. *We have eyes on us.* Smile more, smile less, arch your back.

"You're not my brother," I tell him in the darkness.

"No, I'm sure as fuck not," West mutters. His profile is a dark outline against the city flashing by outside the car window. The sharp jaw is another thing he's inherited. It shouldn't be legal to move the way he does, and also look that damn good doing it.

"I appreciate the security guards," I say. "Truly. But I don't think I'll need a lot of protection, and I'll be very careful. I promise. So thank you, West, but no thanks."

He looks at me in the dim lighting of the car. "Very nice," he says, "but that's not up to you. Tomorrow, you won't go anywhere without them."

•

CHAPTER 2
WEST

Nora Montclair is my best friend's little sister.

And considering Rafe is basically a brother to me, that should make her like my sister. The problem is that the word *should* has never really worked the way it's meant to where Nora's concerned.

She's a problem for me. Always has been. From the moment I first met her, years ago, when she walked into the Montclairs' chalet with a smile on her face and her sketchbook tucked under her arm. Her hair deep brown and glossy, her eyes intelligent, her mouth smiling. Five years younger than Rafe and me, sheltered and lovely.

Only a few inches shorter than me and with a face for billboards and ads.

Now she's a very *immediate* problem. Some godforsaken idiot has decided that he's obsessed with her in an unhealthy way, and Rafe has filled me in about the stalker his security firm has failed to find. How it's escalated from social media comments, to direct emails, to the first letter arriving at her apartment.

She moved to New York to pursue a design opportunity,

and while Raphaël has a great security team trained for his European properties, I know this city.

It'll be fine. Perfectly *fine*.

It'll just mean interacting with her for weeks on end. Monitoring her position and her safety and being on standby for the security team. Nothing can happen to her on my watch.

Exactly how I'd feel if it was my own sister.

Even if the annoyance I felt last night, shoving away the man who was leaning in when she wanted to lean away, teetered on the edge of something else. Something I can't afford, can't indulge in, can't think too hard about.

I'd last seen her at a party Raphaël threw months ago. She looked pretty in a blue dress, with impeccable manners and a smile that looked natural but I often suspected was anything but.

She's always had impeccable manners with everyone *but* me.

Like last night, in a silky black dress and dark eyeliner, arguing with me every step of the way.

I run my hand through my hair and ignore the stares a few of my employees send my way. I'm not usually at Calloway Holdings in downtown Manhattan, but I'm here today, and they're noticing.

For some reason, I annoy her. Have for years.

But I promised Raphaël personally that I could guarantee her safety. Because Rafe is family. Has been since we lived at Belmont Academy together as maladjusted teenage boys with too much free time and no parental supervision.

Someone from the executive team stops me; I told her that I wanted to be informed when the latest financials arrived. *Do I have time now?*

I say yes, even if time is the last thing I have.

This old building has been Calloway Holdings' headquarters since the thirties, after my great-grandfather made money hand over fist in the steel business. Rumor has it he bought this old stone building during the depression for pennies on the dollar. Ruthless.

Then again, that was him. *The Maverick.* There have been two biographies released about him just in the past five years; I've read neither. Having a portrait of him in my own dining room has cured me of any curiosity. I see his stare often enough. I know what I have to live up to.

And after he fucked me over, there's no love lost between me and my ancestor. He was the one who established the trust for Fairhaven Estate on Long Island, the place I call home. I can inherit the business, but the house? Only if I'm married by the time I turn thirty. Which is at the end of the summer.

Time is running out, and now Nora is my problem too. My frustrating, too-pretty and decidedly unsafe problem.

I listen to what my financial officer is saying but only hear half of the words.

After thanking Allison for the financial brief, I head to the elevators. A glance at my watch shows that I'm cutting it close to my next meeting, and I hate being late.

There's a text from Rafe.

RAFE

How's the first full day been?

I hesitate only a second before I type back a response.

WEST

Fine. Everything's under control.

He doesn't need to know that the very first night with her under my protection was a failure. Nora's eyes flashed defiance on the sidewalk, and it sparked my own irritation. But then there was a tremble in her voice when she insisted she could take care of herself.

I've always had that sense with her, that there's one side she shows to others and another she keeps leashed tightly.

Raphaël texts again.

RAFE

Thanks. I owe you one.

That makes my teeth grind. He really, *really* doesn't. Not when he let my own sister use his Paris apartment last summer. Not when he kept me sane through boarding school. Not when he's just asking for a favor in return. And what's a favor between brothers?

We're family, after all. In every way but blood.

Which means that Nora should be like my little sister.

The meeting drags on. Numbers and projections for the different holdings, all packaged together with clear recommendations for the upcoming quarters. We break in the late afternoon, and I see two missed calls from my head of security.

Shit. I'm instantly on high alert. Her eyes flash in front of me again, and I hear that wobble in her voice. If someone has frightened her…

I excuse myself and call him back. "Report."

"The target is fine. But she disappeared for a while," Arthur says. His tone is short, no-nonsense. "She went for a run in Central Park. We maintained visual contact, but she gave us the slip. It took us fifteen minutes to locate her again. My guys are following her back to her apartment now."

"What do you mean, gave you the slip?"

"She ran fast, sir. I had two of my more experienced guys following her, but we were unprepared for… quite how fast she ran. I believe it was at least partially intentional. I'll get some of my faster guys for next time. Won't happen again."

"Shit," I mutter. "And you're certain you have eyes on her now?"

"Yes, sir. She's heading back to her apartment building. Should be there in about twenty minutes."

"Keep me updated."

I make my excuses to the board members and leave the office. The quickest option is to grab a cab, and I'm soon on my way through traffic to Nora's.

I haven't been in a relationship in years. There's no time. But Nora's been in New York for less than two days, and I already feel like I'm following someone around. Trying to coordinate two schedules.

The car pulls to a stop outside of her apartment building. Raphaël sent me the details, and I know my team has scoped out the place. But there are a lot of unknown factors. Neighbors. Multiple entries and exits. Views in through her windows.

One of my security guards waits inside. "Floor eight," Madison tells me. "She's in."

Another guard stands in the hallway outside her apartment. His name is Jason, and he's a new one on the team. His cheeks are flushed with color. Did he have to keep up with her running?

How fast is she, anyway?

I knock on her door. It takes a good while before I hear the lock turn and the door opens.

Nora is in her workout clothes. Her deep-brown hair is in a ponytail, her slim chin turned up as she looks at me. Her fair skin is flushed, too, and it makes her look—

I shouldn't notice. *Practically* my own sister.

"Nora," I say.

"West." She peers out past me, at the security guard. "Hey, are you sure you don't want a glass of water?"

He shakes his head. "Thank you, miss. I'm fine."

"Just knock if you change your mind." Her smile fades when she turns to look at me, but she opens her door fully to let me in. "Would you like that glass of water, maybe?"

"No, I wouldn't." Her apartment is spacious and modern, with floor-to-ceiling windows offering a stunning view of the city. Tasteful artwork adorns the walls, and sleek furniture fills the open-concept living area. It's nice, in that short-term rental kind of way. "I heard you went for a run."

"So that's why you're here." Nora leans against the back of a couch. She's in a pair of black tights that hug the length of her toned legs. "Yes, I did. And I brought my security guards. I don't think I did anything wrong."

"You promised you wouldn't run from them again."

"I didn't run from them," she protests. Then she throws up a hand. "Well, technically, yes, I did, but they were running after me. I don't think it's my fault if they can't keep up."

I walk past her to the windows. There's a clear view here from the apartment opposite, even with the street between them. "You have to adapt or adjust your routines. Do you draw your curtains in the evening?"

"Yes. Your guys have already been here and checked everything." Her crossed arms push her tits up, and she's in some tight, black shirt. The sight makes my teeth grind together. *Should* be like a sister.

But she's not. I've never been able to see her that way.

"I know they have."

"Don't you trust them?"

"I trust myself more." I walk into the bedroom and give it a quick once-over.

The room is as tastefully decorated as the rest of the apartment, with a large bed dominating the space. Only one window here, and it's above the courtyard. It's a good thing she's high up.

"This is a bit invasive, don't you think?" Nora remarks behind me. "What are you even looking for?"

My eyes snag on a tank top draped over the back of a chair in the corner. A black bra hangs beside it.

"Your brother trusted me," I say. "I'm being thorough."

"Want to go through my dresser?" she asks acidly. "Open my drawers? Look at my calendar? I've already shared all of that with the security team. A team of mostly men, I should add, whom I don't know. And now they're outside my door twenty-four seven."

Her chin is turned up, her green eyes meeting mine. The makeup from the other night is gone, and it makes her look softer. Younger. There are freckles dotting her nose and her lips are pressed together in a tight line.

She's finding this tough. Genuinely tough.

I cross my arms over my chest. "Have they introduced themselves to you? My security team."

"Yes," she says. "After I asked."

"Has anyone made you feel unsafe?"

"No," she says. But she runs a hand over the back of her neck. "I hate needing them."

"Yeah, I get that. Rafe had a team for you as well, right? Before you came here."

"Yes. I became good friends with some of them." She takes a deep breath. "I don't think the stalker will follow me to New York."

She says *don't think*, but I hear the word she's not saying. Hope. She hopes that's the case. I study her for another quiet beat. "You have my number. I sent it to you. You'll use it if you feel unsafe. Doesn't matter the reason."

She nods, and some of the vulnerability leaves her face. "So you can come charging in and complain about babysitting like you did last night?"

"I take my job seriously."

"Take it a little *less* seriously," she says.

That makes my lips twitch. "Do you have anything against me that I don't know about? Did I break a family heirloom? Accidentally run over a pet of yours?"

She rolls her eyes. "None of the above, thank you very

much. I'm twenty-four. I can take care of myself, and I know how to live with guards. I've already done it."

"Did you run from them, too, and give your brother a heart attack?"

Nora smiles sweetly. "You're in great shape and in the prime of your life. Your heart can take it."

"A compliment? I should come inspect your apartment more often."

She walks toward her front door. "You've already seen my bedroom once. Won't happen again."

Well, she's damn right about that. I have no business getting closer to her than is absolutely necessary. I head to the door. Nora watches me, her eyes still just as defiant.

"I won't stop going for runs," she says.

"I'll get you faster guards."

CHAPTER 3
NORA

West Calloway has never liked me.

I know this for a few distinct reasons. First of all, he is the only one of my brother's friends who never smiles at me. Even James, quiet and serious, has done that. But never West.

Second, I once came on to him, and he turned me down.

It was at a Christmas party my father threw. Rafe was there, and he brought all his friends along. It was right before New Year's, and they were headed off to the alps the day after to ski. Rafe, James, Alexander... and West.

I'd just turned nineteen. I had a bit too much champagne, and I gathered up my courage just before the clock struck midnight.

He was there alone, standing by the chateau's large fireplace, a glass of brandy in his hand, and I walked up to him. Smoothed a hand over my hair to double-check that it was in place... and I suggested we grab a drink together.

He looked me over once, and then his gaze landed on my face. There was nothing but dismissal in it. "You're drunk, Nora. Go to bed."

Mortifying. I'd never initiated anything with a man before, but I did with him that night, and it was an idiotic idea. I walked away without saying a word, tears pricking in my eyes.

The humiliation didn't stop there. A year later, I overheard him tell Alex that I'm pretty enough, but boring, and the last person he would ever date.

Since then, West has barely acknowledged my existence. We haven't been in the same room often, but every time, he looks through me like I'm not there.

Their other friends aren't like that. Alexander jokes around with me every chance he gets; James is terrifying but civil. Not West. And I've seen him laugh with others.

So I know it's personal. It's *me* he doesn't like.

And because I don't like being disliked, I've made a point of *not* liking him back. He's arrogant. He's competitive. He thinks he's better than everyone else. The way he carries himself, like he owns every room he's in.

That kind of confidence borders on conceit.

The times we've been around one another since then, it's become a hobby to catalog all the reasons he's not a great person. The way he smiles, rarely and crookedly. That he's never completely clean-shaven.

His clothes always look like an afterthought, yet still fit him perfectly. Thick cable-knit sweaters and loafers. His thick brown hair pushed back, that scar through his eyebrow that he's had for as long as I've known him. Where my brother likes looking expensive, West looks like he's always ready to play some kind of sport.

He probably doesn't even think twice about what he wears and is still the most eye-catching man in the room. It's infuriating.

He makes me feel small, young and insignificant. Like I'm still the girl by the fireplace, asking my older brother's best friend if he'd like to have a drink with me and being told off.

And now he's somehow decided that it's his job to keep me safe here, in one of the world's largest cities. Rafe told me he would be hands-off. He assured me that West would just oversee the security detail.

Right. Because looking into my bedroom is so very *hands-off*.

The next morning, I walk to the atelier space I'm renting two blocks away, carrying the giant bag of fabrics I've already sourced.

There are two men trailing me, dressed in jeans and navy jackets, courtesy of West. One has a backward baseball cap over his auburn curls. I spoke to them earlier. Sam and Miguel. They're a constant reminder that someone might be watching me.

It scares me more than I've told anyone.

Because if I tell people, they'll worry more than they already do, and I don't like that. It's the currency of my life: being well-liked. Making others happy. Maybe that's why West bothers me so much.

I haven't been able to figure out how to make *him* happy.

And I always figure that out. I know exactly what buttons to press to make my mother ecstatic. She loves beauty, for example. Loves my modeling career. Loves achievements. I'm a master at reading her expressions and her tone of voice.

When I was eighteen, she took me to get a nose job to help the modeling career she had willed into existence for me. My mom rejoiced in my slimmer, slightly upturned nose. My father didn't notice.

When my parents got a divorce, after my oldest brother's death, Rafe had just been sent away to boarding school. It left me to handle the fallout alone. I listened to the screaming matches, the threats, the demands, and the protracted settlement in court. By that time, my father had already moved in with the woman who would become Wife Number Two.

There's a Wife Number Three, too, and I've tried to be friends with them all.

I'm good at that: being nonthreatening. It's easy to make people feel at ease when you can read their signals so well.

The problem with being a chronic people-pleaser who hates conflict is that life is nothing but constant conflict. From *you didn't want sesame on your sushi?* to *I can't believe you didn't call me when you said you would.*

Intimate relationships are, as my therapist Zeina loves to say, a constant negotiation of boundaries. But when you're scared to set those boundaries, you can't have intimate relationships. Not without bending over so far it's practically a yoga pose.

Too many times I've gone out with men who wanted things from me. "Smile for me, Nora. Go out with me, Nora. Let me kiss you, Nora." It's a constant barrage of their wants. I've heard it all my life—with men, with my family, with the photographers I pose for. *Do this, do that, stand here.*

It drowns out my own feelings and overwhelms me with what *they* want. I turn down all men, and with the few I haven't, my experiences haven't been particularly fantastic. So it's easier not to bother with dating at all, which means here I am at twenty-four with my life in order except for these two very small details: I have never been in love, and I have never had sex.

It's my most embarrassing secret. No one knows except my two closest friends and my therapist. When asked, I've always, always lied about it. It feels easier than the inevitable follow-up question of *why?*

But things are going to change. I'm in a new city, and I have a list of three things to do.

1. Sew twelve cohesive pieces to compete in the Fashion Showcase.

2. Survive West Calloway's overseeing of the security that I hate needing. Also, don't let the stalker kill me.

3. Lose my virginity before I turn twenty-five, which is exactly seven months from now.

So far I've gotten a jump on the first of those. As for the second one, the stalker hasn't made an appearance yet. I'm four days into my new life in New York, and I finally feel light again. Like I might have left the fear behind me on the plane ride over.

And tonight I'm getting a jump on the third.

After waking up far too early again because of jet lag, and too sleepy to get a jump on designing for the fashion showcase, I opened my own personal nemesis. The little square on my phone that promises connection.

The dreaded dating app.

I've been chatting with a guy for the past two days. He looks cute, normal, a little nerdy. Says he likes running, so we chat about that for a bit. I'm rarely on the apps, but when I decide to practice dating, that's where I go.

I like vetting them beforehand.

We decide on a place to meet for dinner that night, and I spend the rest of the day with a knot in my stomach. This is why I *hate* dating. The anticipation and the nerves. I never feel like I can truly be myself.

Be present. Let them see the real you. You don't have to perform for them.

Great advice from Zeina.

And really, really hard to do.

When it's time to leave, there are two new guards outside my door. A short woman with curly blonde hair and a no-nonsense stare who introduces herself as Madison, and a tall man with a wide smile and tight braids named Amos.

"Going out?" he asks me.

"Yes," I say with a smile back. "And don't worry; no running involved."

But as it turns out, that won't make the night any easier.

CHAPTER 4
WEST

I get the text between the main course and dessert.

> **MICHAEL**
>
> She's on a date. We don't know who the guy is. Currently running an emergency background check on him.

I excuse myself from the conversation I'm in and type back.

> **WEST**
>
> Do you have eyes on her?

My head of security answers immediately.

> **MICHAEL**
>
> Yes. She's safe.

Maybe, but she's also reckless, and that's a problem. I give my regards to the host of the private dinner and leave the Fifth Avenue apartment with quick steps. She's out with a man? She's on a *date*?

That guy could be anyone. It could be the stalker, presenting himself as someone new here in New York. Rafe warned me that they'd had more than a little trouble pinning down the guy, and that's not a good sign.

An obsessed, crazed fan doesn't fit the profile of someone meticulous and smart enough to outwit a team of trained professionals.

Watching over Nora is going to take all my time, and I have too little of it to start with.

My car is already waiting by the curb. I get in and find Arthur already typing her last-known location into the GPS. We're a smoothly run operation, and I've never been more grateful for it than now.

"We'll be there in ten minutes," Arthur says.

"Thanks." First I had to pull her out of a club. Now I have to interrupt what must be a date. She's going to be so angry at me.

The idea shouldn't make my blood run hotter.

But it does, because *should* really *never* works around her.

We pull up to the Midtown restaurant. I walk past the line of people waiting for a table. The waiter gives me a tight smile, but I tell him I'm meeting a friend inside. My tone doesn't invite any questions, and he wisely asks me none.

I don't see her right away. I do see one of the security guards I hired through the window. His gaze meets mine and he nods toward the back.

And there she is.

Nora is wearing a red dress, her brown hair swept up and away from her face. She's looking directly at the man in front of her. He's got sandy hair, and his hands move as he talks.

She looks at him with a small engaged smile that she's never once given me. Though I've seen her use it on others. It's charming. It also looks fake.

I'm nearly at their table when she looks up at me.

Her eyebrows lift with shock. But then her mouth presses into a thin line. "West. What are you doing here?"

"I need to cut your evening short." I put a hand on the

back of the man's chair and don't give him a glance. "There's a car outside."

Her date looks between us, confusion evident on his face. "I'm sorry, who are you?"

"He's not important," Nora says. "I'm so sorry, Mark. It's just a misunderstanding."

I level her with a glare. "No. It's not. Look, Mark, is it? The evening's over." I pull out my wallet and put a few bills on the table. "Nora. We're leaving."

Her eyes flash, but she's all gracefulness as she apologizes to Mark. "I'll text you later," she tells him, and my hands clench into fists at my sides.

He looks at me again, then back at the money. I wait until Nora walks past me before turning my back to him.

"What the hell?" she hisses my way. Her heels click against the floor. "Why are you here?"

"I could ask you the same thing. What were you thinking?"

"I was in public *the whole time.* I didn't run from my guards. I asked them to wait outside. I was *doing* what you told me to. What Rafe is telling me to."

I pull open the door and let her walk out in front of me. The cool air feels good. Her anger? Less nice. But at least it's real. I can work with that. No practiced, easy smiles.

She whirls to face me. "You had no right to do that. No right at all."

"How well do you know that man?"

She crosses her arms over her chest. "That's none of your business. Mark is nice."

"Right. And how long have you known Mark?"

"Em… three days?"

I look up at the sky. The tall buildings around us, the never-ending light. "God help me. You have no sense of self-preservation."

"Yes, I do."

"This is the second time I've had to pick you up late from this area. You can't try to stay inside for a *single* night? Do you just crave constant attention?"

Her eyes flash. "I'm not giving up my life."

"I'm not asking you to."

"Yes, you are," she says fiercely. "I didn't do anything wrong tonight."

My face settles into stone. "You're well-known, Nora. You were on a billboard in Times Square a few months ago, for fuck's sake."

Her eyes widen. "You saw that?"

"Hard not to." She was half-draped over luggage made by one of the storied luxury brands her family's company owns, her hair mussed like she'd just gotten out of bed, and her eyes staring straight at the camera.

Straight at me every time I passed by.

"Who I date isn't your business."

"Why do you want to make my job harder than it already is?"

"Keeping me safe isn't your job. That task belongs to your security guards, and they're doing a great job. They were standing outside that restaurant, keeping a steady eye on us the whole time. They were probably bored out of their minds."

"It *is* my job. Your brother made it mine," I say. "That man could be *anyone*. He could be your stalker. Did you think of that?"

She takes a deep breath. "He is *not*. I matched with him on an app."

"Which proves nothing," I say tightly. She's on online dating apps? She's far, far too well-known. "This is serious. Did you act this spoiled with Rafe too?"

"I'm spoiled?" she asks. "Remind me where you're living. Did you build Fairhaven? Did you buy it? Or did you *inherit* it?"

Twisted amusement makes my lip twitch. *There she is*, I think. That's all her, the true her. Not the kind and sweet little sister Rafe thinks he has. "I'm trying to help you."

"And I appreciate that. Truly, I do… even if you constantly remind me just how *little* you want to help. But I still have to live my life." She crosses her arms over her chest. "I haven't done anything wrong. I brought the guards tonight and informed them of my plans. You didn't have to get involved."

I take a step closer and lower my voice. "Whether you like it or not, trouble, I am involved. And until we catch whoever is… obsessed with you, you're stuck with me."

"Do you want me chained at your hip? Glued to your side? West, I have things to do, people to meet, places to be." She takes a step back, like she needs to put distance between us. "I understand the threat, trust me. But I can't change everything in my life because of the letters. I moved here to start fresh."

"We don't know yet whether it's stopped," I say. If her stalker stayed across the Atlantic, or if they followed her here.

"Maybe not." Her voice trembles a little, but her eyes are fierce. "But I'm not giving up my life."

"Your life of nightclubs and dating strange men? You can still go to work. You can do all kinds of things. Just don't go to dark places with strangers, which includes *dating* them." I shake my head. "Not until you've been here for a little while longer."

"But I have to date." The words slip out of her like a confession.

My eyes narrow. "You *have* to?"

"Yes. I *have* to."

"And why's that?"

"Because I'm practicing." There's color on her cheeks now. "Not that it's any of your business, but I haven't dated a lot in the past. I don't have a ton of practice, and I'd like to one day be in a relationship, so this is important for me."

"You don't have a ton of practice," I repeat.

Her cheeks flame. She looks like she wishes she could take back every single word. "No, and I'm not going to let this stalker keep me inside for another few months. I moved here to…" She shakes her head and looks away, like there's no point in continuing the sentence.

"I know why," I say. "For the Fashion Showcase you were chosen to compete in."

Her eyes dart back to me. "You know about that?"

"Yes. Your brother told me. Impressive." I run a hand along my jaw. "How the hell can you not have any dating experience?"

"I didn't say that I don't have any. I said I didn't have *enough*." She crosses her arms over her chest. "That guy was perfectly nice, and you were rude to him."

"Was he as perfectly *nice* as you were?"

Her eyes narrow. "He might have been the love of my life."

That makes me chuckle. "Right, and you left him because I told you to, did you? You have never had a problem being yourself around me. If he was the love of your life, you'd still be in there. Or the two of you lovebirds would be on the phone all night after this. I'd be a good villain to bond over."

"Fine, so maybe he wasn't all that fun. Or nice," she says. "But that doesn't mean it wasn't still important to me."

"I don't see how practicing dating can help you actually find a relationship."

"No, I suppose you wouldn't." She looks past me, at the people in the distance. Her expression is shuttered. "Is this the way to disrupt West Calloway's day, then? Go on a date that he hasn't been informed about beforehand?"

"Don't abuse it, trouble."

"Stop calling me that." Her eyes flash again.

"That's what you've been these last few days."

"Only because you're overly concerned with what I'm

doing and who I'm with." She walks past me to the car and stops by the door. "Are you going to drive me home?"

The annoyed expectation in her voice makes my lip twitch again. "If you stop going on dates with random guys."

"I promise," she says, and tilts her head up like a queen without a court, "to stop going on dates with *random* guys. The next guy, I'll make sure your team vets. How about that?"

I walk past her and pull open the door to her car. The idea of her with other guys, other dates, makes the smile die on my lips. But I just gesture for her to enter the car.

"I'll take that as a yes," she says, and slides into the darkness of the car.

Because it *should* be a yes, even if I feel like it's a *hell no*.

CHAPTER 5
NORA

I'm not defeated the next day.

I might have lost the battle, but not the war. And there's no denying that West showing up saved me from a date that had turned sour almost as soon as I sat down. He started by telling me about his tech job, about cryptocurrencies and how much he could bench, before slipping into conversation about how his ex was a model, too.

I hadn't gotten that impression from our chat. Then again, I'd only matched with him a few days prior, and what I need is practice in person. Not texting.

It's easy to be nice in texts. It's harder to be authentic in person.

Zeina and I have tried to trace where my issues started in our sessions.

When my friends and classmates were bubbly and excited about boys, and I was too, until I tried it and found their wants and needs like a cage that closed around me. It was like a dance that took too much energy and drowned out my own burgeoning feelings of excitement for a boy.

When I was sixteen, I was at a party in Paris. My friend's older brother was cute, and we'd been talking all night about nothing and everything. Mostly teenage bluster and a few fumbling jokes.

He took my hand and pulled me into his room on the second floor, and I ended up on his couch, watching him put on some music.

He locked the door behind us.

He wasn't a bad kid. Only a year older than me. We kissed for a long time, wet and warm and sort of nice, even though he tasted like whiskey. But when I pulled back with a giggle, his eyes were hot with desire.

He looked at me like I held the entire world in my hands. I could make or break his night.

If I made the wrong move, I would disappoint him. And disappointing people felt like dying. With parents like mine, it was the most terrible thing that could happen to me as a kid, and the fear reared its ugly head again.

Any excitement or desire I felt died right then. Withered behind the expectations and the pressure and the words that couldn't, wouldn't, form on my tongue. *How about we wait? How about we go slower? How about…*

He went to the bathroom, and I snuck out through his window onto the terrace. Left the party entirely and called a taxi to take me home. Then I snuck back into the apartment in the 16th arrondissement that I shared with my mother and fell asleep with a pounding heart.

I said no a lot after that.

No, no, no. No thank you. No, please. Thanks but no thanks. When I tried dating at twenty, and the guy was lovely on a first date, but then texted just two days after to ask if I wanted to come to his place for dinner. I was still trying to decide whether I liked him, and he already wanted me in his apartment.

At twenty-one, when my model friend's nerdy brother asked me out, and I thought it was time to try again. We were on our second perfectly nice date in London when he surprised me by kissing me wetly against a brick wall outside my apartment. Then he asked me with shining eyes if he could come inside.

I sputtered something about an early morning and ran off.

And finally, at twenty-three, just last year, when I searched for therapy online and found Zeina's practice. Opened up to her in a two-hour session about how much of a failure I was, only for her to hand me a tissue with a kind smile and say "let's do this again next week."

Because paying to feel all the emotions you usually suppress is a fantastic pastime. Very fun.

It took two more sessions for her to issue her verdict, and it fell over me like a scythe. *You only see relationships as* taking *from you. You bend, because you've been taught that if you don't, a relationship will break.* It won't.

You *can* say yes and then change your mind.

You *can* say no and not have it kill you. Or them.

You *can* negotiate boundaries and compromise.

Apparently she has more belief in me than I do, because I feel like I can't. I don't do arguments, or conflicts, or disappointments.

Like my mother calling the next day and spending almost thirty minutes venting to me about the frustrations she's having with my brother. I try to softly end the conversation four times before she finally asks me how I'm doing. We say goodbye when I've already left my apartment, two guards in tow.

Madison again, and a curly-haired, ruddy-cheeked guy named Sam. He's tall and has a puppy-like quality to him. Like he's a bit gangly and his paws are too big.

They follow me as I walk to the place that'll be my workspace for the next few months. I'm renting one of over a dozen worktables in an atelier near my apartment. I need all the time I can get to work on my collection.

Only twelve designers can compete in the Fashion Showcase. I was selected after submitting my designs anonymously online, and now I have less than two months to perfect and put together the final collection.

The judges will be industry leaders, and they'll rank us without knowing who we are. Not our names, ethnicities, backgrounds, age or gender.

I've never wanted anything more than I want to be there.

Several new designers have been discovered that way, and I'm going to be one of them. Based on the power of my designs. Not on my last name or because of my connection to my brother.

Not that Rafe's particularly supportive. He said *good job* when I got into fashion school, but only in the way you are with a child who has a dream.

When I applied for the Fashion Showcase, I did it without telling him. And when I got accepted and told him I was moving to New York, he called it my little pet project. He assumes that, sooner or later, I'll come back to the family business, work in an office every day, and look at numbers the way he does.

That's not going to be me. I just haven't told him that yet, because again, *conflict. Boundaries.*

Just as I haven't told my agent or my mom that I'm done modeling. It's what I've done since I was fifteen, when my mother took me to the first audition and told me it would make her so happy if I booked it.

Since then, I've been in campaign after campaign for Maison Valmont. The company my father started, that my brother now runs, which owns most of the world's largest luxury brands. I've been in campaigns for all of them. *Brilliant,* my mother says about her own idea, that one of the Montclairs should be photographed for Montclair-owned brands.

But I want to feel fabric between my hands and a

sketchpad beneath my fingers. I want to work for no one but myself.

When I'm designing, I don't care about anyone else. I care about the garment and the woman who's going to wear it.

It's sacred.

When I arrive at the shared atelier, I nod hello to a few designers hanging out in the lounge. There's a woman in a bright green dress behind a reception desk, and I give her a smile.

"Hi. I'm Eléanore," I say, extending a hand.

"I know." She smiles broadly back at me. "Diana. It's a pleasure. You're at table number twelve. Let me show you." She stands and strides away. "It's right by the big, beautiful windows."

"Oh, that's amazing. Lots of natural light." I hitch my giant fabric bag up on my shoulder and follow her. She glances past me at Sam and Madison, but they stay outside the workspace. Sam seems to be doing his very best to look interested in a poster for a thrift sale pop-up.

I follow Diana into the buzzing room. The sounds of several sewing machines echo. "We got a delivery for you this morning," she says over her shoulder. "I popped it in some water and set it on your workstation."

"A delivery?" My steps slow, and then I see it. The giant, over-the-top bouquet that's standing on the otherwise empty countertop.

"Isn't it gorgeous? We've all been eyeing it." She gives me a wink. "A boyfriend?"

I feel faint. "Yeah," I say. "Something like that."

"Well, I'll leave you to get settled in."

My smile stays on, and I nod at her as she returns to the desk. A few of the other designers give me curious looks. I return them all with a smile and walk slowly, foot by foot, toward the workstation like the flowers might bite.

There's a card attached.

I won't touch it. I *can't* touch it. After the first three letters in Paris, I stopped opening them. Just sent them all to my brother's security team. But it's half-opened, and I can see the words clear as day.

New York is nice, isn't it?

It's not signed. They never are, but I know who sent it. How did he know I'm starting work today? That I'd be *here*?

I look at the beautiful sewing machine at my desk. The people around me, who I've been so excited to meet. To get to know. To be accepted by.

I close my eyes for a few long breaths, and then I call in Sam and Madison. I want to ask them not to involve West, but I know that's futile. Everything I do these days, it seems, has to involve other people.

He's going to see me as even more of a nuisance than he already does. I hate being an inconvenience. Hate bothering other people.

I feel like screaming.

I settle for wrapping my arms around myself and stubbornly fighting back tears. My brother is convinced the stalker is someone I went on a few dates with in December. The letters started up shortly after, and then the texts, and the anonymous DMs. The occasional picture.

And now the stalker has followed me to New York?

I hoist up my big bag of fabrics and say *no thank you* when Sam offers to carry it for me. He already has the bouquet in a large plastic bag tucked under his arm, while Madison is reporting on the phone.

I walk in front of them back to the apartment, choking back the tears. The last thing I want is for either of them to see. They'll probably report that to West too. I bet everything I do now is reported to West.

I already *have* a stalker. It's funny, how little I treasured my freedom before it was taken from me. Now I'm constantly monitored.

I'm barely through the door of my apartment when my phone rings. I answer, and in French, my brother asks, "Are you okay?"

"Yes. It was just flowers and a note." I take a deep breath. "I'm just a bit shaken. I thought…"

"I know. I hoped too. West is on his way." Rafe's voice is tight. "This asshole knows where you work and probably where you live. I don't know how the fuck he figured it out so fast, but I want that changed."

"Changed? I just got here." I close my eyes against the sadness. I thought I was done with the fear. "And I like where I live, and where—"

"West's place is a fortress," Rafe says.

"You want me to *move in* with West?"

"Yes, and it's not up for debate." We're not that far apart in age, but over the last few years, it's felt like a chasm. He had to fight to gain control of Maison Valmont after our dad died. He's finally in the CEO position, but the board is making him work to keep it. "Nora, please," he says, switching to English. Having one Swiss parent and one American has made our conversations a constant negotiation between the two languages. "Mom is worried too. We're all worried. This isn't forever. My guys will work with West's, and we'll find this asshole."

He's said that for the last several months. But the special investigators he's hired haven't found anything yet. Everything is *inconclusive.*

It's the worry in his voice that convinces me. As much as I hate being a pushover, I hear myself agree. "Okay. But for a short period of time, right? And only if West agrees to it. I need some time to pack up my stuff."

"He will," Rafe says. "Stay by West's side tonight. I don't want you out of his or the guards' sights." Then he hangs up, the line going quiet on the other end.

My stomach knots. He *will* agree? So they haven't spoken about it yet?

West is already annoyed at having to "rescue" me from innocent situations. He's overbearing and annoyingly handsome, and he doesn't like me. And now I have to live with him?

We're going to kill each other.

CHAPTER 6
NORA

There's a knock on my door a few minutes later. I'm barely there before the handle rattles, and there he is. West looks me over, his eyes dipping from my toes all the way up to meet my eyes. His face is carved in stony lines.

"Are you all right?" he asks.

"Yes. It was just the flowers."

He doesn't wait for an invitation, just strides in, his eyes scanning the room. "It was *just* flowers that shouldn't have been there. I saw them on the way in; my head of security has them now." He's wearing a charcoal gray suit that fits him perfectly, and his hair is mussed as if he's been running his hands through it repeatedly. "We'll trace them to the store where they were ordered and get their logbooks."

All the air leaves me, disappears, and all that's left is a pounding headache and annoyance. "That's good. I just can't believe he found me so fast."

"Me neither." West crosses his arms over his chest. There's anger in every line of his body. "Rafe may have a leak."

"A *what*?"

"Someone in his team that has been feeding information, either on purpose or accidentally. Apparently this isn't the first time he's suspected it, just not in regard to you." West shakes his head. "We've decided that your brother won't be informed about most of the details going forward."

"He won't be informed," I whisper.

"Not in writing, and not over email. No locations, plans, or the configuration of my security team."

I feel cold. "He followed me to New York, then."

"Apparently he has." West's eyes are narrowed. "So it seems like you're moving in with me tonight."

"I've been informed."

His eyebrow lifts. "The happiness in your voice takes my breath away."

"You can't be happy about it either," I say. "Your place is far away, right?"

"An hour or so. On Long Island." West lifts up one of the pattern books I left on the counter and leafs through it. "The timing isn't… ideal. I'm hosting a party tonight. The place will be packed."

"You're hosting a party?"

He looks at me. "You sound surprised."

"I've heard of the parties you, Rafe, Alex and James used to throw. Didn't you all trash a villa once?"

The tightness around his eyes softens. "We were nineteen."

"Old enough to know better."

"That's what my parents thought. And no. I'm not throwing that kind of a party. But it's good to hear that you know about all of my teenage mistakes."

That makes me scoff. "Not *all* of them. I'm sure Rafe has censored most of them."

"Thank god." He looks down at his watch. "We should leave in fifteen minutes or so. Pack your bags."

"Wouldn't I be just as safe here? Sitting on this couch for a few hours, with the guards surrounding me? I can join you when the party is over."

West crosses his arms over his chest. He's large like that, too large for this space, and I hate that he looks good when he does it. "We need to keep you moving and unpredictable."

He's serious, and that seriousness makes my stomach tighten. I thought I'd gotten away. That I'd be safe here. "But the person sent me flowers. Not a death threat," I protest. It feels weak, half-hearted. I *hate* that I'm scared.

"Nora," West says. "You think I'm thrilled about this? We'll get through it."

"Thanks for your enthusiasm," I say sweetly, and push off the kitchen counter. I walk toward the bedroom. *Make yourself at home* dances on the tip of my tongue, but I don't say it. I don't say anything at all. He stays in the living room, and I close my bedroom door tight.

And finally take a deep breath. Tears hover hot, pressing behind my eyes. This was meant to be a new start. A new beginning. But with their soft petals and delicate smell, the beautiful bouquet dashed all of it to shreds.

I count to ten, then get to work with shaking hands. Just the other day I hung all my dresses on hangers, and now I'm going to have to pack them all up again.

Annoyance runs like a current beneath my skin. I grab one of the dresses, a vintage velvet thing that my mother wore in the nineties, and throw it on the bed. It'll have to do for the party West is throwing.

He's right on the other side of the door.

She's pretty enough, but she's boring. The last person I'd ever want to date. He said all of it to Alexander, too, one of his and Rafe's best friends. It was late. I was standing on the balcony and overheard them from where they stood in the garden by Lake Como. They'd both been drinking, their voices low and amused.

But they carried.

Alex asked if I was single. It sounded like an off-hand comment in his casual Scottish drawl.

West chuckled. I remember that sound to this day. His chuckle, and then his deep voice responding. *Pretty enough. Boring. The* last *person.*

But I've never forgotten it. Conceited, arrogant man.

I slip the dress over my head and pull up the zipper. I've always loved this dress. It's sleeveless, with a scooped neck, and it hugs my body right down to my knees.

Right now it feels like armor. I push my feet into a pair of low heels and look in the mirror. My makeup is intact, but I touch up my lipstick and run a brush through my hair. It'll have to do.

I start throwing clothes into one of the large bags. I don't fold them, just shove them down.

This is not what I wanted. *None* of this is what I wanted.

The thought of staying at West's estate makes my stomach churn, and it fights with the anger. That this stalker, this stranger who can't seem to stop bothering me, is *yet again* changing my day-to-day life. It's so deeply unfair.

When I finally open the door, West's eyes widen for a fraction of a second before his face settles back into its usual mask of indifference. "You look… appropriate."

"Wow. Do you compliment all women that way?" I ask.

"Only ones who are my best friend's sister." He reaches for my bag, but I take a step back.

"I can carry it."

"You don't have to." He steps closer and takes it out of my hand. "Here."

He leads the way out of the apartment. Right outside are the two guards, who fall into step behind us.

I nod a hello to them both. This must be the world's most boring job. I should ask them if they get to listen to podcasts, at least, while they work. They'd blast through audiobooks watching me be boring.

The silence between West and me feels thick and uncomfortable. The elevator ride lasts an eon, longer than I've been alive, and I breathe a sigh of relief when we finally emerge into the lobby.

His car is outside again, with that familiar kind-looking older man as the driver. He gives me a smile, and I smile back.

West hires staff nicer than himself, it seems. I don't know if that's a mark against or for him.

When we slide into the back seat, West finally breaks the silence.

"Look, I know this isn't ideal for either of us," he says. "But we need to at least appear to be on good terms tonight. People there will know you."

The nerve. I turn to the window to get away from him. But there's nowhere to run in this small space. "I can be civil. And what do you mean, *know* me?"

"You're a famous model," he says dryly. "Though you seem to think otherwise."

"I'm not *famous*."

"Well-known, then? Choose whatever word you like. People know you're a Montclair."

I wonder if it's the same for him. That wherever he walks, people know he's a Calloway. *The* Calloway. Each generation has one heir that gets it all, and he's this one's. He must have jealous cousins and siblings lurking in the wings. Blessed and saddled with a last name that makes him a constant target.

It might be one of the few things we have in common.

"What kind of party are you throwing?" I ask.

West's voice turns low. "It's a fundraiser. There will be... people there I'll need to talk to."

"You're networking tonight. Private or business?"

He's quiet for a short beat. "Both. I need you right next to me. The guards will blend in when we arrive, and I don't want you farther than an arm's length away."

"There's absolutely no way my stalker has magically

gained an invite to your party in less than an hour," I protest. "Just so we're both aware of that."

He glances over at me, something like delight in his eyes. "I like it when you bite back. And no, probably not. But I'm not taking risks."

The car slows down at two large, ornate wrought-iron gates. There's an intricate C in the middle. They swing open as the car inches forward.

And there's Fairhaven.

I've never seen the house that the Calloway family has called home for over a century. West's famous ancestor, the Calloway who started it all, built it during the Gilded Age on North Shore's famous Gold Coast.

Fairhaven lies at the farthest edge of King's Point, right by the Atlantic Ocean.

The house itself sits at the end of a long, well-lit driveway. It's all red brick, white columns and green ivy, and is several stories tall.

A testament to a family that was once America's richest, when the glittering New York society built mansion after mansion along the North Shore. Not many remain. Those that do are museums, hotels, college campuses. Very few are still in private ownership.

Arthur stops the car right outside the main steps up to Fairhaven's double doors. The house is even larger up close. Symmetrical, well-kept, stunning. I step out onto the gravel. Lit torches line the steps, and there's music swelling from inside.

"Welcome," West says beside me, "to Fairhaven."

I roll my shoulders back. His house will be filled with guests. I can already see some of them, spilling out through the open door, moving behind large, white-trimmed windows.

We walk into the foyer. White marble tiles echo faintly beneath my heels, drowned out by the sound of live music and chatter. The ceiling is arched, tall, with grand staircases curving on either side of the foyer.

A few people turn to us. Smiles are thrown West's way, a few *hellos*, *wondered where you were at*s. I put on my best smile beside him. It's one thing I've learned in modeling over the years. Smile. Look happy. Never let anyone know that you're uncomfortable, or upset, or hurting. Never let anyone see you.

Let them see what they want to.

West shakes hands and makes his way to a large sitting room.

"This is your home?" I whisper beside him. I know he inherited Fairhaven, but I didn't realize it was quite *this* large. There's an ornate stone fireplace that curves in the center of the sitting room, flanked by people holding drinks and talking.

"I'll be sure you get a proper tour later."

Then he stops in his tracks. I follow his gaze to the other side of the room, where a woman sits on a futon beneath two bay windows. She might be in her fifties or sixties; it's hard to tell. Brown hair a shade lighter than West's.

And she's looking straight at us.

Around her is a group of women my age. They're different ethnicities and all beautifully dressed. Some seated, some standing. It looks like she's a queen holding court.

"Your mother?" I guess. The resemblance isn't striking, but it's there. And I've spent more time looking at West than I would ever admit out loud.

"Yes." He looks down at me, and there's a tightness to his expression. "You wanted to practice dating?"

"Erm, yes. I told you that, didn't I?"

"You sure did." He looks across the room again. His mother is on her feet now, and is walking toward us. The women she's been entertaining stay put over by the bay windows. More than a few eye West speculatively.

"Practice it with me," he says. "Now."

"Be your… you mean, pretend that we're together?"

"Yes," he says tightly. "You want to date more. I want to date less. Let's help each other out tonight."

I blink up at him. Whiskey eyes look back down at me, and that left eyebrow with the scar through it, and it's suddenly hard to breathe. Pretend to date… West.

The guy I once had a stupid, silly little teenage infatuation with, until he crushed it beneath his boot. *Too boring*, he said. *The last person I'd ever date.*

"Say please," I tell him.

West's eyes flash with amusement, and he leans in another inch. "Please, Nora."

"Thought you'd never ask." I slip my arm through his and turn to face his mother.

CHAPTER 7
WEST

Cordelia Calloway is on a mission. It's clear in her measured steps, her calculating eyes. She looks between Nora and me in a low, assessing sweep.

Her smile is sharp. "West. You made it."

"Of course. Mom, this is Eléanore Montclair. You know her brother, Raphaël. Nora, this is my mother, Cordelia."

"It's a pleasure to meet you." Nora shakes my mother's hand. "This is such a beautiful house."

"It's a pleasure." Mom's voice is warmer than it was only a moment ago. "I've met Raphaël many times over the years. It's lovely to meet his family."

"Nora just moved to New York." I put my arm around her waist, and she doesn't move away. Doesn't flinch either. Thank god. "She's my date."

"I didn't know you were seeing someone, West."

I look down at Nora and make my voice teasing. "It took her a while to agree to go out with me."

"You wore me down," she says with a pretty, fake smile.

"This is wonderful news," my mother says, as if we've announced a pregnancy. There's genuineness in her voice, and god knows she's probably analyzing how great a Montclair-Calloway union would be.

The estate safe, and a wedding to rival the royals.

"I hope you'll enjoy yourself here tonight. And West, darling, when you have a moment, there are a few people I'd like to introduce you to."

My hand is pressed flat against the velvet of Nora's dress. "Later, perhaps," I say. "I'm going to show Nora off first."

Her eyes narrow. It's tiny, but she heard my *no* for what it was. "Of course. Enjoy yourself, darling. Both of you."

She walks off, disappearing into the throng of people she's all personally picked. It doesn't take long before someone pulls her into a new conversation.

Of course she still wants me to chat with the eligible young women she's invited, just in case Nora and I don't work out. Doesn't matter that I've told her over and over again that I don't welcome, want or favor her interference.

That the more she pushes, the more I'll resist.

But Cordelia Calloway has never said no to a little manipulation. I'm sure at least six women here were specifically invited for me to meet.

My arm is still wrapped around Nora. She turns to me, and my hand finds the curve of her waist. In her heels, she's only a few inches shorter than me.

"Why are those women over there," she murmurs, "staring at me like I'm the enemy?"

"Because they probably think you are."

Her teeth dig into her full lower lip, and heat shoots through me at the sight. There's something unexpected in her beauty, something unique. It hits you right beneath the breastbone.

She's not someone you look at and forget.

"Explain it to me," she says. "If I'm going to play this part tonight, if we're… dating tonight… tell me."

I look past her. There are too many people in this room,

too many ears that might overhear. So I nod toward the opening leading to the dining room instead. "Come. Let me show you around."

She nods, but her eyes are still narrowed.

"And yes, I'll explain it to you."

"Good."

My home has been transformed over the past few days.

There was a line of cars on the tree-lined driveway coming in. Fairhaven rarely has this many guests anymore. After my father died, and since my mother moved into the city, it's mine. *For now.* I'll lose it in five months if I don't find a way out of the damn marriage rule. Like the controlling bastard he was, the Maverick is still dictating the family's decisions from beyond the grave.

I've never been less grateful to John F. Calloway.

The usually quiet rooms are filled with a low hum of voices of laughter, of music, creating a background swirl of noise. There's a champagne tower flanked by the open French doors to the terrace and the ocean beyond it. Champagne coupes all stacked upon one another with the golden liquid overflowing.

I reach for two from the top and hand Nora one. "My mother," I say, "loves to play games."

Nora looks at me through long lashes. "Like you?"

"She enjoys a different kind. The social ones. This fundraiser is for a charity she's on the board of."

The people around me are vaguely familiar, and I know it's only a matter of time before we'll be set on by the hordes. There was a time in my life where this sort of thing energized me. The social game, the connections, the strategies. I was young and eager to prove myself.

Then my father died, and I took on the helm of Calloway Holdings, and I had to make sure I don't become the Calloway that fucks it all up. That Cal Steel doesn't fail, that the family wealth remains diversified, that our thousands of employees are well-treated.

Making small talk with my second cousin twice removed over the latest political dealings in Washington feels like a waste of time after that.

"But you don't like being here." She looks at me with eyes that see far more than I'd like. "Do you?"

"This is my house."

"You know what I mean. The party."

"Not particularly." I'd been the heir for years before Dad passed. But that day was far in the future, until it suddenly wasn't, and now all of them want access to and influence over me. Leveraging old family or friendship connections into *donate to my gubernatorial campaign.*

"Huh." She takes another sip of her champagne and looks around the room. She's tense, even if she's wearing that soft, serviceable smile. Such a pretty liar. She doesn't want to be here either.

"You mean something by that *huh.*"

"No, I don't."

"Yes, you do."

She rolls her eyes, and the placid smile breaks. "Fine, I do."

"Tell me."

"Just that I always assumed you and Rafe, Alex and James too, had all the power in the world. That you never did anything you didn't want to do." She lifts one shoulder in a shrug. "I guess everyone bends in some ways."

"This is my house. It would look bad if I wasn't here."

"Right. You know, I can't help but feel like none of this is an explanation as to *why* your mother is trying to present an entire harem to you."

That makes me scoff. She wants nothing of the kind. She wants me with a ring on my finger, and not in a courthouse kind of way. No, my mother wants the spectacle. Another giant Calloway wedding, just like her and my father's.

She's just as committed as I am to making sure I fulfill the clause of the trust. She's just determined to go about it in a different way.

"My mother believes in tradition," I say. "She loves legacy, which means she'd love for me to produce an heir and a spare." My voice comes out dry. It's a half-truth, but the details of the trust aren't publicly known. And lord knows the last thing my mother wants is for me to find any kind of happiness or love. Not that that can be found in marriages, anyway. I've seen what society matches look like.

It's all manipulation and games.

And not the fun kind.

"So she's trying to set you up?" Nora asks.

"She's trying to engineer somewhat organic meetings between me and single women she's vetted."

Her eyebrows draw close. "And you're not interested in any of them?"

"In being pushed together with someone I don't know by my *mother*? No. You're my shield tonight, trouble. Just like I'm yours."

"Stop calling me that."

"Trouble? It's the truth, isn't it?" I look through the open doors and past the terrace. The sun has long since set and the ocean is just a sea of darkness at the end of the property. "You've been trouble since you arrived in this city."

The practiced, easy smile she's worn all night is nowhere to be seen. I feel a dark satisfaction at seeing the real her again.

"I'm not trouble," she says. "I'm just trying to live my life."

"And causing chaos in mine," I reply. "But we're allies tonight, and we have an audience." I lean in closer; I can't help myself. "You're not wearing your lovely fake smile right now."

"I don't fake smile."

"Yes. You do it all the time."

"You're impossible." She takes a sip of champagne and runs a hand over her neck. The movement sweeps her hair to the side, revealing a curve of pale skin.

I look away.

Like my little sister, I remind myself again. It sounds mocking now. She's always been pretty and off-limits. Pretending tonight doesn't change a thing.

A group of people across the champagne tower watch us with undisguised interest. I almost never bring dates to parties like this. Haven't for years, at any rate. But here I am with Nora by my side.

There will be talk in the morning.

We move through the crowd, stopping to chat with various guests. I introduce Nora as my date, watching as eyebrows raise and whispers start. She plays her part well, laughing at the right moments and charming everyone she meets. Most people recognize her last name; her brother is no stranger to these parties, even if he's not here tonight. Some recognize her from the campaigns and the billboards she's graced during her years as a model.

We get separated during a discussion with some of my business associates, and I find her again a few steps away, sampling from a tray of bacon-wrapped dates.

"Stay close to me," I tell her.

"Are you worried about the safety of your own party, in your own house?" She grabs another glass of champagne from the tray. "That doesn't sound great if I'm meant to stay here. Rafe called this place a fortress."

"It is. When it's not filled with people." I lead her out of the house and onto the terrace. The spring air is cool, and it smells like the ocean. Our dock is lit up with a few lights at the far end. "The entire perimeter is controlled. You're safer than in your apartment."

She raises an eyebrow and nods out to the ocean. "The *entire* perimeter?"

"We have naval mines in place, yes, and a state-of-the-art ballistic submarine operates out of the boathouse."

Her lips part. "What?"

"My guards patrol the outer fence and the shoreline."

"Asshole," she mutters, turning to face the water. A breeze catches her dark hair, lifts tendrils of it.

My hand tightens at my side. She'll be staying here, week after week. Night after night. I'm going to have to ask Ernest to give her the wing farthest from mine. I need to put space between us.

Entire *corridors* of space.

"West!" My sister walks toward us, her strawberry blonde hair loose around her shoulders. "There you are. I've been dying to meet your date."

Nora turns too. Her smile is back, like it never left, serviceable and charming. "Hi!"

"Hello." She extends a hand to Nora. "I couldn't believe it when Cecil told me that Mae had told him that my brother brought a date tonight."

"Amber," I warn.

"I have so many questions," she tells Nora.

I narrow my eyes at them both. "No, you don't."

"Yes, I do." Amber takes a step closer to me. "You should head into the library. Cecil is here, and he has news for you. Something about Calloway Steel and an investor meeting?"

Damn. That might actually be important. I find the closest security guard, who's standing by the edge of the terrace, and nod to bring him over. "Keep your eye on these two," I tell Sam. "You don't let my sister or my… date out of your sight."

"Yes, sir," he says.

I give the two women one last glance. One dark-haired and one reddish, looking at each other with barely disguised curiosity.

How much trouble could they get into?

CHAPTER 8
NORA

I watch West's tall, retreating form through the masses. This ought to be interesting. The woman in front of me is about my height, and probably around my age too.

She smiles widely. "Nora, was it?"

"Yes, that's right. Amber?"

"The very one." She steps past me to the low stone wall that runs along the edge of the terrace. She puts a hand on the stone, considers, and then jumps up to sit on it.

In her luxurious silk dress.

Amber crosses her long legs, her heels high, and pats the spot next to her. "Come join me?"

I like her immediately.

I look back at Sam. He's watching, glancing from Amber down to the dark garden below. He doesn't like this. But maybe that doesn't matter.

I jump up beside her and raise my glass to hers. "You have a beautiful home."

She touches her coupe to mine. "I'd say thank you, but I didn't build it and I didn't decorate it."

I chuckle. "Yeah. I can imagine. It's been in the family for a while?"

"Over a century," she says. "Are you really dating my brother?"

I take a sip of champagne to hide my surprise at her bluntness. Is she someone we need to pretend in front of? Or is that limited to his mother? "We've been seeing each other, yes," I say cautiously. "But it's… new."

Her eyes sparkle. "New, is it? I thought you lived with your brother in Europe."

"I grew up mostly in France, yeah, and I earned my degree in London. Our mother is American, though. We spent a lot of summers here." I clear my throat. "I just moved to New York for work."

Her eyebrows lift. "But you're not one of the women Mom loves to chuck at West. You're different."

"I… what makes you say that?"

"Well, first of all, you're sitting out here with me in a designer dress on this lovely stone hedge, drinking champagne, instead of clinging to his side like a lost puppy."

I think of my issues with intimacy, my dislike of men on dates who want to touch me all the time, and smile into my champagne. "Well, I'm not the clinging type."

"No, I can see that. But you're still dating West." She lifts an eyebrow. "Tell me, what's your favorite thing about him?"

"Well," I begin, and lean back with my hand on the stone hedge, "that's a great question. I really like his… work ethic."

"Oh. Interesting," she says. "That's usually the first thing I notice about a man, too."

"He's a very devoted friend," I admit. Everything he's doing for me, he's really doing for Rafe. As much as it might drive me nuts. "And I think he's got a pretty dry sense of humor, too."

He often uses it at my expense, but he does have one; I have to admit that.

Amber swirls her champagne in her glass. "That's a very diplomatic description."

"Thanks?" I fumble for another compliment, trying to think of anything else. That he's painfully handsome but seems not to care about his appearance. That he's intimidating and scowls a lot, that he's powerful. That I'm aware every single time he steps into a room.

He's magnetic.

But I can't tell his sister that.

Her face breaks into a wide grin. "Relax," she says and nudges me. "I know you two aren't really dating. Let me guess; you're here to help him score a point against Mom?"

I hesitate for a second. There's no good answer here, so I just lift the glass to my lips and drain the last of the champagne.

Amber laughs. It's a warm, easy sound, and my own worries slip away with the bubbly burn of the drink. "Don't worry, I've got your back. He's never brought a girl to one of these parties on his own before, and I can't imagine him doing it with someone he's just started seeing. But if it gets Mom to stop trying to set him up with women he has no interest in, I'm all for it." Her eyes glitter again, and the cool wind brushes her strawberry blonde hair back. "How did his best friend's sister get drawn into all of this, though?"

I blow out a breath. "That's a very long story."

"I've got time." Her eyes dip to my empty glass. "But we're going to need more to drink. I'll grab a bottle. Stay right there, will you?"

I pat the stone. "I won't move."

She jumps down, landing on the balls of her feet. She walks on practiced, smooth strides to the bar and gives the bartender a winning smile. He just nods, and she swipes an entire bottle of Dom.

I stare at her, mouth half open.

She holds it up in triumph as she returns. "I hunted, I gathered!"

"Wow."

"Hold this for me." She hands me the bottle and jumps up beside me again. There are other guests around, and some send us curious glances, but we're far enough away to be left mostly alone. Except by the security guard standing several feet away with his earpiece and serious expression.

I nod to him. "We can't share the champagne, can we?"

Amber chuckles. "I've tried in the past. I had a particularly attractive security guard my third year of college…" She undoes the steel cage to the champagne bottle easily. "But he had been trained too well. Never so much as looked when I wore a push-up bra and a low top."

I laugh. "You did that?"

"Of course." She uncorks the bottle with a loud, familiar sound and holds it out to me with a flourish. "There we go. Now you can tell me the whole lurid tale of how you ended up right here, right now. Pretending to be in a relationship with West."

I take a fortifying sip of the champagne first. "Okay. So… it started a few months ago, with a letter on my doorstep."

"Wow. Not what I expected." She fills her own glass and then wiggles her eyebrows. "Watch," she says, and extends the glass to Sam. "Want a glass?"

His eyes slide to hers, and his stoic façade doesn't break for a second. He just shakes his head firmly.

"Right. If you change your mind!" she tells him.

"You weren't lying," I tell her. "Have you had guards often?"

"The last decade or so, yes," she says with a shrug. "On and off. Mostly West will assign me a driver with security training to give me a little freedom."

I sigh. "God. I'd love that."

"You have the whole team?"

"Yes, and they're around constantly. For the last week, my schedule has been monitored every single minute."

Her mouth thins into a line. "Oh. I'm sorry. What happened with the letter? I derailed your story completely."

"No, no, it's okay. It's just... I started getting threatening letters. I think it was just someone trying to scare me, but I told my family, and Rafe hired guards."

"Threatening letters," she repeats. "Oh my god, that's terrifying."

I laugh a little. I've become so used to laughing it off, to pretending to be strong, to seeming like it doesn't really bother me all that much. Like all my hopes weren't dashed today with a beautiful bouquet of flowers.

I don't want people to feel like they have to comfort me.

"Yeah, it hasn't been the best. It started with all these online messages, really. Texts and comments. But when the first letter arrived, that's when we knew it was serious. It escalated to a few pictures in the mail. Pictures of me doing things. Walking around the city. Waiting in line for a casting."

"Shit." She glances from me to the security guard and then back again. "Okay, he should not be drinking, and it's very good that he turned me down. I'm sorry."

"I'm getting... used to it, I suppose. I wanted to move to New York, specifically for a job, and I didn't want this to stop me." I lift a shoulder in a shrug. "My brother asked his friend to help with the security."

"Ah," Amber says, nodding sagely. "And my brother doesn't do anything by half measures."

"No, he most certainly doesn't."

"Is he smothering you?"

"A bit," I admit, looking at the doors to see if he's nearby. I don't want to sound too ungrateful.

She laughs. "He's not all-powerful, even if he likes to think he is."

"I'm just... it's not that I'm not grateful," I tell her. "I'm just struggling with all of it. The stalker sent flowers to my new workplace today, and everyone freaked out. That's why

57

I'm moving in here tonight. Apparently Fairhaven has excellent security and lots of space." I take another sip of champagne. The bubbles are quick, delightful little things, and my head feels lighter than it has in a week.

I'm going to have to figure out a new kind of atelier. Maybe buy a sewing machine and see if I can set it up in the guest room I'll be staying in. There's no way I'm missing my shot at the Fashion Showcase.

"It's a beautiful place." Amber's voice turns a bit wistful. "I love this house. The ocean, the orchard, the library… I spent most of my childhood here."

"It's incredible. It's a little hard to believe it's where you grew up. Both of you."

She glances at me with a smile. "Yeah. I know we were lucky that way."

"Do you still live here?"

"No, I haven't for years, but I still consider one of the guest rooms my own."

"West said I had to be by his side all evening, for security reasons…"

Amber lifts her shoulders in a shrug. "But you became the convenient solution to avoid Mom's matchmaking tonight."

"It seems like it, yes. And so much for the whole 'Nora, do not stray from my side' talk he gave me earlier. He's the one who just strayed!"

She laughs again. "God, you're going to be so good for him."

"I'm going to drive him insane. He already complains that I'm trouble, that he doesn't have time for this." I roll my eyes and take another long sip. The air is getting colder, and a shiver races across my skin. But I can't imagine moving away from this ledge, right here, with her. It's been a long time since I've spoken so freely to someone. "But I'm just trying to get by in what's already a really weird situation."

"Hey, you know what you need?" She turns to me more

fully on the hedge, a smile playing across her lips. "A girls' night out."

"Oh, I'd like that. But no nightclubs."

"No nightclubs." She holds up her glass to mine. "We'll bring the guards. We'll be safe, but we'll have fun. I've had years of practice sneaking out from my brother."

"I'd really love that." I touch my glass to hers, a true smile breaking out. Maybe this whole thing won't be so terrible after all. Maybe there's a way to still be my own person here.

Another shiver races across my skin, and I take a long sip of champagne. My head spins a tad more.

"I leave you alone for what, half an hour?" The voice is deep, male, and very clearly frustrated.

I look over to see West standing in front of us. He's looking at the half-empty bottle of champagne between Amber and me.

"Careful, or your new girlfriend here will think you're a total bore," Amber says. She jumps down off the ledge. "We had a wonderful heart-to-heart. I'm happy for you." She pats his arm. "I didn't know how truly romantic you could be."

His eyes narrow and slide to mine.

I hold up my hands. *Not me.*

Amber looks over at me with a wink. "We'll talk later?"

"Absolutely."

She heads off, and West doesn't spare her another glance. He looks at me instead, his lips turning down in a faint frown. I've probably committed yet another grave offense. Maybe this particular stone was laid by a founding father and I'm desecrating it.

But I can't find it in me to care right now.

"Don't worry," I tell him. "She figured out you and I aren't really a… couple."

"I suspected," he mutters, and he shrugs out of his jacket. He steps closer and hangs it around my shoulders. It's big and warm from his body. It hangs stiffly off my shoulders, and I grip one of the front pieces, pulling it closed around me.

"You're cold again," he says.

"Just a little," I say. "Is this your move? Giving girls your jacket? This is the second time."

West's eyes narrow as he looks at me, his gaze flickering between my face and the champagne glass in my hand. "How much have you had to drink?"

"I don't think that's any of your business."

"I think everything about you is my business right now."

I shrug and look past him to the others on the terrace. "Have you been off mingling with eligible women?"

"Hardly. Everyone knows I brought you tonight."

Oh. "And that's apparently a big thing, is it? Your sister told me that you never bring dates to these events."

His face hardens. "Spoke about my dating life, did you?"

"It came up," I say primly. "Is it because you scare women away? Because I can see that."

Something flickers in his eyes that looks weirdly like amusement. "Yes. That's exactly it," he says. "No woman in history has ever been attracted to wealth, power or prestige."

"Well, not this woman, at any length." I gauge the distance to the ground. It looked so easy when Amber jumped down, and I'm very used to being in heels, but I don't think I've ever jumped in them before.

I scoot forward on the stone.

West sighs and steps forward. "Let me help you."

"I can do it."

"You're not breaking an ankle the second day I'm in charge of your safety." He puts an arm around my back and bends a bit. "Come on. Arm around my shoulder."

It takes me only a second to obey. The touch is clinical. Practical. He slides his other arm under my knees and then he lifts me squarely off the stone ledge. For a moment, I'm suspended in the cradle of his arms, my face close to his chin. Wearing his jacket.

My head spins again, and this close, I catch his scent, cologne and something darker, smokier. He sets me on my feet but keeps his hand on the low of my back. "You all right?"

"I'm fine," I say. "Perfectly fine."

He looks at me for a long moment. "It's time we made our exit. Enough excitement for one night."

"But I'm just starting to relax."

"My mother will try to corner you for an interrogation, and I can promise it won't be very *relaxing*."

"Okay. Am I staying in this… house?"

"Do you think I'd exile you to an outhouse? Fairhaven has dozens of rooms."

"I didn't mean to insult you," I say, and turn my chin up. "Just a question."

His lips twitch, like he finds this amusing again. "I know. Ernest has made sure your bags are already in your room. I'll show you the way."

I hesitate before reaching out to grab the bottle of champagne. "I'm keeping this."

"Wouldn't dream of taking it from you. Come on, let's go."

He guides me through the crowd with his hand still on my lower back. I notice how people part for him, their eyes following us curiously. A few women give me appraising looks that make me want to shrink into West's jacket.

Because I'm still wearing it. If people didn't think I was here as his date before, they all certainly know it now.

My annoyance at him sparks again. I wonder if it'll ever go away completely. *She's the last person I would date.* Except when it's very convenient for him, apparently.

We're walking through the large sitting room when his attention lands on something in the corner. Someone. "Wait a second," he mutters, steering us toward a photographer in the corner.

I walk on autopilot, but I'm confused. "You want to memorialize this night?"

"I want to be photographed beside you, yes," he says in a low voice.

I want to stop right then and there. What the hell? Just so he can do what, exactly? Send an even stronger message of just how off the market he is?

"West," I protest. "I don't want to be—"

"This photographer was hired by my mother's party planners. I can make sure a photo of us ends up in the local paper."

I shake my head slowly. "Why on earth do you care so much if people think you're single or not?"

"Not me," he says sharply. "You. If you have someone watching your every move, I want them to know that I'm next to you now. That you're not alone and that you've got a powerful friend in your corner. People here will talk, but an image speaks louder."

"Oh. I didn't realize… That's smart."

His lips twitch again. "Thank you very much."

"Okay. Let's do it."

He takes the champagne bottle from my hand and puts it on the windowsill behind me. Then he holds out a hand for his jacket.

"Oh. Right."

He tosses that beside the champagne bottle, and then the photographer's attention is on us. I shuffle beside West, and he reaches for the low of my back again, wrapping an arm around me.

It doesn't feel so bad.

It feels… good, and warm, and strong. And he's not trying to charm me, to get me into bed. There are no expectations here. It's an act, and I know how to act.

I tilt my head against his shoulder and smile at the lens. It's one of the smiles I've perfected over years of modeling. The secret smile, a photographer once told me. *Like you're happy and thinking about a secret only you know.* Or in this case, a secret only West and I know.

I think of him sitting alone in the armchair years ago, nursing his scotch and looking up to meet my gaze. Me asking. *Want to grab a drink?*

A flash.

I look up at West and keep that smile in place. He looks down at me, his eyebrows knitting together. His eyes really are the oddest color. The deep shade of whiskey or honey, so unusual beneath the scarred eyebrow. He looks at me like he's trying to figure out what I'm thinking.

Another flash, and the spell is broken.

I step away from him.

West's jaw works. He thanks the photographer and reaches for the bottle of champagne. "Come," he tells me. "We're done for tonight."

CHAPTER 9
NORA

I wake up with a headache the next morning.

Sunlight streams in through the curtained windows. The space is large, sumptuous. I didn't get a proper look at it last night, after West dropped me off outside the door to my rooms. Plural.

I sit up slowly, my head throbbing. The bottle of champagne is still on the big dresser beside my bed where I left it. My bags are on the other side. Neatly stacked and waiting for me, just like West told me they would be.

The furniture in here is ornate, the dresser mahogany, the walls a light blue. There's a nook on the other side with windows that open up to… is that?

I slide out of bed and walk over to pull the curtains back.

The windows open up to the large gardens on the back of the property. I can see parts of the terrace, where I chatted with Amber. The next level down is all green and hedges and a pool. Another staircase down the terraced gardens leads to a boathouse built on the shoreline.

And then there's the ocean.

The expanse of blue stretches out past the edges of the

property, waves softly roaring. The sky is a lighter shade of blue and dotted with clouds.

This nook might be the best thing about the entire room. I walk across the padded floor to the double doors. They open up to my own little sitting room, the first space in the "rooms" that are my own. Two couches, a TV, a desk. Decorated in the same classic, traditional blue colors. It's understated and rich at the same time.

I head into the en suite and straight into the shower. It's right next to a beautiful claw-foot tub that overlooks the ocean.

I'm going to have to try that one.

When I get out of the shower and look at the clock, it's almost eleven, and I feel only marginally better.

And I'm in West's house.

The knowledge feels like a splinter beneath my skin. He might be just a few rooms away. Right now. He's close, and he'll always be close.

But there's no denying that I feel safer now, too. Maybe that's what annoys me the most. My own fear after seeing that damn bouquet.

I haven't been fighting West or Rafe because I'm not afraid. God, I wish I wasn't. But because their concern makes me feel like I'm imposing on them.

Rafe especially, and my mother, who I have to call later today or she'll freak out that it's been twenty-four hours without contact. Managing everyone else's feelings about my situation is like walking a tightrope, leaving no space for me to feel my own. My brother's obsession with my safety started years before the stalker entered the picture. My mother's paranoia, too. It dates back to over a decade ago, when the avalanche caught Rafe and Etienne in its claws and left me with one brother instead of two.

I rummage through my bags and find some clean clothes. I

get dressed slowly, wincing when I bend down to pull on my socks. Yeah. I need water and food, and to never, ever indulge like that again.

I'm braiding my damp hair when a soft knock on the door to the sitting room makes me freeze.

"Um. Hello?"

"Miss? Mr. West asked me to check on you," a male voice says. It has to be one of the staff.

"Just a moment."

I pull on my favorite cardigan, sky blue with small embroidered roses, and open the door.

It's the man I met last night. He's slender and in his mid-fifties, perhaps, with his peppered hair brushed back.

"Good morning, Miss. We spoke briefly yesterday. My name is Ernest, and I'm the house manager here at Fairhaven. Would you like some breakfast this morning?"

"I'd love a glass of juice," I say.

"Of course. I'll be happy to show you around later today and help you settle in."

"I'd love that, thank you." Maybe I can ask him, too, if it's okay if I move some things around in the little living room outside of my bedroom. I'll need to buy a sewing machine and a working table.

Ernest leads me out of my rooms and down the grand staircase. I let my hand run along the polished wood banister. It's smooth, worn from decades of use.

Fairhaven is a memory from the past.

It's a testament to a kind of wealth that doesn't exist anymore, to a time when America's premier families made their fortunes in railroads, steel and stocks. When giant houses like these were erected along this shoreline, over-looking the ocean like bastions. A memory from a sliver of time that's come and gone.

I saw so little of Fairhaven last night.

Ernest leads me down one of the curved stairs to the foyer, where we entered last night. The marble flooring and the wainscoting, the high ceilings, are all stunning.

I saw the outside of the house yesterday. The red brick and white columns make the house look as if it's caught between the Old World and the New.

"You're already familiar with your wing," Ernest says, walking into the sitting room. Other people are there, cleaning, moving things. Resetting the place from the party. "I want to reiterate that no one will enter past the first door without your permission, with the exception of the scheduled cleaning."

"Thank you," I say. "I appreciate that."

He walks me through the sitting room, the dining room, and into the butler's kitchen. There's a large family kitchen too, with a massive center island and French doors that open to the terrace.

"Lunch is available in the kitchen around one p.m. every day. It's served to all guests at the manor and available for the staff. Nothing fancy," he tells me, "but it's good fare."

"That sounds lovely," I say.

Ernest leads me back through the kitchen and into a long hallway. "This wing houses the library and Mr. West's study," he explains, gesturing to a set of heavy wooden doors. "The library is open to all guests, but Mr. West's office is private."

I glance at the doors. Is he behind them right now? I haven't seen him around, not since last night, when he dropped me off outside the door to my rooms. He silently handed me the champagne bottle and then disappeared down the stairs, back to the areas with the guests. To conquer, to talk. Had he spoken to those women his mother had brought in?

"And through here," Ernest says, opening a large French door, "is the conservatory."

We step into a bright, airy room filled with plants and wicker furniture. Sunlight streams through the glass ceiling, warming the space. The scent of flowers and damp earth fills my nose.

"Oh," I breathe. "This is beautiful."

Ernest's face softens. "Yes, it is. I was thinking we might have a seat here. I have some documents prepared for you."

"Let's." I sit in a wicker chair, and Ernest takes the one opposite me. Documents? I'm as intrigued by Fairhaven as I am by the house manager himself.

"I prepared a guide for you here." He hands me a booklet. "All the staff information and their on-call phone numbers are on the first few pages. Evelyn Greaves is head housekeeper; Melissa Durham is the chef. You've met Arthur Webb; he handles all transportation and manages the vehicles of the property. But," he adds, his tone sharpening, "I am the house manager. If you're unsure who to turn to, you can always contact me, and I will delegate."

I look from the paper to him. "Thank you. This place is clearly run like a well-oiled machine."

His frown lessens just a tad. "Yes. It is."

"How long have you worked here?" I smile at him, warm and friendly.

"It will be twenty-five years next August."

"That's incredible. You must have known West almost his entire life."

"Yes, I have."

I smile down at the papers and flip through them. There are details here regarding laundry, emergency contacts, Wi-Fi, how to give a guest access to the front gate, historical anecdotes, overviews of everyone in the Calloway family, past and present…

This is a guide, but it's also a love letter to an estate and a family.

"I'm looking forward to learning more about the house," I

say. "It's truly stunning, and I'm very grateful to be living here."

His frown disappears all together. I wonder how much notice he and the rest of the staff were given before my sudden arrival. An hour, perhaps? Two? And yet my rooms had been prepared and I have a personalized guide in front of me.

"Thank you," I tell him sincerely. "For all of this, and for the tour. I appreciate it."

Ernest's lips quirk up. "Well. You're very welcome. If you'd like more of a tour of the grounds, that can be arranged too. The apple orchard will soon bloom. And we have thirty-six different species of roses."

"Really?"

"Yes. The first bushes already have buds, particularly the Margaret Merrils." He clears his throat and looks past me to the hallway. "Your breakfast should soon be ready. I know that—Oh."

I look over my shoulder, following his gaze.

West is standing in the doorway to the conservatory. His tall frame is silhouetted by the bright hallway behind him, and he looks every inch as put together as he did last night. His hands are in the pockets of his dark pants, and an off-white cable-knit sweater stretches across his broad chest.

"You're awake," he says. "I see Ernest is giving you a tour."

Ernest stands. "We've finished with the most important parts."

"Good. I'll take it from here."

Ernest nods and walks out of the room using another exit, leaving West and me alone in the conservatory.

He looks no worse for wear after last night, and I hate him a little for that. And for looking every inch as casually confident as I never, ever have.

He stops with a hand curved over the back of the chair

Ernest just vacated. I catch sight of the signet ring on his finger, the same one my brother has worn for years.

The air feels heavier.

"Your brother and I just spoke," he says. "You and I have more pretending to do."

CHAPTER 10
WEST

Nora is sitting in my conservatory, looking at me with cautious, distrustful eyes, not a stitch of makeup on her face. Her hair is braided back, and she's in a too-big cardigan. It drowns her body, and the sleeves cover half her hands.

She looks young.

She looks annoyed.

"Keep pretending," Nora repeats. "What do you mean?"

I pull up the article from Page Six on my phone and hand it to her. The image is the one of us two. She's looking straight at the camera with a smile, like she knows something the rest of us don't.

She looks like a model.

Which she is. Pretty as a fucking painting, and trouble if I've ever seen it.

"This is already out?" she asks.

"Yes." I pulled some strings to make sure it was. It wasn't hard. Privacy is usually a high concern around all parties thrown at Fairhaven, and pictures rarely emerge into the public. They were happy to get a call from one of my executive assistants with the offer.

She's well-known, and so am I. As much as I dislike the scrutiny most days.

"Oh," she says. "Rafe has seen it too, I'm guessing."

"Yes," I say. He's a few hours ahead of us, and I just spoke to him from my office. "He thinks we should make this charade a more... permanent thing."

Her eyes flash to mine. "What does that mean?"

"He thinks we should keep pretending to date in public."

"Absolutely not." She pushes my phone back to me across the table. "That's ridiculous."

I grit my teeth. I told Rafe she wouldn't agree to any of it, but he promised he would talk to her. Clearly he hasn't gotten around to it yet.

I sit in the chair opposite her, like we're two poker players gearing up for a game. "It's not ideal. But Rafe thinks—and I agree—that it would be best for your safety."

She crosses her arms over her chest. "How?"

"Your stalker," I say. Rafe was very clear. *I want you by her side twenty-four seven.* "If we're dating, it'll explain why I'm always by your side."

I want to send this fucker a signal.

A blush creeps up her cheeks. "I'm already living here. In your house. I have your security guards. How could it possibly help if we have to pretend... pretend all the time? Like we did last night."

"If the stalker thinks you're dating someone... You're unavailable. We're trying to puncture his fantasies." I rest my hand on the table and feel the coolness of the glass beneath my palm. "If you're publicly dating, you become less accessible in his mind."

Her eyes flash. "So I trade one man's unwanted attention for another?"

"I'm not asking to actually date you, Nora," I say. My voice comes out low and harsh. Actually dating her isn't an option. Never has been, never will be. I have no time for relationships, and younger sisters have always been off-limits.

Dating her for real would end my friendship with Rafe.

Nora draws her arms tighter around herself, like my comment hurt. "I know that. I wasn't implying that you were. I don't want to date you either."

"Good. We're on the same page."

"But I don't see how this is going to deter the stalker."

"It might. It might not. Regardless, it'll explain why you're staying here and why I'm always around. If you want to go to a party or a club again, I'll be by your side."

She takes a deep breath, and her gaze slides back to mine. She's annoyed again. Good. I can handle that. "For how long?"

"Rafe and I thought a few months would be best." We discussed more than that. He hopes my presence will make the stalker reckless. That it'll cause him to make a mistake, to leave a trace. Then we can get him. That we can goad him into revealing too much.

Life won't be great for him when he's caught.

I'm not taking any chances. Not when I've been the one entrusted with her safety. If there's one thing I hate, it's failure. And I'm not going to fail at this.

"A few *months*?" Her voice is high. "I can't pretend to be your girlfriend for months."

I grit my teeth. "Stopping you from dating, is it?"

"Yes, actually. It would interfere with that, now that you mention it." She takes a deep breath. "What would this even mean? To keep pretending in front of your mother? Your *family*?"

My mother has already called, asking when Nora can come by for dinner. "Yes," I admit. "It would help me."

"Because you're drowning in beautiful, single women, and it's *such* a problem for you." Nora's voice is acidic, and the heat of it makes a smile twitch at the corner of my lips. "What a problem."

"You get tons of male attention," I point out. "You can't tell me you don't. Men ask you out all the time, right? And you still want to practice dating."

"That's different."

"Is it? We have the same issue, just different ways of dealing with it."

She narrows her eyes at me. "I told you that I'm not willing to give up my practicing."

"If you're pretending to be my girlfriend, you're *only* dating me." I press my hands flat against the table. "So if you want to practice? You'll practice with me."

CHAPTER 11
NORA

His words won't make their way through the haze of hungoverness. I blink at him. "You can't be serious."

"I'm always serious."

That makes me roll my eyes. I know enough about West Calloway to know that's not the least bit true. *Practice with me.* He doesn't know what he's suggesting. Doesn't know *just* how inexperienced I am, thank god. I'll never tell him that.

"You want expensive dinners, Nora? You want flowers, and chocolates, and to flirt with no consequence?" His eyes are that amber color, the one that makes my stomach tighten. "Do it with me."

I shake my head slowly. "You don't mean that."

"Why wouldn't I?" He doesn't look away from me, and his full focus is a terrifying thing. "Tell me, then. Why do you want to practice so badly?"

He's too intimidating to tell this to, and yet the words tumble forth. "I'm not good at dating. I almost never do it, but I want to fall in love. I want a relationship... So I need to get comfortable with it." This is humiliating. I want to sink through the seat, and that humiliation makes my voice testy. "I need to practice."

"You must have men asking you out all the time," he says. His face tightens, draws together with confusion, like what I'm saying is idiotic. Makes no sense. I know I should laugh— or giggle—and brush this away. Say the thing he wants to hear.

But I'm so tired of pretending.

"Guys ask me out sometimes. But I say no." I curl my fingers into a fist, my nails digging into the flesh of my palm. "They want things of me, they have expectations… and I can't relax. Can't have fun with them when I feel like they just want a performance from me."

He's quiet for a long moment. Just looks at me.

Any moment now, he's going to laugh. Give me a sneering response.

Instead, he just nods. "Right. Come, we're going to the library."

He stands, and I look up at him. "Why?"

"We need pen and paper." He shoves his hands into his pockets. "Consider it another stop on your tour."

I follow him down the adjoining hallway and through the large oak door.

The library is huge.

It has a high ceiling, twice as high as a normal room in the house. There's a ladder along the dark wooden bookshelves leading up to a mezzanine. A frayed oriental carpet covers most of the floor, and several leather couches are centered in the corner around a stone fireplace. The other side has a pool table with a rich velvet cloth.

There's a bar cart too. Tucked into the corner with an array of liquor on it.

The library looks like something out of an old film set. I love it immediately and follow him into the old space.

West doesn't seem floored.

He walks to an ornate desk and grabs a notepad and pen out of one of the drawers. He hands it to me. "Write a list of everything about dating that makes you uncomfortable. Everything you want to practice."

"You're…" I look down at the piece of paper and back up at him. "Seriously?"

"Yes," he says. "Look, you don't like me, right? You've made that clear. So you don't have to worry about hurting my feelings. You can practice rejecting me over and over again, if you need to."

There's a weird kind of logic to it.

I take the pen he's holding out. Thick steel, engraved. *Calloway Holdings.*

"There's no way you're going to agree to this," I say. "There's no way *I'm* agreeing to this."

"Then we'll negotiate for it." His voice is gruff. "If we're going to pretend to be a couple anyway, why the hell not? Might as well get something you need out of it."

Why not, indeed.

I write things down. My handwriting is sloped and slightly sharper than usual. I get granular. It's pathetic, really, to see it all written down, but I'm past caring. I want to prove to him just how *little* he will want to do this.

When I talk about practicing dating, I mean it. Everything.

The dinner or the drinks. The conversations. Saying no, saying yes. The way they look at me, their hands on my waist, the conversation. And then the goodbye.

I write that up and underline it. The damn goodbye after a date. When I just want to leave, but they want to linger, looking at me with those intense *I'm about to kiss you* eyes. I even add that to the list.

I glance over at West while I'm writing. He's leaned back, eyes on my pen. His eyebrows are drawn down low.

"That's all?" he drawls, looking at where my pen's stalled.

"No." I add a few more points. *Rejecting a man in person. Pushing him away if he tries to kiss me. Rejecting a man over text. Arguing.*

That part I won't mind practicing with West.

Handling conflict without running away. Setting boundaries.

Receiving and accepting compliments and gifts.

Going out on romantic dates.

Asking for what I want.

Zeina's words ring in my head. She wants me to practice being present and showing my true self, not the version I think they want to see.

Being authentic, I add.

There's more I could write. *Kissing. Making out. Having sex.*

But I'm not adding that. It feels like far too much of an ask, and glancing up at West, the idea of pressing my lips to his makes my entire body tighten.

I wonder what he'd be like as a kisser. I wonder if I'd even be brave enough.

When I'm done, there's almost no space left on the back of the sheet of paper, and West's mouth has pressed into a thin line.

"That's it, I think." My voice is casual, like I haven't just written a bullet-pointed essay.

He holds out his hand. I hand back his pen but don't let go of the note. I hold it between us instead. "This is everything I want to practice. If you agree to all of this, then... I'll pretend to be your girlfriend, including in front of your family."

I raise an eyebrow.

"Wouldn't you like to keep your mother's matchmaking at bay?"

"You're better at this than you give yourself credit for." He heads to the bar cart in the corner. It's only noon, but he pours himself a finger of whiskey. "Want some?"

No. Not really. But if we're going to talk about this, I need something in my hand. Something to do. "Yes. Please."

West's lip curls, like he sees my reasoning. But he pours me a drink. I curl up on one of the sofas, but he stays leaned against the desk.

And then he starts to read my list.

I take a long sip of whiskey. God, I don't like it. Never have. I tap my fingers against the crystal and look away from him. To wall after wall of books. The whole place is dark, but in a comforting way. It makes me want to stay here longer. Curl up on one of the armchairs.

The wooden door to the side must go to his home office. The one Ernest told me was off-limits.

The silence is deafening.

I take another sip of the whiskey just to give myself something to do. "Is this Alex's whiskey?" I ask.

West doesn't look up from his list. "Yes."

"Mhm. Thought I recognized the flavor."

His eyebrows are drawn together, a furrow between them. A few more long seconds pass, and I click my fingers against the crystal tumbler again. The whiskey doesn't work well with a stomach tied in knots.

"Just say something," I ask him.

His lips quirk. "It's a long list."

"It's not that long."

He lowers the piece of paper. "This is everything involved in dating."

I shake my head. "No. Not everything."

His eyes snap to mine. Warmth floods my cheeks, and my stomach lurches the way it always does when anxiety comes knocking. *It doesn't include sex.*

"No, I suppose it's not everything." His jaw works, and he looks back down at the list. "But damn near. So you want to practice this."

"Yes," I say. "And like you said… rejecting you. Or arguing."

He lifts an eyebrow. "Good thing my ego can take it."

"Are you sure about that?"

"I am," he says. "But there's only one way to see if I'm

wrong. So this is what you want, then. In return for us pretending to be a couple."

My fingers tighten around the glass. "Yes."

He puts the paper down on his desk. "That's a tall order."

"It's not that tall."

He crosses his arms over his chest. He looks broader when he does that. He's so different from any of the men I've ever gone on a date with. Maybe that's good. It will make it easier to pretend. "The dating thing in public, that's for your safety. But this?" He holds up the list. "If we do this, trouble, then I need our relationship to look ironclad in private too."

"Ironclad," I repeat.

"Yes. Parties. Events. Investor dinners." He taps his knuckles against the desk. "My family."

"You want us to pretend all the time."

"Yes. Like you said, I want to… keep matchmaking attempts at bay."

I dig my teeth into my lower lip. He wants us to sell this, then. I've never been in a relationship. But I know how to pretend. How to smile for a camera and make people feel at ease.

"How often will we practice?"

"Once a week," he says.

"Three times a week." The next words slip out, tight and teasing. "You don't really do relationships, so I'm not sure if you're really an expert in all of this."

His lips curl at the corner. "We've already established that you're not, so I'm willing to bet I have more experience than you."

Damn it. I drain the last of my whiskey. "Three times a week. That's my final offer."

His eyes narrow. "Three times a week, then."

Victory makes it hard to think. I'll be practicing. With him. *With West.*

"One final thing." He braces his hands against the edge of

the desk behind him. "These lessons? Your brother can never know about them. They stay between us."

"I'm not in the habit of discussing my private life with him."

"Don't start." He throws back the last of his whiskey. "Or I'm going to be in deep fucking trouble."

GROUP CHAT

ALEX

Saw the pictures of you and little Montclair in the news. Something you want to tell us?

JAMES

Send the picture.

ALEX

Attached below.

JAMES

Rafe, if you're on your way to kill West, consider that he's the only one of us with a house in America. It's convenient when I have to visit New York. Much better than a hotel.

WEST

Thanks for having my back because I'm convenient.

JAMES

You're welcome.

RAFE

They're only pretending to date. It's to draw the stalker out, or to deter him. Either works for me.

WEST

And explain why I'll be by her side nonstop for the next few weeks.

RAFE

I think I have a leak in my team. West will take over Nora's protection in hopes that nothing else comes out.

ALEX

And here I thought something salacious happened.

JAMES

There's still time.

WEST

No.

RAFE

It's just for show. West would never.

CHAPTER 12
WEST

"Everyone's watching us," she says beside me. Her smile never wavers.

"Some of these people were at the party the other night. They're curious." I hand her a glass of champagne and ignore the onlookers.

She hasn't been here before, but they certainly know who she is. Daughter of Francois Montclair and Rafe's sister. Not to mention heiress to the largest luxury conglomerate in the world.

Her eyes return to mine. "Because you never date publicly. Why not, by the way?"

"It's not like I have a rule about it," I tell her. I just haven't been interested in attempting long-term relationships or the way they always turn toxic and manipulative in the end. They hurt and they embarrass, and I have no interest in either of those things.

Her eyes search mine, like she's trying to make sense of that response. "You date in private?"

"You're very interested in my dating life."

"Well. I think it's only fair, considering what we're doing."

I put a hand on her back and guide her over to the VIP area. "I'll answer your question if you answer one of mine."

"You're bargaining again," she says.

"It's what I do best."

"Fine. What do you wanna know?"

I lower my head, closer to her ear. We pass an elderly couple who stare at us as we walk by. "Why did you choose Mark for your date?"

Nora looks up at me. "I'm still annoyed at you about that, by the way."

"No," I say. "You're not."

Her eyes narrow. "And why do you think I'm not?"

"Because I saw the relief on your face before you hid it," I say. "Didn't make sense at the time, but now it does. You didn't want to be on that date to begin with, and you were glad I ended it."

She turns her face forward, her narrow chin pointing up. Her full lips are pressed tight together.

I smile, because I'm right, and she hates that I've read her correctly.

"If you want me to say thank you…"

"I don't need thanks," I tell her. What I need is her honesty.

It's exhilarating.

She steps through the white picket gate that opens up to the grassy VIP area. Over on the green, the players have already lined up, four horses in each team, ready for the first chukka to start. Polo season has begun.

Nora sits on a chair in the front row. Her green floral-patterned dress hugs her shape perfectly as she looks out at the riders. They're all in colorful jerseys—green and white for one team, and red and yellow for the other.

"My question," I remind her. "You still haven't answered it. Why did you swipe right on him?"

"Because he seemed normal," she says. "And not intimidatingly attractive. And besides, I need the practice."

My eyes narrow. *"That's* why?"

"What more could there have been?" She shrugs and glances at me briefly before looking back out at the game. We're close enough to hear the snort of one of the horses and the shake of its head.

"I don't know," I say acidly. "That you liked him? Found him attractive? Wanted to talk more to him? Found him *interesting*?"

She looks back at me. "Is that why you date so rarely? Because you never find women interesting?"

"You're making a lot of assumptions about me, trouble, but you don't know me. Not really."

"No. Clearly not." She takes another drag of her champagne, and her sheet of brown hair hides her face from view. It looks glossy beneath the bright spring sun.

It's the first game of the season, and the stands are full.

She said yes to him because she needed to practice, and that was it. Nothing else.

"Did you have fun? Before I showed up?" I already suspect the answer.

"No," she admits. "He wasn't… it wasn't fun."

"You could have left," I say.

That makes her chuckle. "How? That would have been rude."

Rude.

She has men fawning over her. She must have. She's stunning, and kind, and smart. And if she struggles to leave or set boundaries? Well, that's a problem. And it's not one I want her to have. She may be sparkly and beautiful and smiling with the world, but she has fangs. I've seen her use them with me.

It's my favorite version of her.

The whistle goes off, and the game starts. The beating of

hooves fills the air, rises up to a melody. They gallop past us in pursuit of the ball.

"My turn, Calloway," she says. "Why don't you date?"

"Wrong question." My arm brushes hers, and I lean in closer so my answer will be heard by her and only her. "I'll tell you why I don't date *publicly*. Because once you step into the public eye with someone, it's not just about the two of you. It becomes a spectacle. Just like you and I are a spectacle today."

"And you don't like spectacles," she repeats. "The famed Calloway heir, who throws giant, glittering parties and balls?"

"I stomach them when they're on my terms. But I won't be in a relationship that is on anyone else's."

She crosses her arms over her chest. Her champagne glass hangs from two long fingers close to my arm. "Of course. It's your way or no way."

"Exactly."

"Must be lovely for the women you date privately," she says. "To know that you won't compromise or bend. To be a secret."

I think of Mark, and of the smiles she didn't mean. "I'm up front about what I want, trouble. People are free to take it or leave it. Can you say the same with the men you go on dates with?"

Her eyes track one of the horses as it races past us, the bay coat shining with health. "You don't know anything about my dating history."

"No. But I know you stayed on a date you didn't enjoy. That doesn't sound like someone who's up front with their wants."

"No, it doesn't," she says finally, her voice short with annoyance. "But I'm trying to learn. Hopefully there's a middle ground between being an asshole and being too kind."

"Asshole, you said?"

"Yes. It's only fair I get a shot in."

"Take your shots. I can handle them." I look back out at the game. Excitement makes the air vibrate. There's nothing quite like a game of polo. Nothing as big or powerful as the synchronization between eight riders and horses.

The beat of so many hooves sets a steady rhythm, so deep when they gallop past that it resonates in my bones.

She leans forward. "Alex is playing?"

"Yes."

"Oh. I didn't know that."

"He subbed in last minute." And he's not staying at my place. He told me he was only passing through. He's one of the men I consider brothers, together with her own brother and James.

Boarding school friends who decided to become the family none of us had.

"I love Alex," Nora says. It falls off her tongue so naturally, the endearment. Like he's one of her favorite people.

I look at her. "You do?"

"He's fun." She glances at me. "I thought he was one of your best friends."

"He is. I've wagered on his team to win."

"Of course you have. You four love to play games." She turns back to watch Alex race across the field on a chestnut, wearing a 3 on his back. He's ridden since he could walk. His family operated one of Britain's finest stud farms. "He's good."

"Yes. He is," I say. We all played, up at Belmont. Even if it's never been my preferred sport. "You see him a lot?"

"No. Just through my brother every now and then." She looks at me again. "Just like you."

Just like me, yeah.

Nora watches the game, and I drape my arm along the back of her chair and watch her. Her list was long. Extensive.

It includes everything involved in dating, but beneath it all, I can see the pattern. It's all about expectations. That's what she hates, the expectations that rest heavy atop all dating interactions, like a blanket that smothers her.

"Tonight," I say, without taking my eyes off the gray horse in the lead. Its rider hits the ball toward the goal at a frenzied pace. "We'll go on a date. Just the two of us and the guards."

The crowd roars as a player scores. Despite the sound, I hear the small hitch in Nora's breathing beside me. It takes a few seconds for her to respond. "Good."

"Lesson one, I think, will be saying no to me."

Her lip curves. "Oh."

"I bet you'll enjoy that."

"Yes," she murmurs. "I think so too."

When the second chukka comes to an end, we all clap. The score is even, and it's set to be a good game. I stand and hold my hand out to Nora. She hesitates for only the faintest of seconds before putting her hand in mine.

Eyes track us as we walk to the bar, following our movements. I know there will be more talk about this. Talk that will reach investors, business partners, family friends and family enemies alike.

Calloway has a girlfriend.

It's that Montclair heiress.

Isn't that sweet?

Not only will it get my mother and her asinine matchmaking attempts off my back, but it will reach others in my family. Like my cousin, who stands to inherit Fairhaven if I'm not married by thirty. He's been having conversations with investors for months, discussing how he might sell it, gut it, monetize it.

As if I'll ever let that happen.

We're stopped to chat three times before we get to the bar. Everyone wants to say how lovely the spring weather is, and to ask how my family is doing, and say thank you for the party last week if they were invited. And then they want to meet Nora.

She's graciousness personified.

She laughs and smiles, asks about someone's dog. I didn't even realize they had spoken about that at the party. Wouldn't have remembered even if I had.

We walk over to the fence. I lift an arm to wave at Alex, and he comes trotting over. There's a huge smile on his face beneath the helmet.

"Calloway!" he says. "And little Montclair!"

I roll my eyes and reach over to grip his hand across the fence. The horse he's on is fresh and prances with energy. "You're in the lead."

"Of course I am." His voice has only a hint of Scottish left in it, softening the edges, lengthening some of the vowels. If he wants to, he can make it disappear entirely, become more English than Scot. "Hey, Nora."

She shades her eyes and looks up at him. "Are you coming by West's place for dinner?"

"I wish I could. I have to fly out of here in a few hours." He looks between us and tugs gently at the reins for the horse to stay still, energy or not. "So you two are to be congratulated, then."

"Alex," I warn.

"Cheers to the lovely new couple! I'd drink if I had anything on me." He's broad-shouldered and puts a hand against his hip. "How is it, pretending to love West?"

The words tumble out of him like a joke.

"I haven't had much practice at it," Nora says. She's still smiling, and it looks real. She does like Alex. "You've been his best friend for over a decade. Do you have any tips?"

Alex looks over at me. "I don't know. Have we ever been lovers?"

"No," I say placidly. "Don't listen to anything Alex might say."

"I know him pretty well, to be fair." His horse tosses his head beneath him, and Alex leans forward to pat the sleek neck. "He loves it when you eat off his plate. You should do that all the time."

"I think you're giving me terrible advice," Nora teases.

"He is."

"I am not," Alex protests. "Do me a favor and spend a lot of his money, okay? And make sure to take him to something he finds boring. Go to the ballet. Often."

"Are you really my friend?" I ask Alex. "Because right now I'm starting to wonder."

He grins, a deep smile in his auburn stubble. "A real friend wants you to suffer a little."

A whistle sounds out, and we all look at where the game is about to begin. I nod. "You should go change ponies."

"I know. You bet on me?"

"Of course."

He grins again and tips his helmeted head to Nora. "My lady. I shall win in your honor."

She laughs a little. "I'll have a rose ready for you."

"It will be my honor." He winks at her and then turns his horse, setting off in a canter across the field. Flirting with her is easy for him, I'm sure, because he's not actually considering crossing that boundary. It's harmless fun.

He's never thought about what her lips might taste like or how her body felt when he lifted her down off the ledge.

Not like me.

We make it a few steps back on the grass when Nora stumbles beside me. Her left leg folds, and I reach out on instinct. Catch her with an arm around her waist.

"*Merde*," she breathes. "My heel just snapped."

I look down at where the bottom of her dress kisses her ankles. Sure enough, one of the thin heels on her strappy shoe has broken off. It dangles, half loose, from the sole of her shoe.

She's balancing on one foot, her hand gripping my arm.

"This is so embarrassing," she mutters. "Good thing I got them for free after a shoot."

"Can you walk?"

She puts her foot down gently, balancing on the balls of her feet. "Yes. But it will look like I've had way too much champagne. I'll take them off and go barefoot, I guess."

I glance around, noticing the not-so-subtle looks from people around us. We've been here long enough. We've been seen and we have seen in return.

"We can call it a day," I tell her. "I'll carry you to the car."

"Carry me?" Her voice comes out thin. "West, you don't have to do that."

"I know." Without waiting for her response, I sweep her up into my arms. One locked beneath her knees and the other behind her back. "Hold on to me."

She gasps and grabs a hold of my shoulder. "West," she protests, but her hand is tight around the back of my neck. Her feet dangle to one side, the broken heel clearly visible. She's warm, and soft, and a comfortable weight in my arms.

I start walking toward the exit.

She glances over my shoulder. "Everyone's staring."

"Good," I tell her.

"For someone who hates spectacles, you definitely turned this into one."

My lips curve. "Yes. But I told you, trouble. I'm fine if it's on my terms."

CHAPTER 13
NORA

For our first practice date, West texts me to wait on the steps to Fairhaven at eight. *I'll pick you up.*

I put on a pair of black pants and an asymmetric top that opens over one shoulder and down over my arm. I let my hair fall straight around my shoulders and add a bit of red tint on my lips.

I focus on that so I can't focus on my nerves.

They're not quite as hot and uncomfortable as when I'm going on a real date, when I know there's a man sitting opposite me expecting something. Wanting me to laugh at his jokes, smile, hint, be interesting and interested. When I want to feel something for him but never, ever do.

How will all this work with West?

A few minutes before eight, I walk through the grand entrance and push open the front door, and there he is. Leaning against a car parked on the gravel courtyard, hands in his pockets, watching me. Like he's been standing here just watching the door and waiting for me to arrive.

I pause on the steps.

West's eyes dip down in a slow look over my body, all the

way down to my feet and all the way back up to my face. He's never looked at me like that before.

Like he's savoring the sight.

"Hi," I manage.

"You look beautiful tonight, Nora."

I look at my feet as I take the stairs. It's a welcome break from his eyes.

"You're playing a part tonight?" I ask. One foot in front of the other.

"I remember your list," he says. "You don't like compliments."

I look up at him, but there's no judgment on his face. He opens the passenger door for me. "Ladies first."

He gets into the driver's seat, and it's *him* I'm doing this with. Sitting here beside. Is this how he usually picks a woman up? Will I get to see West Calloway the way his dates do?

The nerves in my stomach tighten.

His right hand curves over the wheel, and I catch sight of the ring. The signet ring. Same one my brother wears and a good reminder of just who he is. He's still the guy who turned me down years ago. Who told Alex that he would never date me.

My nerves settle a little, and it's easier to breathe. I've been on first dates before. I'm good at first dates. It's one of my skills. *I shine*, if I may say so myself. They always ask for a second date.

But my therapist Zeina tells me that's not the point. *You're not yourself. You're performing for them and you come home exhausted. You don't leave any space for your own emotions.*

She's good at saying hard things and making them sound easy.

West pulls down the long driveway to the wrought-iron gates and reaches to turn on the radio. Dulcet tones spread in the car.

"Where are we going tonight?" I ask.

"You'll find out," he says, voice low. "But I think you'll like it."

Damn. I don't like not knowing. "Oh. That's fun."

West glances at me once and then back at the road. "You don't mean that. Push me on it. Make me tell you where we're going."

I cross my legs at the ankles. Right. "Can you tell me, please?"

"Better," he says. "But too polite."

"I am polite. Usually."

His lips quirk. Like he knows the part I'm not adding. *When I'm not with you.*

"It's a surprise," he says, voice deepening again. "But you'll like it. I promise you."

"I'm not good with surprises," I say. "Tell me."

West chuckles, hand tightening around the wheel. "You're so demanding, Nora. You have to learn to be patient."

He's not making this easy.

God, he's so arrogant. And he doesn't seem to mind when I push back. He just speaks his mind and expects the world to adjust to it, to shape to his wants and his needs. I hate him a little for that, and I envy him for it, too.

"I don't like being kept in the dark. Tell me where we're going."

His scarred eyebrow lifts. "Or what?"

"Or I'll get out of this car."

His lips curve. "Well done," he says. "Much better. We're going to the movies."

The praise rolls through me like a warm wave. *Well done.*

And then I realize what he's said. The movies? I was expecting him to do something extravagant. A dinner, seated opposite him, forced to make polite conversation with him for hours. But the movies? I can handle that.

"Oh," I say. "That's really nice. Nearby?"

"Yeah, it's a fifteen minute drive." He looks at me again, and then back at the road. "Tell me about yourself. What's it like to be a model?"

I answer his questions on the way to the cinema. They mirror ones I've gotten many times before, and I wonder if he knows that, too.

If this is also a facet of the part he's playing.

I smile at him and do my best to answer truthfully, adding a little joke here and there. Like I usually do on dates. The talking is not the hard part. It's everything else. The expectations beneath the sentences, the hope and want for something more. That we're two single people constantly evaluating the other, and that I can never decide whether I even like them before they've already made up their mind.

West's expression doesn't change. He nods as I speak, asks follow-up questions. But I don't see that smile on his face. I don't get another *well done.*

At the movies, West and I sit in silence beside one another. The lights dim, and darkness settles like a thick blanket over us. He's taking up the entire armrest between us, and I wonder if that's on purpose. If it's another test for me to push back, like he told me in the car.

Maybe. But it wouldn't surprise me if he's the kind of man who takes up the space available because he's used to doing it.

Because he always has and has always been rewarded for it.

The movie is okay. It's some kind of buddy-cop movie. I can't fathom why he chose it. He asked me before we went in if it was okay if we saw it, because he'd loved the first movie.

His face was blank when he said it, no facial cues other than his words. *It's one of my favorites.*

So I nodded and said yes. *I'd love to.*

But my mind drifts off during the movie, and I'm making lists of all the fabric I still need to buy. I found a great new sewing machine the other day, so at least that's sorted. But I need to find a really good stretch jersey…

By the time the end credits roll, I realize I missed the ending completely.

We walk out of the theater, me still clutching the giant bag of candy he bought me. I prefer chocolate, not gummy bears. But he said they were his favorite and asked me if I wanted to share, and I nodded and said yes.

Outside, the spring air is crisp. Perfect running weather.

He stops beneath the marquee. "So," he says. "This is the part you like the least."

"The end of a date?"

"Mhm. Pretty obvious from your list."

"Yeah," I admit. He looks nothing like the guys I usually meet for dates. A little nerdy, nice, some shy and some too talkative.

But West is the kind of guy I usually say no to right off the bat. Handsome, tall, smooth. They come with expectations, compliments and gifts.

He looks up and down the street like he's surveying a kingdom. The guards are somewhere behind us, too, a shadow we can't escape. I wonder what Sam and Madison think about what we're doing.

"Let's practice, then. We're not West and Nora. You met me two hours ago, when I picked you up."

"Right. And you're… Paul."

"Paul," he repeats.

"It's a normal name," I say. "I've been on dates with at least one Paul before. I actually think my cousin is named Paul."

West's eyebrows lift. "Right. I don't know how to interpret that, except that you're nervous, so this is working."

"I don't babble when I'm nervous."

"Yes," he says, putting a hand at my elbow, "you do."

We start walking down the sidewalk, and just like that, the familiarity is gone. He's a stranger again, and I try my hardest to pretend he is indeed a Paul. Any Paul.

Except cousin Paul.

"I'm walking you to your taxi." His voice is smooth in the darkness. He's West and he's not; a version of himself I've never seen until tonight.

"Thank you." I fall into step beside him. This is always what the entire night hinges on. The goodbye. Men will look at me with those searching, wanting eyes. They'll ask for another date. They'll want to see when I'm free, if they can kiss me, if I want to follow them back home.

And I hate the awkwardness that happens when I say thanks but no thanks.

"The movie," West says. "Did you like it?"

"Yeah, I thought it was pretty good. Did you?"

His hand brushes against mine, and heat rushes up my arm. "Yeah. But I was distracted by the beautiful woman beside me."

I glance up at him. He's smiling a bit, but he looks straight ahead. *He's playing a part.* I have to remember that. He's only pretending, and he's laying the compliments on thick.

I usually feel like they increase expectations. Some guys use them like rain, when I haven't even decided whether I like talking with them yet. It's like they're always five steps ahead of me.

"Thanks," I say. "Um, I was distracted by the guy two rows in front of us who ate his M&M's so loudly."

"He was inhaling that bag, but it never seemed to end."

I smile. "No. Do you think he had several?"

"At least a dozen." West glances my way. We're almost at the car. "Are you free this weekend?"

Oof. This is the moment I'm so bad at, where I feel awkward and tongue-tied and struggle with saying what I want. "I might be," I say. "But I have some plans with friends, and I might be having dinner with family on Sunday. What are you up to?"

West turns so that my back is to the car door. "I'm not doing much," he says. His voice is low, eyes locked on me. "I'd like to see you again, Nora."

I've seen this expression on other men before, but never on West.

There's an intensity in his features, a focus I've never seen directed at me. It makes my throat dry.

He looks at me like he wants me.

It's similar but it's not *the same* as I've experienced before, because it's West. The man I once had a little crush on before he crushed it beneath an arrogant boot.

"You want to see me again," I repeat.

There's a shift in his eyes. A brush of humor. "Yes, this weekend. I'll come pick you up on Saturday. Same time."

"Okay, yeah. That might work," I hear myself saying.

He leans over and puts a hand on the car door beside me. Locking me in on one side. With only streetlights around, his face is cast in shadow. Broad shoulders turned to me, eyes on me, and dear god, is he leaning in?

He is.

His lips quirk, and there's just a foot separating us. I catch the scent of the same cologne I caught the other day, when we were pretending in front of his mother. He smells good. And he's looking at me. He just won't look away. My heart is pounding—

"Trouble," he says. His lips are only inches from mine. "This is when you reject me."

"Oh."

"Push me away," he murmurs, now only an inch from my lips. I feel his warm breath, and my eyes flutter closed on instinct.

I wonder what it would feel like, to be kissed by him. If he closed the distance, would I like it? All his focus, all his strength, directed at me. Maybe it would be ni—

"*Damn it.*" He pulls back. "What the hell was that?"

I blink a few times. "What?"

"You *agreed* to a second date when you didn't want to, and you would have let me kiss you." His brows are drawn low, and the smirk on his lips from a minute ago is gone. He's dropped the role he was playing, and he's West again, the West I know. Not the one who looked at me like I was everything he wanted. "Let's get in the car."

"Okay." I get into the passenger seat and wait for him to walk around. I still feel out of sorts, my heart beating too fast. I've never seen West so close up before.

His amber eyes looked almost dark brown in the low lighting.

He pulls out onto the street without waiting for the guards to get into the car behind us. The silence is heady, a thing with teeth.

"Do you often do that?" he finally asks. He's looking straight ahead, one hand on the steering wheel and the other in a fist on the console between us.

"Do what?"

"Freeze. You just froze when I gave you those eyes you mentioned and leaned in."

My knee bounces. "It happens sometimes."

"Do you let them kiss you even if you don't want to? Like you were about to with me?" He blows out a breath. "Fucking hell, Nora. We need to keep practicing. Next time you're going to push me away so hard I take a step back."

"Next time?"

"Yes." His hand tightens around the steering wheel. "We're going to need more practice here."

I close my eyes, only to see West's face again, so close to my own. His arm braced against the side of the car. Is that how he always is on dates? Is that his real charm or some-thing he turned on just for tonight?

Is that how he looks at women he actually dates?

I froze. But I'm not sure why.

"I think tonight went well. I just didn't… do the last part. I'm going to push you away next time."

"Good," he says. "I asked you about this weekend. You should have told me you didn't want to see me again."

"I can't just say that to someone's face!"

"Of course you can," West says. *"No, I would not like to see you again.* There."

"It's easy for you to say that."

"You must turn down guys all the time."

"Yes, for a first date. But I struggle with the rest of it. Like once I'm seeing them, it just feels like…" I blow out a breath. "How do I tell them to slow down? That I might want to see them again, but I'm not sure yet? That I don't want dinner, I want a walk in the park?"

"I'm not surprised by that." He glances my way, and I can see his jaw working. "You were masking the entire night."

"Masking?"

"Wearing a mask. *Performing.* You didn't want the candy. And that movie? It was terrible, but you said yes because I stated a preference."

I turn to him. "That was on purpose?"

He chuckles darkly. "Well, I wasn't exactly enjoying myself. Of course it was on purpose."

"You were testing me."

"If you'd be honest about what you want? Leave halfway through? *Do anything?* Yes." He shakes his head. "You're too nice. You're nice to everyone except me. I want you to show them the person I see."

It's something I've heard before. But it's not an easy habit to break when making people happy feels so *good* in the moment.

"I'm not nice with you because I know you can take it," I tell him.

"So can the others," he says. "And when you're being overly nice to them, Nora? You're not showing them the real you. And the real you is someone with teeth."

He's right. And I didn't push him away.

But I think that's because I wanted him to kiss me.

CHAPTER 14
WEST

Nora is a beautiful actress.

She's sitting opposite me now at the long walnut table in Fairhaven's dining room. The perfect girlfriend, the attentive guest.

The annoyed Nora she shows me sometimes, green eyes blazing and claws out, is nowhere to be seen.

Now she's wearing a polite smile, her eyes dancing around the table at my family members. Her hair is back in a low bun, and there's a string of pearls around her neck. She's in some kind of light blue sweater and skirt combo.

She looks bright. Brimming with positive energy. The perfect date to show off to the people around this table.

Which is exactly what I asked of her. A statement to my mother. Nora obliged, and *still*. I look at the mask she's wearing, and I want to tear it off.

My sister is having too much fun with this. While my mother asks Nora questions and my aunt and uncle regale her with stories of Fairhaven, Amber shoots me too-long glances.

"West," she says.

I turn to her. "Yes?"

"Can you pass me the salt?"

I hand it to her and hold on to it one second longer. *Behave,* I tell her with my gaze. Her smile widens. "Thank you, dearest brother."

She's never once called me that, and I resist the urge to roll my eyes.

My mother has already asked Nora about Rafe, about her upbringing, her job, what she came here to do. She's the picture of a benevolent queen in the house she used to live in. Once, this room was in constant rotation, she and my father entertaining night after night.

That was then. Now it's mostly empty. The family fractured and none of us willing to pick up the pieces. She lives in the city now, closer to friends and the world she can control. The opera. Luncheons. The ballet.

"The house is stunning," Nora says. I think it's the third time. "West told me that you oversaw the last round of renovations?"

Mom's smile is genuine. "I did, yes! About a decade or so ago. A house of this size, it takes a lot of work. The windows had to be completely refitted—and all according to code."

I haven't told Nora that. She must have read up about Fairhaven.

"Well, it turned out beautiful," Nora says. She's wearing that smile again, the pretty, placid one.

I cut into my steak harder than necessary.

"So, tell me," Mom says. "When did you two start dating? You've known each other for years, surely."

That's what she's here for. Why she ambushed me with this lovely, cozy family dinner that we never have. To find out just how serious this is.

Nora's eyes shift to mine, and she smiles a little. "Well, it's pretty recent."

"Not that recent on my end," I say. "I wanted to ask you out for a long time."

Her eyes widen. "You did?"

"Yes. But being my best friend's little sister, well… It wasn't easy." I look at Nora for another long moment before turning my gaze to my mother. "We connected this past winter, when I was at Rafe's chalet in Switzerland."

"Yes," Nora says. "That's right. I didn't even know he would be there!"

My sister looks between the two of us. Her eyes, so similar to mine, are long-lashed and glittering with too much fun. "I have to ask you something," she says. "I've never really met one of West's girlfriends. Well, not the ones past high school, anyway."

I shoot her a warning glare.

She doesn't look at me.

"Of course," Nora says. "What do you want to know?"

"I *think* I know West pretty well," my sister says. "He hates when people are late, he thinks he's always the smartest person in the room, and he has a pathological need to win at everything. That part's exhausting. The one thing he's *not* is sentimental." Her smile widens. She's doing this on purpose, to make my life harder. "Tell me. What's he like as a boyfriend? Do you get flowers, presents? Does he take you out on fancy dates?"

Not helping, I think. But by the glittering of her eyes, she's not trying to. She's having fun.

I look at Nora, like the rest do. But I bet they don't catch the calculated little tilt of her head or how she laughs softly, as if Amber has said something brilliant.

She's thinking about the right thing to say. Buying time.

"He does. He might not seem romantic, but he has his moments. In fact…" she draws out the syllable, and even my mother leans forward a little, as if she can't wait to hear the rest. "Last night he surprised me by taking me to see a new movie. A sequel to one of his all-time favorites."

I reach for my wineglass. *One of my favorites,* indeed. She's trolling me while still playing her part.

"West went to the movies?" Amber asks.

"I am capable of doing things other than working, *dearest* sister."

"Sailing and traveling," she says. "That's it. What movie was it?"

Nora smiles. "*Hot Pursuit II.*"

My aunt and uncle laugh. Amber grins, and even my mom looks at me with raised eyebrows. The buddy-cop franchise is aggressively mediocre. I don't think anyone has ever described it as one of their all-time favorites.

Nora is blinking at me with those long lashes, a soft smile on her lips. Like I'm her favorite person in the world. Like this is all real and true and not a beautiful lie.

"I knew you would enjoy it," I tell her and turn to the others. "You'd think Nora loves luxury, but she loves a bit of normalcy."

"You know her so well," Amber says. "What's your favorite thing about her?"

I'm going to strangle my sister after this.

But I can't right now, so I look back at my fake girlfriend. "She's the most perceptive person I've ever met."

It's the truth. I saw it the other night, when she was by my side at the party. Perceptive about what other people want from her... and how to give it.

"Ouch," my sister says.

Even my uncle chuckles. "West, you have to come up with something better than that."

But Nora just smiles, running a slim hand along the table-cloth. "Thank you."

"She's sarcastic, too," I say. "Beautiful, of course. And she doesn't shy away from arguing with me. Which... I'm finding I quite like."

Her eyes flash to mine. There's surprise there. If we

weren't pretending, if we didn't have an audience, I wouldn't have been able to say any of those things.

Wouldn't have been able to confess that I wanted to ask her out for a long time. She'll believe my words are just for show.

Mom tops up her wine. "My son needs someone who can speak her mind. What do you like, Nora? About him?"

"You don't have to answer that," I tell the woman opposite me.

But she smiles at me again, and damn it, I hate how convincing it looks. Like she really does like me. "He's funny and caring. He takes really good care of me. Especially now with my… with the security issue I'm having."

"He is good at that." Mom tops up her wine. There's a glint of victory in her eyes. I'm sure she can already hear the wedding bells. "And Nora, how do you feel about children?"

I set down my knife. "That's not an appropriate question."

"It's a perfectly appropriate question," she says, and skewers her meat. "There's no right or wrong answer. I'm simply getting to know your girlfriend. That's not a problem, is it, Eléanore?"

"Not at all," she says smoothly. "Yes, I think I do want children, but not for a while."

"Good," Mom says. "Would it affect your career?"

"If I was still a model, yes, it might. But I'm planning to transition away from that. I want to be a fashion designer."

"And you will be," I say before turning to my mother. "You just said *good*, but before she replied, you said there was no right answer."

"I lied." She gives me a short look before looking back at Nora. Her expression is too sharp, too triumphant. I wanted her to back off, and instead, she's sunk her teeth in further.

I'm going to have words with her after.

"For what it's worth, I want to get to know you too," Nora

says. "All of you. You're important to West, and, well… he's important to me."

My eyes narrow. That voice was gentle. Like she was admitting something that was hard for her. Both my mother and aunt make soft, happy sounds. *Aw.*

"I want more details," Amber says. "You two are the cutest, and Nora, I promise you, this is the *first time* he's brought a girlfriend home. Okay… West. What's Nora's go-to drink?"

"A negroni," I answer without missing a beat. *Shut up,* I tell her with my eyes.

My sister just smiles. "What's Nora's middle name?"

"He doesn't know it because it's embarrassing," Nora answers with a little laugh. "Don't make me reveal it now. Next!"

"What was her first pet?"

"A dog named Titou," I say. "She took him everywhere."

Nora's eyes widen. She didn't know that I knew that.

Well, I've listened to her brother's stories. She got that dog on her fifth birthday. Rafe went with his mom to pick out the shepherd puppy.

"And what was your first date?" my sister asks. "I mean, I can imagine it must have been hard, with Rafe being one of your oldest friends."

"Amber, no need to quiz them," Mom says. She sets down her cutlery. "But yes. Tell us about the courtship."

Jesus fucking Christ.

I look around the table. This isn't something I'll force her into telling. "Like I said, we were both in Switzerland over New Year's. Rafe, James, Alex and I were only skiing for a few days. Nora showed up with her girlfriends."

This part is true enough. But we only crossed paths for a day, nothing more, and there was almost no conversation between us. She smiled at us all, kissed Alex's cheek, hugged

James. Gave me a short look that had none of her pleasantness or soft smiles.

A *real* look.

"On the last day I asked her to ski with me," I say. "Rafe had business to attend to; Alex was hungover, and James had already left. No one knew that we headed out, just us."

"It was unexpected," Nora says. Her eyes flick up to mine, and there's a challenge there, too. "I wasn't sure if he'd be able to keep up with me on the slopes."

My lips curve. She's got the Alps in her blood. "I kept up."

"He didn't tell me it was a date until we were down the slope," Nora says. She's looking at my mother, smiling. "As for my brother... we spoke with him together a month later."

Mom makes a low, thoughtful sound. "Interesting. How did Rafe take it?"

"He was surprised at first. But ultimately, he's supportive," Nora says. Her smile doesn't waver, but her voice grows tighter. "He wants me to be happy."

He would never react like that.

But the others don't need to know that. Nora's hand is tight around the glass when she lifts the wine to her mouth, like she heard the lie as clearly as I did.

The servers come to clear out the dessert course. My mother looks around the table. "Shall we move to the living room?"

"Let's," my uncle agrees. "Do you still have some of that whiskey, West?"

"I do. Help yourself."

I stand behind my chair and roll up my sleeves, waiting for when Amber has to walk around and pass me.

"What," I mutter, "the hell was that?"

She smiles. "I was just showing an interest in my brother's love life."

"Well, stop being interested."

"I'm just having fun," she says. Her face is all innocence,

and I give her a glare. "If you're going to perform for Mom, why can't I?"

"You're a brat," I tell her.

She pats my shoulder and glides past me. "Yes. And you love me."

That leaves just me and Nora, who's standing opposite me, at the large dining room table. She's flanked by the two large French doors behind her, closed to the patio and the ocean beyond.

Her face isn't placid or soft anymore. She glances over her shoulder and takes a step closer. "I hate negronis," she says in a low voice.

I shift to rolling up my right sleeve. "Too bad. They're now your favorite drink."

"West, we don't know anything about each other!"

"I think you did very well," I say dryly. "I'm never going to live down *Hot Pursuit II* being my favorite movie."

"When we're together, yes. But before we sat down, when you were in the other room, your mother asked me a million questions. And I'm sure that as soon as we walk in there with the others, your uncle will ask you things too. And we won't know what the other has said."

I take a step closer, catching her scent. Oranges and something else, something floral. "You're saying we need to get our stories straight."

"Yes," she says. "Our first date was skiing?"

"You would have let me win, too, wouldn't you?" I brace my hand on the back of the same chair as hers. Only inches away. "Just like you said yes to a shit movie yesterday and ate candy you didn't like."

Her eyes narrow. "Tonight isn't about me and my... issues. It's about you and yours."

"What did my mother ask you? Before dinner."

"How serious we are. If I'm planning on living in the US

permanently." Nora's voice lowers even further. "If we've spoken about marriage."

My hand tightens on the back of the chair. "She asked you that?"

"Yes."

"What did you answer?"

"I said no. We've only just started dating," she says. "But I said that I could see a future with you."

The words sink like a stone inside me. She's looking at me with narrowed eyes, annoyed at the situation I've put her in. She doesn't mean the words. Didn't mean them when she said them. And I'm certainly not fit for marriage.

And yet. *I could see a future with you.*

"You're the prettiest little liar I've ever seen," I tell her, and lean in closer. Like I did the other day, when she didn't push me away. When she looked at me like she *wanted* my lips on her.

Like I wasn't alone in wondering what it would feel like.

Her eyes narrow. "Save the compliments for our next practice date."

"Tomorrow," I say, "we go over our stories. We get them straight, and we'll do it while we box. We can work on your issues while we work on mine."

CHAPTER 15
NORA

The estate has a gym.

I hadn't seen it on the tour Ernest gave me, but that shouldn't surprise me. Fairhaven has everything.

Tucked into hidden corners of the sprawling estate, the house reveals itself slowly. The manicured gardens, the tennis court, the pool at the base of the tiered gardens. Only a stone's throw from the ocean itself.

I read the booklet Ernest gave me, flipping through pages that detail its storied history as the jewel of King's Point. According to the story, West's ancestor, the Maverick, built it as a love letter to his wife. I wonder if that was true, or if it was as a testament to his own wealth. I wonder if he asked her beforehand.

Maybe she would have preferred flowers.

Ernest showed me a spare room on the top floor with a tall slanted roof and a giant round window overlooking the gardens and the oceans. *Your atelier, Miss Montclair,* he had said. It took me a moment to remember to breathe.

It's *stunning*.

I spent most of the day setting up my workspace and cutting fabric before going in search of the gym. West texted me to meet him there. *Wear workout clothes.* I haven't seen him since the other night at dinner with his family. Fairhaven is so big, it can swallow up anyone. Does he work from here? Does he go into the city during the days?

I push open the door to the bright space, and he's already there.

He's curling his right arm with a heavy weight in hand, but stops when he sees me. A gray T-shirt stretches across his chest, and he's in a pair of black shorts.

"Hi," I say, hating that I'm still affected by the sight of him. That I can't help noticing how good he looks.

He sets down the weight. "You made it."

"Yes. You want us to *box*?" I put my water bottle on a side console. "I thought we needed to get our stories straight."

"We can do them at the same time." He looks at me with that focus again, the one that makes my mouth dry. "Have you been taught self-defense?"

"The basics."

"Tell me what they are."

I cross my arms over my chest, mirroring his stance. This feels like a pop quiz. "Prevention, really. Always share my location with others. I have a smart watch with a button I can use to call for help quickly. Yell loudly for help. One of the guards I had in Paris told me that the best self-defense isn't to fight. It's to run and run fast." I give him a triumphant smile. "You know I'm good at that."

He runs a hand through his hair. It looks a darker shade of brown today, like it's damp. Did he shower before this? "And if you're cornered?"

"Then I suppose I'll fight. If I have to."

"But no one has taught you how to."

"No."

His face sets in disapproving lines. "Why did Rafe not get you a private instructor?"

"He always told me that the stalker wouldn't get that close."

"He won't." West's voice is steel. "But you knowing how to defend yourself is for *your* peace of mind. Knowing you can get physical if need be."

I run a hand along the back of my neck. I put my hair up in a ponytail, and I feel strangely exposed. "Yeah. I guess... there's logic to that."

"The other night. You didn't push me away at the end of the date, so we'll practice that today."

"If you want me to knee you in the groin over and over again, I will," I say. But there's a nervous ball in my stomach, and I glance at his broad shoulders. This would mean getting to touch him. Putting my hands directly on his chest.

Feel if he's as firm as he looks.

"Yes. That's exactly what I want." His lip is curved. "I want you to have some muscle memory. Have you ever pushed away a guy who tried to kiss you when you didn't want to?"

I pick up my water bottle and focus on unscrewing it rather than meeting his gaze. Because no. Of course I haven't. I've avoided situations where that might even happen, said no to dates, and on a few rare occasions, let a guy kiss me for a bit before I extricated myself with a polite smile.

"Fucking hell," he groans.

"I didn't say anything!"

"You didn't have to. Right. Let's start by warming up." He picks up a pair of boxing gloves and hands them my way. "These are probably too big for you, but they'll do."

"We're boxing." I look at the large, vinyl things in my hands.

"Yes, to start with."

"I know you and Rafe do this. It's... it's James's thing, right?"

"Yes, he's obsessed with self-defense." West rolls his neck, like he's preparing himself, and holds up his hands, large palms facing my way. "And for good reason."

"I bet you wish I was his problem instead of yours," I say. "Imagine how much time you'd have on your hands."

West's jaw tenses. "Bend your knees a bit," he instructs, like I haven't spoken. "Yeah, that's it. Now I want you to hit my hands. A jab and a cross."

"Your hands? Shouldn't you have a pad or something?"

"I can take it," he says. "Want me to get a pad? Prove to me that you can hit hard enough for me to need it."

"You really are pathologically competitive."

"Don't listen to a thing Amber says." He lifts that scarred eyebrow. "Hit me, trouble."

I bend my knees a bit and take sight on his right palm. "Why did she quiz you like that last night?"

"Because she lives to annoy me," he says, "and she wanted to see me sweat. Don't procrastinate. Hit me."

I give him an annoyed glance and then hit his palm with a jab. The glove connects softly.

"Weak," he says.

I hit his other hand harder. Twice in a row. I tried boxing at the gym a few years ago, and this is just as thrilling.

"Better. But I know you have more anger inside you."

"I'm not angry," I say.

"Sure you're not."

I hit him harder. He doesn't budge, just follows my movements with his hands, pushes back against my hits. And he keeps looking at me with those narrowed, intense eyes. Like he sees far too much.

"What are your hobbies?" I ask while hitting his right hand as hard as I can with a jab. He doesn't even flinch.

"Sailing," he says. "Working out. Traveling. If it ever comes up in conversation, you can use one of those."

"Your favorite cocktail?"

His lips curve up. "Negronis."

"Great. You can finish all the ones I'll have to drink now."
I hit him again, and he takes a small step back. Taps his finger against his chin. "What do you work with?"

"You know that. I run Calloway Holdings, which owns Cal Steel and a few other companies."

"Do you work from here?"

"Here, from the office in Manhattan, or I'm traveling for business." He tilts his head back. "Aim for my head now."

"You can't be serious."

"I'll duck." He lifts an eyebrow. "I thought you'd like the chance to hit me. Get some of your frustration out, trouble."

"I don't hate you *that* much," I say.

His smile curves. "I think you do."

"I'm very *indifferent* regarding you." But I drop back down into the stance he showed me and try to punch his head. He does exactly what he said. He drops down, hands raised. I jab twice in a row. We haven't done this long, and my shoulders are already aching.

"Why do you live here and not in the city?"

It's the first time he's hesitated before answering. It's brief, but I catch it. "I don't like being far from the ocean. The city doesn't let you think."

I pause for a moment. "Fairhaven is beautiful."

"It is. And it's mine." He rolls his neck.

"What about your pet? The cat I've seen around?"

"I don't have any pets," he says.

That makes me pause. I saw a sleek gray cat running through the library the other day. I saw it again lying outside by the apple orchards, bathing in a speck of sunlight.

"Well, the estate seems to have one."

"Maybe one of the staff feeds it." He nods at my hands. "Come on. Hit me."

"You're a masochist," I mutter, but I do hit him. Again and again.

He blocks them all, moving in a graceful line around me

so I have to stay on my toes. A jab, a cut. Another hit to his head. He ducks it easily, sidestepping.

"Why have you never brought anyone home to meet your family?"

"You met my family," he says dryly. "Why would I put a woman through that?"

"Except me."

"I knew you could take it. We come from the same world." He holds up his palms again, and I cross jab one of them. My breath is coming faster. It's a good workout, this. Being on my toes. Moving in tune with him. "My turn," he says. "How have you never been in a relationship?"

"I'm not telling you that."

He narrows his eyes. "Right. Then tell me why you think you're not angry."

"Because I'm *not*. I'm never angry." I hit his right hand a bit harder, and his lips curve up again in that frustrating, arrogant smirk. Like he knows best. I hit his left hand as hard as I can, and the smack rings out loudly. "People don't like it when you get angry, and I can't stand it when they do. So I'm *never* angry."

West's eyes are a pool of light brown, of scotch in the sunlight. "You can get as angry as you like with me. We're locked together on this. So practice getting angry with me."

"I don't need to practice getting angry. I need to practice *dating*."

"And why can't you practice both, you little over-achiever?"

I aim a hit straight at his head, at that smug smile. He ducks, and the smile only widens. His hair is messy now, falling in brown tendrils over his forehead. I've never seen him like this with me. Half undone and half exhilarated.

He looks like he does when I've seen him with my brother and their friends. When he comes to life, when he relaxes into himself. Mischievous confidence in a rich, handsome package.

He sidesteps, forcing me to follow him across the gym. "You need that anger," he says. "You need it so you can stand up for yourself if a guy tries anything you don't like. If he insists on taking you to see a movie you don't like."

"We're supposed to get our stories straight." I aim another punch at him, and he blocks it. "You just winged the first date story!"

"Of course I did. And they bought it."

"I'm *perceptive*. What kind of compliment is that?" I hit him again and again, and he ducks effortlessly. Why won't he go get the pads? Haven't I proven how hard I can hit? My arms ache now.

"A true one," he says. "I wasn't pretending. Now come on. Don't get lazy."

I aim a hit to his left palm. He captures my gloved hand instead and starts undoing the Velcro around my wrist.

"What are you doing?" I ask.

"Moving on to the next stage." He pulls off my other glove too and tosses them both to the carpeted floor. "Keep this energy and use it to argue with me. Push me away."

Oh.

West takes a step closer, and the inches between us vanish into nothing but a sliver of heated air. He's still wearing that expression that makes my chest tighten—the focused eyes, the curve to his lips. I reach up and put my hands on his chest.

He's warm beneath the fabric of his T-shirt. Firmer than anyone has the right to be.

"That's it," West says. "Now push me away."

I shove. He moves two inches, if that, but a smile spreads across his lips.

"What's wrong? You don't want to see me again?" His

voice drops into the low one from the other night, when he pretended he was into me.

"No. I don't." I shove harder this time, putting my entire body into it. This whole thing is stupid, and I'm sweaty and excited. This time he takes two solid steps back.

"Well done," he says, and the praise feels like the taste of sugar. "You're doing really good. Do it again, trouble."

My heart is beating fast. I can hear it, the pounding in my ears, when he steps up close again. This time, he brushes a hand along my cheek and rests it right beneath my chin. It's a faint touch.

But he's never touched me like that before.

He tips my head up and looks at me with half-hooded eyes. The same he gave me the other night.

Like I'm someone he wants.

"So pretty," he murmurs, and his head drops another inch in my direction. The words make my breath catch. I've been called that before. Brushed it aside, ignored it. Now it lodges beneath my skin like a warm caress.

I put my hands back on his chest and shove. "No thanks."

West laughs. The sound heats up the room. "You're so polite. That was very good. How does it feel?"

"Strange," I admit. And good. *Look at me like that again.*

"We'll do it over and over again until it feels like second nature," he says. "And then we might work on getting that politeness out of you, too." He runs a hand through his hair, and the mirth on his face falls like a curtain dropped. "Mark. Did he try to kiss you?"

"No," I say. "You interrupted, remember? Besides, guys often wait to try until the end of the date."

"Which is why that's the part that stresses you out."

"Yeah. But it's not just the kiss. It's the questions." I shrug. "I'm not good at those kinds of conversations. Deciding whether we're doing it again. If they ask how I feel…"

"We'll practice them too." He lifts an eyebrow. "Again?"

"Again."

We do it a few more times. Each time, he tells me how good I'm doing, until I come to crave the sound of the compliment in his low voice.

When he lowers his face the next time, I decide to try something different. With his lips only inches from mine and my chest tight with anticipation, I turn my face to the right. Offer up my cheek instead.

He pauses, inches from my skin. "You've done that before."

"Once or twice," I say. "It always works."

"I want you to try one more thing," he says. This time, he's right in my space, all six foot two inches of man and muscles beneath his T-shirt. "Slap me."

My eyes widen. "Of course not."

"You were the one who spoke about kneeing me in the groin." He lifts an eyebrow. "This is milder than that."

"I've never... I can't... I've never done that before."

"Then this is the time to start."

"Why do you want me to do that? Do you get off on pain?"

He chuckles. "No. We'll work on proper self-defense tomorrow. For now, I think you have a lot of mental blocks. You won't even let yourself get *angry*, for fuck's sake. If you needed to, could you defend yourself? Lift your hand?"

"I don't know. I'm not a violent person."

He blows out a breath. "No. Really? You could have fooled me."

"Sarcasm doesn't suit you," I say primly.

"You're lying, but that's fine. Everything suits me." He puts a hand on his cheek and looks straight at me. "Slap me when I come at you this time. So if you're ever in a situation where a little shove on the chest doesn't work, you know what to do."

He's pushing the limits.

He's pushing *my* limits.

Irritation slithers down my spine. Irritation at him for correctly reading the situation so quickly. He identified one of my core fears within one lesson. I'm terrified of making people upset. I'm a people-pleaser to my core, with everyone but him. And he's challenging that.

When someone is in front of me, asking something of me... I don't know how to handle it. That's why I just say no to dates, or say yes to my family and friends. I don't know how to find the middle ground. To say *no, I don't want to kiss you yet, but I do want to go on another date with you.*

To negotiate. To *what if we do it this way?*

The easiest way to handle a conflict is to avoid it.

Works every time.

"Nora," he says, his voice darkening. "You've been so good today. Can you do this too? Remember how annoying I am. How I control your life. How I've forced you to date me in public. You can hit me. You don't even like me."

I roll my neck. "Not right now, no."

His grin flashes. Then he takes a step forward. And another. We've ended up close to one of the large machines in the gym, and my back hits the machinery.

He's crowding me in.

"Do you want me to pretend to be the stalker?" he asks. "Or a date who won't take no for an answer?"

I think of the way it feels when he comes close. Of his breath against my lips and the fluttering in my stomach that happens each and every time. The wondering of what it would feel like if this was different.

"The second one," I whisper.

He puts a hand beside me, locking me in on one side. My heart picks up with speed when he lowers his head. His eyes drop to my lips, and he's watching me like I'm all he's ever wanted. All he's ever needed. "You're so pretty, it destroys me."

Oh my god.

He's upped the levers by ten.

"Can I kiss you?" His lips come closer, and there's a pounding in my head. "Nora, let me kiss you."

My eyelids flutter like they want to close. *Please do,* I want to say. But he doesn't mean it. He's pretending, just like we're both meant to be pretending. This is all fake.

And he wants me to slap him.

I put my hands on his chest instead, and I push him away like I've done before. Except he barely budges. He just chuckles and runs his fingers over my hair. Pushes a tendril behind my ear.

I once dreamed of him looking at me like this.

Now he is, and it undoes me. And I *hate* that I'm still attracted to him after everything. After what he said. After agreeing to help me out only to do his best friend a favor. I *shouldn't* wonder what his kiss would really feel like.

And right now I hate that part of me.

So I slap his cheek with my right hand. The sound rings out in the space, and before I can think, I push him back and lift up with my knee. It hits his groin. Not very hard, because I'm still holding back. But it sends West backward, and I stumble after him, my free hand still on his chest.

I don't know who loses balance first. But we fall to the ground, and he wraps his free arm around my waist, softening the blow with his body. We hit the ground with a groan.

I'm half draped over him. My leg between his, my chest pressed to his.

"Fucking hell," he groans. He lifts his free hand and runs it over his face, hiding his eyes from view.

"I'm sorry!" I quickly pull my hand away from his chest. "Did I hurt you? God, I'm so, so sorry."

West starts to laugh. He slides his hand up through his hair and then locks his arm behind his head. "That," he says, "was a triumph. You do have some anger in you, don't you? You showed me your fangs."

I turn over onto my back beside him. And something in his own mirth brings out my own. "Oh my god. I can't believe I just did that."

"Feel good?"

"Yes. Is that terrible?" I close my eyes, still smiling. "Am I a violent person?"

"No," he says. "And you did real well, trouble."

He props himself up on an elbow, his dark hair hanging over his forehead. I let my gaze run over that scar of his again. The one through his left eyebrow. I've always wondered how he got it.

But I've never been close enough to him to ask. It's one of the many secrets behind West Calloway, the rich-boy heir turned bachelor king. "Why does your mother want you to get married so badly?" I ask instead.

"Why have you never been in a relationship?"

We stare at each other. His eyes look honeyed, the color of thick syrup. We both know we're at an impasse. We may be locked in this together, but that doesn't mean all the truths should come tumbling out.

There's a sharp knock on the door before it opens. West's jaw tenses, and he rolls away from me, pushing up into standing. "Ernest?"

The dignified estate manager looks from West to me, still on the floor. "I'm sorry to interrupt, but there's been another incident."

CHAPTER 16
WEST

The *incident* is an envelope.

The experts I hire spend the next few days analyzing it. The manila envelope is post-stamped in New York, and it contains pictures of Nora from the past week. Out running. With her guards outside a fabric store. The picture from the *Long Island Tribune* of the two of us is attached, too, cut out in precise lines. There's a note with handwriting that immediately gets sent off for analysis.

He won't keep you from me.

It's unnerving. Unsettling. It's also a clear escalation from what she received back in Paris. There were letters, but sometimes weeks went by between them. Now it's barely been a week since the bouquet incident.

The plan might be working. Annoying him, drawing him into getting more reckless. I need more moments like the polo match or the party. *He won't keep you from me.* Yes, I will. And I need to goad this obsessed stalker into making a mistake... and then I'll catch him.

The day after, when we're back in the gym, I tell Nora about it. Show her images of what was sent and what I'm going to do with it. What my team is looking for and analyzing.

She nods through it all, asks a few follow-up questions. Her hands are balled up and her expression is tight. Like she's holding back what she's really feeling. But she can't hide the effort it takes.

"Okay," she says finally. "Thank you for telling me."

I raise an eyebrow. "That's it?"

"I really do appreciate it, West. Rafe doesn't usually share this much with me. And I want to know. It's my life, after all."

I shake my head. "Not that. I don't need thanks."

"Then what do you mean?"

"Are you angry? Scared? Annoyed? He knows you're living here. He's been watching you," I say, and *I'm* angry. The idea of someone thinking they have any right to her...

"It wouldn't be productive." She locks herself back under control, and the effort I saw on her face disappears. She becomes a still lake again. "Let's continue with the moves you taught me."

I narrow my eyes at her. "It's not *productive*?"

"I can't do anything about it," she says. We've been practicing self-defense maneuvers for an hour already. How to get out of a grip, how to twist a man's arm. How to break out of a chokehold.

I want her to feel competent. Empowered. Even if I'll never let that bastard get close to her.

I approach her again, and this time, she doesn't hesitate. She ducks from my lazy attempt to catch her and shoves her knee between my legs.

I stop it only an inch from making impact. "Good," I tell her. "That was really good."

A smile flashes over her lips. She likes these kinds of compliments, I've noticed. Maybe not the ones that make her feel ogled or like an object. She's had enough of those.

But she loves being praised.

Good thing I fucking love praising her.

"Again," she says, her cheeks flushed with color. "And I *know* anger is productive. My therapist tells me all the time."

"Your therapist?"

"Yes." She jabs my way, and I raise my palms in time to catch her attempts. She's not holding back today. "I've tried to work through all of this. I told you."

"In a therapy room."

"Yes, but she wants me to get out there, too. She tells me I've said no too many times and that I need to learn to say yes and have the tough conversations that follow."

"Have you told her about this? About us?"

Nora hesitates only a second, but it's long enough for me to hear the answer. *Yes.* "She won't tell anyone."

"I'm not worried about that." I approach her again and wrap my arm around her upper body. Fix my forearm against her throat. We've done this before, and I'm not applying any pressure. "What does she think?"

Nora is warm beneath my grip. She's also quick, reaching up to find the spot on my hand, between thumb and index finger, that hurts like a motherfucker when you press down.

"She thinks this is good for me." She presses down. Sharp pain radiates up my arm, and I release her.

"Well done," I say through gritted teeth.

"I'm sorry," she says. I fix her with a look, and she shrugs a little. "I know you tell me not to apologize to you, but I have twenty-four years of practice. It's hard to break."

"I know. Which is why I'll remind you. That was really good. You found it immediately."

"I've been practicing."

"On yourself?"

"Yeah." She must see my look, because she rolls my eyes. "I don't do it *hard. I'm* not the masochist."

I hold up my hands again, and this time she jabs twice before giving me a cross. "So I've been given the stamp of

127

approval from your therapist," I say. The idea of Nora talking with someone about me, about *this*, fills me with curiosity. That there's a space where truth floods out of her. "What have you told her?"

"That's privileged information."

I can't help teasing her. "She's probably on my side, you know."

"About what?"

"*About what?* she asks," I say and shake my head. "About this. You learning self-defense and embracing your anger."

Color spreads along Nora's cheeks. "She was shocked when I told her about that. Our practice with... Well. Practicing dating."

"Shocked at the *brilliance* of it. Don't forget to move your feet."

She glances down and then shifts around me, her hands still raised. Tendrils of dark hair have escaped her ponytail and frame her face. "She said she'd never heard of anyone using that approach before."

"We're innovators."

"Apparently." Her lips tug. "Let's try the thing you did earlier."

"Grabbing you from behind?"

She nods and turns like she's walking away from me. I move closer and sling one arm around her waist; the other covers her mouth. My movements are slow, and I don't hold her hard. I wouldn't even if she asked me to.

We've done this several times already.

She's soft against me, and warm, and her lips part beneath my palm on an exhale. There's a brief second where I wonder what that would feel—

And then her hands come up to grip my arm. She drops beneath me into a wider stance and puts all her weight into pulling down my arm. Then she swings her leg back and bends it into the back of my knee.

I'm pushed forward, off balance, and can't hold on to her anymore or I'll fall. She dances back and out of my arms with a wide smile. "That was the best one yet!"

"That was magnificent," I tell her honestly. "And now? What would you do?"

"Run. You know I'm fast." She's still grinning.

"Yes, you are. You'll run and you'll call for help. You'll call me."

"And you'll come?"

I push up the sleeve of my shirt. "Always."

She glances away, out the windows and toward the green spring lawn. But just as quickly, she looks back at me. "Okay."

"Promise me," I say. "You'll call me if you need help."

"Yes, I promise." She rolls her eyes. "Sometimes you're worse than Rafe."

That feels like a barbed spear in my chest. I haven't reminded myself of just how much she *should* be like a sister to me in days. It has been futile, since I clearly can't see her that way. I've never been able to.

But maybe she does.

I switch tactics and study the fire in her eyes, the flush in her cheeks. She's comfortable around me, at least.

"You said you don't like arguing with people," I say. "But you must have done it plenty of times."

She rolls her neck, like the question annoys her. "No, not really. I guess I just never learned how to. I never argue with anyone—not with my family, not with friends."

"You have siblings," I say. "You and Rafe never argued?"

"No."

"Funny," I say. "I argue with him all the time."

"We're five years apart, and then he was away at boarding school with you and Alex and James. And after the accident, when we lost my oldest brother... it felt like my job to keep everyone happy." Behind her, the ocean is stormy today, the

129

sky gray. "My two younger siblings weren't born until Dad was on wife number three, and the age gap in that direction is large, too."

I cross my arms. "What about friends? Guys you've dated? Have you ever argued with them?"

"Ever?" Her voice comes out testy, like she's embarrassed by the question. She runs a hand through her ponytail. "No. Not really. I avoid it; I *told you*. I give them what they want, or I remove myself from the relationship entirely."

"Right. Either it's a hard yes or a hard no."

"Yeah," she says. "I guess you can teach me how to argue, then."

"Weird kink, but okay," I say. "If you want to, we can fight all day long."

Her heartbeat picks up—I can see it in the way she shifts, the way her breath changes. "It's not like… I mean, I don't *like* arguing."

"People usually don't like doing things they're not good at." I grab her water bottle and hand it to her. It feels like she needs something to do, something to hold. She gets nervous even at the thought of this. "But that's where practice comes in. Repetition. Just like with you saying no to men."

She uncorks the bottle. "Who made you an expert at fighting?"

"I can handle conflict," I tell her. "Everyone fights with the people they're close to. My parents did a bit too much. Rafe and I, and Alex and James, well… you think four teenage boys always saw eye to eye?" I lean back against one of the weight machines. "What do you want to fight about?"

"There's nothing on my mind right now."

"Nothing? I doubt that very much."

"Fine. Maybe there are lots of things, but nothing that we can argue about."

"I've met your mother. I met your father, too," I say. "They don't strike me as people who never fight."

"I never said they didn't."

"You said you never learned. I don't believe you," I tell her.

Her gaze snaps to mine. There's a glint of irritation in her eyes. It feels like victory. She knows exactly what I'm doing with my goading.

"Yes, *they* fought. The entire family fought. But it wasn't productive. It wasn't efficient. And it always, always meant I had done something wrong. And it was never truly over. They didn't fight *with* me. They fought *at* me."

"It was never over?"

"No, there was never a resolution. Mom loves bringing up disagreements that happened months ago, reminding me with little barbs of things I've done—things that still hurt her. My father, when he was alive, didn't argue at all. You either agreed with his perspective, or the conversation was over and you could leave. There was no in-between. And there was certainly no making up afterward." She takes a deep breath. "I just had to quietly wait it out, test the waters, prove myself to them again, until the argument was swept under the rug and hopefully forgotten."

"So you never knew when it was over."

"No."

"We'll practice that too." I hold up my hands. "Do you do the same things with guys, then?"

"I guess," she says. "I know what to say to ensure there's no argument, to bend to what they want to hear, because the idea of not doing it…"

"You'd get punished if you didn't," I finish. "Your mother. She's…"

"Yes," she says with a groan. "You know her."

"I've met her a few times. She's a character," I admit. Rafe and Nora's mother was once an actress. She nurtured attention and craved it, a circle that sustained her, until it stopped. Until she pushed that onto her children instead.

I've seen the exasperated way Rafe has dealt with her over the years.

I've never witnessed the way she takes it out on her daughter. It rearranges some of the things I've heard, things I've seen.

"Was she the one who wanted you to model?" I ask.

Nora looks down at the water bottle. "Yeah. It was her dream for me. She made most of it happen."

I shake my head slowly. "Don't say that. You did the work."

"Yes, sure, but it was…" She shrugs a little. "I'm grateful. I don't mean to say that I'm not, and I know that my life—"

"For fuck's sake," I interrupt. "There are no cameras here. Do you think I'm going to hold you to anything? Say what you really feel. Without the caveats."

Nora's eyes flash again. "*Fine*. It was her dream, and I did it to make her happy. All of it. The auditions, the dietitian, the nose job, the sessions with a coach on how to walk, how to pose. And it made me feel good for a while, to know that I was making her happy. That I was making photographers happy. My father, my brother. Everyone thought it was so *clever*, that I could model the brands Valmont owns."

"I'm sure they did." My arms are crossed over my chest now, like that might stop my muscles from tensing with anger. Every single thing she's saying makes my blood heat another degree. "A *nose* job?"

"The week after I turned eighteen," Nora says. Her face is calm in a way I'm not. Like I'm the only one burning with anger. "She found the surgeon, booked the time."

"She did *what*?"

"To set me up for success, she said." Nora shrugs. "It was years ago."

"You never needed it."

She chuckles a little, but it's polite. Strained. "Right. Thanks."

"Do you enjoy it? The work?"

"Modeling? Not really. I loved getting to work with beautiful designers, though, and wear their clothes. It's taught me a lot." A real smile spreads across her face. "It's what made me realize I want to be the one creating the pieces. I don't want to model anymore."

"You want to design."

"Yes." She meets my gaze with one of her own. "Even if my mother and Rafe think I'm throwing away an opportunity by turning down modeling jobs."

"They've told you that?"

"Yes. Repeatedly."

"I wonder what your therapist says about your mother. And your father," I say darkly. The image of much younger Nora, caught between two arguing titans, pressured in every direction, makes red descend. *They didn't argue with me.*

They argued at *me.*

"She has a lot of opinions there too," Nora says. She raises her hands. "Shouldn't we practice again?"

"*Should* we?" I ask her. "What do *you* want, Nora? It's your list of things to practice, and so far, I've decided on the self-defense classes. That wasn't on your list."

"No, I guess it wasn't," she says slowly. "But I like the idea of defending myself. If the stalker ever… Well. Not to imply that your team isn't great."

"You can imply it if you want to. I've told you, my ego can take it."

That makes her laugh a little. "I'm not so sure about that."

"Test me," I say. "Get angry with me, argue with me. As long as you're being yourself. Okay?"

She nods, and a small smile curves her full lips. Lips I've come close to kissing far too many times, all under the guise of helping her. *I'm an asshole*, I think. But at least I can help her practice standing up for herself and being honest.

It's a fucking tragedy that anyone ever made her feel like she couldn't.

CHAPTER 17
WEST

The next day, I'm waiting outside the front doors when she returns home. I've spent almost a solid six hours in remote meetings, discussing the latest expansion of Cal Steel, and the sight of her washes it all away. Chases away the headache that's been drumming at my temples.

She gets out of the car with two large bags, a pair of sunglasses on her head, and parted lips. "West?"

"Welcome home."

"You're here? Waiting for me?"

"I am."

She lifts up one of the bags and gives me another curious look. "You're not here to tell me off, are you?"

"And why do you think I'd do that?"

"Because I left Fairhaven."

"It's your right to." She took her guards with her, and despite what she might think, I'm not her jailor. Never have any intention of being so, either. I open the door for her. "I'm not angry at you. But we can pretend that I am, if you like."

Her lips part. "You mean..."

"Practice arguing. You haven't had much issue standing up to me in the past, so it shouldn't be too hard for you."

"That's different. You're different." She pauses in the doorway to my home, and then her shoulders straighten. "Okay. Tell me off."

The determination in her voice makes my lips twitch. But I don't let any of that amusement bleed into my tone. "Where were you?"

"Out," she says. She puts her bags down on the checkered marble floor. "I brought guards. Amos and Miguel. I even stopped to get us all burritos between errands. I went to two fabric stores, one bookstore, and a coffee shop. I made sure the guards were feet away the whole time." She turns to me, fitting her hands to her hips. "Are you pleased, my fearless leader?"

My lips curve. "That's an exaggeration, wouldn't you think?"

"You're right. Despot. *Dictator*." She takes a step forward, and her smile morphs into something sweet. "Is that better?"

"You're doing spectacularly," I tell her. "And who said you're allowed to go out?"

"I did. You don't set my schedule. I followed every single rule." She grabs one of the large bags stuffed with fabric. I take it from her and shift it to the hand farthest away so she can't steal it back.

"Feeding your guards is not part of our deal."

She rolls her eyes. "That's ridiculous."

"No. It's practical. Do you know whether they have allergies? What if Amos has a severe gluten intolerance and your kindness puts him out of commission for three hours? Who will guard you then?" I step past her to grab the bag of books. It's far heavier than the one stuffed full of fabric.

"Where are you going with those?"

I head for the stairs. "Your workspace."

"Amos isn't gluten intolerant."

I look over her shoulder. "Why do you know that?"

"Because he ate bread. And he was able to perform his

very boring duties of walking five feet behind me without keeling over in pain. I asked what they'd want, and he said he loved a place down the street." She follows me up the stairs, her heels clicking against the wood. "Why wouldn't I be allowed to buy lunch for my guards? That's ridiculous."

"They're not your playthings."

"I don't treat them like they are. Which why I fed them!"

"Not your pets, either." The irritation in my voice isn't entirely staged. Amos is tall, handsome. He has an easy smile, and he's around her age, too.

"I bet they do a better job if they're well-fed. Also, unless any of them file an HR complaint, it's officially none of your business."

"I hire them. I pay them." Shouldering open the door to her studio space, I tilt my chin to tell her to go first. "It's decidedly my business."

"You're being an ass."

"Did you want to go to the place Amos suggested, or did you please him by choosing it?"

"Don't overanalyze everything I do," she snaps.

I set the bags on the large table Ernest must have put in here for her. In the center of the room, right next to two mannequins and a sewing machine. "Did you buy half the store?"

"I bought some books. For inspiration." She takes a deep breath and glances at me. "And I've agreed to the guards. I want the guards. But how I interact with them is up to me, not you."

I look down into one of the bags to hide my smile. "You should have let me pay for all of this."

"What? No. This is my collection."

"And you're my girlfriend."

"*Fake* girlfriend."

"Fake or real, you're mine," I say. The words feel better than they should. "Take my card next time."

"I'm perfectly capable of funding this collection. It's mine." She takes a step closer, and I catch the scent of her. Flowery shampoo and clean woman. "If you're so eager for me to spend your money, I can think of more fun things to buy."

"If that's meant to be a threat, it's only making me intrigued."

"So if I spend it on buying lunch for all my guards every day," she murmurs and tilts her head. "You'll love that, will you?"

My jaw works. "As long as it's my money you're spending and not your own."

"I've been a professional model for years. I have a savings account."

I reach into my back pocket and slide out my wallet. Grab one of the black cards and set it beside her on the working table. "Use mine."

"You know that I don't like it when men pay."

"I know. It's on your list."

She grabs my card, turns it over, and runs a finger over the embossed name. *Weston Calloway.* "People think it's stupid. A few of my girlfriends tell me I should accept any free dinners and drinks that come my way."

"Do you think it's stupid?"

"No." Her fingers curl around my card, and she looks back up at me. "I've told you—I hate when men have expectations of me. If they buy me stuff, well…"

"You don't owe them shit," I say. We're supposed to be arguing, but this is too important. "You don't owe your mother a career, and you don't owe a man kisses or another date just because he chooses to pay for a meal."

"I know it intellectually. But it's not that easy."

"It is that easy."

Her eyes flash. "No, it's not. Disappointing people is *not* easy. If it was, do you think I'd be the way I am? Maybe it's easy for you. You've never struggled with speaking your mind."

"Which is why I know it's easy."

She rolls her eyes. "Just for that, I'm going to take this card and spend it on all kinds of stupid stuff."

"No, you won't. You'll think about it. But you'll be too afraid to upset me for real to make good on it." I take a step closer, and she braces her hands against the worktable behind her. "I wish you would."

"If I do it, it won't be to make *you* happy."

"Well done." I slide a finger under her chin and tip her face up. Her eyes spark with the look I've come to crave. Surprise. Excitement.

Curiosity.

"You're so good when you're fighting back," I tell her.

"I'm starting to like it." Her words are whispered, laden with guilt. Like it's an admission.

I slide my thumb over her lip. "You're pretty when you stand up for yourself."

"That's not why I do it."

"I know. But that doesn't make it any less true."

Her breath warms my thumb. "Is this when we practice ending an argument?"

I drop my hand. She's not mine to touch. I know that. Not outside our practice sessions, outside the fake game we're playing in public. And I've forgotten.

"Yes." My voice comes out gruff. "You were right. You're free to do what you like with your guards."

She nods a little. "I'm sorry I didn't listen to your concerns. And that I got so heated."

"I got heated, too."

"I guess we have that in common." She looks at me like

I'm something new, something she's never seen before. "Are we good?"

"We're good," I tell her. "And I mean it."

"I mean it too." She digs her teeth into her lower lip for a second, distractingly pretty, beautifully earnest. "I won't bring it up again. Or hold it over your head."

"I won't either."

"Good," she says.

"Great," I say.

A smile breaks out over her face, and it makes something tighten inside me. Like a ray of sunlight peering in through the large half-moon windows in this room that was forgotten, the furniture covered with sheets, before it became hers. "I've never had closure like that before."

"How did it feel?"

"Good. A bit silly." She shrugs again, and the smile stays in place. "We weren't really arguing."

"No. But can your nerves tell the difference?"

"Not really." She glances down at my card, still in her hand, and then slides it into the back pocket of the white jeans she's wearing. "Thank you."

"I meant what I said about that. Practice getting used to men paying for things for you too. If you want."

"Yeah. Thank you."

I shouldn't ask her for this. Have been considering it for days, whether it's a good idea or not. But the glittering of her green eyes is an invitation, a door ajar. "Want to pretend for me tomorrow night?" I ask. "We can combine a lesson with being seen in public again."

She tilts her head. "You need a date?"

"I do."

"Where are we going?"

I open my wallet again. This time I pull out the playing card that was delivered a few days ago. It's an ace, and scribbled on it in a flowing cursive is a date and an address.

And on the back it says *come play* in red ink. Beneath it are two words. *Paradise Lost.* The party's theme this time. Considering the address, the theme has been very deliberately chosen.

Nora turns the card over, her eyes narrowing. "Oh my god. This is the invite?"

"Yes." I hesitate only a moment. "It's a... special kind of party. People go there to gamble."

"Will we play?"

"No. But we need to be seen." The stalker won't be there. He *better* not be. But some of the world's most powerful people will be. They always show up to these parties, and in the haze of the night, they'll all see that Nora is with me. That she has my protection. It'll filter down the chains, back out through the network. The Calloway and the Montclair.

"We'll need to put on a show," she says, and her gaze slides back up to mine. "Won't we?"

"We will, trouble. Will that be a problem?"

"No. It's just..."

"Just what?"

"Maybe we should practice that," she says. "I've never been a girlfriend before. Never engaged in... PDA."

Everything in my body tightens. "You want to practice the physical part of dating."

"No." Her cheeks spread with the most delicious color, and she looks back down at the books she bought. "Well, yes. Sort of. Apart from fighting, we haven't... touched."

I'm undone.

By her voice, by her asking for what she wants, and by the openness in her expression. She's not sparring with me right now. She's offering up another truth.

"When we're in public, when I'm pretending to be..."

"Mine?" The word feels better than it should.

"Yes." She worries her teeth between her lower lip. "What would that look like?"

"How would I touch you?"

"Yes," she whispers.

I reach for her hand.

I've touched her before when we practiced self-defense. I had my hand on her low back at the party. But threading our fingers together between us, in the silence of the large room, feels like the first time we've touched.

"Like this. I would be touching you. Often."

"Holding my hand?" She's looking down at where we're joined.

"Yes. I'd have my arm around your waist. Like this..." I do just that with my free arm, sliding it around her narrow waist and flattening my palm against the low of her back. Like she's actually mine to touch. Like there's not a million reasons why I shouldn't.

Nora's eyes land back on mine. "That's good."

"Yeah? It's good?"

"I mean, it's okay. I can do that." She's nodding a few quick times, now, like she's embarrassed.

"If we're sitting next to each other, I might do this..." My hand trails up her back, finding the soft ends of her hair. I wind them through my fingers. "Make sure everyone knows that we're together."

"That you're mine, too," she says. Her pupils are wide, and her hair is soft between my fingers.

"Mhm. You've got pretty hair."

"Thanks." She places her hand flat on my chest. Carefully, gently, like she might hurt me. It would make me smile if I wasn't so dialed into this moment. If it didn't feel like I might shatter with one word.

"I could touch you too?" she asks.

"Yes. You can."

Her fingers spread a bit, pressing firmly against me. But not pushing me away. "If we want to sell this, it would be good if we kissed."

THE FAKING GAME

It's like she's punched the air right out of me. Want shoots down my body, electrifies the nerve endings it passes by. My eyes dip to her full lips.

If she only knew how much I've thought about doing just that.

It would send her running.

"From what you've told me, men have kissed you when you didn't particularly want them to." I reach up and slowly push a tendril of her hair back. Her eyes are on mine, and the air grows taut, like before a storm. "I'm not going to be one of them. You're done kissing men just to be nice."

"It's more that they sometimes just *lunge.* I never understand why they do that."

"They lunge. What do you mean?"

"It's like they think this is their moment, and if I meet their gaze for a second too long or smile too nicely and there's even a *hint* of intimacy in the air, they just pounce." She shakes her head, a flush creeping up her cheeks.

"Sounds like you've kissed the wrong men," I say.

"Maybe, yeah. Probably. It's like I always end up two steps behind the pace they're setting." Nora looks back at me, and there's a question in those eyes. A question I'm not sure she's brave enough to ask.

So I ask it instead. "If you want to practice kissing, trouble, practice it with me."

"You wouldn't mind?"

The question would make me laugh if it wasn't asked in such an earnest way. If the blood in my veins didn't immediately rush south, if my hands didn't tighten into fists at my sides. I'm a bastard for taking any pleasure in this.

"No. And from what you told me, I'm guessing you've *been* kissed. You haven't kissed someone. Is that true?"

She sways closer, just an inch. Nods once.

"Then this is all you." I tilt her head up. "You decide,

Nora. You decide when, how long, in what way. You don't think about me. Okay?"

Because I'm going to enjoy this regardless of what she does.

Because I'm going to hell, but I need to make sure that this is about her.

"I can... kiss you?" she asks. Her voice vibrates, half excitement and half nerves. But her deep green eyes don't stray from mine.

"Yes." It's all I can do not to add *please*.

CHAPTER 18
NORA

"Is it okay if you just… stand there?" I ask. It's hard to hear over the pounding in my ears.

West's lips curve. "Yes."

"Like, stand perfectly still."

"I won't move," he says. "My hands will stay in my pockets. How's that?"

"Good." I can't seem to take a full breath. He's *right there*, and I have wondered, have considered, what kissing him would be like. But it's always been hypothetical. Theoretical.

I've never been in charge before. Never been allowed to set the pace.

"Relax," West says.

"I'm trying!"

His lips twitch again, but he stays true to his word. He just stands there, his chest rising and falling with even breaths. He smells good up close. Like that cologne and something fresh, ocean and spring and safety.

I put my hands on his shoulders and have to stand on my tiptoes to reach him. He doesn't bend his head much. Just a slight tilt forward to make it easier for me, but he doesn't close the distance.

He's letting me do this on my terms.

I've never hovered this long before, had this much time before the kiss happens. My eyes close, and I can feel the faint heat of his breathing.

I brush my lips against his.

It's quick, brief. I pull back quickly, but he doesn't follow. He stands stock-still, just like he promised me he would.

I've never, ever been able to do this before.

I kiss him again. Warm, dry lips against mine. It sends little thrills of energy shooting through me. *West.* I'm kissing *West.* He doesn't move, doesn't kiss me back. But beneath my hands, his shoulders are tense.

"This is so… interesting," I say.

West gives a tight, huffed laugh against my lips. "Good."

"Can I keep going?"

"Yes," he breathes.

I press my lips more firmly against his. I tilt my head, and his lips move gently against mine. Just following my pace. Not pressing, pushing, invading.

It's better than just nice. Heat spreads through me from that warm press of his mouth. I walk my fingers back to the edge of his shirt. Find the smooth skin of the back of his neck. The short strands of his hair tickle my fingers.

I pull back an inch. His eyes are closed, and he takes a deep breath before opening them. They're a dark amber now, and when they meet mine, we're closer than we've ever been.

His body is tense under my hands.

"Was that okay?" I ask him.

"Yes." His voice is low, his hands still tucked into his pockets. "You're doing so good."

I wind my fingers through his hair. "You keep telling me that."

"Because it's true."

"It's not because I told you that I find compliments hard?"

His gaze drops down to my lips, and he swallows hard. "No. I wasn't thinking about that."

"Really? Maybe you're just doing it to make my lessons easier." I shift closer. Drawn to touching him just one more time. "Is it okay if I try again?"

His jaw flexes. "Yes."

I kiss him more confidently this time. I've never realized just how nice this can be, when I'm fully present in the moment. To know that I can pull back when I want, deepen it when I want. There's no hand moving to suddenly touch my ass, no tongue about to thrust into mine.

It's just sensations. His warmth. His taste. His lips move against mine in a faint mimic of my own pace, and I lose myself in a way I never have before. Forget the expectations. My fingers thread through the short hair at his nape, and a tremor runs through him.

I touch my tongue lightly to his bottom lip. He groans, and the sound travels to my stomach, hooks inside me.

His lips part. Inviting me in, if I want to.

Maybe I shouldn't, but I do anyway, because I have to have more of him. So I deepen the kiss. He's hot against me, and when his own tongue brushes mine, it's like something sparks inside me. Electricity, or maybe a crashing wave. Something that surprises and thrills.

He tastes minty and warm and like himself somehow. I trail my fingers down the side of his neck and feel the strong, fast pulse there. Is he affected too? Or am I alone in wanting?

I break off and drop back down on my heels. West's eyes are darker than I've ever seen them. My breath is coming fast, but he looks like he's barely breathing. Like he's made of stone.

I just kissed West Calloway.

Was it supposed to feel that good?

My body feels tingly, and my cheeks are on fire, and he's

looking at me like there's barely leashed irritation beneath his skin.

Maybe he didn't like it.

I know he isn't interested in me, not like *that*. He still rejected me years ago. *Boring. Last woman I would date.* But I feel suddenly desperate to know that he enjoyed that just as much as I did. That while we're not real, while I don't want him and he doesn't want me, *at least* I wasn't alone in liking that kiss.

"That was... very good." His voice is rough, like it's unused, even though we only kissed for a minute. "Did it help?"

Right. This was practice. To kiss on my terms. "Yes. It helped."

West's jaw works. "Good. Just say the word when you want to practice again."

"You sure you don't mind?" I ask. He looks far tenser now than before we kissed. He was fake angry before, but now... I can't read him.

"Yeah," he says, "I'm very sure. When you want to practice, you practice with me. Any time. Any place."

"Thanks. That's generous."

He chuckles. The sound is warm. "Don't thank me too much. It's not a hardship."

"It's not?"

"No." His face transforms when he's smiling. Comes alive, becomes almost hard to look at. "It's not hard to kiss you."

Oh.

Oh.

My fingers twitch by my side. I know enough of West to be sure he never says things he doesn't mean. He's the opposite of me in that way. Doesn't hide, doesn't obfuscate. There's never any fake politeness.

I don't know how to handle that information.

He doesn't mind kissing me. *He doesn't mind kissing me.*

"Don't think too much about it." The smile on his face dies. "I'm walking a fine line here. You want my reassurance, but you also don't like it when guys want you too much. Right?"

"Right." My voice sounds wooden, coming out between tingling lips. *Kiss me anytime. Anywhere.* "But I don't feel that way with you."

It's meant to be reassuring.

Instead, the hint of a smile disappears entirely. "Good. Because we're only practicing, right? For when you date after this. When you're looking for a real relationship."

"Yes," I repeat. "But it's good to know. Good that you're not... that you find it... tolerable. Letting me kiss you."

He looks up at the ceiling, and I can see his Adam's apple bob. I wonder if he's counting to three. "Don't think about me," he finally says, eyes returning to me. "Only think about what you want. Can you do that for me?"

I nod quickly. "Yes. I can."

"That's my girl," he says, and the praise feels almost as good as his lips did.

GROUP CHAT

RAFE

Have you recovered from the last trip, Alex?
We can't have a repeat of your meltdown.

WEST

Even if it was hugely entertaining.

ALEX

Fuck off.

RAFE

As the victor of last trip's poker game, I'd like
it noted that I handled Alex's poor
sportsmanship with grace.

WEST

Yes, you cursed him out very gracefully.

ALEX

And you? Have you recovered from your
hangover? I haven't seen you mistreat
whiskey like that since boarding school.

RAFE

I don't know what you're referring to.

WEST

I have video footage of that, too.

ALEX

Will you even have time, West? Our next trip is only a few weeks away. Considering you have a new girlfriend and all.

JAMES

We've lost him to the dark side.

RAFE

These jokes are going to get old fast. They're not REALLY dating.

JAMES

Of course not. Sisters are off-limits.

ALEX

I'd personally kill West for you if it was true.

JAMES

Hung and quartered?

ALEX

Feathered and tarred.

WEST

Thanks.

CHAPTER 19
NORA

The Paradise Lost party is held at an estate not far from Fairhaven. In every other way, it seems to be its complete opposite.

The old building is tall, with two towers that rise up toward the night sky. The entire driveway is covered with burning lights. There are no stately columns or red brick like Fairhaven. The house is gray, ornate. Something that might belong in a Scottish fairytale.

West is silent beside me in the car. There's something inward about him tonight, like he's drawn tight beneath the dark gray suit. No cufflinks, the top two buttons of the white shirt undone. Like he was in too much of a rush to coordinate the little details.

Like he's deep in thought.

He told me a bit about the party. That invites to them are highly coveted, phones are forbidden, and locations always change.

"Who will be here tonight?" I ask him.

He looks out the window at the estate. Everything about him radiates a coiled sort of readiness that makes my own stomach tighten.

He doesn't answer until Arthur pulls to a stop next to a circular fountain. It has a fallen angel at its center, half kneeling, wings raised and head bent. I've never seen anything like it.

"Everyone," West says shortly. "Stay close to me?"

"I promise."

"The guards can't follow us in, but this place has heavy security. You'll be safe." He steps outside the car and holds out a hand to me. I take it, and his long fingers close around mine.

The air smells thick of burning candles. They line the steps up to the estate and into the space beyond. Milton's *Paradise Lost* is about redemption and temptation. Angels and devils, heaven and hell. I designed my own dress for the party. It was a distraction from the pieces I have to create for the showcase, but a welcome one, and a chance to test out a design in person.

I'm wearing a draped white fabric that flows over my body and cinches at the waist. It would be angelic if it wasn't for the dark eyeliner I'm wearing and the slightly mussed waves of my hair.

"Who throws these parties, anyway?" I ask West. He's tucked my hand into the crook of his arm.

"Someone with a twisted sense of humor," he says.

"There's more to this than you're telling me."

"Yes." He sighs. "She throws a few parties like these a year. She has an... appetite for games, let's say. And she's very well connected."

"This location is incredible."

"It is," he says tightly. "She chose tonight's location for a reason."

The massive oak doors creak open before us. They reveal a large hallway teeming with figures in various types of costumes. A few are dressed as actual angels. It takes me a second to see the trays they're carrying around and realize that they're servers carrying food. There are devils, too, I realize. I catch sight of one walking around the living room with a tray of shots.

A few people stop and say hi. I smile at them all and say thank you when a woman compliments my dress.

West hands me a glass of champagne. I take it gratefully and strike up a conversation with two of the people standing next to us. They're a couple in their forties, perhaps, and I vaguely recognize one of them from the movies. He's eating an oyster, and when he sees me looking, nods toward an adjoining room. "Freshly shucked in there."

"That sounds delicious," I say. West is still silent beside me. It's unlike him; at the fundraiser at Fairhaven, he commanded the room. He spoke to everyone like he knew them, or at the very least, knew of them.

Now he's stiff. His eyes wander up a spiral staircase in the hallway, past old family portraits hanging on the walls. They look like they're oil portraits of a family. One of them has a long gash down the center. The entire place is decorated with flowers, with vines, with wine. It's Paradise.

I wonder where hell is.

Before I can press further, an Asian woman in a shimmering gold dress approaches us. Her hair is midnight dark, piled high on her head and adorned with what looks like diamond studs. She looks ageless; she could be thirty-five or fifty-five.

"West," she says with a wide smile. "You came. How lovely." Her eyes flick to me, and her smile doesn't move an inch. "And who is this?"

"You know exactly who it is," West says. Despite the tension, his voice is smooth. "This is Eléanore Montclair. My girlfriend."

I lean into his side and smile at her like I'm the happiest girl in the world. "It's a pleasure to meet you."

She takes in my dress, my hair, my face. Her scrutiny takes so long that it must be on purpose.

"Vivienne Cho," she says. "It's a pleasure to finally have you at one of my little parties. Your brother has been here often enough."

"I'm sorry about that," I say jokingly.

"Now I finally have the full set." Her glittering attention shifts to West. "Do you like the location I chose for tonight's party? I had to pull some strings, but once I had the theme, it had to be at Thorn Hall. And it couldn't be closer to you."

"Distasteful," he says.

The woman laughs again, and I look up at West in surprise. His face is carved in stone. I've rarely seen him look like this; his expression is angry, resigned.

"Oh, but that's the fun!" she says. "It fit the theme so well, don't you think?"

"You're right about that. Is he here tonight?"

"I had to invite him, of course," Vivienne says. "He's been clawing his way back. Slowly building another fortune."

"I've seen," West says tightly.

"Maybe we'll get a little show out of you two, hmm?"

"I think not." His hand falls to my low back. "I don't like performing for crowds."

"That's a shame, because I so love it." She reaches into her pocket. She pulls out a large brass key with a red ribbon on it and hands it directly to me. It's heavy in my palm. "Don't forget to pay the downstairs a little visit."

Vivienne walks away, her hips moving through the crowd. "Who," I ask, "was that? And you're not allowed to answer with *no one*."

West takes the key from me and puts it in his pocket. "She hosts these parties a few times a year. She's... very well connected. And she's not someone to be angered."

"I think you did just that when you told her that her party was distasteful."

"I said the location was. Not the party."

"You're arguing semantics." I take another sip of my champagne. "And why is the location distasteful?"

His jaw tightens. "Not something we're going to discuss right now."

I push. Like he told me to. "You told me to make you angry. To practice it. So maybe I won't let it go."

His eyes flash down to me, and then his lips curve. Just a hint. "I did, didn't I? Are you going to make me regret those words?"

"Maybe I'll try."

He lets his hand lie flat against my low back, then his eyes sharpen. Like he just realized my dress is open and his hand is against my bare skin. It's warm, too, and a shiver runs through me at the touch. "Good," he says. "You're doing very well."

"By annoying you."

"Yes. And you're doing a damn good job of distracting me, too."

"Do you need distractions tonight?"

"It wouldn't hurt. We need a few people here to see us together." He guides me through the crowd, into another room. This one is large. An old stone fireplace is in the center, but no ordinary furniture. Like the hallway, the place looks mostly abandoned.

There's a bartender in one corner and a large poker table in the center.

"Who are we pretending for?" I ask. "Your mother isn't here. The stalker isn't here."

He looks out over the space. "Some of the world's most powerful people come to Vivienne's parties. Whispers always spread. And I want them to."

I look out over the poker table, the hazy room. More than a few people glance our way. Just like the polo game. "People are watching us."

"Want to put on a show?"

"You're not carrying me again."

"Break a heel and I might," he says.

"I'll be careful, then."

He guides us past the poker table. There are people I recognize in here. Famous faces, a few familiar ones. People I've seen my brother talk to on occasion.

"Do you play?" It's a stupid question. I know he does; my brother loses a lot of money on the trips he goes on with the guys. When they spend half a week in a far-flung location doing dares, and making mistakes, and ending it all with a poker game.

"You know I do," West says in a low voice. He's turned us so I have my back to the game, and he's looking across my shoulder at the guests. "There's someone from my family here tonight, I think. He never misses a game."

"Who?"

"My cousin."

"Is he part of the matchmaking scheme?"

"In a way," West says.

"So you want us to put on a show," I murmur, and reach out to run my hands along his chest. Flatten them like I've done in our self-defense sessions.

"Do not," he says, "practice rejecting me right now."

"But you want me to get good at it."

"I do. And we'll practice more. In private."

My fingers close around his lapels. He wants people here to think we're a couple. *Whispers always spread from this party...*

"Don't reject me either," I whisper, and I rise up to brush my lips against his cheek.

West stands stock-still. I've never had a guy react like that before. It's always been a rush to capitalize on the moment, mouth on mine, tongue too fast.

I sink back down onto my heels and smile in delight.

"Playing for the audience?" His whiskey eyes are unreadable.

"I'm putting on a show. That's what you wanted, wasn't it?"

He chuckles. It's a dark sound, and it's just as scratchy as his beard. "Trouble, if you think that qualifies as putting on a show, we're going to have to work on our definitions."

My eyes briefly dip to his lips, and then quickly away again. "You don't strike me as the kind of man who loves PDA."

"You seem to spend a lot of time thinking about my dating life," he mutters, sliding his hand back around my waist. Where he told me he would keep it. "Come. There's only one place we have left to look."

I reach into the pocket of his suit jacket and pull out the brass key. "Let me guess. It goes to hell?"

"You've caught on to the theme," he says. "I shouldn't take you there, but I will, and I'll pay the price for it."

Excitement makes my blood drum. "I can handle it."

"I know you can." He reaches down to take my hand. Threads his fingers through mine the way we practiced the other day, warmth against warmth. "This way."

"You've been in this house before."

"Many times."

"You knew the person who used to live here."

"Yes. But we're going to get in and get out before he might show. That's not the person I'm looking for." He pulls me down a corridor and through an old wooden library. The whole place is gothic, so different in design from Fairhaven.

He stops by an ornate wooden door flanked by a server with rainbow colored hair and a devil's outfit. Red leather pants and a tight red vest. Horns peek up through the hair.

West holds up the key.

They smile and push the door open to reveal a dark staircase straight down to a basement.

We walk down the dark space and into a cavernous room bathed in red light. The ceiling is low, supported by thick stone pillars. Smoke hangs in the air. The scent hits me first—incense and sweat and some kind of thick perfume.

We've made it to hell.

CHAPTER 20
NORA

The space is lit by red lights. Thick smoke rolls along our feet, and the air feels heady. I make out a few bodies dancing to the pulsing beat. Others are sitting on futons, and a couple is draped over one…

Making out lazily.

A goblet hangs from the man's hand while his partner kisses his neck. I look at them too long and flinch when a waiter approaches us. He's dressed in a red leather suit and has dark-rimmed kohl around his eyes. "Welcome to hell." The tray he holds up has shots, a few drinks, and… are those pills? "Be careful down here, angel," he tells me with a smile that encourages me to be anything but.

"Thanks." I reach out and take one of the shots. It burns. Whiskey with some kind of spice.

West takes the empty cup from me. "You don't know what that was."

"Alcohol," I say with a grimace. "And liquid courage. God, I don't like whiskey."

"Be careful what you drink down here." The darkness casts shadows over his sharp cheekbones.

"You sound like there's danger down here."

"There is." He takes my hand again. Fingers curve over mine, and we start walking through the party.

Like we hold hands all the time.

His palm is warm and a bit dry in mine, and it sends a shot of heat through me. I kissed him yesterday.

Kissed West Calloway.

And he let me do it, set the pace, run point.

He leads me past the bar and past another velvet couch with two women making out so vigorously that it looks like the prelude to something that should be done behind closed doors. Except that's probably the point.

Virtues rule in paradise above.

But down here, all is lost.

And West brought me here. He didn't avoid this, he didn't come here alone, in some misguided attempt to protect me. He let me come.

Excitement courses through me.

This place is electric.

The air grows thicker in the next room, warm with incense. He's clearly been here before; he knows to turn around a pillar and move down a few small steps. This place is huge... and yet there are people everywhere. In various states of undress.

His hand is warm around mine.

I can't stop noticing it. How it feels to have him holding on to me like we're together. I know it's an act. But I'm not *not* liking it.

Another couple stops us. The man smiling widely and leans in to talk to West. I can't hear what he says, but I can practically feel West's irritation at being stopped.

I look around, my hand still grasped in his. People are milling about, drinking, talking. Two are making out. There are curtains hanging from the low ceiling, creating little partitions, hidden alcoves.

A woman with strawberry blonde hair stands by an opening across the room, holding a martini.

Is that…?

She turns, and her eyes find mine.

Amber.

She looks past me at where West is still talking to someone. She holds a finger to her lips.

I nod. *I won't tell him.*

Amber smiles quickly and then slips out around the corner, disappearing from the room, unseen by her brother. I'm more curious now than ever. Amber's here? Vivienne didn't mention that, but she mentioned Rafe. And if West shouldn't know either…

Maybe she snuck in somehow.

I have to ask her about it one day.

The music is too loud to make out West's conversation, so I keep looking around. There's a man leaning against the wall right beside us. He's got dirty blond hair, and his black silk shirt hangs open, showing off his abs.

He crooks a finger, motioning for me to join him. There's a wide smirk on his lips.

Oh.

I give a little shrug that's neither yes nor no.

"You look parched," he says. "Let me grab you a drink. Come play with us."

He nods toward an alcove I hadn't spotted before. It's half hidden with draped fabric, and there are already two people inside. A woman is sitting between a man's splayed legs, and his large hand is gripping one of her breasts.

They're both looking our way.

"Um, you and your friends?" I ask.

"We have room for you too, gorgeous."

The hand on mine tightens suddenly, and then West is beside me again. "She's taken."

The other man holds up his hands with a grin. "You're welcome to come play too."

"I don't share," West says darkly and pulls me along. I follow him with a small wave goodbye at the handsome blond. He was willing to have a... fivesome? I don't even know how that would work logistically.

Maybe after four people, it stops being called a -some and becomes an orgy. I don't know what the etiquette is. I haven't even had sex with one person.

We walk beneath an archway, and a large room opens up. At the center is another poker table, mirroring the one above, and I realize it has to be in the same position as the one we saw upstairs.

As above, so below.

The table is full. Some players look at their cards, others at their opponents. A Black woman wears a gorgeous dress, with red feathers attached along sleeves that drape over her fingers where she grips her cards.

And they're all quiet. The only sound comes from the spectators. Because there's plenty of those, too, draped along the walls.

People are looking at us.

West isn't a stranger to these games, I'm sure of it. He leads me through the stares to the only seat still free. It's a single high-backed chair in an alcove, velvet curtains pulled back.

We pass a tray on the way.

I grab another one of the spicy shots and down it when he's not looking. It tastes better now and burns alongside the excitement pounding through me.

"Showtime, trouble," he says. "There's only one chair. Think you can sit in my lap?"

The pulsing beat of the music reverberates in my breastbone. Makes my heart speed up. "Yes." I can sense the people watching us from the back. I'm blocking their view of West...

and giving them a good shot of my backless dress. "I'll play the part if you're prepared to get kneed again during our next lesson."

His lips curve. "By you? Any day."

He sits, legs spread, and puts his hands on my hips. *I'll touch you in public,* he told me. I sink onto his lap. It's more of a perch than a sprawl, and it only takes a second for West to chuckle behind me. His hand finds the curve of my waist, and he pulls me back until I'm leaning against his chest. "Relax," he murmurs.

People are still watching us.

His hand is warm, steady. I can feel the rise and fall of his breathing behind me.

I lean my head back, resting it against his shoulder. "There are two poker games?"

"Upstairs," West says, "they play for money. Down here, they play for far more interesting things."

"You've played here before," I say.

It takes him a while to answer. "Yes. When I was younger and dumber."

"You can lose a lot down here," I guess. The tension at the table is thick. Some of the players are silent. Others are drinking heavily or chatting to someone sitting behind the poker table.

"You can lose everything," West says.

I look from the table to the futon in the corner, where the couple is going from making out to… hands between legs. I've never seen anything like it before.

He notices my gaze and turns his mouth to my ear. "Have you ever watched people have sex before?"

That answer is an easy one. "No. Is that common at these parties?"

"No. Not unheard of, sure. But I think everything has been heightened tonight. Especially down here."

My eyes land on the couple in the corner again. A man has

a woman clutched against him, half reclining on the velvet chaise. Her skirt is rucked up, and his hand is between her legs. I can't make out anything clearly in the hazy red lighting, except that his hand is covering the spot between her legs perfectly. And judging from the way her head is thrown back in bliss, he's touching her well.

A hot flush creeps up my cheeks. They don't seem to mind the other people in the room. If anything, they like it. Being watched.

West's fingers curve over my waist, and I can feel his breath against my ear. "Your brother will *kill* me when he finds out I brought you here."

CHAPTER 21
NORA

"Does he have to know?" I ask.

"People will probably tell him. People who see us here."

Oh. "Good thing no one can photograph us, at least."

"Thank god," he mutters.

But his words make me think. "Have you done... *that*? At other parties?" Then I stiffen. "Oh my god, has my brother? Wait, don't tell me."

He chuckles. "I told you, spectacles aren't for me."

"And yet here we are," I say. There are several people at the poker table who have clearly taken notice that West is here. One of them is a man a few years older than us, sitting dead center and in our line of sight.

He looks up with wide eyes and then back down at his cards.

"Yes, but we're not going to do what the others are doing." West's other hand comes to rest on the side of my thigh, his arm draped over me. It's a possessive, casual gesture. He's resting his arm around the woman he brought here.

The shots have helped make me feel lighter. Less in my head. I run my fingers along his forearm where it rests on the side of the chair. I've never touched a man like this before. Casually, no expectations, just to explore.

His sleeve is rolled up, and his forearms are thick, dappled with dark hair.

"Because you don't date," I say. "That's why you've never been on one of those couches."

"No, trouble. Because like I said, I don't share. And that includes letting others watch when I make a woman come."

His hand is big and curved over the end of the armrest, and his words whisper through me in a heated echo. *When I make a woman come.*

I've only come by myself. Heated touches in my own bedroom, to fantasies with nameless, faceless men. To stories and my own imagination. His hand, though... what would it feel like if it was him?

I run my nails lightly over his skin, from wrist to elbow. "Who are we performing for?"

West's mouth shifts to my ear. "The man in the pin-striped suit. He's sitting directly opposite us."

The man who can't stop watching us.

"That's your cousin?"

"Yes." Beneath my searching fingers, his hand tightens on the end of the armrest. "He's a nuisance."

"You're not close."

"No. We're not."

"And he needs to think you're committed? Or in love?"

West's head turns, and I catch sight of his narrowed eyes. "Is there a difference?"

"Of course. Why would he think you're committed and not just... bringing a date here to have fun?" I shift in his lap. This isn't unlike a few of the modeling gigs I've done, when I'm posing with male models. It's choreographed. Clinical. Acting.

To tell a story.

"He should think we're serious."

"I'm in love with you. That's what you're saying." I put my hand flat on his chest and smile like I'm charmed by something he's saying. My forehead is pressed against the warm, bare skin of his neck. He smells good.

His hands tighten their hold. "Yes."

"I'm good at pretending," I say.

"Yes, I know you are."

"I've posed like this before for shoots." I reach for his hand, the one around my waist, and pull it more thoroughly into my lap. I play with his long fingers, weave them around my own, and look like I'm the happiest, laziest, most content woman in the world.

It's not a difficult mask to wear.

It might not even be a mask at all.

West's voice is by my ear. "You pose with male models a lot?"

"Sometimes. But I'm turning down most modeling gigs now." Or trying to, at least. It's hard sometimes, when my brother is asking. I have a shoot for a Valmont brand just a week from now that I wasn't able to get out of.

"They must ask you out."

"Sometimes," I say again. My finger brushes over his signet ring. The golden *B*, for the Belmont Academy. The school in Vermont. The one he attended with my brother and Alex and James. I don't know what happened there. But Rafe was sent away a rowdy teenager and returned ready for university with three best friends, a ring he never took off, and a purpose.

"Do you ever say yes?" he asks. His other hand is on my low back now, brushing over the bare skin.

"Almost never. I say I would have loved to, but I travel so much…"

"You lie." His voice holds only wry understanding. Not judgment. "You turn them down, cloaked in niceties."

"Yes."

"You're the prettiest little liar I've ever met." His large hand is warm around mine, where it lies on my thighs, fingers woven through my own. "And you make it look so easy. But it's not, is it?"

"Not always." I look out at the game again. "Why your cousin?"

He's quiet for a long moment. "I told you that there's an expectation that I need an heir. If I don't, the next Calloway in direct line is my cousin Dave."

"Not Amber?"

"No. She hates that. I hate that. I'm working on getting it fixed," West mutters. "But I dislike him immensely, and I don't want him to think he's close to getting… everything."

"He might kill you. That's motive right there, isn't it?"

He laughs. The sound makes me turn to him fully. "West?"

"Your mind works in wondrous ways sometimes."

"But I'm not wrong."

"No, you're not. Too bad I couldn't bring the guards inside tonight." He doesn't sound troubled. He sounds amused, and his hand tightens around mine. "Everyone's looking at you. You've never been here before. They're interested. And you look…"

My breath catches. From somewhere left of us, a loud moan cuts above the music. "Like what?"

"Like you don't belong," he says. "Like an angel that's wandered into hell."

His hand is tan against the silky white of my dress. It's ridden up, showing off most of my legs from just above my knees. My heels dangle from my high spot on his lap.

"I dressed on theme."

"Devastatingly so."

Another moan echoes from somewhere in the space, followed by a low, masculine groan. My cheeks burn, but I can't help glancing toward the sound.

His fingers brush over my neck, my cheek. Push my hair back. "Would you like to get closer? Watch more?"

"No," I say. Too quickly.

"You're too good for this party. I should feel bad for bringing you here. For corrupting you."

"But you don't," I murmur. My eyes land on the couple on the other side, and my entire body tightens.

They're having sex now.

He's on his knees, and she's laid out in front of him on her back. He's thrusting into her in slow, rolling motions. Her eyes are closed and her arms stretched up above her head. I can see the thickness of him disappearing and reappearing between her legs with each thrust.

"That can't be normal," I say.

My fingers are still playing with West's idly, and at my incredulous tone, they twitch.

"Having sex?" he asks.

"No, but she looks like it's the best thing she's ever experienced." My head is swimming again, and my tongue feels loose. Looser than it's ever been around West. "He's not even touching her... her... god. Never mind."

"Continue that thought."

My entire body is too hot. "I don't think I should."

His lips brush my ear. "Some women can come from penetration alone, but it's rare. Even if she won't, she can still get pleasure from it."

"Mhm. Or maybe she's performing," I say, "for her partner, and the people in the room."

"Has that been your experience with sex?"

"I don't think we should talk about my sex life."

"But you seem so very interested in mine," West says back. "You asked me just a few minutes ago if I've done exactly that at one of these parties."

Damn it.

I make my voice teasing. "I don't care."

"Mhm. I think you're lying."

"You think far too highly of yourself."

"Or I'm good at reading you," he says, his hand flattening against the curve of my waist. It's big and steady, pressed against my body. His thumb is only inches from the underside of my breast. "Don't perform in bed. If that's what you've done until now."

"I'm not taking advice from you on what to do in bed." My voice is all bravado. Another lie. If only he knew that I've never had sex. The most I've done is make out with someone.

That's my greatest secret and largest shame, and I'll be damned if I ever let West in on that.

"Good." His voice is rough, at odds with the velvet curtains and the swirling smoke. "You and I shouldn't be having this conversation."

"Don't worry. I'm not about to call Rafe and recount it word for word."

"If you do, let me know before so I can up my security." He rolls his neck a little and looks straight ahead.

At his cousin Dave with the pin-striped suit. His eyes are narrowed and his skin is flushed and ruddy. I wonder how much he's been drinking and how much he's already lost at that table. West said they play for more than money.

My heart is beating fast. Maybe it's the place, the moans around us, the shots I've taken, that cause butterflies to swirl inside me.

"He's watching us," I say.

West's breath is hot against my ear. "Time to really sell it, trouble."

His hand slides up my bare back, leaving goose bumps in its wake. His fingers tangle in my hair, and he curves my head up, bending his own face to my neck. His lips brush my cheek and then move down to my neck, like he's pressing soft, barely there kisses.

Except he's not.

His lips aren't touching my skin.

I wrap my hand around his neck. My fingers dig tentatively into the short, thick strands of his hair. He's warm. And his face is still buried in my neck, hovering there, lips close but not touching, stubble brushing my skin.

Playing to the audience.

We're both pretending.

"He's still watching." I shift in West's lap, turning to face him more. My legs are now fully draped over his thigh, and my dress rides up dangerously high. His hand is there, on the bare skin of my knee, a finger beneath the ivory silk.

"The fucking pervert," West mutters against my neck.

It's so unexpected that I giggle. His hold tightens around me, and I slide my hand down to his cheek and stubbled jaw.

I kissed him yesterday and I liked it. It's the safety of that, and the pounding of heat through me, that makes me ask for more.

"We should kiss. To really sell it."

His eyes darken. "You're done kissing men just to be nice."

"I'm not being nice. I'm going to knee you again tomorrow." I lean in another inch, breathing his air. "You told me I could practice with you. Whenever, wherever."

"I did, didn't I?" His eyes dip to mine. "I'm not going to stand still this time, trouble. Not if I'm kissing my fake girlfriend in public..."

He leans in slowly. Giving me plenty of time to pull away.

I don't.

His lips brush over mine in tantalizingly faint contact that sends goose bumps down my arms.

No one has ever kissed me softly before.

It's always been a rush of contact, a face against mine and the taste of expectation and demands. This is nothing like that.

He lifts his lips, hovers half an inch from mine. Like he's checking that I'm still with him.

My fingers tighten in his hair in response. *Yes.*

He kisses me stronger, his lips moving over mine with practiced heat. I'm hyperaware of every point of contact between us—his hand on the bare skin of my back, his fingers around my knee, his strong body beneath mine.

I can't think beyond the feeling of his lips. It's like my thought process has stopped. My hand tightens in his hair, my nails brushing over his scalp.

West groans. The sound reverberates through his mouth and into mine. His tongue brushes over my lower lip, insistent, seeking, and the heat inside me slides down and settles between my legs.

Oh. *Oh.*

He's not kissing me softly now.

It's hard to breathe, but I don't need air, anyway. I just need more of this.

But he lifts his head from mine. "Fuck," he mutters. My eyes are locked on the spot at the base of his throat where his Adam's apple bobs. He smells good. *Tastes* good.

It's like the other day.

And it's also completely different.

West looks past me and back at the room, his gaze sweeping over it all like he's surveying his kingdom. He's not trying to catch his breath.

I turn my face against his warm neck again, like I'm just playing the part. Try to hide my quick breaths.

Maybe he doesn't feel like his world changed. And why would he? He said I was the last woman he'd date. He's doing this for his own reasons, and it's not because he wants to.

My old crush needs to stay dead. I will just have to remind myself of that.

West's thumb brushes over the skin of my thigh. "That was good," he finally says. "You did very well."

The praise warms me. Maybe it shouldn't, maybe it's patronizing, but maybe it doesn't matter what someone else thinks. Only that it warms me down to my bones and lets me relax against the strength of his body.

I don't have to worry about pleasing him when he reassures me that I do.

"What are they playing for?" I ask, like he didn't just give me the best kiss of my life. Like I'm back to pretending. "Do you know?"

"Tonight?" His mouth is by my ear. "Houses. Companies. Boats. Planes. Sex."

The last word makes my eyes flit to the chaise in the corner and the couple. They've switched now, and the woman is on top. She's discarded her clothes and is riding him slowly in a confident roll of her hips.

Maybe she enjoys performing, I think. Maybe she enjoys knowing people here are watching her and liking it. The man beneath her has his arms beneath his head and looks at her like she's hung the moon.

Maybe she enjoys that too. The power of giving someone else pleasure.

"You can't look away, can you?" West's voice is tight.

He's caught me again.

I let my gaze grow hooded and look back at the game. "It's hard to," I admit. "How long are we staying?"

"We'll leave soon. We've done what we came here to do."

I shift a little in his lap and look around for one of the waiters. I wouldn't mind another spicy shot. But that's when I feel it, the distinct hardness beneath me.

It takes me a few seconds to realize what it is.

Holy shit. He's just… sitting here. Breathing low and steady, his hand on my bare back, the other curved over my knee. Holding me against his body.

I shift against the hardness, and he grinds his teeth together.

Oh my god. West Calloway is hard. The knowledge shoots through me like one of those shots, warming every place it touches. What would that hardness look like? What would he feel like?

Is it because of our kiss?

My gaze wanders back to the naked woman riding her partner. She's gorgeous, with large breasts and curvy hips. She has to be it. He's watching people have sex. Sure, he's seemed pretty disinterested in them, but he's a person. A man. It's normal for that to affect him.

That has to be it.

CHAPTER 22
WEST

I'm in hell.

Nora is draped in my lap, a warm, soft weight. Her hair tickles my neck as she watches the couple in the corner with a kind of focus I've never seen in her before.

I'm hard as a fucking rock.

It's more than inconvenient. It's *indecent*. She has asked me to help her practice so she can feel at ease around dating and men, so she can learn to ask for what she wants. She's told me that men sometimes act like creeps around her.

And here I am, blood painfully rushing south at the first taste of her lips.

I started by kissing her carefully. Slowly. A tempo she could follow along with and not be overwhelmed by. But then she scraped her nails over my scalp, and I couldn't resist tasting her with my tongue.

She's sweeter than I ever thought she might be.

And now that I've tasted her, I know I'm never going to get enough.

At the poker table, Dave is staring hard enough at his cards that I know he's wishing they were different. He's going to lose tonight. Just like he loses all the time.

He's a Calloway, but only through my father's cousin. And he can't stay away from these parties… or the other privileges that his last name provides. Not that he'll ever take on any responsibility.

I only told Nora half the truth.

Over my dead body will he gain access to Fairhaven. I know he's already planning what he'll do if my thirtieth birthday comes and I'm still unmarried. My home will show up in one of these games, gambled away because he thinks he has great cards when he doesn't. It'll be turned into a hotel or a college. The grounds desecrated and an elevator installed.

Nora shifts again, and I bite down on my tongue to hide a groan. I need my body to get a fucking grip.

After she kissed me the other day, hesitantly, sweetly, gloriously, I had to take a cold shower. Gripped myself and painted the tiles to the image of her face behind my eyelids.

I shouldn't think about her that way. But *shouldn't* doesn't seem to work.

She was so sweet, kissing me carefully first and then in delight. Like she actually enjoyed it and was surprised by the whole thing. It took every ounce of control in me to not move. To keep my hands in my pockets.

"There's another couple beside us." Nora's voice is breathless. "They're the ones we've been hearing."

"Oh? What are they doing?"

She leans forward to see, and my lip curves. Her excitement is charming. It's rare that Vivienne's parties have open displays of sex like this. If I had known… but now we're here, and there's no denying that there's a dark, twisted pleasure in watching Nora fascinated by sex. It makes my cock throb beneath her thighs.

"He's eating her out," she whispers.

Fuck. Her voice, saying those words… I could eat her out. It would be so easy to slide my hand up beneath the virginally white angel dress and brush against her pussy.

To see if she's wet from watching the others.

She's Rafe's little sister. She's mine to protect and mine to teach how to date, but she's not mine in any other sense. She's *definitely* not mine to taste.

But the guilt doesn't make my cock deflate.

"I never knew you were such a deviant." I grip her tighter and shift her forward off my lap. "Time to go, trouble, before you start asking to join in."

"I wouldn't," she says. But her voice is high, excited.

I reach for her hand again. "Think that woman is just performing too?"

"No. I don't. Her pleasure looks… real."

I wonder what she looks like when she comes. If the kind, polite, practiced charm falls and she's just herself again. I don't think she would be a screamer. I think her breathing would hitch, and she would grow tense, and her back would arch.

"Take your mental picture to use later," I tell her, "and then we'll leave."

Her eyes flash to mine. "I'm not… I wouldn't…"

I raise an eyebrow. "Everyone does it."

"I can't believe you're talking about that." She looks flushed. "That's not something people just mention!"

"You're watching people have sex in front of you, but you can't handle talking about masturbation." I narrow my eyes at her. "Is talking about sex something we need to add to your lessons?"

She bites her lip, and I have to look away. The image of those perfect teeth sinking into plump flesh is doing nothing to help my erection. Thank god it's dark in here, and thank god the zipper is digging in painfully.

"Maybe, but I'm not sure it's necessary," she says.

"Your goal is to date more, right? Get into a relationship?" My words come out a little harsh as I lead her out of the room. Back toward the pulsing bodies on the dance floor and curve toward the staircase.

"Yes," she says.

"I hate to break it to you, but in relationships, you talk about sex and intimacy. Now let's get you out of here before you spontaneously combust from curiosity."

"I'm not curious!"

"Sure you're not."

"Maybe a little," she says, walking in front of me up the stairs. The ivory clings to her slim, curved shape, and that backless dress… Her dark hair plays at her shoulder blades. And her ass is now *right* in front of me.

My fucking hard-on was *just* starting to surrender.

"But aren't you, West?" she asks with a small chuckle. "How could you watch that and not *care*? Not be curious?"

"They're exhibitionists."

Heaven upstairs has soft blue lighting, and there's fake ivy draped along all of the walls. Some of the Whitman family's paintings are still up but torn in places. Most of their once ornate furniture is gone, too.

The place I once visited as a boy is now a wreck.

Sold and repossessed in a lengthy court battle and scandal that consumed the city. The boy who was once heir to it all hasn't shown up. I hope he stayed far, far away, whatever Vivienne might say.

I haven't seen Hadrian in years. Not since that night at Belmont, not since everything unraveled like the threads in a tapestry, spinning out of control. We're four now, but we were once five.

Nora dances a little in front of me in the large hallway by the front door. Other people look at her, smiling.

She doesn't seem to realize.

She holds my hand and lifts it up. Twirls under my arm. A smile spreads across her face. It's so unlike the way she's been with me so far that it makes something tighten in my chest.

It's not a mask, either. It's a real smile, and it lights up her face like a sunrise. "I like this party," she tells me.

I brush a tendril of her hair back. "How much have you had to drink?"

"I've had a few shots."

"From upstairs or downstairs?" I ask.

"Both, I think."

Vivienne's parties are known to break every legal rule there is. Lord knows what was in the shots. "We're going home," I order.

She pouts a little, but dances backward toward the front door all the same. Her hips sway in a way that speaks of hours spent perfecting her movements. "Fine."

I push open the door for her. "You're in a good mood."

"Yes, I guess I am. I'm also a tiny bit drunk."

"You don't say?"

"Tonight was very educational."

I scoff. "That's what we're calling it?"

She laughs again. "It was! I've never seen anything like… *that* before. It was fascinating."

"I'm corrupting you."

She waves a hand, like that's neither here nor there. "No you're not. But I'm surprised by you, actually."

We walk down the long, candlelit driveway. I've already texted Arthur that it's time. "Surprised how?"

"I used to think you went wild. You and the guys, like on your trips."

I shove my hands into my pockets. "You shouldn't know anything about those."

"I've heard enough from Rafe. Including stories about *you*." She walks to the large gate that guards the old Whitman property and peers out through the iron. "You flipped a water scooter once."

"Yeah, yeah. Come on."

"And you cliff jumped in Ibiza. At midnight!"

"That was a long time ago. And I was very drunk."

"So you've mellowed out with age?" she asks. "I'll admit, I've really only seen you all stern and serious and arrogant."

"Arrogant?"

She puts a hand to her mouth, laughing behind her fingers. "Yes. I'm sorry. I guess I'm taking the whole 'you can't make me angry' thing to heart."

"Good. I meant it." Arthur pulls up, and I open the car door for her. She slides in with a cheery hello to my driver. They chat a bit as he drives the short way from the old estate back to my home up in King's Point. There was a time when I came here often. A lifetime ago.

When we get home, Nora doesn't wait for me to open her car door. She walks up the steps to Fairhaven with a hand lifting the long skirt of her dress. The moonlight bounces off the ivory silk, and she does look like an angel.

A smiling angel with slightly smudged lipstick. Smudged because of my kiss.

I open the front door for her, and she walks inside. She drops her clutch on the center table and steps out of her tall heels. "Finally," she says with a happy sigh. "Do you have any snacks in the kitchen?"

"I have no clue."

She giggles again. "It's your kitchen. That's silly. What... oh! Look!" She hurries to the open doorway between the twin staircases. "Did you see that?"

"No."

"Your cat! It's inside again!"

I follow her, rounding the corner into the hallway. She's half running toward the library wing.

"I don't have a cat," I say.

"Yes, you do," she protests. I catch the hint of two gray back legs and a tail held high before the cat disappears into the half-open door to the library. Nora disappears in after it.

I follow at a slower pace. When I open the door fully, she's crouching near the large leather sofa and talking softly to a feline I can't see. "Hi, sweetheart. Don't be scared. We won't hurt you."

"Don't speak for me," I say.

She looks at me over her shoulder. "Don't say that! He's your cat."

"I don't have a cat."

"Well, the cat has you. Or Fairhaven does, at least. I've asked Ernest about him, but he didn't know either." She smiles a little. "If he's a lodger, we'll have to get him properly moved in."

"He might belong to someone."

She makes more soft, beckoning sounds. "Then we check if he has a chip first."

I walk toward the bar cart in the corner. I pour myself a glass of whiskey, but I don't offer Nora any. She's had enough.

There's a small basket here filled with bags of bite-sized snacks. I grab what looks like a small bag of nuts and a bag of chips, then sit on the couch near where she's trying to lure out the cat.

"Here," I tell her and toss the snacks on the table between us. "Eat… and answer some questions for me."

She sits on the thick oriental carpet and looks my way. "Questions?"

"Yes. I want to know exactly why dating is so hard for you."

CHAPTER 23
WEST

Nora looks away quickly, reaching for the bags of snacks instead of answering me. "We've spoken about this," she says, and tears open a small bag of chips.

"Not enough." I brace a hand against the leather couch opposite her. She's leaning back against an armchair, white silk pooling around her curled legs. "Why have you never found a guy that interests you?"

She eats a chip and looks over at the bookshelves, where the cat has disappeared. "It just hasn't happened for me."

I shake my head. There's more here. There has to be. She was clearly intrigued by the sex we witnessed tonight. *Affected*, even. "You're not attracted to men?"

"No, I am."

"What is it, then?"

"I have issues." She shrugs a little and stretches out her legs beneath the coffee table. "You know that. I'm working through them. I'm just not very good at feeling something quickly. It seems like everyone else just *knows* right away. Sometimes, at least. And I feel like I almost never know."

"Know if you want someone?"

"Yes."

My hand tightens around the leather armrest. "It's not a contest. You don't have to know right away."

"I guess not." Nora rests her head against the armchair. "Once I'm comfortable with someone, I don't think I have a problem. But I struggle with the *getting to* the comfortable part. You know? Like opening up, talking about emotions, dating, all the expectations..." She shrugs, her movements just as languid as her voice. "Having all those conversations freaks me out. I don't do it, so I don't end up in relationships."

I take a deep drag of my whiskey and think of what a fucking travesty it is that this woman has been taught that her mask is more valuable than what's beneath it. That showing her teeth means someone might not want her.

"Say something."

"Like what?"

"Anything. React to what I just told you, or I'm going to imagine that you're thinking the absolute worst." She laughs a little. "I mean, you already do. I know that."

"You've had sex before?" I ask her. The idea that she might not have, and I took her to the party tonight... What she saw. The practice lessons. Being Rafe's sister. My hand tightens around the glass. *Please don't be a virgin.*

It would make me far shittier than I already am.

"Of course I have," she says with a small laugh. "I've had moments where the stars aligned. I can get turned on."

"Thank god." I run a hand along my jaw. "You're outspoken in other areas. With me, all the time. And you're clearly ambitious. You work on your designs every day. I've watched you while you work." When she's not pretending for someone. "It consumes you."

"That's different."

"Is it?"

"Yes. With you, well, we're not *dating*." She looks back over at the cat, where a twitching nose emerges out from a bookcase. "And when I'm designing, it's just me. Me and the clothes. I don't know... It's like people always want things from me, and I'm not always willing to give it."

"Because you've been taught that relationships are either-or," I say. It feels right, the words. "Either you present the image you think they want, or you don't bother at all. Because the middle ground, of having hard conversations? You don't know how to do that."

"Yes. You and Zeina should talk. You both have it all figured out."

"Your therapist?"

"Yes. Identifying an issue is great and all, but I still have to do the work, and the work sucks." She reaches for another of those little bags. "Nuts! Sure you don't want one of these?"

"They're all yours." I walk around the couch and sit in front of her. "So your therapist also wants you to practice. Your list isn't just your own."

"Yes. It's called exposure therapy." She says the term ironically and then laughs a little. Her hair has all fallen to one side, exposing her long neck. I pretended to kiss her there tonight. Caught the warm scent of her skin and grew hard beneath her thighs and still somehow kept my lips from ever touching her.

Now, curled up against the dark leather and oriental carpet, she looks distractingly good. A light in this dark space. "It freaking sucks, though. Sometimes I think that life itself is just one long exercise in exposure therapy. God, these cashews are good."

My lips curve. "You really are drunk."

"Oh, yes. Very," she says, and chuckles again. "I can't believe you aren't."

"I've been to those parties before."

"Right. When you were younger and dumber," she says.

I stretch my legs out and ignore that. It's too true. "So all the stuff on your list. It's not so much practice as exposure therapy."

"Yes." She shrugs a little and turns toward the bookcase fully. My eyes trail down the length of her back and the soft skin on display there. The silk curves all the way down to the small of her back, and with the way she's moving now, it gapes a little.

I look away.

She lowers so she's eye level with the cat and makes soft little cooing sounds. A gray paw emerges, and then a small gray face too, the pink nose twitching carefully. "Hey, aren't you pretty?" she says in a low voice. She switches to French, murmuring to the cat.

It walks out in full view and carefully sniffs her hand.

"Look at your cat," she tells me.

I shake my head. "Still not mine."

"Your roommate, then. He's living here rent-free." She scratches the cat behind an ear, and slowly, it comes closer. Rubs itself against her bent legs.

"Tell me why it freaks you out."

"I've told you already," she says. Her voice lowers. "Oh, you're so soft."

"Tell me again," I demand.

Nora sighs and turns to look at me. "It stresses me out when a guy is into me," she says. "It just does, and I can't explain it more than it makes me feel like he's *expecting* something from me, and now I have to perform, or let him down. And between those two emotions, there's no space for *me* to actually feel attracted to him."

"You care too much about what people think."

"Yes, obviously." Her voice rises. "I don't know how it's so easy for everyone else. It's like somewhere along the way, my friends got so cool with it. They learned how to do it, you know? How to fall in love and how to have fun dating. How to get to know someone. And I just never did."

"It's not easy for everyone else."

"It sure seems that way." She takes a deep breath. "Anyway, that's why I avoid dating most of the time. It takes so much time and energy. I'm trying to navigate how to make them happy while trying to figure out my own emotions, and most of the time I can't bother."

"Which is why you turn down all men."

"Yes," she admits. But then she strokes the cat's back, and a smile crosses her face. "Except you, of course. If you are a man. I'm not sure yet."

"I assume you're not talking to me," I say and lift my glass to my lips.

She laughs. "No, I'm not. I'm very aware that you're a man."

I brush my hand over the edge of the couch. The leather is well worn beneath my fingers, but it's nowhere near as soft as her skin. "You want it, though. A relationship. Love."

"Yes," she says softly. "I do."

"So you've thought about it. There's a version of it you think you'd like."

Her summer green gaze wanders over to mine. "Yes."

"Tell me," I say, "how you would want to be courted. How you'd like to be kissed."

"How would I prefer to be kissed?" she repeats softly.

"Yes. Tell me what your ideal date would be. How you'd want it to end, if it was a man you were attracted to."

She bites her lip, considering. "I... I'm not sure I can put it into words."

"Try," I urge. She's never going to be able to get what she wants from men if she doesn't know what that is herself.

The whiskey burns going down my throat.

I deserve it. For this night. For this conversation.

"I guess I'd want it to be slow. Like we're both savoring

the moment, not rushing to claim a prize." Her gaze drops to the cat in her lap. "I'd want it to be... a bit teasing. Like it might end at any moment, instead of a race toward..."

"A finish line."

"Yes." She smiles a little. "Like you kissed me earlier tonight."

There's an old grandfather clock in this library. In the sudden quiet, I can hear it ticking loudly. Once. Twice. Three times.

I can't look away from her.

Nora breaks our staring contest first, a blush rising up her cheeks. "Please forget that—"

"Like I kissed you," I say roughly. "What about it?"

She lifts a shoulder in a shrug and looks down at the cat now purring in her lap. He's going to ruin her pretty silk dress, and she doesn't seem to care at all. "You started slow, and then it grew deeper. Better." She shakes her head and presses a hand to her forehead. "I need to shut up."

"You're drunk," I say. "I won't hold you to this."

"But you will remember it. That's the part you're not saying."

I can't forget it even if I tried. And there's not a single part of me that wants to try. Triumph flows through me, dark and heady.

Like you kissed me.

"If you want to feel what it's like to date, to be courted, to be in a relationship? To kiss? I'll give you all of it. On your terms."

Another smile ghosts across her lips. "Exposure therapy."

"You ask for what you want with me," I say. She's had so little of that in her life. If I can be the one to give that to her, it'll all have been worth it. "So that when you go out into the real world later, you know what you want, and you stop wearing a mask. A man who wants you to pretend for him doesn't deserve you."

"Okay." She tilts her head and looks at me like I'm a surprise. "How come you've always been able to see through it?"

"You're not the only one who's perceptive," I say. And because I've looked far, far too much at her over the years.

And once I saw the real her, it was the only version I wanted.

CHAPTER 24
NORA

It takes me longer than I want to admit to get over my hangover from the Paradise Lost party, and there are stains and claw marks on my dress I'll never get out. I don't resent a single one of them.

There was a magic to last night. I felt alive around the idea of *real* men and sex, when it's not just in my head, but right there in front of me. West kissed me again, and I liked it.

It wasn't just pleasant or nice. It was amazing.

I talk to Zeina about it over video call, and despite her professional tone, she's amused by the whole thing. Especially by West's insistence that I practice dropping the mask. *How did that make you feel?* she asked me. *Do you think he's right?*

It was a leading question, because of course he is. It's something Zeina herself has told me over and over again. I people-please too close to the sun, making people like an image of me. Not actually *me*, with my truth and my flaws.

I never thought West Calloway would be the person to see it so clearly. He was raised in a world that prides itself on surface, on legacy, on appearances. And yet he seems to be obsessed with getting to the truth of things.

My truth, at any length.

When I've made myself come in the past, it's never been to a real guy. It's been to some vague fantasy, to an idea of a man, but not someone I know. That has always felt too intense. They're too clearly another person with wants and needs that might clash with my own.

But last night, beneath the covers, I imagined West and his lips against mine. His voice in my ear telling me how good I'm doing. Thought about how hard he had been against me. All the fantasies I've ever had came roaring to life with him in the starring role.

I came twice and fell into a dead sleep.

He isn't in the house the next day. I know this time, because I ask, and I find out he left Fairhaven on business.

It's just me and the staff, a bustling crew that I'm getting to know more with each passing day. Melissa in the kitchen is talkative and funny, and I take to eating my breakfast at the island so we can chat while she bakes bread or meal preps. She always has a crossword on the center island and the radio playing.

"The cat?" she says when I ask her. "I've tried to catch him for weeks!"

"I saw him in the library. He let me pet him, but I didn't feel a chip." I grin at her. "We should get some cat food."

"Do you know who he belongs to?"

"Fairhaven," I say. Despite West's protestations, the cat has looked supremely at home here every time I've seen him.

Ernest is a harder nut to crack. I get the sense that he walks through the estate like a captain of a ship, checking and double-checking that everything is up to his exacting standards.

I throw myself into my work for the rest of the day. Half of my pieces are already done, but I'm trying a new design for a skirt and blazer set, and I can't get the pattern quite right. It takes me all day to cut and measure and perfect the patterns.

By the time the sun sets, my shoulders ache from sitting hunched over, and there's a faint headache at my temples. There are also two texts waiting for me on my neglected phone. I shouldn't get excited at the name, but I do anyway, remembering the press of his lips against mine.

WEST

> Out of town for work. Will only be gone until tomorrow evening. Stay with your security detail at all times. I'd prefer it if you don't leave Fairhaven, but I know I can't convince you of that.

The phrasing makes me smile. No, he knows I don't respond well to orders. Even if the idea that the stalker is out there, combined with the sprawling beauty of Fairhaven, makes me more than happy to stay on the grounds.

The house feels like a living entity, history carved into every wall. It holds secrets to West. And he is so loath to share any of his own.

Funny, how I thought this place would feel like a prison, and instead it's become a sanctuary.

There's a second text sent a few hours later.

WEST

> I know you're home. I remember that texting with men was on your list of things to practice.

Nerves simmer in my stomach. He's right, it was. The plans, the conversations, the asks. It all takes so much energy.

NORA

> Do you have the list memorized?

WEST

> I have it in my wallet.

NORA

Do you read it daily?

WEST

Of course.

NORA

I'm not surprised. You feel like an overachiever.

His response is quick.

WEST

Takes one to know one, gorgeous.

My eyes zero in on the word. He's pretending. I know he is, and still, I can almost hear the compliment in his low, warm voice.

My phone buzzes, signaling an incoming call, and his name flashes across the screen.

"Hello?" I say.

"Hey." His voice is familiar in my ear, and I close my eyes at the deepness of it. There's faint music in the background and the chatter of voices. "I'm glad you answered."

I swallow. "Yeah. I was just… working."

"Designing? How is it going?"

"It's… going. I'm struggling with a pattern, but I think I finally solved it."

"Of course you did," he says. "You're talented."

The praise, said so matter-of-factly, makes my stomach tighten. "Thank you. Where are you?"

"Boston."

"Having fun?"

He scoffs. "Not even a little bit. I'm in constant communication with the security team too. You're safe."

"I know," I say. "Thank you. Are you out somewhere?"

"Yes. An executive corporate retreat for Calloway Holdings. I had to make an appearance." He sounds annoyed by that fact, and my smile widens.

"Maybe you should practice boundary-setting," I tell him sweetly, "and learn how to ask for what you want."

He's quiet for a beat, and then he laughs. It's a low, warm sound that skitters across my skin. "Is the student becoming the teacher?"

"I can handle a little role-play from time to time."

"Can you? Interesting." His voice is suggestive, and my stomach tightens again. "Go out with me tomorrow, trouble."

His voice is a low slide over my skin, demanding, soothing. "Tomorrow?"

"You're free," he tells me. "I'll pick you up. We'll have fun."

I take a deep breath. "Okay."

"No. You're supposed to push back. Tell me you can't but would love to go out another day. Tell me you want to drive yourself."

"But that's hard."

"I know it is. That's why we'll practice," he says. "I'm picking you up tomorrow. Wear something pretty."

I close my eyes. "Thank you, that's a very nice offer, but I'm busy tomorrow night. How about Sunday?"

"You're being too nice."

"No, I'm using affirmative boundary-setting! It's a tool my therapist and I have been working on."

"What did you call it?"

"Affirmative boundary-setting, and I know you heard me the first time."

He chuckles again. I like the sound more than I should. "I did. See, that's good. You calling me out. And you don't need to affirm someone before drawing a boundary."

"Sometimes I do. It's very helpful, actually, especially with people I care about." I take a step forward, looking out the window. The ocean is calm today. A perfectly shiny surface. "It makes me feel less awful."

He's quiet for a beat. "Right. But do you care about a random guy asking you out?"

"Maybe," I say. "But maybe… I just want to make sure he doesn't get too disappointed. Or mad at me."

"Do they get mad?" His voice drops, and there's an undercurrent of irritation in it. "Have you ever experienced that?"

"Once or twice. I mean, not angry *angry*, but yeah."

"Fuck them," he says. "If being kind when you refuse makes you feel better, then do that. But I don't want you to feel like you have to. You don't owe me anything, all right? I'm just an asshole you've been on a single date with, who's annoying you to get you to say yes. We'll go again."

We do it three more times, and each time he asks, I tell him what I'd like to do instead. *No, I don't want to go out to dinner. Let's go for a walk next weekend instead.* It's a constant negotiation. And on the final attempt, I tell him that I'm only interested in being friends.

West chuckles. "Even then, you can't help yourself, can you?"

"What? I turned you down completely! I'm good at that!"

"Yes, but you still offered friendship. Do you want to be friends with me?"

"You you, or fake you?"

"Fake me," he says.

"No."

"Right. So don't offer anything. You've told me you worry about living up to expectations. But you can also be the one to set them."

I close my eyes. "Right. If I'm brave enough."

"You are brave." Another nugget of praise. I tuck it away, fold it into the warmth of my chest. There's a voice behind him, closer than the background noise. It sounds urgent. "Damn. I have to go."

"Your adoring fans are calling."

"I have to give a speech."

"Do you have that memorized, too?"

"I'm going to wing it," he says with the perfect confidence I so envy. "And Nora?"

"Yes?"

"I *am* picking you up tomorrow night. We're practicing another date. Our last one was…"

"I failed at it. I know."

"You didn't fail. It wasn't a test, but it was informative," he says. "We'll do it again."

"Okay."

He hesitates for a second. "Stay safe."

"Isn't that your job?" I tease.

He chuckles again. "Yes. It is."

"Have fun," I say. "Good luck with your speech."

"Thank you, trouble."

The conversation stays with me for hours afterward. Even as I talk to my mother, as I do every day, and she urges me toward a new modeling job, all I hear is West's voice. *You can be the one to set those expectations.*

My mother *did* push me into modeling. But I've never explicitly said I didn't want it, either. I've placated and smiled and demurred and quietly tried to pull out of engagements. Maybe that was okay then. I was younger. I was doing the best I could.

But I'm older now, and it's my life.

The next day, I'm sitting in the kitchen with Melissa when I hear the front door open. It's large enough that the sound echoes through the immediate rooms downstairs.

People come and go often here. Ernest. The security guards. The head housekeeper, the gardeners, Melissa herself. I don't react much, focusing on solving the six-down for *mercurial* we've been stuck on.

But footsteps echo on the marble floor to the kitchen.

Ernest appears. His face is half hidden behind a giant bouquet of spring flowers. It's an explosion of green and pink.

He sets it on the counter and places a small wrapped box next to it. "There's a delivery for you," he says.

"Oh my god. For me?" I slide off the chair and then pause. "It's not from…" I let my words trail off, a tightness in my chest. I don't like saying the word. *Stalker* makes it feel so real, somehow, and so predatory. I'm trying not to think about whoever it is.

"No. It's not from *him*." Ernest says the word with barely concealed distaste. "Don't worry."

"Thanks."

His eyes meet mine. "I'm sorry about your situation."

"Thank you. I really appreciate that."

He nods and says hello to Melissa before leaving the kitchen.

I stare at the giant bouquet. The dazzling array of lilies and baby's breath and peonies. *Practice getting gifts.* That was on my list. It always increases the pressure for me. When guys bring flowers or chocolates.

When I was nineteen, I was walking shows in Milan for the spring/summer collections. A man in his forties, and a friend of the designer, wouldn't stop giving me gifts. They'd show up at my makeup station between shows.

Giant, ostentatious things that made saying no to him all the more hard, because now I felt like I owed him gratitude too.

I reach for the card attached to the bouquet and turn it

over with careful fingers. There, in sprawling masculine handwriting, is a single sentence. *I'm picking you up at seven.*

Anticipation makes me smile. He sent me flowers. West sent me *flowers.*

Melissa makes a small whistling sound. "Look at that! That's gorgeous."

"It really is, isn't it?" I reach out for the small wrapped box. "And it came in a vase."

"He knows how to spoil a girl," she says and turns back to the dough she's kneading.

"Oh, we're not… that is… we're not dating," I tell her.

"Of course you're not," she says so quickly that I know she's humoring me. "No need to explain anything to me."

"Thanks."

"You should know, though," she says, "that I've worked here for years, and he never has women staying here."

"Oh. That's… good."

She nods a little and starts humming to herself as she works on the bread. She makes the best rolls; I've praised her so often that she rolls her eyes at my compliments now.

I undo the small package that was delivered alongside the beautiful flowers and carefully open the lid. Inside, wrapped in black silky paper, is a card game. Unopened. Newly bought.

On the front is an illustrated pair of fuzzy handcuffs. Beneath it is the text *Naughty Conversations for Couples* in a pink font.

And I know this date will be nothing like our last.

CHAPTER 25
NORA

West leans against a dark red car parked on the gravel of the Fairhaven courtyard. Dark pants, white shirt, top two buttons undone. He looks lazily elegant, a bit bored, tall and masculine.

But when I walk down the stairs, his focus sharpens. His eyes drop down over my body in a slow, devouring look. There's raw appreciation in his gaze that makes heat spread through me.

He's just pretending again, I remind myself. *We're practicing.*

"Hi," I say.

"Hey." His eyes are still on my body, not on me. Like he can't tear them away. It's so blatant that it has to be another test.

"If you're *quite* done," I say.

"That's my girl," he says with a smile. "Tell a man off if you don't like what he's doing."

"Is everything a lesson with you these days?"

"That's what you wanted from me," he says. "Did you like the flowers?"

I hesitate only a moment before replying. "Yes. I did."

"I have something else for you." He holds out a velvet

case and opens the lid. There's a gold necklace inside. A single gold coin pendant hangs from the thin chain. It's got several small jewels inlaid. An emerald, two sapphires. What looks like diamonds.

"West…" I murmur.

"Turn around." His voice is a command, and I do what he's asked. Lift my hair up for him. A second later, the necklace comes to rest around my neck, the gold cold against my skin.

It's beautiful.

"This is too much," I say. "It's gorgeous. Thank you. But I can't ask you to spend money on me just to help—"

"You didn't ask." His voice is a bit rough, and his fingers linger at my nape. "This is what it would feel like. If you were in a relationship. If you let a man treat you right."

I stroke a finger over the necklace. "Did you pick it out yourself?"

It shouldn't matter, and I shouldn't have asked. Of course he didn't. He's a busy man, and he's been traveling, and it doesn't—

"Yes," he says.

Oh. I smile down at the pendant. "Thank you."

His fingers disappear from my skin. "You're very welcome."

He opens the door for me, and the scent of his cologne wafts toward me. Subtle and woodsy. It feels like him, like the rooms of this house and the deep, dark wood and the constant view of the deep blue ocean.

He drives down the tree-lined driveway and to the wrought-iron gates with the intricate C. "How does it feel?" he asks.

"How does what feel?"

"Leaving home again." West glances up at the mirror, at the car that follows us. Miguel, Sam and Madison are with us tonight. "He might watch us tonight."

"Yes. That's the point, right? For him to see us together."

"Yes. But I asked how it made you feel."

I look out the window, at the dark roads of King's Point. Fairhaven lies at the shoreline farthest out on Great Neck, and from here, it's all hedges and hidden houses. We won't see lights and shops for at least another ten minutes. "It is what it is," I say.

The photos that were delivered last week were terrifying. I stayed composed in front of West, but I broke down afterward in the safety of my bedroom. The stalker had *watched* me.

Anyone can deliver flowers. Even someone halfway around the world.

But taking pictures of me out fabric shopping with my guards…

He was here.

"You can use more descriptive words." West's voice is dry. "I won't hold it against you."

"It sucks. But I won't let it stop me from living my life." My chest feels tight, and I force a smile. "I brought the card game you sent me."

He glances at me, like he knows all too well I'm changing the subject, and not so subtly. But he doesn't protest. "Well done," he says.

The compliment feels like a shot of warmth. Maybe that's all I need. West Calloway telling me how good I'm doing. I've come to crave it. "Where are we going tonight?"

"It's a surprise," he says.

"No. You'll tell me. Won't you?" I ask him. I make my voice low, mirror the flirtation I've seen others do. I've never had a chance to engage in it myself. I've always been on the back foot, two steps behind what the guy wants. "I don't like surprises, Calloway."

His lip curves. "You only use my last name when you're annoyed with me."

"Does it bother you?"

"Since you only do it when you're annoyed at me, whether I like it or not shouldn't matter."

That makes me chuckle. "Sometimes I think you want me to turn into a jerk."

"A jerk is honest," he says, "and not particularly concerned with likability."

"You sound like you have some experience with the subject."

He smiles wide, and it transforms his face. Makes it come to life. "I do, yes. Some might say I majored in it."

"Straight A's?"

"Always."

"Where are we having dinner, Calloway?"

His smile stays in place. "We're having dinner at the yacht club."

"The *yacht* club? Where you used to sail?"

"Yes." He glances over at me and then back at the road. "I didn't think you'd get that excited about it."

I fiddle with the clasp on my bag. It's a piece of him, and it's far better than a fine restaurant in the city. But I can't tell him that. "I've never sailed before," I say instead.

Like that makes any kind of sense.

"Well," he says, "we'll change that at some point."

It sounds like a promise. I look down at the pendant resting against my skin and struggle against the weight of a crush I thought I'd left behind years ago. He still turned me down at that Christmas party five years ago. He still said those things to Alex four years ago.

And yet.

Here he is, making me feel things again.

West pulls into the marina and parks behind a large white building by the ocean. The adjoining restaurant is decorated in nautical themes, and there's not a single white tablecloth in sight. A cheery teenager escorts us to a table right by the seafront windows.

West suggests we both get sirloins, and he does it in front of the waiter. I cut him off and tell him I want the ravioli instead. He nods at me afterward. "Good. You're learning."

"I know that everything is a challenge with you now."

"Just because I know you can rise to them. You're more than people think you are."

I look down at my glass of wine. What *he* used to think I was, he means. *Pretty enough, but boring.*

"Proving people wrong is fun," I say.

His eyes stay on mine. There's amusement there, and something else, something that warms me to my core. "Give me the card game."

"Can you say the magic word?"

His lips curve. "Please, trouble, can you put me out of my misery and let me ask you questions about sex?"

A hot flush surges up my neck. I dig through my bag for the purple card game. *Naughty Conversations for Couples.* And beneath, in smaller font. *Learn more about each other's fantasies, desires and wants.*

He runs a finger over the cover. "You opened it."

"I read some questions. Where did you even find it?"

"You can find anything online." He pulls out the deck. "Why do you think I suggested this?"

"You're going to make me say it?"

"Yeah."

I sigh. "Because of the party. Paradise Lost. Because of what we saw."

"Yeah. When you looked at the couple having sex and said you didn't think she could be enjoying herself. That her pleasure was performative." He raises his eyebrow. "And when you didn't want to say the word. The one that starts with an *M*."

"You're gonna make me say it?" Now my cheeks are burning.

"I'm not going to make you do anything. Your terms, trouble. Always. But if your end goal is to date more and to get into a relationship, learning to talk about these things is important. You've never really learned to ask for what you want. Have you?"

"It's not easy."

"I didn't say it was." He flips through the cards, shuffles them like we're about to play a game.

I rub a hand over the back of my neck. It's hard to think around the length of his fingers as he expertly flips through cards filled with absolute filth. "I'm not a prude."

"Didn't say you were. I saw you watching the other couples that night."

"And you weren't?" I ask him.

"I had more… pressing things to focus on." He finishes his shuffle and extends the deck to me. The cards look small in his large palm. "Ladies first."

I reach for the top one.

"Do you have any kinks?" I read. It's a pretty broad question, and I glance up to see him looking at me. "You go first."

"Some," he says.

"What are they?"

His entire focus is on me, and I feel myself expand beneath it, a piece of paper folded out and smoothed. "I like praising the women I'm with," he says. "You might have noticed that."

CHAPTER 26
NORA

"Praising," I repeat. "That's…"

"Exactly what it sounds like." West reaches for his glass of wine. "I enjoy making my partner feel good and valued."

"Doesn't everyone?"

"They should. They *better*. But not everyone likes it quite as much as me, I think." His amber eyes darken. "Guiding, admiring. Learning what a woman likes. What makes her feel good. Telling her just how good she's doing when she's pleasing me."

"Oh." The word comes out a bit strangled. He's called me good several times in our previous lessons. *That's my girl.* It was unexpected… and unexpectedly nice, coming out in his deep, smooth voice. "You do like doing that."

His hand stops, wineglass halfway to his mouth. "I wasn't sure if you'd noticed."

My mouth feels dry. "I didn't know it was a kink."

"Not everyone likes it. Some women can find it… paternalistic. It's something I discuss first."

"Praise," I whisper. I've lived my whole life craving validation. Chasing it. Fighting for it. Feeling like I'm not good if I don't get it. It's dictated my whole life.

I have to look away from his gaze. It's too knowing. Like he knows just how much I crave that, too.

"I can see how someone might like that," I say.

"Someone," he asks, "or you?"

My eyes flit back to his. It's hard to breathe. "Both. I think."

"Mhm. That's good, trouble. Expressing what you like."

"Anything, em… else? Do you like chains? Whips? Um… role-play?"

He runs a hand along his jaw. "Was that on the card?"

"No. I'm freestyling."

"And the first thing you came up with was whips? Makes me curious about *your* kinks."

"Not whips," I say quickly. "Actually, scratch that one. I don't know where that came from."

"Don't worry. I won't forget it."

I groan. "Of course you won't."

"Does pain interest you, then?"

"I'm not sure I—" We're interrupted by the approaching waiter. West effortlessly swipes the cards off the table and tucks them beneath his palm in time. My ravioli is set in front of me. It smells divine.

"Thank you so much," I tell the waiter and smile widely at him. "This looks delicious."

He hesitates for a second, blinking at me. He looks young. Probably still in high school. "Thank you."

"Tell the chef, will you?"

"Will do. Thanks. Again." He smiles a bit and then hurries away.

Across from me, West chuckles darkly. "You just made his night."

"With a simple compliment?" I shake my head and flip over the card I'm still holding.

"By being the most beautiful woman who's ever smiled to him," West says.

The compliment rolls through me like a thunderstorm.

He didn't say it with his fake voice, his acting voice. He said it matter-of-factly. A little amused. Darkly pleased. Like he means it. "You were talking about pain, and I'm very interested in where you were going with it."

I clear my throat. *Right.* "I don't think I like it," I say. "Pleasure is hard enough to come by, and I don't see how mixing in pain helps. But I've never tried it, so what do I know? What about you?" My question comes out a little breathless.

I have insight into West's sex life. Into what he likes and doesn't like. And he's *sharing* it with me, talking openly about it, and I suddenly understand completely why this is something he insisted on.

It's a terrifying conversation.

And it's exhilarating.

"I don't like inflicting pain," he says. "I don't mind it on my part, and if you want to scratch my back with your nails, I'll wear the marks proudly. It'll let me know you're enjoying yourself. Rough sex, sure, but no pain. I want my partner to come. Repeatedly."

I nod at West too many times. "That's good... to know." I run a hand along my neck. My skin feels hot beneath my thick hair. "I'm not sure if I have a ton of kinks."

"Everyone has something."

Maybe everyone does. Everyone who's actually had sex. I've only fantasized about it. Formed my opinions based on books, and movies, and my own touch. That's something, at least.

"I like... a lot of things."

The skin around his eyes crinkles. "How descriptive."

"Maybe I haven't explored a lot of kinks."

"No shame in that. What would you want to try?"

I'm quiet for a few moments, my brain racing.

West's mouth tips into that smile again. The challenging

one, the one he gave me when we boxed the other week. *Come on. Hit me.* "It's okay to be vanilla, trouble. You can own that. You don't need to think of something just to impress me."

"I'm not *trying* to impress you, Calloway."

West chuckles. "Of course not. Not me. But we're pretending I'm someone you're dating. Someone whose opinion you care about. Even if they push you on something, you can still say no. Or stand by your first answer."

"I know that." I roll my neck and try to shake it off. He's right. Of course he's right. It sounds so natural and so true when he says it. I just can't get there on my own. "I don't think I would mind, actually, a bit of roughness... if it was someone I trusted. Someone I liked." I take a deep breath, needing this conversation to end before I embarrass myself completely.

I've thought about how you'd feel on top of me. I want you to praise me more. I want you to do it while I come. Is that a kink?

"Okay. You take a card," I say.

He does just that, his broad hand between us on the table. "Well," he says, his voice darkening. "This one will definitely come up when you're in a relationship."

"It will?"

"When was your last check-up?" he asks.

My eyes widen. "West."

"It's a normal question with someone you're dating."

"Okay. But..." I glance away from him at the waiters around. There's only a few other tables occupied, and they're a fair bit away. "You answer that first."

West's hand presses flat against the table, big and tan against the white wood. "Fine. Ask me, then."

I clear my throat and force my eyes back to his whiskey ones. There's amusement there. He's enjoying this, just how awkward and uncomfortable it's making me.

"When was your last check-up?" I ask.

"Why do you want to know?"

I groan. "West."

"Come on. Press me on it."

I toy with the edge of my napkin. "I think it's good practice. Generally speaking. When dating someone."

"Mhm. Well, I'm clean."

I smile at him. "Great, thank you."

"No, trouble. You should never accept that response."

"Why not? I got what I asked for."

He shakes his head. "He could be lying to you."

"So I need to press him on it?"

"Yes." He narrows his eyes at me and makes his voice hard. "Don't worry about it. I'm clean."

"Oh. Right. And how do you... know that?"

"No symptoms."

I dig my teeth into my lower lip. "West, I can't demand someone show me a clean bill of health to their face!"

"Of course you can. Argue with them. Never accept their word for it." His voice is dark and just shy of deadly. "You should definitely not let him come inside you without a condom if he doesn't."

"You're making this too hard," I say. "How would you even handle this conversation?"

He reaches for his glass. "Well, first of all, I wouldn't be having it halfway through a first date. A little presumptuous."

That makes my lips twitch, despite myself. "Good call."

"And I'd start with..." He puts down the glass of red and looks at me directly. "Let's talk birth control."

My eyes widen. "Oh."

"Opens the conversation. I'd make it clear that I use condoms, always," he continues in that deep, rasp of his voice. "Protects against all kinds of... consequences. Even if going without is more pleasurable."

I think of his hardness beneath me when I was draped

over his lap. I think of what he might look like and that big hand rolling a condom on.

"Okay. Yeah." I blink a few times. "That's good."

"How've you handled it in the past?"

I look down at my food and lie through my teeth. "Always used condoms. I told you, never been in a relationship."

"Save going without for that. And make the bastard show you a doctor's note." His voice is a bit rough, too, and his jaw works. He cuts into his steak with more force than necessary.

We eat in silence for half a minute. I feel too hot, my legs rubbing together beneath the table. I don't know if I've ever been turned on during a date before. But right now, all I can think of is what his hand would look like gripping something other than a steak knife.

He reaches for another card, his face smoothing out. The annoyance disappears. "Well," he says. "Funny, considering it was the one word you couldn't handle. How often do you masturbate?"

I force out a smooth, polite laugh. "Wow."

"Yeah."

"That's a very personal question."

"That's the point of this lesson, trouble. To get personal."

I curve my fingers around my glass of wine. The surface is cool against my too-hot skin. "I've never spoken about that with anyone before."

"No one?"

"No. It's not something that comes up in conversation." My lips part. "Not mine, at least. Does it for you?"

West runs a hand along his jaw, hiding a smile. "Not daily, at least."

"I guess couples talk about that sort of thing. And this game is for a couple."

"Yes. But if you're dating a man, if you're planning on… if

you're sleeping with him," he says, the words coming out through gritted teeth, "you should be able to have a conversation with him about all these things. Protection, safety, boundaries, safe words, your wants, your needs. Your own pleasure."

My stomach tightens, butterflies fighting with a roiling snake. Funny how I used to run from being uncomfortable. Now it feels like I'm hurtling myself headfirst into it daily.

"Once or twice a week," I say into my wine. "I guess."

West's eyebrows rise slightly. "You guess?"

"Well, I don't exactly keep a *logbook.*"

His lips curve. "All right. Twice a week is good. Toys?"

"I haven't tried one. I guess it's easy to end up in a routine when something… works."

He leans back. "It is. But maybe getting to know yourself more will help with all of this. If you're going to ask for what you want, it helps to know what that is."

I cut into my ravioli. "Yeah. Maybe. But I feel like I need to even get there with a guy in order for it to become relevant. Again." I tack on the last word and hope it doesn't sound too much like an afterthought. "What about you? How often do you…?"

Silence stretches out for a few long seconds. Maybe he won't respond. Maybe he's done with this game.

"More often than that," he finally says. "Especially lately."

"Oh. Is that because of… me?" I ask. His eyes flash to mine, and then immediately narrow. Shoot. "I mean, because you're pretending to date me, and you're busy? So you don't have time for your usual… hook-ups."

He cuts into the final piece of his meat. "You're right," West says, "that I haven't been with anyone since you moved to New York."

"So I'm standing in your way," I say, and the sick realization that he might otherwise be out there, dating, if he wasn't *here* with me—

"No. Don't think that for a single fucking second. Okay? I'm happy where I am."

"You mean that."

"You know I'd never do something I don't want to."

That makes my lips curve, and the fear, the sudden punch of jealousy, melts away. "Yes. I do know you well enough to know that." The tension between us feels so thick it's hard to breathe. I have to cut it. "And do you use... toys?"

His lips quirk. "No. I don't."

"Then it's not fair that you told me I should try."

"Female pleasure can be more complex."

I take another long sip of my wine. "You mean you're perfectly happy with your right hand?"

West's eyes won't leave mine. "I wouldn't say *perfectly happy,* but it works."

"So does mine," I say. Maybe it's the wine, or the questions I've already answered, but I feel braver. His gaze slides to the wineglass I'm holding.

To my *hand.*

"And yet," he says, "you want to date and end up in a relationship. So it can't be all that good."

"I hope men are good for more than just sex."

His smile is sudden. "I've heard some of us can be. On occasion."

"You're enjoying this far too much."

"Watching you squirm over normal topics? Who wouldn't?"

"They can't be *normal.* Do you really talk about this with women you date?"

"I thought you'd decided I didn't date. At all. Just because you've never seen me at a party with someone."

I roll my eyes. "Do you *really* talk about this stuff?"

"Yes," he says. The smile disappears. "Talking about what you like in bed is necessary if you're going to have a good experience. No one is a mind reader."

"Too bad," I say and reach for another card. "It would make things easier."

"Nora." His hand lands on top of mine, pressing it flat against the table. Stopping me from reading the card. "What you said the other night... You're not having mediocre sex with men just because you feel like you're not allowed to ask for what you want. Right? You're not performing in bed too, are you?"

I'm a deer caught in the headlights. Torn between a lie I can't uphold and a truth I can't bear. "No," I tell him. "I promise I'm not."

His wide shoulders sink in a sigh. "Good. I couldn't handle it if..." He shakes his head. "Save the card you just took. We'll talk about it at our next stop."

"The date isn't over?"

"No," he says, and there's a glint in his eye that tells me he's going to enjoy whatever comes next. "Something you said gave me an idea. We're going shopping."

CHAPTER 27
WEST

She'd gotten me hard at dinner with the image of her touching herself *once or twice a week*. It's an image I shouldn't have, shouldn't think about, but now it's all I can think about.

The way her eyes lit up when I mentioned praise... I suspected we'd be a fit there. But her prettily flushed cheeks confirmed it.

But remembering the future men she'll date was enough of a cold bucket to wash away the heat and turn it into ice. I'm jealous of men she hasn't met yet. Irrationally, desperately jealous.

And furious at all the ways they'll fail to deserve her.

Nora is quiet beside me in the car. It isn't until I pull into the parking lot outside Afterglow that Nora makes a strangled sound.

"Oh my god," she says. "Oh my *god*." Her expression is open. There's something wondrous there, and then nervous. And then her gaze flicks back to mine.

"Too much?"

She shakes her head and undoes her seat belt. "No. I've been to a sex shop before."

"When?"

"Years ago. I was studying abroad. A few of my friends and I went into one during a night out. We mostly giggled the whole time." She wets her lips. "Is this because I said I had never tried toys?"

"We'll buy some for you," I say.

The look in her eyes when she watched the other couples has stayed with me. Her fascination with the oral sex. She hasn't been well taken care of in the past, and I'll be damned if that'll ever happen again.

"Oh. *Oh.*" There's excitement in her voice. "We can look at toys for you too."

"I don't need any."

"Fair is fair!" she says and pops open the door. I follow her into the shop, stopping only to nod at Sam and Madison. They've parked next to us, and they follow a few feet behind us into the shop.

They're the best of the best. They won't comment on the location.

Afterglow is all sleek decor and pale pink, with a smiling attendant that says hi as we enter. A display of candy is the first thing we see. Nora's gaze lingers on it, but then she moves on to a shelf that has a dizzying array of condom types and lube. More flavors than anyone has need of.

Her brown hair flows down her back, and I know what it feels like to drag my fingers through it now. Forbidden knowledge.

"XXL," Nora reads on one of the condom boxes. "I think that's a vanity purchase."

"Never been with anyone who needed one of those?"

"No. I know there's size variation, but XXL?" She looks over her shoulder at me quickly, then back at the packages. "What size do you buy?"

Don't get hard again, don't get hard again…

I shove my hands into my pockets. "The ones that are ribbed for her pleasure."

She laughs a little and moves on down the shelf, past the lubes. "Clever way to get out of that question."

"Are you saying you're interested in the size of my—"

"West!" she says, glancing behind me at where Sam and Madison flank the front door. She motions for me to follow her deeper into the store.

I grin. "They've signed an NDA."

"*Still*," she says.

If the stalker watches us here... Dark satisfaction spreads through me, nipping at the heels of my guilt. He should see how well taken care of Nora is. I want the thought of how many orgasms I probably give her to plague him.

Get even more reckless, I think. *Come out of the shadows.*

So I can close the noose around him.

Nora stops in front of another row of toys. These are all in leather. She pauses and tilts her head. "Is that a…"

"I believe so, yes." There's a ball gag on one of the shelves. "Not your thing."

"Are you kink shaming me, Calloway?"

"Never," I tell her. "I'm guessing, though."

Her eyes linger on mine for a second before she turns back to the shelf. "No. Not my thing. Not that I'd even know what my thing is…"

"You know," I say. "Don't do that."

"Do what?"

"Downplay what you want." I step closer, my words only meant for her. "You have fantasies. You've touched yourself for years. You know what turns you on."

Her breath catches. "Yes."

"You know there are things you like and things you don't. And you know what you'd like to try." I lean against the edge of one of the shelves. The blood is rushing south, but I won't let it distract me. "Don't downplay that. Not with me, not with any guy."

She wets her lower lip, and the entire world narrows to that single movement. "Tell me where I should begin in here."

I raise an eyebrow. "We could ask the attend—"

"No," she says quickly. "You."

Me.

I take a step closer and hold out my hand. She doesn't hesitate before she slips hers into mine. Warmth and triumph, one and the same, zing through me at the touch. "Come."

We walk down an aisle of cheap polyester costumes. Nurses and devils and maids and angels. I turn to the right, and we walk by a row of crops, paddles and handcuffs. "Oh my god," Nora breathes. "Look at that."

I pause, her hand still in mine. "Yeah. For people who like the pain."

"I've read about it. The whole BDSM thing. Doms… and subs," she says.

"Yes," I mutter. There's one of them among my own friends, and discovering that about him had been more intimate than I ever thought we'd get. "There's one thing it gets right, though."

"Um, BDSM?"

"Yes." We walk down the aisle and turn past a number of plugs and toys until we get to the vibrators. "It's about trust. And sex should *always* be about trust."

"I don't think everyone feels like that."

"Then they're doing it wrong." My voice comes out harsher than I intend. The idea of Nora people-pleasing in bed makes something inside me turn hard with fury. Not at her. Never *at* her. At the men who might not have listened.

It makes me hate my own gender. The idea of men on a date, seeing her beauty, seeing her kindness and her smiles, and thinking only of their own gratification.

"West," she says. She's looking at me with furrowed brows. "You okay?"

"Yes."

"Is that how you do it, then? Sex?" Her cheeks flush. "It's all trust-based?"

"Yes." *It would be with you,* I think. *Earning your trust and getting to touch you would be a fucking privilege.*

Instead, I reach out and grab one of the small pocket vibrators in a purple box. "You love pleasing others. But good sex is about pleasing yourself, too."

"That one is small."

"That's the point."

She turns it over and looks at the description. "Oh. It has vibrations."

"Mhm." I look over at the selection. "There are better ones, I think."

"Who made you such an expert?"

"I told you. I like pleasure." Reaching for another one, I hand it to her instead. Take the bullet one and put it back. "This one has suction."

There's a small, audible intake of her breath that sends heat rushing straight down my body. My cock hardens and pushes painfully against my zipper.

Fuck. I thought I would be better in this role.

What an illusion.

"Oh," she whispers. "So one would hold it against... one's clit?"

That makes my lips twitch. "*One* would, yes."

"That's interesting..." Her attention is locked on to the toy in her hand, and fuck it, I'm going to have to adjust myself.

I turn from her and scan for something bigger. There's plenty of them, but I settle for a medium-sized curved vibrator. It's meant for internal stimulation too. No suction, if she finds that too much...

"I think," she says, "that I want to buy this one."

She's still looking at the one I handed her. The image of her using it flashes through my mind. I shove it away with nothing but pure force. This is not the time. But I know it'll come back. Along with the hardness that needs to recede. *Don't picture her bent legs, her hand gripping the toy…*

"We'll get several," I tell her.

She looks up at me. "Several?"

"Yes."

"And… we?"

"Pay using my card." I hold up the other one for her. "This one too."

She reads the box like it's a manual, like we're still at the restaurant and she's looking through menu options, and there's such curious focus on her face that it makes me bite my tongue. I need to get a fucking grip.

I don't think anyone has ever turned me on as quickly, as easily, as she does.

"Yes, this one sounds good," she says.

"Do you mean that? Or are you saying it just because I picked it?"

She rolls her eyes, and more heat pulses through me. "I'm *not* just saying that. I'm not trying to people-please around you all the time, you know."

"I know. You do it more with other people."

"Yeah."

"I don't know whether to be flattered or offended that it never really crossed your mind with me."

She takes the vibrator from me and stacks it atop the other one. "Your pick, Calloway," she says with a smile.

My pick.

Flattered, then. More than flattered. It fucking *wrecks* me that I'm one of the few people she feels safe enough to be mostly herself around. That she doesn't preen or pretend for me, doesn't offer me fake smiles or hide her opinion.

She walks along a long line of increasingly outlandish dildos. Ribbed, curved, colorful, sparkly. Fantasy inspired and painful-looking.

She's incandescent beneath the low lighting of the store. A little wine-drunk and high off the conversations we've had.

She's being such a good girl.

I follow behind her and try not to picture her using the vibrators I've picked out for her. I fail.

At the end of the aisle, she stands stock-still and quickly backs up two steps.

"What's wrong?"

"Sam and Madison will see us at the register. They'll see what we buy." She worries her lip between her teeth. "I know I shouldn't care about it. I just need a moment, and then I'll do it."

"Do you want me to ask them to turn around?"

"No."

She's cute, this flustered and hot. Her face isn't the serene, unsmiling picture of beauty she offers when modeling. Now it's a beautiful kaleidoscope of her emotions. Playing over her cheeks, the green of her eyes, her full lips.

"Want me to buy them?"

Nora shakes her head. "I should do it. It's not like I'm doing anything wrong."

"No, you're not." I'm strung taut, the pleasure-pain of being on the edge for hours playing at my temples and the base of my spine. So I shouldn't, but I do it anyway. Reach out and tip her head up. "You've got a body with desires and wants like everyone does."

Her eyes are the deep green of winding ivy and full of trust. I feel heady with it, drunk on the power of it.

I smooth my thumb over her flushed cheek. "You've got nothing to be ashamed of. What other people think of you doesn't matter. You're allowed to be you, trouble. And you're allowed to be a woman who wants pleasure."

Her lips part, and warm breath washes over my thumb.

I could kiss her right now.

I want to.

"I'll buy them," she says. "What's your PIN code?"

I smile at her. "That's my girl. And it's one-nine-one-two. The year Fairhaven was completed."

She smiles beneath my thumb, and I'm lost. Maybe I always was. But this is the moment I know it, wholly and completely.

There's no recovering from her.

CHAPTER 28
NORA

When West finally drives through the gates of Fairhaven, I'm an ember. I've been burning for *hours.* I play with the silky straps of the pink bag in my lap. *Afterglow* emblazoned on the side, and inside, the two vibrators I bought.

We bought.

"You're about to drop me off at home," I say. "If this was a real date… and if this was a good date… maybe I'd invite you inside."

He's quiet. Looks straight ahead at the driveway. "And has it been a good date, trouble?"

"I think it's been a good date." My fingers find the pendant around my neck, smoothing over the gold plate. "Do you?"

He pulls the car up outside the front steps and turns off the engine. Behind us, the security team is meeting up with the others that patrol the grounds. *Our targets are back home safe after visiting a sex shop,* I imagine them saying. *No suspicious activity.*

"Stay where you are," he says. It's not an answer, and I wait while he walks around the car and opens the door for me.

"You're going to spoil me with that, you know," I tell him. "Most guys don't do that."

"A man who's worthy of you should."

"You didn't answer my question."

He shuts the door behind me. His eyes drift down, rest on the gold against my neck. "I had a good time. Hard not to, when I'm with you."

He's acting. I know he's acting, but still… "Thanks for tonight," I say. "I had a really good time too."

He puts a hand on my low back. "Let me walk you inside."

Once inside, we pause in the large foyer. Somewhere, an old clock ticks. Generations of Calloways line the top walls along the double staircases. West's ancestors, looking down on us.

"I want to go out with you again." He's standing closer than usual. We've done this before, and *still* my heart starts to race. "Let me take you out, Nora."

"Maybe," I say.

"Maybe?"

"Mhm. It depends on what you do now." I'm two glasses of wine in and high on the night. "On how well you kiss me."

He brushes his hand over my cheek. Just like he did earlier in the sex shop. "I have to earn another date with you?"

"Yes."

"That's it," he murmurs, and the inches between us close. "You're so pretty when you ask for what you want."

He smells like himself, like warmth and wine, and he tips my head back so he can fit himself against my lips. He kisses me slowly, leisurely, like I told him I liked.

It's wet against wet, a hot slide, and I'm lost to it. A labyrinth I don't want to escape from. Kissing West seems to do that.

It rearranges my world every time.

He lifts his head from mine, hovers just a few inches away. I sway into him, lean forward, but he keeps his lips just out of reach.

He's holding back.

My hand finds the collar of his shirt. "More," I tell him. "Do better."

His chuckle is hoarse, and he finds my waist with his free hand. "That's my girl. Tongue?"

"Yes." I'm too hot, too close, have been for hours. "You're holding back."

"No. I'm not."

I shake my head once. He is. I can feel it in the tense curve of his body, in the tightly leashed energy beneath the starched fabric. "Kiss me *properly*. Like I'm… like I'm a woman you would actually want to date."

His eyes narrow, and the curve to his lip disappears. He looks at me like he's not sure I can take it.

I'm so tired of being underestimated, and coddled, and scared, and anxious.

I don't want any of it from *him*.

"Please," I whisper.

He swallows hard, and his thumb brushes a circle down to my bottom lip. His darkened eyes track the movement. "Like a woman I would date."

"Yes. Like this is *real*."

A muscle flexes in his jaw. "Like this is *real*," he repeats, and his hand pushes back and tangles in my hair. He's never held me like that before.

The space between us shrinks, and he brushes his lips over mine like I did to him the other day. "So pretty," he mutters. "Will you be good and let me kiss you properly?"

I nod. *Please.*

He tugs me forward, fits my lips against his. He kisses me with strong, insistent strokes that send my thoughts scattering like wisps of smoke.

And when his tongue moves against my lower lip, I open for him.

He groans. His tongue is hot inside my mouth, and he's the only thing I can feel, the only thing I can think of. It's gone in the next instant, a teasing touch, replaced by his lips capturing my bottom one.

He's firm against me, wide chest and hard hips, and there's something there, something against my stomach, and is that... is he...?

I never knew curiosity could be this aching, painful feeling.

His hand runs in a rough caress over my hip, down to the curve of my butt. He's touching me like he's wanted this forever; like I've finally given him permission and he's not going to waste a single second of it.

I'm not planning on wasting it either. Not now that I'm *finally* here, when I'm finally feeling this hot, twisted feeling inside of wanting to get closer and closer still. Not when it's *him* touching me like this. Like I'm the best thing he's ever held in his arms.

His hand skims my ribs and brushes over my left breast. His thumb slides across my hard nipple, through the fabric of my clothes.

A live wire goes off inside me.

My hands turn into claws against his neck. *Wow.* I break off from his mouth to take a shaky breath.

West is breathing just as hard. Like I've finally knocked him off-kilter, made his controlled teacher role crash and burn. "Are you okay?"

I arch into him again. "Yeah. It's just that no one's ever touched me there."

"What?"

"It's fine," I say, rising up on my tiptoes. "Sorry, I didn't mean to—"

"Don't apologize." West's hands drop from my body. "You should never apologize to me. But Nora…"

I shake my head again, like this is all just one large misunderstanding. He can't know. "West—"

"Tell me you haven't hidden this."

"Hidden what?"

"Your inexperience with men." He looks at me like I've destroyed him. Like he's coming apart at the seams. "You told me you'd had sex before. You told me… and now… that wasn't true. Was it? You've never let anyone that close."

My face is hot. I can taste my own fear. "West, it's fine. It's all good. We don't—"

"It's *not* fine." His expression is slack. "You're a virgin."

The word lands in the space between us like a curse. It feels ugly. Something I've been working against for years. Not something I want to be, not something I crave or value. It feels like a testament to my own failure with men, with relationships, with love.

A testament to my own fear.

"This doesn't change anything," I say.

"Fuck." His eyes close for a second, and there's color along the tops of his cheekbones. His hair is mussed from my hands, and he's so handsome it hurts. "How could you have lied about this?"

"It doesn't change anything." Embarrassment makes my eyes water. The word *lie* feels ugly too, tossed out between us. Tears at the truce we've built and the trust that's been developing so slowly, so quietly, that I didn't notice it until right this moment.

He's Rafe's friend.

And somehow he's also become mine.

West's face twists with horror. "It changes *everything*. If you're a virgin…" He shakes his head. "Fuck. *Fuck*."

I can't look at him. Can't see that expression of disbelief, disgust. Of anger. He's deciding, right now, what I am and what I need. Changing his perception of me and all of *this*, all these lessons, the practicing… it'll be over.

I can see the decision forming in his eyes.

So I turn from him and rush out between the double staircases, needing out and away. The French doors open easily into the night air and the terraced Fairhaven gardens. I leave the pink bag behind and take sight of the boathouse in the distance, with the light that winks at the end of the dock.

I messed it all up.

CHAPTER 29
WEST

It's guilt that keeps me rooted to the marble floor.

I hear the sound of her quick steps as she disappeared with tears in her eyes. Tears that I put there, about to spill down her cheeks like *she's* the one who's done something wrong.

I run a hand over my face. I can still taste her on my tongue, feel her warm, willing body beneath my hands, and it's all I can do to breathe until the overwhelming *want* recedes.

I'm a fool of a man for not realizing this sooner. For taking her to the Paradise Lost party, and for bringing her downstairs.

Sitting there in her angelic dress. A virgin offering, served up on a platter, for me to use in my war against my cousin. She sat on my lap and watched people have sex, and I'd *promised* her brother that I would take care of her.

There are so many layers of messed-up to what I've been doing.

Kiss me like a woman you'd actually date.

The rush of adrenaline almost made me dizzy. I did exactly what she told me to. Kissed her hard, tasting her mouth, feeling her body mold to mine. Her lips parted, and I brushed against her tongue. Because she's exactly the kind of woman I'd date.

I touched her like I've craved for weeks, finally feeling the luscious curve of her ass and the soft peaks of her tits, and then she tensed.

Froze.

I'd thought she was right there with me. Had felt it in her breathless little moans that sent shockwaves directly to my cock, the way her fingers turned into claws at the nape of my neck.

But I was wrong. Because she *froze* and I missed all the signs.

She's been lying for weeks. She lied all through dinner tonight when we spoke about sex. And then I took her to a goddamned sex shop.

Jesus. I bought her sex toys.

Something winds its way around my legs. I look down to meet a pair of yellow eyes and a pink nose. The gray cat headbutts my calf, tail swishing.

"Hello," I mutter.

I heard from Ernest that Nora has been trying to catch him to take him to the vet. Find out if he belongs to anyone or if he's just here. Made his way through the fence and found it to his liking.

I bend down slowly. If I can catch him for her, if I can—

He doesn't let me pet him. He pads off on quick paws, pausing by the still open French doors to look at me.

"You're going to find her?" I ask, and *great*, now I'm talking to a cat.

He looks at me for a second longer before slipping out into the spring night, into darkness and fresh grass and probably more mice than I care to think about.

I look at the bag of vibrators, forgotten on the side table. It's a mocking shade of pink.

And fucking hell, she told me she wasn't good at arguing and she wasn't good at the making up part afterward. I was the one who told her we'd practice it.

I follow the cat out into the gardens.

Lights illuminate the edge of the terrace and down along the pathway to the seaside pool and tennis court. But she's not there. She's not by the orchards or at the gazebo. I walk the grounds I know like the back of my hand, the places I'd escape to and play in as a child.

Until there's only one spot left.

I walk the dock around the open boathouse. There's a silhouette of a woman sitting at the very edge, next to the lantern that casts a warm glow over the soft waves. They dance around the pillars of the dock, and in the secluded edge of King's Point, there's nothing but ocean in front of us.

Any words I might say feel like ash on my tongue. They burn and die before I can get them out.

"I can hear you." She draws up her knees, rests her arms against them. She looks small against the dark waves. Like she might tumble into them at any point. "Did West send you to stand guard?"

My hand flexes at my side. "I'm not Sam, or Madison, or Miguel."

"Oh." Nora rests her forehead against her bent knees. "There's nowhere I can be alone anymore. I considered leaving Fairhaven, but... that requires inconveniencing at least seven people these days."

"Don't think—"

"I do think," she says, and her voice comes out fierce. "I do think about those things, and maybe that's not always wrong."

"You're upset."

"I am, yeah."

I sit beside her on the edge of the dock. Behind us, the water laps softly against the hull of my sailing boat. "Yeah."

"Please don't say whatever you came here to say. I don't want to hear it. I already know it all."

"And how do you know what I came here to say?"

Nora turns to, and the look in her eyes guts me. "I'm embarrassed enough."

"Why are you upset?"

"Because of you," she says, and takes a deep, shaky breath. "I'm upset because… because… this is a failure of mine. I know that. I'm pathetic, and now you know it too, and it will change everything. Won't it?"

I stare at her, trying to parse the words.

She laughs a little and runs the back of her hand over her cheek. "I know that it's weird and strange that I don't have the experience I should have. Why do you think I lied about it in the first place? You asked me to be honest, and I wasn't. And now this will change how you think of me."

"I'm upset, yeah. I'm angry." My voice comes out hoarse. "But it's not at you."

She looks back out at the ocean. "Right."

"I mean it. The things we've done… I took you to hell at that party. The things you saw there? I would never have done that if—"

"I know that. Of course I know that. Which is exactly why I had to lie. You were already treating me like Rafe's annoying little sister you had to babysit. And when we made that deal, fake dating in exchange for dating lessons, I knew that if I told you…"

"I would have said no."

"Yes." Her eyes meet mine, glittery and proud. "Wouldn't you?"

The truth is there in the silence between us, and the look on her face is ripping my heart out of my goddamn chest.

"Nora," I say.

"It's embarrassing enough as it is, this whole thing. You and me, and now that you know… But the thing is, can you blame me for lying about it? You offered me something I've never gotten with a man before. A chance to practice, no expectations, no pressure. You're the first guy I've ever *really* liked kissing." She looks back out at the ocean like she wishes it would swallow her whole. "That's so embarrassing."

"No." I move closer, my hip against hers on the dock. "Don't be embarrassed. Be angry at me, yell at me, do whatever you want. But don't be embarrassed because of this."

A tear tracks down her cheek. "Don't tell me what to feel," she whispers.

And damn it all, that makes me proud. "You're right. I won't. But I will tell you that you're strong, and smart, and beautiful. There's nothing wrong with you." I reach up with my right hand to brush away the tear. Her skin is rosy. From wine, from emotion. It's terrifying how comfortable I've become touching her.

How addicted I am.

"What's the furthest you've ever gone with a guy?"

"Just kissing." She looks down between us, but she soldiers on. "Making out, you know. One guy put my hand over his jeans when I was a teenager, but that was through… clothes."

I hate him immediately.

"I want to have sex," she says. "So I want to keep practicing dating. I want to be in a relationship one day. I'm turning twenty-five in November, and I've told myself that I won't be a virgin then. I won't—"

"You've given yourself a deadline?"

"Yes." She nods a little, and there's fierceness threaded through her voice. "I've told you I'm working on all of it. I just need to find someone I like, someone I feel comfortable with."

She's killing me. "You want…"

"I want to keep going. We made a deal, Calloway. I need these lessons."

233

I brush her hair behind her ear. I need the contact, need her to stay grounded. "This changes everything."

"It doesn't change anything." Her eyes flick between mine. "You told me that I could practice kissing with you. Anywhere, anytime."

"I did." My hand slides down, fits to the side of her neck. I can feel her quick pulse.

"Am I a terrible kisser?" It's a whispered question, nearly lost in the sound of waves beneath us.

"What makes you think that?"

"Now you know just how inexperienced I am. Maybe I'm..."

"You're *not* a bad kisser." The idea is laughable, preposterous, a joke. "Not even close. You're... no. No."

"Thanks."

My fingers flex against her neck, her silky hair tickling them. "I'm not a selfless man, trouble. I didn't volunteer to help you practice kissing out of the goodness of my heart."

And that's the whole problem.

She's practicing. She's learning. I'm the one taking advantage of a woman who feels comfortable with me and is learning her own boundaries. She doesn't *like* me like that. And I can't stop getting fucking hard over her.

Even now, I can't stop touching her.

"Oh." A small, tentative smile spreads across her lips. "I could go out and try to solve this problem on my own. That's what I've tried to do. But I haven't had much luck, because I don't actually... I'm not actually attracted to those men. If you won't help me, that's what I'll have to do. Go on dates again. Maybe I can try to befriend one of the security guards my age. Sam, maybe, or Amos."

"No."

"Then help me, West."

"Help you." I force the words out through clenched teeth. "I kissed you up at the house, and you froze."

"I didn't freeze. It surprised me, but I liked it." Even in the darkness, I can see the flush that's creeping up her face. She's trusting me with this. With the secret of tonight, with her emotions, with telling me she likes kissing me.

The trust of it all makes me feel ten feet tall. I want all of her, all of it. I told her tonight that good sex is always about trust.

Sex with her would be more than good.

But that can't be my role. I can't be that much of a bastard.

The rest of it, though... maybe I can help her with that.

"You liked it," I repeat. "Is that what you want, then? To practice all the things that might happen after a date?"

"Yes. Maybe." Her words are rushed. "If you're interested, or even attracted to me. I know you're probably used to women who are experienced and who don't need to go slow, but—"

"Sweetheart." My thumb smooths over her cheek. "You've told me that it stresses you out, when a guy wants you early on, right? Do you want us to pretend that I don't, or do you want me to be crystal clear about it?"

She blinks quickly, eyelashes long and wet. "Really?"

"Really. I already told you, I'm selfish. Don't think that you're asking me for a favor here."

"I won't be good at it," she says. "There's a real chance I'm going to be terrible at all of it. Whatever we practice. Like I have been so—"

"No. Don't finish that thought."

She smiles a little. "It's true, isn't it?"

"Why do you expect yourself to be great at something you've never tried before? What kind of unreasonable standard is that?" I want to fit her against me, pull her into my lap. "Don't worry about that for a second with me. Can you promise me that?"

"Okay. Yeah. I think... I can do that."

"Good. I'm not judging you. I'm not keeping a scorecard."

Her lips curve, and the look sends relief flooding through me. "What kind of teacher are you?"

"One who doesn't believe in grades." My thumb moves down over her lower lip. Every muscle in my body is locked down tight, and the want that rolls through me is so strong it knocks the wind out of me. "We'll practice more. At your pace."

"Thank you," she breathes, like I've bestowed a favor on her. Like I'm not the one who will be begging, and burning, and sinning. "I'm sorry I lied to you about it."

"I understand why you did." I'm closer to her now, close enough to see the goose bumps along her arms. "You've been so brave."

Her lips part on a soft sigh. She likes it when I praise her.

I'd suspected, but I asked her tonight, because I had to hear her say it. Wanted to gauge her response. Not every woman wants to be spoken to that way.

Even if I ache to tell her just how sweet she's being. To use that vibrator between her legs and tell her to be good for me, tell me what she's feeling. To let her see just how hard she makes me.

I'd told her I didn't like BDSM, and I don't. But there's a dominant aspect to praise that I do like. Always have.

Slow, I remind myself. And *hell.* That's where I'm heading.

"I like it. When you praise me," she whispers. "I meant to tell you that earlier at dinner. But I didn't."

"Mhm? You do?"

She nods a little. Eager, wide-eyed. "Yes. It helps me relax. Not think so much about whether I'm doing things right or wrong. Because you tell me."

"I'm going to keep doing it. Would you like that?"

"Yes." Her breath is warm against my thumb. "Very much."

"That's my girl. I want you to talk to me, just like that. Can you do that for me?"

"Like what?"

"Honestly. If I'm going to touch you…. if you'll touch me… We have to talk." I tip her head up. "No more lies."

"I promise."

"Good. You did so well tonight. Dinner, sex shop, making out… and then arguing with me. And now making up. Almost like you're in a relationship."

Her eyes glitter. "I did, didn't I?"

"The perfect fake girlfriend," I say.

A shiver racks through her. I want to warm her. Should bring her inside, but first…

"I want to kiss you."

Her eyes dip to my mouth for a second. "Why?"

"Because sometimes," I say, "it's an easier way to talk."

Her lips part, and she sways forward another inch.

I touch my lips to hers. She's warm and soft, and the thought that she's been fearing she's bad at this, that something is wrong with her, is devastating. Her mouth relaxes against mine, and she sighs a little when I deepen the kiss.

Beneath us, the waves continue to softly break against the dock. The same way they always do. The same way they always have.

But everything has changed.

GROUP CHAT

ALEX

Costa Rica next week. I've finalized the list of challenges. Who's ready?

JAMES

Not you, because you'll write that list on the plane over.

ALEX

Can you let me lie for once, please?

JAMES

No.

RAFE

I'm winning again this time. Sorry to call it.

WEST

You say that before every trip. Also, I'm sitting this one out.

JAMES

Because you're wining and dining a potential wife? That's the only excuse I might accept. We book these trips months in advance.

ALEX

Absolutely not, Weston Maude Calloway.
You're going.

WEST

Not my middle name. Not courting a wife
either. With Nora's stalker ramping things up,
I'm not leaving New York. This is too
important.

JAMES

I'll allow it. Family comes first.

RAFE

I'll figure something out.

WEST

She shouldn't be alone.

RAFE

I know. Leave it to me.

CHAPTER 30
WEST

Turns out, when your best friend's little sister tells you she's a virgin who wants *your* help with practicing intimacy, it's a little hard to concentrate on work the next day.

Guilt makes me avoid the group chat, where Rafe and Alex are talking polo. I know well what taking care of his siblings means to him. And here I am... doing something he'd consider a betrayal and not finding the strength to stop it.

I have meetings in the city and another call with the investors from Japan. Nora is busy too. She informed me early this morning, when she was getting ready to go for another run with her guards, that she has a meeting of her own that night. She's having dinner with my sister.

"You two have become real friends, haven't you?" I hadn't been able to resist. I pulled at her ponytail, wound it around my fingers, and kissed her in the grand foyer.

She kissed me back, mouth soft and open against mine, before pushing me away. "Yes," she said with a smile. "And no more, thank you. I have places to be."

"Run fast."

"I always do."

I watched her walk down the steps in a pair of leggings that hugged her long legs and pert ass. Sam and Madison were standing beside her, caps pulled low. They both met my eye and gave a short nod. *Protect her*, I thought.

I know she doesn't want to stay cooped up forever. That it's important for her to still live her life. But I couldn't relax until I had confirmation that she'd returned to Fairhaven.

I don't see her for the rest of the day.

My dinner is with investors visiting Fairhaven, as boring as it is necessary. They're charmed by the place, by the old grandeur, and I nod politely at their questions. They stay longer than I want them to, playing pool in the library. Clapping me on the shoulder like we're friends.

When I finally walk up the stairs that night, I know Nora is back home from her own dinner; my head of security informed me.

It's late. She must have gone to bed.

I slow down when I pass the door to her rooms. It's almost natural, by now, to be attuned to her. To listen to where she is.

That's when I hear it.

A muffled groan.

I'm by the door in two quick strides. "Nora?"

There's a loud yelp in response. I push open the door and find it unlocked. Her living room is empty. Is her stalker inside? *How?* I stride into the open doorway to her bedroom, my hands already fisted at my sides.

Nora is alone. Lying on her bed.

Her eyes lock with mine. "Oh my god!"

There's no intruder. Just Nora, with her hand pushed beneath the waistband of her shorts… and a steady vibrating sound.

"West!" She pulls her hand out, but the vibrator remains there. She pulls the cover over herself, with nothing but her face peeking out.

"Shit." I'm unable to look away from her. "You were making noises. It sounded like you were in danger."

"I'm not." Her voice comes out thin, and there's still that vibrating sound. "God, I need to shut it off…"

I turn away and focus on the dark wood of her dresser. There's another muffled gasp from the bed and then nothing but silence. She's turned off the vibrator.

"You're trying them out." All my blood has rushed south in one fell swoop, and I reach out to put a hand on the doorway. Fuck.

"Yes. I'm not convinced yet."

"You sounded pretty… convinced."

"They're intense," she says. I look over to see her draping an arm over her face. "I can't believe you're here. I was…"

"Don't be embarrassed." My feet move me closer to the bed with a will of their own.

"How can I not be?" She lowers her arm to look at me. "No one has ever seen me do… *that*."

"I know. You could barely talk about it before. But it's a good thing to practice, sweetheart."

She digs her teeth into her lower lip. "You think so?"

"I do. Were you able to come?"

"No. Not yet."

"But you were getting closer."

"I think so," she murmurs, and takes a deep breath. Her cheeks are on fire. "Yes. I was. But I couldn't get the vibrations right. They were too strong, I think."

"Stop being embarrassed."

"I can't!"

I take a step back. "I can leave, if you want to continue… and report back to me later. Or I can stay, and we can practice. It's entirely up to you."

Her eyes are burning, just as strongly as her cheeks. But I see the fire in them that I've come to relish. "Stay."

The word makes me lightheaded.

I sit next to her on the bed, slowly, carefully. No sudden movements. Without taking my eyes off hers, I stretch out beside her.

She's beneath the covers.

I'm on top of them.

"You're using the small one. Right? With suction."

"Yes. It's intense."

"Were you turned on before you put it against your clit?"

Her lips part on a soft exhale. It takes a moment before she responds, and she can't quite meet my eye. "A little."

"Touch yourself now," I murmur, turning so my face is beside hers. "Don't turn the vibrations or suction on."

Her shoulder shifts, and beneath the covers, I hear the faint rustle of fabric. I close my eyes at the rush of need that sweeps through me. Fuck, but I want to see that.

Nora's breathing catches, and damn it, I have to look. Her mouth is parted and her eyes flit from me to the ceiling. I reach out to turn her face to mine. "I'm right here with you. You're so brave," I tell her. "Being so good for me, working through your nerves like this."

She gives a tiny nod, and some of the tension around her eyes relaxes.

"Does that feel good? Touching yourself?"

"Yes," she whispers. She's watching me, her hand moving beneath the covers.

"I won't touch you. Won't do anything you don't want," I murmur. "But I'll be here with you the whole time."

"Maybe… you can kiss me." Her voice is a bit thin, but her skin is flushed.

I smile a little. "I can do that."

Slowly, I shift closer until our foreheads touch. Her breath is warm against my lips, and I kiss her slowly, thoroughly. I take my time, savor her, suck on her tongue. Brush my teeth over her lower lip and whisper how good she tastes.

Her lips follow mine hungrily. The triumph of that makes me even harder. She said she'd never liked kissing a man before me.

I'll wear that compliment as a badge of honor until I die.

I brush my lips over her cheek instead, down to the fragrant curve of her neck, and let her catch her breath.

"You've never kissed me like that before," she says.

"We've been taking things slow."

"Do you… like it? Kissing me?"

The question is so innocent. If she only knew how my cock aches against the zipper of my pants. "You're perfect. I could kiss you for hours, sweetheart."

"Oh." Her entire body relaxes.

No one has likely kissed her neck like this before. I brush the collar of her shirt aside with my mouth and kiss the edge of her collarbone. The scent of her skin is making it hard to think straight.

"Turn on the vibrator," I tell her. "Lowest setting. Press it against your clit, but not the suction part."

"Okay."

I lift up on an elbow to kiss her again. She arches into my touch, her lips parting for me. I can tell the moment the vibrator turns on, with her fumbling under the covers, because her mouth stutters against mine.

A low buzzing fills the air.

"That's it. It's stronger than your fingers, isn't it?"

"Yes," she whispers. There's a current of energy rushing through her, and I want it to burn me. I trail my lips along her cheek. "What were you thinking about? Before I walked in?"

Her eyes flick to mine. "I was… um. Nothing."

"Nothing?" I kiss her neck again, and her breath catches.

Yeah. She likes that.

"I think you're lying." I kiss the hollow of her throat, and her free hand surges up, slides through my hair. The pressure at my scalp makes my cock throb.

I'm going to have the worst fucking blue balls after this.

"What do you want me to tell you?" Her voice is sharper now, tinged with heavy breathing.

"The truth."

"You," she whispers. "I was thinking about you."

I groan against the crook of her neck.

"I'm sorry," she murmurs, her hand stroking up my neck, "if that was—"

"Don't apologize. Never apologize to me, and not for that." I kiss her again. It's much harder this time, driven by my own need. I should be more careful. Go slower.

But Nora only tightens her grip on my hair and kisses me back like she wants it just as much. Just like she's told me she always does with men.

I lift my head, mouth inches from hers. "We need a safe word."

Her eyes are wide. "What do you mean?"

"If you don't feel comfortable anymore. At any point, in any of the… practicing we do…" I lift up and make sure she meets my gaze. "You tell me stop, and we stop. That's it. I won't get angry, irritated, or mad. Nothing will change because you tell me what you want. It won't change what I think of you."

Nora nods a little, and embarrassment flitters over her face. "Yes."

"I need you to promise me, sweetheart. Tell me stop, and we stop. Promise me that the second you think it, you'll tell me."

She nods. Her skin is flushed and warm beneath my lips. "Yes. If I want to stop, I'll tell you."

"And you remember that I won't be angry, right?"

"I know, West."

I kiss her neck again, and her breathing stutters. "Have you ever been kissed here?"

"No. I like it. I like it… a lot."

I smile against her skin. That's something I can work with. "I've thought about you too."

"You have? While you've…"

"Yes. I know I shouldn't, but I have." I kiss the edge of what I can reach with her comforter pulled up like this. Goose bumps erupt across her skin. "You like this a lot."

"Yes," she whispers.

"My sweet, responsive girl. You're doing so well." I kiss her again. "I want you to shift the toy. Put the suction right on your clit. Can you do that for me?"

Her free hand is still on the back of my neck, like she's anchoring herself to me. "Okay, I'm… oh. *Oh.*"

Fire pounds down my spine. "Good?"

"*Yes.*"

I kiss down her neck again, and this time, she pushes the comforter down. I follow the newly bared skin of her chest down to the edge of her camisole. I can see the faint swells of her tits and the hard poke of her nipples through the fabric.

I trail my fingers along the edge of her camisole and watch her shiver. "You're doing so good," I tell her. "So pretty. What does it feel like?"

"I feel hot. It's so intense." Her eyes are locked on mine. "I've never felt this kind of craving before."

"Stay in the moment. Can you do that for me?"

"Yes," she whispers. Her chest rises and falls with a quick breath, and her back arches. "I want…"

"Tell me, pretty girl."

"I want you to kiss my neck again. I want your mouth on my…"

I glance down at where she's arching her chest. The hard outline of her nipples. "I know where you want me." I kiss down her chest. "Increase the vibrations."

Her breath catches, but a second later, I hear the noise

ramp up. I kiss her breast through the fabric, up to the hard point of her nipple.

I suck it through the cotton.

She moans again, a soft, drawn-out sound that makes my cock throb. I imagine her hand between her legs, under those covers. Her sweet pussy, her swollen clit.

"That's it," I murmur, and lift my mouth long enough to meet her gaze. Her pupils are blown wide. "Can I push this fabric down? Suck your nipple without the shirt?"

There's a quick nod.

"I need to hear you say it."

"Yes," she quickly says. "Please."

Fuck, I could get used to her begging. I slowly inch the fabric down over the soft swell of her tits until two tight pink nipples wink up at me. I groan at the sight. "So pretty," I mutter. "Pink is my new favorite color."

I lower my head to take one of them into my mouth. I suck strongly, and she moans again. I glance up to see her face pushed back against the pillow, her neck arched. She's sensitive here, too.

I switch tits, giving the other the same hot, sucking treatment. And then I brush my teeth over her nipple.

Her breath turns loud, catches. The fingers threaded through my hair tighten with an almost painful grip. "That's it, baby. Let it take you."

She's panting, and then her body bows beneath me. I slide my arm under her and hold her as she comes.

"Look at you," I say, because I can't stop, because I'll never forget this. Because it's the hottest thing I've ever experienced.

She shudders, and there's movement beneath the covers. The vibrations continue, but the sound is more muffled. She must have pushed it away from her sensitive clit.

Nora buries her face against my neck. "Oh my god."

I pull her closer, so she's curved into me as far as she can be with the cover separating us. "What a good, fierce girl. You did so well."

"I can't believe I just did that," she says. "I just came with someone else."

I smooth a hand over her silky hair. "You did, sweetheart."

CHAPTER 31
WEST

As it turns out, it's even harder to concentrate at work the day after you've helped your best friend's little sister have an orgasm. I was so hard after I left her in her bed, drowsy and dazed, that I had to jerk off twice before falling into exhausted sleep.

I still woke up aching.

I'm short with my assistant and my colleagues all day. They pick up on it, but no one comments, and I'm counting the minutes until I can leave Fairhaven and drive to pick Nora up from a fashion shoot in the city—one she booked far in advance and couldn't cancel.

I'll take her directly from the shoot to the Fashion Institute's fundraising event after. She really wants to go, and we need to be seen in public. Win-win.

Arthur drives me into the city when it's time. Nora's fashion shoot is in downtown Manhattan, in an old brick building with giant windows. Looks like some kind of converted warehouse. I take the stairs two at a time and catch sight of my guards standing outside a door.

"Everything all right?" I ask.

"Yes," Miguel says. He's a prior-service marine and excellent at his job. "They're inside. Seems like the shoot is running late."

"Thanks." I push open the door.

The room is huge. It's teeming with activity, people bustling about. There's a makeup station and a giant rack of clothes. I spot the other two guards first. One is by the windows, and the other is standing closer to the photographer.

And there she is.

I stop dead in my tracks.

She's in lingerie… and *only* lingerie.

There are other models around her, but she's all I see. Her hair is tousled, falling dark around her face. Pale, golden skin on display with only a few scraps of dark lace that cover almost nothing.

She's stretched out on a velvet couch, legs curled slightly. One arm is draped over the back, the other resting on her bare hip. She looks at the camera and slowly changes her pose. Where she looks, the tilt of her chin, her outstretched leg.

She makes it all look fluid. *Easy.*

Her bra is lacy and ornate, and a small pearl hangs between her tits. My eyes zero in on it, dangling there. As if her beauty needs accessorizing.

A man in a suit stands behind her, holding out a tray with a glass of champagne on it to her, like he's a waiter. He's young. Face clean-shaven, all hard angles.

Another male model is lying on the ground in front of her, holding up another tray with a bowl of grapes.

The photographer calls out directions, and Nora shifts, reaching for the champagne glass. Her fingers brush against the man's as she takes it. She looks up at him with hooded eyes, and there's nothing virginal about that gaze.

She looks powerful. A woman who knows what she wants and knows she's wanted in return. It's convincing.

But I know just how convincing she can be.

She arches her back. My gaze drifts to the perky tops of her tits, the perfect handhold, and I have to ball my hands into fists. I want to cover her up.

I want to end this entire shoot.

She doesn't want to be here. Didn't even want to model, has been trying to phase out of it, and yet *here she is*, doing a beautiful job of it anyway. Because she was asked to. Because she's kind, and supportive, and doesn't want to inconvenience anyone.

Madison is standing on the left side of the shoot, past attendants and the photographer click-click-clicking. I force my locked muscles to move and reach her.

"Sir," she says.

"How long has this been going?"

"Most of the day. No deliveries from the suspect."

I nod. After the letter that was delivered with the photographs, we're all expecting the stalker to make further contact. And whenever that happens, I want it intercepted before it reaches Nora.

Nora's reclining all the way now, her head propped up on an arm.

It hurts to look at her. That's the way her beauty is: a dagger, sharp and piercing. And yet the pain doesn't stop me from looking.

There are so many people here. All watching her and the two male models who are still so fucking close to her. I want to order everyone else to look away. But I can't, and the jealousy is a painful thing inside me. It's not right, to feel like that. I have no fucking right to it. And yet here it is.

Nora tilts her head up, looks off into the distance…

And spots me.

Her movements falter. The graceful, slow change of positions stutters, but then she remembers where she is and looks back toward the camera.

It takes about ten more minutes before the photographer yells "cut." Every single minute feels like an eternity.

"That's a wrap!" the photographer calls out. "We've got it!"

The music is immediately turned down. Voices rise in volume, and two people high-five in the back. Up on the set, Nora relaxes. She smiles and starts chatting with the male models. Their expressions were blank before. Now they're smiling, two statues suddenly come to life.

Nora stands, still wearing just a pair of lacy underwear, the fabric hugging the curve of her ass. I cross the space to her.

One of the models sees me coming. "Didn't know you had a boyfriend, Nora," he tells her. He has a lilting European accent I can't place.

I'm already shrugging out of my jacket and wrapping it around her. "Hey."

"Hi," she says, and the smile she gives me makes me breathe easier.

I look over at the guy. "She does. It's pretty new."

"Well, you make a cute couple," he says.

Nora pulls my jacket tighter around her. "Thanks for today," she tells the models. "You can finally eat one of those grapes, Pawel."

"I've been dreaming of it all day."

"Gentlemen," I say to them both. My chest is tight, and I can't make myself sound nicer than that. Even if they haven't done anything wrong.

"See you later, guys," she says. They return her warm smile. One of them holds out the tray with grapes to her, and she laughingly grabs one on the way past. "Finally!"

We walk off the lit set, my jacket still draped over her. People are packing, rolling away a rack of clothes.

But plenty of them are looking at us too.

She's a name in this industry. Has done plenty of these

shoots since she was only a teenager. Maybe the stalker worked on a shoot like this. Handled lights, sound, styling. Gained an unhealthy obsession...

I should ask her for a list of all of her modeling jobs. Give them to my security team. *Check every single staff member.*

"You okay?" I ask her.

"Yes. I could ask you the same thing."

"Me?"

"You look angry. Did something happen today?"

"No. Everything's fine."

Nora gives me another long look, her eyes searching. "You're annoyed about something. The shoot went a bit long, and I'm sorry. Didn't want you to have to wait."

"I was early. It wasn't a problem."

She stops at a leather duffel bag in the corner. Next to it is a half-finished smoothie and a phone plugged into the wall outlet. "You sure? You said you're always honest." She pushes up the sleeves of my jacket so she can rummage through her bag.

"Yes. At least they gave you snacks."

She looks over at the smoothie with a small laugh. "That was my lunch."

"You haven't even finished it."

"I've been in my underwear all day." She rolls her neck. "God, I can't wait to grab a burger. And fries."

Cold anger rolls through me. I'm getting her a proper meal as soon as this is over. "Is there a dressing room somewhere?"

"Yes. I'll be right back."

"I'll follow you there," I say.

She chuckles. "Are you my new guard now? Madison and Amos are here, you know. Miguel and Sam too."

"I'm always your guard." We walk to a makeshift changing room in the corner. She disappears behind a drape, and I lean against the wall outside. My hand is clenching and unclenching.

But I can't resist the urge.

"Why did you do this shoot?" I ask her.

There's silence on the other side of the drapes. "I told you, it was for a new brand that my brother bought. It's up-and-coming."

"That's not why I asked."

"They needed models."

"There are thousands of models in New York."

There's a rustle of clothes behind the curtain, and I imagine the slide of lace off her hips, the release of her tits. "My modeling agent works closely with my brother. He just bought this brand for Maison Valmont, and it shows… confidence in them if I'm in their first campaign post-acquisition."

They're words she's been told. Probably by Rafe.

"But you don't want to model anymore," I tell her.

There's another long few seconds of silence. "Are we practicing arguing again?"

"I'm arguing with you for you."

"That doesn't make a lot of sense."

"It makes perfect sense." My eyes catch the faintest of movement behind the microscopic slit of the curtain. "You performed up there, with those male models. Didn't you?"

"Of course I did."

"Did they touch you?"

"Only a few times." The curtain is pulled back, and there she is, handing me my jacket. She's in a black cocktail dress. It hugs her body, coming down almost to her ankles. Her hair is in big, bouncy curls, loose around her face like she's spent an entire afternoon in bed. "It's what I've been trained to do. There's an expectation, yes… but I know I can meet it." She shrugs a little, but there's high color on her cheeks. "I'm in control because I'm playing a character."

"And the men?"

"We're acting," she says. "There's no real intimacy."

"Did you want to do the shoot today?" I ask her.

"It doesn't matter what I want. I was asked, and I said yes. And now I'm done with the shoot." Her voice is annoyed. Good.

"But what will you do the next time your agent, or your mother, or Rafe asks you?" I put out an arm and brace it against the other side of the opening, blocking the way. "What will you tell them?"

Her lips part on a sharp exhale. "I don't know. I'll figure it out when it happens."

"You'll stand up to them," I tell her. "Because it's your life, and you're the only one allowed to decide what you'll do with it. Doesn't matter if they think it's a great opportunity. Doesn't matter if it would make them happy."

"You're pushing too hard." Her words are sharp, but the spark in her eyes isn't. "They're my family. They're not guys I'm trying to date."

"Doesn't matter, does it? You want to please them all. But you can't please everyone, sweetheart."

"I know that. Of course I know that."

"So what will you say? When they want you to model again?" I lean in an inch. "Please, Nora. Your face would help sales. It's just one afternoon."

She puts a hand on my chest. "You're in my way, Calloway."

"That's my girl."

"I'm done modeling," she continues. "Thanks but no thanks."

My lips curve. Always so polite, even when she's drawing a boundary. "That's it. And if they push even more, you know what you'll do?"

"What?"

I lean in closer. "You'll get angry."

CHAPTER 32
NORA

If I didn't know better, I'd say West was jealous.

Standing in the corner and watching me with Henri and Pawel.

I'm used to lingerie shoots. They're not my favorite, but I know what's expected of me, and I'm used to the impersonal way I'm touched by the makeup and wardrobe department. *Stand here. Lie like that. I have to moisturize that calf.*

I carry those expectations like a cloak and turn performance into my armor.

It's not me being photographed. Not really. It's a projection of myself that can become what the viewer wants.

But I've never done it while West watched, and it was *his* gaze on my near-naked body. Not a photographer or a DP's. And then he'd covered me in a jacket that still carried his warmth and his scent, like he was marking his territory.

Maybe it's wrong, but I liked that. Someone coming to pick me up afterward, reminding me of who *I* am.

Not who they want me to be.

Now he's beside me, my arm threaded through his. He was the one to take my hand and put it in the crook of his arm. We're standing at the base of the steps to the Fashion

Institute fundraiser. This is what I've been looking forward to all day. Not the shoot. *This.* The pieces on display here tonight are legendary.

We walk the red carpet together, looking in the direction of every photographer. The cameras flash bright and dizzying, and he's there every step of the way.

"Mask on?" he asks by my ear.

"Yeah. Yours looks good."

"I'm not as smiley as you."

"Doesn't surprise me at all."

When a photographer yells at me to look his way, West says in a half-amused drawl that *Nora will look wherever she wants*, to the laughter of the photographers.

I look up at him in surprise as another bright flash explodes.

Inside, the Fashion Institute is huge and storied. A legendary building. When I was a child and we spent summers at my grandparents' in Maine, we'd occasionally spend a few days in the city. My mom and I always came here.

Beautiful, well-dressed people watch us enter the fundraiser. There are plenty of people I recognize. Designers I know, photographers I've worked with. West stays by my side as we mingle about.

More than a few people cast him speculative glances.

One designer winks at me openly and tells me that I've done well to catch myself the Calloway. Not a Calloway. *The* Calloway. He has plenty of family—distant cousins, a sister, aunts and uncles—but West has become this generation's main Calloway, the way his father was and the previous heirs before him.

When I spot the exhibit, I slide my hand down to grip his. "Come!"

He lets me drag him over to the items for sale. "Is this what we're here for?"

"Yes. Look at this. Isn't it incredible? These are archival pieces. This dress right here? It doesn't look like much, but it revolutionized the industry. Grace Kelly wore it in 1972."

He gives a low *hmm* beside me. "Are you planning on bidding on one?"

"No, no, they're way too expensive."

"But if you could?"

"Maybe this one… this emerald dress. I remember when it was worn at the Cannes Film Festival when I was a kid, and I was floored. I used to sketch it in my notebook, over and over again, trying to get the drapes in the fabric just right."

West's eyes are on me, not the dresses. "And what about this one?"

We move down the row, my voice getting more excited with each passing design. I'm halfway through telling him about how the slit in a dark navy gown was the first of its kind *ever* when I put a hand over my mouth. "Sorry. I'm boring you."

"No. You're not."

"Really?" I ask. "Because people who don't like fashion don't usually find this interesting."

"I find you interesting." West's hand runs up my back, and his fingers tangle with the ends of my hair. The light tug at my scalp feels good. "Keep going."

"You're good at this," I tell him. Maybe he won't see how flustered this makes me, his full attention, the hand playing with my hair, if I disarm him first. "Pretending."

"Maybe I have a good scene partner," he says.

"Thanks for coming here tonight. I wouldn't have been able to go without you."

Somewhere behind us, the music picks up, shifts from a classical piece to a modern cover. "Tonight serves us both," he says. "This will be in the papers tomorrow."

"The Calloway heir and the Montclair heiress," I murmur.

I saw some of the chatter online after the last pictures of us surfaced. "They seem to like it. The public, I mean."

His hand slides forward, fits against the side of my face. It's warm against my skin. "We're a good match."

"Mhm. Your mother still happy?"

"She is, yes."

"No harem of women thrown your way?"

His lip curves. "No, not since you moved in with me."

"I must be the most hated woman in New York," I say. There's flirtation in my voice, and it feels *good.* It feels good to reach up and fix the stiff collar of his shirt. "You're the most eligible bachelor in the country, and here I am, taking you off the market."

"No one could hate you."

"I don't know about that," I say with a smile.

"And if anyone should be on the receiving end, it's me." His Adam's apple is so close to my fingers. I brush the back of my knuckle against it. His skin is warm. "You're beautiful. People want to buy what you model, look like you, date you. I'm the one taking you off the market."

"I'm not that famous." My fingers trail up, along the edge of his jaw. It's still a wonder to me that I get to touch him like this.

"Mmm?" His free hand fits against my waist, warm and big. "I want one person to hate me very much."

My breath catches. "The stalker."

"Yes. I want him to look at the photos tomorrow, of us out on that red carpet, and I want him to burn up inside with hatred for me. To wish he was where I am right now, holding you." West's eyes drop to my lips. "I want him to imagine the things you do for me that you'll never do for him."

"You've thought about this."

"I have," he admits darkly. "Because I want him to get reckless, and stupid, so I can catch him."

The fierceness in his eyes makes me feel like when he

draped his suit jacket around me. Enveloped, warm, taken care of. For years, I hated it when my brother tried to do that sort of thing. When my mother complained I was moving too far away.

But with West, it makes me stronger.

A few people are looking at us with interest. It's not every day people engage in this kind of public display of affection.

And it's never been me.

But here I am, the other half of a couple. Even if it's just a fake one.

I dig my teeth into my lower lip. "Can I kiss you?"

"You don't have to ask anymore."

"It still feels right. I don't want to—"

"If you're going to say take advantage," West says, "after I just saw you in nothing but lingerie in front of a crew of twenty people, knowing you were uncomfortable, I might break apart."

"That bothered you?"

His jaw works. "Yes."

"I'm used to it. And I'm going to turn down more shoots." Once I gather the courage to tell my mother, brother and agent that my modeling is fully over and done with.

"Good," he says. "You do what you want, trouble."

"What did you think? It was their collection. The lingerie." I brush my hand into his thick hair, and it helps ground me against the flood of excited nerves.

West's teeth grind together. "Nora…"

"I never know when your compliments are real and when they're part of the game we're playing," I say. "But maybe it doesn't matter. Maybe I want to hear it anyway. Maybe I want to pretend I'm an adored girlfriend tonight."

His hands come to fit around my waist, and the tenseness in him could be shattered with a single blow. "You looked fucking incredible. Is that what you want to hear? You know you're beautiful. But it broke my brain, sweetheart, to see you in nothing but that lace. To know how easy it would be to slip it to the side..."

"Oh."

"Too much?"

I shake my head, and his lips curve into a dark smile.

"You're brave tonight. And if you want to be adored, well... I'd adore you. Tell you how pretty you looked, how perfect, in lingerie that no other man but me should see. You had a little pearl hanging between your tits. Did you notice that? Because I did."

"Yes. It's part of... of their signature look." I feel hot beneath the dress again. "What would you do? If we didn't have an audience."

Something glitters in his eyes. A question and delight, and he knows exactly where I'm going with this. "I'd keep you on that couch. Ban the others from the room. I told you, I don't like others watching when I make a woman come."

"And you'd make me come."

"I'd ask you to show me how you touch yourself first. Tell you how pretty you look, how good you're doing, how well you're pleasing me." He bends closer, brushes his lips along mine. "You liked the suction on that vibrator, didn't you?"

"You know I did."

"I could do that."

There's a throbbing between my legs. "Do you mean..."

"I do mean, yes."

It's hard to breathe. Hard to focus. His lips brush over my temple. "That's what I'd do with you on that couch. Worship you the way you deserve to be."

"I... I..."

"Too much this time?"

I shake my head in a tiny *no*.

He groans against my temple. "You get me hard at the most inconvenient times, sweetheart."

"Really?" I glance down between us.

"Really. Fuck, don't draw attention to it. And don't sound so damned happy."

I laugh. "Why wouldn't I be? That's cool."

"I can't believe you just used that word," he mutters.

"What other word do you want me to use?" I rise up, brushing my lips against his ear, and whisper in French the things I wouldn't tell him. That I think I like being his adored girlfriend.

He groans again, and his hands tighten around my waist. "I have to brush up on my French."

Something vibrates against my hip. Insistent, incessant. It's not a call. They must be texts. Once, twice. Then a third time. Like someone is texting me nonstop. "I'm sorry," I say. "Someone's trying to reach me, I think."

I open my bag and pull out my phone. My mother sometimes has her episodes, when she demands my attention with all the fervor of a mosquito. *Is this the right couch for my decoration projection? Blue or white? Tell me!*

But it's not Mom.

The texts are from an unknown number. Seven *hello*s in a row, no punctuation, no capital letter.

Another text follows quickly. *Good. I have your attention now.*

My stomach drops, and I turn my phone to West. The three little dots appear, signaling that the person is typing.

I can't look away.

You look beautiful in that black dress. But you shouldn't let him touch you like that.

"Shit," West growls beside me. His arm is around me in the next instant, and he waves our guards forward with a quick hand.

My hands are shaking, holding the phone. I keep staring at it, but the three dots don't appear again. There's no other text.

"Nora," his deep voice urges by my ear. "Come. We're leaving. Hand me the phone."

My eyes flick from face to face in the room as we walk. From person to person. The stalker is here. Inside. There's no other explanation.

How many people are there in here? A hundred? Two hundred?

Amos and Sam are there too, walking behind me. West gives orders in a low voice. He taps something on my phone and then hands it to someone and tells them to trace it.

And then I'm in the back of the car with Arthur in the front seat and West beside me, and it feels like I can finally take a breath again.

"Home," West tells the driver, and it's the most beautiful word I've ever heard.

CHAPTER 33
WEST

Nora is quiet the whole way home. It's not a short drive, but she keeps to herself and gives few answers. It's past midnight in Europe, but Rafe is awake and calls us both within the span of five minutes.

I listen to her talking to her brother in low, consoling tones, reminding him of how good her security guards are and how safe she was all night.

It makes my knuckles whiten.

She's taking care of *others* when she's the one whose evening was ruined. I'm the one responsible, and it was my team who got an opportunity to catch him tonight. Half of them stayed there to keep scoping out the place.

Tonight, we made him more reckless than he's ever been before.

But she's the one who paid the price.

When we get home to Fairhaven, she's still on the phone with Rafe. She walks the curved stairs up to the second floor landing, her voice calm and reassuring.

It's another performance. I'm sure of it.

I stand there for a solid minute after she's disappeared, thinking. Then I get to work. My head of security spends ten minutes debriefing with me. The entire night will be analyzed. Security camera footage hacked into, turned over, investigated. We've never gotten an opportunity this good before.

He blasted her phone and waited for her to pick it up before he said what he wanted to say. Because he'd been watching.

"We traced the number," Michael says. "Burner phone."

"His pattern is changing."

"Yes, but he's never *had* a pattern. It's like the whole thing is deliberately meant to throw us off."

"Keep me updated."

"Always," he says.

After he hangs up, I rest my hands against my desk, feeling its stability beneath my clenching fingers. I've hired some of the best people. People who won't mind bending the rules if needed. But this stalker still seems to slip through our fingers like sand.

It's too good. Too professional.

This can't just be a regular guy who's become unhealthily obsessed with a beautiful model. It's a guy with resources.

There's something I'm missing.

A puzzle piece that doesn't quite fit.

And I'm going to figure it out.

The house is quiet. Most of the staff is home by now, except for security. And Nora didn't get a chance to eat properly. I order food, and while I wait for it to be delivered, I make a call directly to the Fashion Institute's auction.

That emerald dress will be hers.

I wait until the food arrives before going to find her. I walk up to her rooms on the second floor, down the long, long hallway from my own. It seemed like a brilliant move when she moved in, to give her the guest wing as far away from my own as possible.

As if space would have worked.

I knock twice. There's no response, so I knock again, heavier this time. I shouldn't have left—

Nora opens the door, her phone tucked beneath her ear. She's traded the long black dress for a pair of sweats and a tank top.

"No," she says on the phone, her voice low and soft, "you don't have to worry."

My hand tightens around the bag of food.

Nora steps back, leaving the door open for me. "I'm fine, I promise." She sighs quietly. "No, it wasn't a close call. I was safe the entire time... No, Mom."

I put the food on the living room table and watch her walk across the plush rug. Her shoulders are drawn up tight. "Rafe is keeping me safe, and so is West. His team is really good... No, no, that won't be an issue. I promise. Please don't worry."

I hold out a hand.

Nora looks at me. "I can reassure her," I say. "If she's concerned about your safety."

She hesitates for a moment, but then she nods. "Mom? West is here. He's happy to tell you about the security team that's—yes, exactly. Okay? I'll put you through to him now."

Her fingers brush mine when she hands me the phone. They're cold as ice.

"Miss Beaumont," I say. "It's a pleasure to speak to you again."

Her shrill, almost transatlantic accent fills my ear. "Weston?"

"Yes." I've spoken to Rafe's mother several times over the years. She's a former actress—tall, willowy, gorgeous. After a disastrous divorce with the king of luxury, she flitted around Europe and terrorized her children, manipulating them to spend time with her on her terms. "I understand you're concerned about Nora."

"Concerned? I'm frantic," she says. "The stalker got too

close tonight. When Rafe called me, I nearly had a heart attack. He's never been this close before."

"The security team currently protecting your daughter is one of the best in the country, if not the world," I say. "I've personally vetted every single guard assigned to Nora. There are two former Navy SEALs, a prior-service marine, and three men with extensive experience protecting high-level celebrities. All well-paid and good at their jobs. None of them take their responsibilities lightly."

"Oh," she breathes. "Okay. I like the sound of that. But what if the stalker tries to—"

"She's never alone." I look at Nora. She's watching me, her teeth digging into that full lower lip. "I'm never far away. If the stalker tries something, we'll grab him. She's not in any danger."

"Good, Weston. Very good." Lauren Beaumont gives a long, dramatic sigh. "She's very lucky, having a man like you to protect her."

I glance at Nora. "And I will. Whatever happens."

"That's darling," she says. "I think I'm finally able to get some sleep now."

"You do that. Nora will call you tomorrow." I don't give her a chance to respond before I hang up.

Nora's mouth drops open. "*Hey*," she says, but there's no energy behind the affront.

"She's fine. She's been reassured. Now eat."

Her eyes drift to the brown bag. "Whatever that is, it smells amazing."

"You said you wanted a burger."

She sits on the couch and rips open the bag. I take my time walking around her rooms. I double-check the windows. There are alarms installed at every entry point, but I make sure they're all functioning too. Not taking any risks tonight.

"Aren't you having any? There are two burgers in here," she calls.

I finish my last check—at the nook in her sitting room that overlooks the dark ocean. "Does your mother always fret like that?"

"Yes," she says with a sigh. "It was stupid of Rafe to tell her right away."

I sit opposite her, and she pushes the other burger my way. I pick it up, turn it around in my hands. It's still warm. "You had to comfort her."

"Yes." Nora eats a few fries. There are tired lines around her eyes. "She's very emotional."

"You shouldn't have to comfort other people. Not on a night like this."

"My mom is... well..." She sighs. "I had to make sure she was okay."

"I know how your mom is. I've heard it through Rafe. But that's not your job."

She takes another bite of the burger. It's nearly gone, and a dark satisfaction unfurls inside me at the sight. I don't want her barely touching her lunch at shoots she doesn't like doing. I want her here.

In my house, with me, eating whatever she wants.

"It's the way things are. Rafe was concerned too."

"They're concerned, but that still doesn't make it your job to comfort them." I eat my burger and watch as she draws back into herself. Pulls her knees up onto the couch and tightens her hatches. It's not another performance. But it's something similar, a kind of withdrawal I know all too well.

"Yeah," she breathes. "Well. It is what it is."

"What do you really feel about tonight?"

Her eyes drift to mine, and then out toward one of the windows. "It is what it is. I had fun, before... *that*. Thanks for coming with me."

"No. That's not what you really feel," I say. "You don't have to comfort me. You don't have to cater to whatever you think *my* feelings are. Tell me how you're doing."

"If you know me so well, why don't you tell me?" Her voice is testier now, and my lip curves at the sound. Good.

"I think you're scared. I think you're frustrated. And I think you're angry at having to spend an hour being brave on the phone with your family instead of being the one comforted. *You're* the one who got those texts tonight. Not me. Not Rafe. Not your mother."

Her eyes flash. "Maybe I feel all of those things, but what good would it do to say it?"

"Do you need to box again? Because I'll get the gloves right now if you do."

"No, no, I just need…" She stands and wraps her arms around her chest. She walks over to the nook but turns immediately, pacing the length of the couch. "I'm frustrated. I'm annoyed. I'm… Not once did Mom ask how I was feeling. That shouldn't be surprising, after twenty-four years."

"Tell *me*, then. I'm asking. How are you feeling?"

"Terrible. We had to leave early." She takes a deep breath. "All these security guards have to stand out in the cold because of me. I hate it. I hate all of it, and I'm angry at whoever he is for making me do all of that."

"Those are other people's feelings," I say. "Not yours."

"I've spent so long taking care of everyone else's feelings. I don't even know what mine are anymore." She puts her hands over her face and takes a deep breath. "I hate bothering all those people. I hate, hate, *hate* it."

"Fuck inconveniencing others. It's not your fault."

"But it feels like it is, and I *hate* being a burden. I know I'm a burden to you." She paces behind the couch. "Or at least I was, before we agreed to the whole fake dating thing. At least now you're getting something out of it too." Her voice rises. "And I hate that everyone seems to be looking at me, to see how I respond, in order to decide how they're feeling. If I was upset on the phone with Mom tonight, she would have been catatonic with stress. If I told Rafe that I'm *terrified*, he would be on the next plane here instead of finalizing the deal he's worked for years on."

"You're not a burden. Not to anyone." My voice comes out low and harsh. "You're allowed to be terrified."

"I don't feel like I'm allowed to be. Because if *I'm* not okay, others won't be either... and they'll make *me* feel bad for it." Her chest rises with quick breaths. "I'm so angry at whoever is doing this for putting me in this position. I'm angry at myself for not being stronger. I'm angry at my brother for not including me in decisions, for still thinking he needs to protect me." Her eyes well up, and she blinks that away. "And I hate that with this whole stalker thing, I've proven that he's right. I do need protecting."

"Good," I say. "Get angry."

She paces again, eyes blinking furiously. "I am. I'm furious that this man thinks he has the *right* to influence my life. The right to make me feel scared and unsafe. I hate that I can't go for a run in the morning without guards, without looking over my shoulder. And you know what else?" She stops in front of where I'm sitting, her eyes blazing.

"Tell me," I say.

"I'm tired of pretending to be so fine and strong about the whole thing. Tired of smiling and shrugging and saying 'yes, isn't it crazy?' to downplay it, to say that the stalker is probably someone harmless. Because he might not be, and I spend so much time worrying about the situation being far, far more serious than that." A tear tracks down her cheek. "He was in the same room as me tonight, West."

My hand tightens at my side. "I know."

"It's terrifying. I'm terrified." She closes her eyes, and another tear joins the first. "And I feel like I'm not even allowed to say that out loud."

It takes me two strides to get to her. I cup her face and brush away one of the tears. Her summery eyes are a deep green, and they glisten in the lighting. "Listen to me," I tell her. "You have every right to be scared. To be angry. To feel whatever the hell you want to feel."

"Now I'm angry," she whispers, "at how I always cry when I get mad."

I pull her against me.

Her head finds the crook of my neck, and she's warm, pressing against my collar. Something fractures a little inside me at her fear. She'd hidden it so well. I thought she was silly that first week. For taking the risks she did. *Didn't she understand?*

But she did.

Of course she did. She always has.

"Good," I say. "I like you angry."

"You're strange."

"I'll take it. Trouble, you don't have to pretend. Not around me. *Never* around me." My voice comes out fierce. I know what it's like to live with crushing expectations. My solution was to remove myself from relationships altogether.

But I hate watching Nora get crushed under them. Bend over backward and play to an audience that doesn't appreciate her true beauty.

"I'm getting your shirt wet," she whispers.

"I have a hundred more. You've seemed so brave since you came here." Her hair smells good. Floral. "Foolish sometimes, even, like you wanted to push the limits. Losing your guards in Central Park."

"I didn't mean to lose them that time. But I couldn't tell you that. I was… I was trying very hard to be brave." She takes a deep breath and pulls back a little to look at me. Her eyes are glossy. "I don't want this man to stop my life, you know? I want to prove to him, to myself, to everyone, that I'm more than what they think of me. But that doesn't mean…"

I stroke a thumb over her cheek again. There's no tear this time, just soft, rosy skin. "It doesn't mean you're not scared."

"Yes." She whispers it like a shameful secret. She's close

enough that I can see her wet eyelashes sticking together. She's not wearing any makeup now. Gone is the Nora I saw today on stage, in her lingerie, performing for the camera.

"It's normal to be scared."

"You're never scared," she says.

My lips curve. "And why do you think that?"

"You always seem so in control. Like tonight. You made sure we left, and you didn't seem rattled. Even if you might be in danger because of this." She swallows. "Because of me."

"I'm not worried about myself. Don't you dare be worried for me either," I say. "Okay?"

"Okay."

"And maybe…" My thumb brushes her lower lip. "You're not the only one who's good at performing."

A soft breath escapes her, warming my thumb. It sends heat down my spine. *I'm scared for you*, I think. *And I'm terrified that you'll wreck me when you leave. When this is all over.*

"Are you tired?" I ask.

"Yes. But I doubt I'll be able to sleep much." Her hand finds mine, fingers curving cautiously along my palm. Like she's not sure the contact is allowed.

"Are you scared now? Here?"

"A little." She looks over at her bed. It's in the other room, through the open doorway, neatly made. Covered with a light blue coverlet. "Even if I know Fairhaven is safe. But I still feel…"

"Shaken. I get it," I say. "Do you want me to stay with you here tonight?"

CHAPTER 34
WEST

Her eyes widen in relief. "Yes, please. Will you?"

"I'll stay all night." She has two couches in the adjoining living room. They're not long enough, but being uncomfortable will be a small price to pay if it means she'll feel better. And it'll damn sure make me feel better too to know she's not alone in here. That she's not crying.

"Thank you. If you're... if you're okay with it." Her hand tightens around mine. "The bed is big."

The *bed*.

She wants to share the bed.

It takes me a moment to find the words. "Sweetheart, you know me well enough by now to know I never do anything I don't want to do," I say. "I'll take the side closest to the window. Will that make you feel better?"

She smiles. It's a tiny thing, but it's real. "Yes. You're annoyingly honest. I never have to worry about bothering you."

I think of Rafe. Of the regular calls I have with him to check in about her security. Honest is the last thing I'm being. "Are you tired?"

She nods, her hand still in mine. "I've never slept in the same bed as a guy before."

Shit. Of course she hasn't. "Consider it a lesson."

"A lesson," she says, and maybe it was the wrong thing to say, the wrong thing to offer, but then her smile widens. "Okay, that's good. Distract me."

"I can do that." I brush her hair back. "Go get ready for bed. I won't go anywhere."

She narrows her eyes at me, and there's a hint of playfulness there, beneath the emotions of the evening. "You promise?"

"I promise."

"Okay. I'll be right back." She disappears into her bathroom, throwing me one last look, like she needs to reassure herself that I really am staying.

I'm left standing in the room that's been hers since she moved in. There's a stack of books on the dresser and a set of clothes thrown over the back of an armchair. On the ground beneath the window, I catch two silver bowls. One with water and one with what looks like cat food.

The rage that works its way through me steals my breath.

That someone so good, and *kind*, who works so damn hard at pleasing everyone all the time, should be made to feel like this.

I hadn't realized the stalker scared her this much. She kept it all bottled up, and she did such a beautiful job of hiding it that even I hadn't seen the full extent of it until now.

Whoever it is, I'm going to make them pay. I'm going to spend nights, *days*, dreaming of how they'll suffer for making a night she was excited about turn ugly. For every single one of her tears.

Water runs in the bathroom, and I force my breathing to calm. To lock the anger down. She needs a protector tonight, not yet another person to comfort.

Her bathroom door opens. "Oh. You really did stay in the exact same spot."

"Promised you I would."

She smiles a little, shy and tentative, and pads across the space barefoot. She's in a camisole and a pair of shorts, and the makeup from the photoshoot is all washed away. It's freckles and big green eyes and a mouth I love kissing.

"Do you need anything from your rooms?"

"Yeah. But I don't want to leave you." I hold out my hand. "Come with me?"

She digs her teeth into her lower lip. "Yes. Is that okay? I know I'm safe here, but still... tonight has..."

I tug on her hand, and she laughs a little. "Okay, so it's fine."

"Of course it's fine."

She examines my room while I brush my teeth and change out of my suit. The door to my closet is open, but she keeps her back turned the whole time. I pull on a pair of sweatpants and a black T-shirt and watch her look around.

She looks good in my bedroom. The words are on the tip of my tongue. To praise her for standing right there, waiting for me like I asked her to.

I take her hand instead. "Looked your fill?"

"Mhm. Your room is a mirror of mine."

"It is. Let's get you to bed, sweet girl." The endearment slips out anyway, and her fingers flex around mine.

"Say that again," she whispers.

I tug her close as we walk to her room. "Sweet girl? You did so well tonight. Getting angry. Crying. Showing me how you really feel."

She draws a shaky breath. "You really don't think less of me."

"Of course I don't. You're brave." I open the door to her room, and she walks in front of me to her bed. *And you take care of everyone else all the time.*

Let me take care of you now.

She pushes back the covers and climbs into bed. I pull her curtains closed over the windows, and when I finally get into her bed, she's watching me. Lying on her side.

Her hair is a brush of warm brown against the blue of her pillow. She's pulled the cover up beneath her chin, a bare arm resting above it.

"Hi," she says, brushing her fingers over the edge of the comforter. "I might kick in my sleep. Or snore. Or cough."

"Maybe. But you won't bother me."

"What if I have to use the bathroom fourteen times?"

I try to hide my smile. "Then I'm sorry for you. But I've already told you, trouble. You don't cater to my feelings."

She tucks her hand beneath her head. "Why are you so different from anyone else I've ever known?"

"Because I'm much, much better."

Nora laughs a little and plays with the edge of the coverlet. Her fingers brush over the seam of the fabric. "You've always been arrogant."

"My only flaw."

"All four of you are," she says. "You, Rafe… Alex and James."

"Mhm. It's what we bonded over."

She smiles again, a true smile, and fuck if I couldn't do this forever. Distract her with silliness. "That and being sent away from home," she suggests. "And causing problems."

"Don't forget being incredibly handsome. That's what cemented our friendship."

"You're an idiot," she says softly, and it sounds like the first compliment she's ever given me. "Tell me about high school."

I groan. "Of all the questions you could ask."

"I want to know. I've only heard it from Rafe's perspective." Her voice is soft. "I know he showed up in Vermont and planned on getting kicked out in a week. It was right after we lost Etienne, in the accident... But instead, he was given this annoyingly smug American roommate who became his friend."

"That's how he told it, huh?"

"Mhm. What was it like for you?"

"I was angry when I got to Belmont too. But I liked it pretty quickly." I put an arm behind my head. Being sent away from Fairhaven was a punishment, sure, but I discovered a world of freedom between tightly regulated academic schedules and completely unregulated free time. "Rafe and I argued nonstop for the first few weeks. Then Alex showed up late, this bedraggled Scottish guy who wanted to be kicked out, too. That's how he and Rafe bonded."

Nora giggles. "I can see that."

"Rafe was never truly serious about it, though. Alex was. We discovered him breaking into the headmaster's residence one night."

"Really?"

"Mhm. We pulled him out of there and made it look like a raccoon had gotten into the trash. Worst cover-up in history."

"But he wanted to get caught."

"Yeah. We told him he was an idiot. I guess he listened, because while he still paid no attention in class, he stuck around us after that. His first few months at Belmont were..." I shake my head. "That's not my story to tell. But he got better. He's a genius when it comes to math, do you know that?"

"Math?"

"Yeah. You wouldn't think it, but he's smart."

"When did James join?"

"He was always in the library when we were slacking off. He'd study advanced Latin. Used to smoke back then too. God. Glad he stopped."

Her hand is on the pillow between us. I want to reach out and thread my fingers through hers again.

"I pulled him into our circle to help with our Latin homework."

"West!"

I chuckle. "He made it *very* clear that he would help no one without getting something back."

"Good for him."

"Mhm."

"The fifth guy," she says. Her voice is tentative. "That's who used to own the house for the Paradise Lost party, isn't it? I remember that you were five, back then. Rafe didn't share much. But he shared that."

I don't want to talk about this.

How Hadrian and I were the only ones who knew each other that first year at Belmont. What happened that unraveled it all, threads pulling at a tapestry.

"Yes. But things changed," I say. "I thought you were tired."

"I am. But I'm also…"

I lift an eyebrow. "Also what?"

"You're here. In my bed." She smiles again. "I'm not sure I know how to relax."

"Has anyone ever held you?"

"No. I've never cuddled with anyone." She doesn't say it with any sadness. Just a statement of fact.

I reach for her. "Come here."

She lets me tug her closer. "Like this?"

"Almost." I curve my arm, pulling her closer with an arm around her waist. She comes to settle with her head on my shoulder and her hand on my chest. "That's it. Let me hold you."

She's a warm weight against the side of my body. Slowly, breath by breath, she relaxes into my arms. Tension leaking out of her. "Oh. This is nice."

"Mhm. Don't sound so surprised."

There's a smile in her voice. "You're warm."

"It's not every day I'm complimented on my homeostasis."

She laughs. Her leg finds its way over mine, and she burrows against me. Like I'm a pillow. The luckiest damn pillow in the world.

It's distracting how good she feels in my arms. Distracting because I'm not supposed to have these thoughts, not tonight. I can't get hard.

It'll ruin everything.

"Will your arm fall asleep?" she asks. Her finger traces circles on my chest, almost like she's not aware she's doing it. Sketching through the fabric.

"Maybe. But that's my concern, not yours."

"Okay. If you say so."

"You sound skeptical. Between the two of us, who's the expert on how men think?"

"I'm not sure I'd call you an expert," she says. Her warm breath ghosts over my neck. "You know how *you* think. I'm starting to suspect that's not representative of most men."

"Coming from you, I know that's a compliment," I say dryly.

She smiles. I can feel it, the movement of her lips against the edge of my T-shirt. "Maybe, yeah. I just feel like... most guys wouldn't be okay with *just* this. I mean, I know you are, because we're just practicing. This isn't real. But if it was, they'd be expecting this to lead to more."

I want to tell her she's wrong.

But there are guys who would be lying where I am right now and hoping. Letting their hands wander. And I'm a fucking asshole for craving that very same thing too.

"They might hope," I tell her, "but a man who cares about you will listen to you and your signals. And believe me, I'm not alone in wanting to hold a beautiful woman close. Any guy would be lucky to be me right now."

She relaxes against me once more, her body molding to mine. "Thank you."

Her eyelashes brush my neck when she blinks, and that brief, teasing contact sets my nerves on end. I'm aware of every point we touch. The curve of her breast against my side, her leg draped over mine... her hand on my chest.

"Do you think he's out there right now?" she asks. "Living in a hotel nearby, driving outside the house regularly..."

It was too much to hope that I managed to distract her entirely.

"Maybe," I admit. "And if he is, my team will catch him."

"I don't like how close he was tonight."

I hold her tighter. "You're safe here, trouble. I won't let anything happen to you."

"Thank you," she whispers, and I've never given someone comfort like this.

Her breathing turns deep and even. I can feel her torso expanding with every breath beneath my curved arm. The trust she's placed in me is enough to make a man addicted.

She's asleep.

I press my lips to the silkiness of her hair, just once, and then settle back against the pillow. For all of our talk, I rarely share a bed with anyone either. It's easier to be alone. It always has been.

I've been afraid of ruining her, but here she is, ruining me.

Lesson by lesson and day by day.

CHAPTER 35
NORA

I wake up to a room bathed in soft light leaking in through the covered windows. The bed is warm and soft. The person behind me is certainly also warm, but not soft. And he's cradling me into the curve of his body.

West.

Who spent the night in my bed because of my breakdown last night.

I close my eyes again and try not to shift an inch. His chest rises deep and steady behind my own. This has never happened before. I've never once done this, and the joy of it makes me almost giddy.

I slept in his arms the whole night.

Even if we must have shifted in our sleep. Because now he's holding me tight, the small spoon to his big one, and he's got both arms around me. One beneath my neck and the other around my waist.

It feels good to be held like this. Even if I'm very warm. It's like he runs hotter than I do, because where his hand rests against the bare skin of my stomach, my shirt ruched up, his palm is hot.

And there's something thick pressing against my low back.

He's hard. *Again.* Like he was when I sat on his lap at the poker game, and like he got last night when he told me how he'd make me come. He helped me practice talking about sex and grew hard at the same time.

He's clearly enjoying what we're doing too.

I focus on the feeling of him pressing against me. He feels big. But what do I know? Our bodies fit well together like this, mine in the curve of his, but what would it be like to practice… all of it?

To take him inside me?

I've never wanted it with a real guy the way I do now. Never been curious this way. But now, with him…

I shift a little to glance over my shoulder.

It's a mistake. West groans and pulls me closer against his body. The hand that's been relaxed by my stomach flattens against my skin, fitting me neatly against him.

Against his erection.

His breath is hot against the back of my neck, his thumb moving in small circles on my stomach. He's not asleep. But he's not quite awake, either.

Heat spreads through me at his touch. What would it be like if his hand moved farther south? Just a little… and his thumb kept rubbing those circles? What would it be like to hear him call me his clever girl? If he told me that I felt so good, was doing so good, while he coaxed my body through orgasms I've only given myself?

Just like he did the other week when he kissed me while I used the vibrator.

"Mmm," he mumbles, and his hips shift forward, grinding his cock against the curve of my ass. "Morning."

"Morning," I whisper.

His hand shifts down just an inch. His pinky brushes the waistband of my pajama shorts.

I try to stay perfectly still.

"You smell good." His voice is rough with sleep. I feel the brush of his lips against my neck, and my breath catches.

His hand stops on my lower stomach. And then he groans, but it's far less pleased now. "Shit."

"It's okay," I whisper. "I'm okay."

The grinding pressure of his erection disappears, and West twists away from me. The warm cradle of his body is gone. I turn onto my back to see him looking up at the ceiling.

"That went well," I say. "We practiced cuddling. It's okay. On my end, I mean. That happens."

He runs a hand over his face. "Yeah."

"And there's no need to be… I mean, I know it's usual for men to get hard in the morning. I know it had nothing to do with me." I'm babbling, and I know it, but I can't stop.

"Jesus," he mutters. "Nothing to do with you?"

"Yes," I say. "Which is fine! I mean to say… it's okay."

He laughs, voice still a bit rough. It doesn't sound like a particularly happy sound. He's still looking up at the ceiling, and I study his profile, the shadow along his jaw that's grown stronger overnight. "I don't have expectations," he says. "But I'm a man, Nora. Of course I'm affected. And it most definitely has everything to do with you."

"Oh," I breathe.

He turns to look at me, his eyes unusually light in the soft glow of the morning. "That doesn't change anything, though. You don't start thinking about me now. We only do what you want to do."

"Have you been… I mean… it must be uncomfortable. To be hard. Right?" The cover is down to our waists, and I can't resist glancing down. "And not get to…?"

He groans again. "I can't believe you're asking me this."

"Do you want me to stop?"

"No. You're curious, and I've promised to teach you

things." He turns to look at me. "What do you want to know?"

A flush races up my cheeks. "Anything. Everything. You got hard last night too. At the party. And at the poker game."

His eyes darken. "I wasn't sure you felt that."

"I did."

"Mhm."

"Does it bother you? Not to get to…"

He lifts an eyebrow. "Not to come? Yes. It's not pleasant, but I manage. And I make sure to finish myself off when I'm alone."

My throat dries. He said that on our date. *More recently.* I glance down again and wonder what he'd look like. I've already felt him against me.

"You've got those eyes. Like you did in the sex shop." He reaches over and tips my head back up to his. "Do you want to see it? No expectations, sweetheart."

"I'm just… I mean… yes." It comes out a little strangled. "Yes. I've never been close to a man before. I've never…"

"I know." He pushes the covers down off the both of us. There's a thick outline in his sweatpants. I sit up on my knees beside him and feel like I can't breathe, can't think around the excitement.

"Remember you can always leave if it becomes too much," he says. He pulls up his T-shirt and reaches down to hook his thumbs in the waistband of his sweats. "No hard feelings. I'll never be angry."

"I know."

"Repeat it back to me."

"Yes, Calloway, I *know* I'm safe with you. I can leave if it's too much. I can throw the covers back over you and kick you out of my bedroom."

He chuckles a little. "That's my girl."

He lifts his hips an inch off the bed and pulls down his sweats and the boxer briefs peeking out beneath.

His cock emerges thick and heavy against his stomach. It's a dusky color, and it looks so big. Are they always that big? I've seen erections before, of course. Just never in person. There's a vein that snakes up along the hard shaft.

West groans. "I've never been looked at like that before."

"Like what?" I look away from his cock to meet his eyes. A languid heat hangs in the air instead, in every relaxed line of his body, in the flush in my cheeks.

"With such focus," he murmurs.

I look back down at him. At the thick, curved head. Beneath my gaze, his length twitches. I smile in delight. "I've heard they do that."

"You've *heard*." He lets out a low sigh. "Jesus Christ."

I inch closer to where he's stretched out on my bed. The urge to touch him makes my fingers tingle.

"I want to touch you," I say. "Can I?"

He reaches up with his hands and puts them behind his head. "I'll keep my hands right here for you. I won't move."

"Good. And you're not allowed to touch me either."

"I won't, sweetheart."

I inch forward on my knees, my eyes already moving across his torso. I've never been able to just study a man like this before. Lazy, unbothered, without urgency. With this much trust. He has grooves in his stomach, a hint of a muscly six-pack. Dark hair that runs below his navel to meet his cock.

I reach out to run a hand along his carved stomach but stop just shy of his skin. "What about a safe word? You said that was important."

His eyes are hooded. "I don't need one."

"Yes, you do. I want you to feel safe. Like you've done for me."

"I am safe. Well," he amends and looks down at himself, "I'm going to be in pain, but it's the kind I like."

"Safe word," I repeat.

His lips twitch. "Fine. My safe word is Nora."

"You can't use my name!"

"Why not? It's *my* safe word, isn't it?"

"Take this seriously, please."

West looks up at the ceiling, and a smile breaks out. "I am taking this seriously. Fine. My safe word is pink."

Pink.

That's what he said was his new favorite color, the other night. When he had his mouth on my nipple, murmuring praise that soaked into my skin.

He looks back at me. "That shut you right up."

"Quiet," I murmur, but my blush is fierce.

He smiles again and settles back against the pillow. "Ready when you are, brave explorer."

I inch closer and put my hands on his chest. He's firm beneath my touch, such a wide expanse of skin. I spend a solid minute just running my hands over his body. Through the hair on his chest and down his stomach, across the pebbled nipples. His arms are thick, too, and corded with muscle even when he's not flexing. I poke at his bicep and find it so curiously hard, unlike my own.

"I feel like I'm on an operating table," West says.

I trace his open palm, past his ring finger and the gold band that circles it. Continue over the top of his thigh, to where hair thickens and is darker than on his forearms. He works out. I've seen it in action, and I can see it now, in every long line of his body.

"Incision here…" I murmur and run my finger over his skin.

He huffs a quiet laugh. I turn up, toward where his erection lies against his flat stomach. The head looks almost purple, swollen and a little shiny.

I run a finger along the length. It's hot to the touch and soft, so much softer than I thought it would be. I smile up at him in delight, only to find him looking at me with a tense face.

"You okay?" I ask.

"Yes. I'm fine." But it comes out through clenched teeth.

I trace one of the veins, smooth over the velvety head, and listen to every careful intake of his breath. "Are they always this big?" I ask him. My fingers just barely wrap around him. The idea of all of this inside me… it makes me ache.

"I know you're inexperienced and it's wrong of me, but fuck if that isn't flattering," he grinds out. "They come in all sizes. Like you saw with the condom options."

"But is this an ordinary size?" I stroke him from base to tip. The skin may be soft, but there's a hard core to him. Unbendable and unbreakable.

"If you want an honest answer, never ask a man who wants you that question."

That makes me giggle. "So you'd say above average, then?"

"Of course I would. There's a pretty girl touching my cock."

"It just seems so big. Like how would all of this possibly fit? I mean, I know it does. That it would." I brush my fingers down his shaft.

"It would fit, sweetheart." His voice is rough. "If you're turned on enough, and I'd… if a man warmed you up properly. Fuck, trouble."

I pause, my fingers on the soft skin of his balls. "Not here?"

"Yes, *there*. You can do anything." But his breathing is more shallow.

I continue my exploration, gently cupping and rolling them in my palm. They're heavier than I expected, and I'm fascinated by how they shift and move under my touch. West's breathing grows faster with my touch, too. He likes this.

And I suddenly realize the rush of power that can come with this.

"What does it feel like? To come, as a man?"

West groans. "Jesus."

"I mean, aren't you curious about women's orgasms?"

His eyes open, dark on mine. "I'm very curious about one woman's orgasms."

I look back down at his length and the twin balls that are now drawn up tight beneath. He's responsive. His entire body is, large and taut beneath my gaze. There's a small scar above his right knee and thicker hair here at the base of his cock.

I return to stroke him. "Tell me."

"It's intense. Like it is for you. Builds and builds, and there's a single-minded focus on releasing all that pressure." His chest heaves with a deep breath, and I get the sense that it's harder and harder for him to keep up this conversation. "What does it feel like for you?"

"Usually it's a pleasurable, warm feeling. It's sometimes intense, sometimes not." I look back down at him in my hand. "It was stronger with you, though. The other day. Much better than usual."

West's arms tauten, the muscles flexing. Like he's having to really think to avoid reaching down and touching me. I speed up and use my thumb to rub back and forth over his leaking head on every upturn. His cock twitches in my grip.

"Oh!"

He huffs a hoarse breath. "Yeah. Oh. If you keep going, sweetheart…"

"You're close? Already? I don't even know what I'm doing."

"Already, she says. As if I haven't been blue-balled for a week straight, and you're telling me I'm big and that I make you come so well." He looks up at the ceiling, his jaw tight. "Yes, sweetheart. I'm close already."

It's there for the taking. I can give him what he wants and

what his entire body is tightening to prepare for. I can make him happy.

But we're practicing changing old habits.

I let go of his cock and sit back on my knees.

He lets out a groan, and his cock jerks against his stomach again. It looks even bigger than before, the tip weeping against his skin.

"Fucking hell," he says.

I'm in control, and his hands remain beneath his head. He's not breaking his promise. Maybe I can…

"West," I tell him.

He looks down at me. There's color high on his cheekbones. "Yes."

"Hands stay where they are," I remind him and reach for the hem of my camisole. I pull it up and off.

I'm not wearing a bra beneath.

His breath stutters, and he curses. "You're so goddamned pretty."

I smile a little. "I want to give you something to look at."

"You always do." His whiskey eyes burn where they trace across my skin. "Your nipples are hard. Look at you, sweetheart, kneeling beside me. You're doing so good."

I reach for him again. He groans when I stroke him. "Tell me what you like. The way you've made me do," I say, gripping him tighter. Watching his face for his reactions.

West's eyes are locked on mine. "There's no way you can touch me that won't turn me on."

"Tell me," I insist.

"All right. The speed you're going right now?" He looks down, his abs drawn tight. "That's good. That's perfect. If you speed it up just a bit, it'll be game over. If you want to draw it out, you can slow down or grip my balls."

I slow down and grip his cock tighter. "Like this?"

"Yes. Exactly like… that." His chest expands with another

deep breath. "Look at you being such a good girl, learning how to please me."

A hot flush spreads up my chest, and I press my thighs together tighter. "And if I speed up…"

I do just that, the skin beneath my grip smooth now with the wetness already dripping off his head. West groans again, his hips shifting up and into my grip. "Fuck. Yes."

"You're close."

"Very," he grits out. His eyes are locked on mine, his breathing labored. Every muscle in his large body looks locked down. Like he's a coiled spring, ready and aching to move, but he remembers his promise that he won't.

He groans loudly, like he's ripping apart with pain. His hips buck up once in my hand, and then he comes in thick spurts up his stomach. His cock twitches in my grip, and I stroke the base of him, watching until the very last drop leaves him.

He relaxes against the bed. The body that was wound so tightly just a few moments ago is loose now.

I've never seen so much spend before. I've always been fascinated by the idea of a guy coming inside me, but that much? Surely it would drip out.

I reach out, curious, and run a finger through the fluid on his abdomen. It's slick and warm between my fingers. "There's so much of it."

West is watching me. His pupils are blown wide, his arms still locked behind his head. He looks like he's run a marathon. He looks like he's won the lottery. "Just when I think you can't make my ego any bigger," he says.

"What do you mean?"

"Nothing. You're pretty as a fucking picture," he says, "and you just killed me."

His cock is still half hard, resting against his thigh. I reach out and run a finger over it, and West grits his teeth. "Careful. Sensitive."

"Right. Just like me."

"Just like you. Can I move now?"

I sit back on my haunches. "Depends on what you're planning to do."

"I want to hold you," he says, and pulls his T-shirt down to wipe himself off. "That's what I'm planning to do. And tell you how good you just did."

I stretch out beside him. "Yes. You can do that."

"Thank fucking god." He turns his face against my hair, and mutters absurd, ridiculous praise that seeps into my bones like warm honey. How good I was, how proud he is, how well I did. How I'm a natural and his cock has never been that hard before. How he felt like he might die if I didn't let him come.

"My brave, beautiful girl. I didn't know seeing your curiosity would be such a turn-on. But it was. Did it help that I couldn't move?"

"Yes," I say. The butterflies turn over in my stomach. I love the feeling of them now. We've become friends. "But I think you can move the next time."

He kisses my neck. "Thank god."

WEST & RAFE

RAFE

I don't like that he came that close. That he
was in the same room as her.

WEST

You think I do? He's getting reckless. That's a
first.

RAFE

Has your team found anything?

WEST

We're working on it now. Triangulating cell
towers. Not legal, strictly speaking, but it's
untraceable.

RAFE

I hate this. I should fly over.

WEST

No, let me handle it. If you think you have
some kind of leak in your organization, this is
for the best.

RAFE

How is she handling it?

WEST

Beautifully.

RAFE

What does that mean?

WEST

She isn't letting it stop her. She's scared, but brave. She's working on her clothes for the fashion showcase. I think she's good here, man.

RAFE

Thanks again. I owe you one.

WEST

Don't mention it.

RAFE

And you're going to Costa Rica next week. I have it sorted.

CHAPTER 36
WEST

Fairhaven used to be quiet. It was that way since I moved back after Dad died, after this house finally became my own again, when parties became fewer and dinners rarer.

But it's not quiet anymore.

Knowing she's upstairs. Seeing her walk through the gardens outside my window. Hearing Ernest tell me that she successfully caught the cat and that they're driving to the vet to see if it's chipped. Her presence is now everywhere, slotting into the mosaic of the place and turning it alive.

All of it makes the place feel like a home again.

And I realize that it never really felt that way before—not really.

It was a place of quiet when I was growing up, then a place of anger when my parents fought. I loved parts of it— the nooks and crannies, the places I could escape to: the boathouse, the orchard, the sailing boat, the pool, the tennis court. I loved running around the grounds, the library and the space in the attic where she now works.

But now I'm starting to like all of it. Talking to her over dinner in the conservatory, catching her in the kitchen when she and Melissa chat. And I start to resent the obligations that take up too much of my time. Take me away and into meetings, and phone calls, and off the grounds.

One evening, I'm entertaining the board of Cal Steel. It's by far the largest of Calloway Holdings' companies, and the one that my great-grandfather founded. The board members sit around my large dining table and we shift from business talk to small talk.

Nora didn't join.

I asked her if she wanted to come and told her, quite frankly, that it was going to be very boring. She kissed my cheek and told me that she'd rather be working on her clothing line.

I told her what a good girl she was for setting her own boundaries.

She danced out of my office with a smile that left me unable to focus for a solid five minutes. I'm constantly on edge around her these days—hard all the fucking time. After the other morning, when she gave me the most erotic hand job of my life, I've had to start jerking off twice a day. If not, I'll go mad.

The relationships I've had have been short, pleasant, mutually agreed upon. With women who want the kind of fun I can provide—along with my wallet and my access. Smart. Educated. But it's never gone deeper than that. The barrier has never fully come down.

And I never craved their presence the way I find myself craving Nora's.

It's late when the last few board members finally leave Fairhaven. I walk over to the library, rolling up the sleeves of my shirt. A headache pounds at my temple.

But there's one last thing I need to look over before the day is over. My lawyers have a few more days to test our final approach, but if it doesn't work, I'll have to be married by September.

It's that or lose Fairhaven forever.

When I was thirteen and angry, that would have sounded like the perfect solution. But now this place is home. I've reclaimed it, and I'll be damned if anyone forces me out.

I open the door to the library and stop in my tracks. Nora is sitting on the couch. The gray cat is curled up next to her, and she's wearing nothing but a thin silk dress. It leaves her arms bare, most of her chest. And those long legs.

"Hi," she says, a glass of whiskey in her right hand. "Are you done with your dinner?"

If I have to get married, why can't it be to her? The thought is traitorous, and I shove it down as quickly as it came.

Because I won't be a good husband to her. That's why. And because she's not looking for a husband—she's trying to learn how to *date*.

Because she's my best friend's little sister.

There are a thousand reasons why what we're doing is wrong, and each one of them sours my mood. What we have belongs in the shadows. Rafe can never find out.

"Hey," I say. "Have you been sitting here waiting for me?"

"Just for a little while, yeah," she says.

Dark delight sparks through me at her words. "Did you eat dinner?"

"Yes, I ate up in the atelier. Melissa made really great lamb tonight."

I frown. "You're drinking Alex's whiskey again?"

"Trying to get used to the taste," she says. "And it felt cool."

I roll my eyes. "It felt cool?"

"Yeah. I'm trying on what it's like to be West Calloway," she says, her voice grandiose. "It's not that bad, actually."

"And that's all it takes to be me?"

"No, I think there are a few more things to it. But I haven't learned all of it yet," she says, and looks down at the cat. It's male, Ernest informed me, and he isn't chipped. "Like sailing."

I head over to the bar cart. "I'll teach you this weekend."

"Really?"

"Yeah. If you have time."

She rises and follows me, leaning against the pool table beside it. "I'd like that. So… how did the dinner go?"

"It went okay."

She studies me, her eyes warm and kind. "You seem…"

"Yeah," I say. "I'm not in the best of moods."

She sets her glass down on the velvet of the pool table and motions for me to come over. I do, draining half the glass as I go.

"Dinner didn't go well?"

"It went," I say. It's the legal stuff with the house that's infuriating. Gnaws at me like a dog with a bone.

She reaches for my shirt and pulls me forward. I brace my hands on the pool table on either side of her. "Poor West," she says, running a hand along my cheek. "So complicated, running Calloway Holdings."

I narrow my eyes at her. "You think you're so funny."

"That's because I am." She smiles a little. "Will you tell me something?"

"Mhm."

Her thumb slips up, finds the edge of my eyebrow. "Will you finally tell me how you got this?"

"Finally? You've never asked before."

Her teeth dig into her lower lip. "But I've wondered. There are a lot of things I've wondered about you."

It's dangerous, the game we're playing now. Dangerous because it doesn't feel like a game at all. Her finger brushes along my eyebrow. "It was a fight," I say.

"With who?"

I breathe her in, and it's soap and perfume and whiskey. "The fifth guy we spoke about the other night."

"Who used to live in that house. Who went to Belmont with you and the guys."

"You were friends." Her finger smooths down my cheek. "Until he hurt you?"

"Until he hurt all of us." His father ran the largest Ponzi scheme in history. Millions of dollars lost, a public trial, the storied family drawn through the mud. All of our families lost money, and Hadrian told us he'd known about all of it. That the friendships were all false. "And he fooled around with Amber."

Her touch stills. "Oh."

"Sisters are off-limits. They've always been off-limits." It was one of the things we agreed on almost fifteen years ago, five boys in a dorm room in wrinkled prep school uniforms and a window cracked open for the smoke.

When it all happened... The fight was bad. Hadrian was expelled. Left Belmont and our lives, and it was years before I saw him again.

At the time, Amber insisted that what happened wasn't wrong. That he liked her and she liked him. But that was before we found out the friendships had been a ruse.

"That's not fair." Nora runs her hand down, finds the nape of my neck. "Don't the sisters in this equation get a say?"

"Rafe would still see it as a betrayal."

"He wouldn't end your friendship. You're like his family."

I look down at the silky fabric barely covering her, and I'm angry, and frustrated, and half hard again. I've never liked things I can't control, and right now there's almost nothing in my life that I can.

Nothing except the way I treat her. I can control that, and I can give her what she needs. As long as I do that, I'll handle whatever pain comes my way.

"West," she says. "He won't find out."

"He can't." My hands find the silky fabric at her hips. "This dress. It's almost nothing."

"Mhm. I know. I made it out of scraps earlier today."

"You *made* this?"

"Yes."

I find her waist and fit my hands around it. She's so lithe beneath my touch, and only half a head shorter than me. "You're so good at what you do."

"This one was stupidly simple."

"And you decided to dress half naked and wait in here for me?"

"Maybe I want to practice being a good fake girlfriend," she says, "and cheer you up. What do you want tonight?"

A good fake girlfriend. I wind my hand into her hair and tip her head back. I kiss the fragrant skin of her neck where I know she likes it. "This is about what you want."

"I know. But… what if…" Her breath catches, and I know she likes that spot. I suck on her skin harder than I should. *"Oh.* What if I want to know what you want? What would you do right now, if I was… if this was real?"

"If this was real," I mutter. "Does this feel real to you?"

"Yes. But you know what I mean," she says, and I do, and I hate that I do. If she were mine. If this wasn't all preparation for some other asshole she'll want to date after this. For the love she wants, the relationship she wants.

All the things I can't give her.

I grip her thighs and lift her up onto the pool table. Her knees part for me.

"Let me make you feel better." She's breathing hard, my mouth still on her neck. Her words close like a fist around me. As if there's a single moment where being around her doesn't make me feel better. "Tell me what to do."

I lift my head, and I'm going to hell, but when she asks me so prettily… "You know what would make me feel better, sweetheart?"

"What?"

"You, naked on this table," I say, "and my head between your legs. Can you be good and let me make you come?"

CHAPTER 37
NORA

He's standing between my splayed knees, hands on my waist, his honey eyes a deep color. His words make it hard to breathe. Hard to think. "You want to…"

"I want to see you." His hands slide up my bare thighs.

I've never been naked with a man before.

He kisses me again, the deep, searching touches that set heat off like slow-moving honey through my veins. I've touched him. He's seen me half naked, he's held me as I came… this is what I wanted. This is what I've always wanted.

I nod, my lips brushing his. "Yes."

"I need to know I can trust you." His hand comes up, plays with the fastening of the silk slip by my neck.

"Trust me?"

"Yes." He tugs on the knot, and it falls in a ribbon of silk. Goose bumps race over my bare breasts. "That you'll be honest with me. That you'll say no, yes, stop or more. To push me away like you've practiced so beautifully." He runs a thumb over my hard nipple, and there's something drugged about his gaze, his eyes glazed. "Can you do that for me, my clever girl?"

"Yes, I can do that," I promise. There's a pulsing between my legs, so close to where his hands are inching my fabric up. I'm not sure I can handle it if he touches me there.

I'm not sure I can handle it if he doesn't.

"Good. Because your body tells the truth too." He kisses down my skin, and I have to brace my hands behind me on the velvet table to keep from falling over. "Your nipples get hard. You might get wet for me. All of that is honest."

He kisses along my tits, my nipples. He pulls one into his mouth, and the wet, warm feeling makes my breath stutter.

"When I did this last time, while you used your vibrator?"

"Yes?" I struggle to find the word. It's a hard one. Just one teeny syllable.

"I wanted to see all of you. Wanted to touch you more than I wanted my next fucking breath." His hand slides up between my legs and brushes over the fabric of my panties. "Right here."

His fingers stroke up and down in slow, exploring touches that make me shiver. And when he brushes over my clit, my breath catches. "That's where you usually touch yourself?"

"Yes."

"Good. Tell me if I can keep going. Tell me if I can pull these panties down and look at you." He brushes his lips against my ear. "Do you remember your safe word?"

I nod, and I think *this is it*. I've wondered what his hand would feel like, if it was *him* and not my own and not a vibrator. His hands slide up beneath the silk of my dress.

He grips the sides of my panties.

"Good. Lift up for me, sweetheart."

I do what he says, and he slides them down my legs, hooks them over one of my feet, and then leaves them on the other.

My knees close on instinct. I'm still covered by my silky dress, and there's nowhere to run, but I don't need to run. Because he's him, and I'm me, and there's trust in this.

"Lie back for me… Just like that. That's my girl." He stands between my bent legs, and I'm stretched out on the pool table. It's hard beneath my back, the velvet soft under my fingers. "Look at me."

I do. At the width of him, the dark eyes, the scar through his eyebrow. He looks like a man ravenous. He looks at me in a way that would have made me nervous if it was anyone but him.

Any situation but us.

I asked him what he wanted. I pushed him, and here he is, showing me just how much he wants me.

His hands are warm on my knees. "Open for me."

I do, my bent knees splitting, and I can't look at him, but I can't look away either.

"A bit wider… and there you are." His eyes are locked between my legs, and the world ends. But then it restarts with his rough voice. "Fuck, you're so pretty. Look at that. *Look at you.*"

But I'm watching him instead, and the look on his face. His large hand runs down the inside of my thigh. "So fucking perfect. You're already glistening a bit for me. That's what I meant, baby. Your body doesn't lie. Your perfect pussy is honest." He brushes a finger along me, and my breath catches. "Look at all that pink."

"West…"

His hooded gaze meets mine. "Does it feel strange, being so exposed to me?"

I nod. Heat pools in my stomach, the only part of me covered by the scrap of silk I made to tease him. I put it on and felt brave, and wanted, and daring. "But good too."

"You're doing great. So brave, showing yourself to me." His fingers feel like fire against my bare skin. No one has ever touched me there, no one but me, and it feels so different when it's not your own hand.

When he brushes over my clit again, and I moan at the

sensation, his lip curls. "Perfect little clit," he says. He makes a soft drumming motion over it, and the sudden rhythm makes me gasp. "That's it. See how beautifully you're reacting? It lets me know what you like and what you don't."

He starts circling, a steady motion that slowly makes my joints relax and pleasure spike through me. It's better than when I do it. It's better because it's his hand, and his hooded gaze, and he's murmuring to me, telling me how good I'm doing. How much I'm pleasing him, stretched out like this in front of him, how pretty I am. How me getting wet for him is making him hard.

I didn't know that it could be like this.

I hoped. I wanted.

But I didn't know, and now that knowing settles beneath my breastbone, rearranges something inside me. This is what it's meant to feel like. To be wanted and to revel in that wanting.

I'm close when he slides his finger down, brushes it along my entrance. "Look at you. You're soaked now." His voice is hoarse. "I need to taste you. Want to try that, trouble? My mouth on you? We can see if you can come that way, and if not, we can grab your vibrator."

Nerves shoot through me, but there's excitement too. "Yes."

"Yes, what?" He runs large hands along my thighs, spreading me farther. "Tell me."

"Yes, I want you to… go down on me."

His lips curve. "That's my girl," he says again, and I love it. I love all of it.

He starts by kissing down my thighs in slow, open-mouthed kisses. He's warm against my skin and he's *there*. Kissing across my sensitive skin.

I look up at the lamp in the ceiling and focus on breathing. West Calloway is eating me out.

The absurdity of it makes my head swim. That I'm actually here, letting someone do this, *enjoying* someone doing this, and that it's *him.*

My teenage crush. My grown-up annoyance. My fake boyfriend and protector. And he's groaning against my skin like there's nothing he would rather do than be pressed against the most intimate part of me.

West's tongue flicks against my clit, and I look back down at him with widened eyes.

"Stay with me, sweetheart," he says. "Don't go off in your head."

"I'm here," I whisper. He's bracketed by my bare thighs, his eyes darker than I've ever seen them.

He takes my hand and draws it toward his hair. "Hold on to me. Can you do that for me?"

I nod. My voice isn't strong enough for speech.

"Good. You're doing so good." He kisses my clit again and uses his tongue to tease it from the sides with a steady pressure. It's intoxicating to watch him do this. To see his brown hair between my thighs, his forehead. My fingers tighten in his hair.

"That feels… good."

There's a faint chuckle against my skin that makes me gasp, and then his tongue resumes its movements. His free hand holds my thigh back and open for him as he works me over, and every now and then, he'll lift his lips to tell me how good I taste. How pretty I am. How he could do this all night.

My body feels heavy and taut at the same time. It's good he's holding my thighs spread, or I wouldn't keep them bent.

His fingers stroke over my pussy, and then he slides one inside me to the first knuckle. He groans, like he's the one being touched to an inch of orgasm. "You're clenching. Can you relax for me, sweetheart?"

I take a deep breath, and he slides in another inch. The

intrusion is delicious, too much and not enough at the same time. He keeps sucking on my clit, and I'm so close it should be illegal. "That's it. Let me inside…" He groans. "Fuck, this is my new obsession, your tight pussy around my finger. Pink is absolutely my new favorite color."

It feels like my insides are aching, and the slow pump of his finger is the only thing that can soothe it. "West," I tell him, my fingers tightening in his hair. "I think… I think I might…"

"That's it. Be a good girl and come around my finger."

His tongue speeds up over my clit, flicking back and forth against the sensitive underside, and it's all it takes to send me tumbling.

My breath catches and my thighs tighten around his face. I let go of his hair, stretch my arms out wide on the pool table. I brush against the cool weight of a billiard ball. It's too intense and it won't stop and I never, ever want it to.

West's mouth stays on me through it all. He kisses me slowly after it's over, avoiding where I'm most sensitive.

I smile. It's a wide, lazy one. "I think you like giving me these lessons," I tell him, and watch as he stands up. He hooks his arms underneath my knees to keep me spread for him. "I think you like being a teacher, Calloway."

"Calloway again?" He looks over me in a slow sweep, and there's that confident, arrogant look on his face. I hate that I love it so much. "Of course I do. Do you know what a thrill it is, that I'm the first man you've let between your legs? The first man you've truly wanted this way? I want to make every single experience earth-shattering for you, to set the bar too high for anyone who comes after me. I want you to be disappointed in them all."

I laugh a little and lift up on my elbows. "In that case, maybe I'll reach my deadline after all."

His smirk doesn't disappear. But it freezes, and he smooths the silk back down over my thighs. "Not with me."

"What do you mean?"

He gathers me up, pulls me against his body and off the pool table. I slowly glide down his body until my bare feet land on the oriental rug.

"It can't be with me." He finds the edges of the silk and lifts them up, ties them back around my neck until I'm covered again. My legs feel weak and maybe he knows that, knows how wrung out I am, because he holds me close.

"West…"

His whiskey eyes look dark brown in this light. "You want a relationship. You want love. That's what you told me, right from the start."

For the first time since he touched me, I feel too bare. "Yes. That's my… that's the end goal. One day. With someone."

His jaw works. "Your first time should mean something."

The sudden embarrassment that floods through me makes my eyes prick. "I didn't ask you to sleep with me, you know. I just said that maybe—"

"I know that. I'm not implying anything." He kisses my temple, my cheek. "But the day you do it, it should be with someone you love. Someone you won't regret."

I wouldn't regret it with you, I think. *I won't regret anything we've done.* But I can't find it in myself to admit that to him. Not now.

"You know I want to." He tips my head up. I do know that, and he's not letting me run away. Not letting me close in on myself. "My beautiful girl. You know that. And look at you. You just did so well."

"I did, didn't I?"

"Yes." He slides his hands down and lifts me up. I wrap my arms around his neck to avoid tipping over. "Let's go upstairs. It's been a long day."

I hold on to him as he walks us through the library and out toward the stairs. "Thanks for staying with me the last few nights. If you would rather move into your own room, I get it."

He doesn't answer. I close my eyes against his shoulder and wonder if that's that. If he'll take this moment to retreat back to his wing. Create space between us.

"I'll stay," he says.

CHAPTER 38
NORA

I wake up to a sharp knock on the door.

I squeeze my eyes closed and burrow deeper into the warmth beside me.

Another knock. The pillow I'm tucked against vibrates with a groan. West's chest. The arm slung over my waist shifts. "Are you usually woken up like this?"

He smells good. "No."

The sound returns, more powerful this time. Five sharp, insistent knocks. It sounds like someone who's done this many times before.

"That's Ernest." West groans, and his hand slides down to pat my hip. "We've slept in."

"He's never knocked before."

"Something must have happened." The roughness in West's voice sharpens, and he slides out of my grip and the bed. I watch him walk across my bedroom. He's in his sweatpants, but no T-shirt this time. I pull the cover up to my chin and watch him, in the daylight, walking through my sitting room.

I glance at the time. We *have* slept in.

West opens the door. I can't see past it, but I can see him, his profile and the mussed hair from sleep. This is the fourth time in a row he's slept in my bed. Ever since that night, with the stalker...

And I've slept surprisingly well each night.

I used to wonder about that. What it would be like to share a bed. But he's made it easy. Night after night, I'm growing more comfortable with his body against mine. Learning the little places he's rough that I'm not, finding the soft skin at the base of his throat, the way his chest hair feels against my fingers.

"Yes?" West asks.

"Sir." It's Ernest's voice, dignified and controlled. "I suspected you would be here."

If there was ever a hope of keeping this quiet... I draw the comforter up to my neck.

"What's happened?"

"Mr. Montclair is here."

My smile freezes in place.

"Rafe? Where?"

"He's in the kitchen as of now, where Melissa and I are distracting him with food." There's a short, tense pause. "When I informed him that you had not yet started your day, he wanted to go upstairs."

"I bet he did, the bastard," West mutters. "Keep him in the kitchen. I will be down."

"He's asking for his sister."

"She will be down too."

Shit. I hear the door close, and I race out of bed. Rafe's here? "He didn't tell me he was coming," I call to West. He's leaning against the open doorway to my bedroom.

His jaw is clenched. "He didn't tell me either."

"What do we do?"

"Take your time," he tells me. "I'll head down."

"Okay. Thanks."

West turns and leaves, and I wait for the sound of my door opening and closing before I jump into the shower. I hurry through the motions, skip washing my hair, and get changed into a pair of jeans and a tank top.

Classic Raphaël. He'll show up, smile, and tell us in that smooth, suave voice he likes to affect that *aren't we glad to see him?*

I run a brush through my sleep-mussed hair and spread it out around my shoulders. A quick glance in the mirror will have to do. I stick my feet in a pair of mules and walk past the cat, who's stretched out in the nook that overlooks the ocean, looking just as peaceful as I wish I was feeling right now. He still doesn't have a name.

I hear their voices halfway to the kitchen and take a deep breath before rounding the corner.

Rafe is leaning against the kitchen counter where I usually spend my mornings. His eyes meet mine, and his handsome face breaks into a smile.

"Hey. It's not like you to sleep in."

I cross the space to hug him. My brother is six-foot-two, just as tall as West, but with messy black hair he inherited from our father.

"But it is like you to make an entrance," I say and kiss his cheek. "Why didn't you tell us you were coming?"

"I wanted it to be a surprise." His hand finds my shoulder, and he looks at me with narrowed green eyes. "You're doing well?"

"Yes."

"West is taking care of you?"

I can't look at the man standing beside us. Try not to think of his face between my legs, of all the ways he's treating me well. "Yes, he is."

"You're smart to stay here as much as you are," he says. "The stalker is getting… closer. But that's good."

"We want him to overplay his hand," West says. He pours

himself a cup of coffee, his hair damp and the sleeves of a navy shirt messily folded up his arms. He looks the picture of athletic ease. Relaxed. Nothing to hide.

"The other night was weird," I tell them both. "That never happened before I moved here."

Rafe runs a hand along the stubble of his jaw. "I've had profilers working on the stalker's pattern. But this guy... he doesn't fit a lot of established archetypes out there."

"Great," I say. "I had to go and get the *weird* stalker."

Rafe gives a surprised chuckle. "Yeah. Anything to make my life more complicated."

"Yes." I roll my eyes. "Because it's *your* life that's been upended, isn't it?"

"You woke up with claws today," he says. There's surprise in his voice. I rarely talk to him that way.

"I've been sharpening them." I walk over to the coffee machine, and West, who's standing right beside it. He doesn't move, and my arm is only an inch from brushing against his.

I've never been more aware of an inch.

"Don't take this the wrong way," I tell Rafe. "But why are you in New York?"

He sighs. "And that's the welcome I get from dear, dear family."

"I know you're busy with the negotiations to buy Mather & Wilde." I take a sip of coffee and move to stand between them. I lean against my own little slice of cabinetry, like we're all three fighters in a battle, squaring off. "How is that going?"

"Terribly," Rafe says in a smooth voice. "The Wilde's have dug their heels in. I'm offering to make them millionaires and their brand a worldwide success, but they're arguing over minutiae."

"Probably not minutiae to them." I blow on my coffee.

"They know you have the confidence vote with the board

coming up," West says. "Do you think they're just waiting for the clock to run out?"

"They might be." My brother's face hardens, and those green eyes glitter. "But I'm not about to lose."

"Of course you're not," West says. He crosses his arms over his chest. "You're here about the trip, because you hate losing, and that includes a walk-over."

Rafe ignores his friend. He looks at me instead. "Tomorrow, Alex, James, West and I are heading out on another trip."

"A lost weekend?"

"We haven't called them that in years," West says, "and I'm not going anywhere." His eyes are steady on mine. "I told Rafe that with the stalker situation ramping up, I won't leave the city."

He won't leave me.

That's what he's really saying.

I look down at my coffee and try, and fail, to stop from feeling the kinds of feelings that will get me hurt around West. To remember that this is only a temporary arrangement.

"How chivalrous," Rafe says dryly. "Which means there's only one possible solution." He looks at me with a wide smile. "Want to go to Costa Rica for a few days?"

"Costa Rica? That's where you're going this time?"

"Yes. Sun, sand, sea." He nudges me. "We'll explore some caves, hit the seas. It'll be good for you."

"A trip… How long?"

"Four days."

"Nora has things to do." West's arms are crossed over his chest. "You know she has the fashion showcase in a few weeks."

"A few days off will be good for her."

I do have work to do. I've been working long hours each day, sewing, draping, making patterns. But I've got more than half of it finished… and I have no shoots coming up.

For weeks, for *months*, I've been so afraid and focused on living life despite it all. This is an escape for a few days. Away from the stalker and from regimented schedules.

And it's an opportunity.

West's gaze rests heavily on me. If I don't go, he won't go. And Rafe so wants me to say yes. But maybe it's not about them. Maybe it's about me.

"This is unexpected." I brush my hair back, collect it at the nape of my neck. "Which means the stalker won't see it coming. He might not even realize I've left the country if we play our cards right."

Rafe looks at me. "You're thinking strategically?"

"We can set a trap." West's voice is low, and his eyes drift to the exposed left side of my neck. He looks away, but he moves a step closer.

"Yes," I say. "Keep all the routines here at Fairhaven the exact same, but relax security a bit. Provide an opening. See if he takes it."

"And if he does, we'll catch him," West says. "Clever girl."

I've just begun to smile when Rafe laughs, and I realize what he's just said. *In front of my brother.* But Rafe just walks up to the kitchen counter and looks through the bowl of pastries Melissa has left out. "That was smart," he agrees. "We should have a meeting with the security team."

"I'll set it up." West closes the distance between us with a few strides and looks over his shoulder at where Rafe has his back turned. He pushes my hair forward, pressing it against the left side of my neck.

I blink up at him.

"Hickey," he mouths, and just as quickly takes a step away from me.

My cheeks heat up. I've never had a hickey in my life.

West looks like the picture of ease again, hands braced behind him on the stone counter. "We'll take my plane," he tells Rafe. "I'll call the controller, see what slot times we can get."

Rafe smiles at us both, a muffin in hand. He was the one to suggest his best friend and little sister fake date, and he's now the one person who can't find out what's happening in private.

"It'll be fun," he says.

CHAPTER 39
NORA

West's plane is waiting for us on the tarmac when we arrive. Attentive staff welcome us when we climb onboard. I'm already in a pair of sweats and ready to curl up in a seat in the corner. Despite the warm spring air, I'm wearing a sweater with a high cowl neck.

West noticed it and smiled. I narrowed my eyes at him. *A hickey?* That was all his doing.

The plane is beautiful inside. The details, the colors, it's all familiar. It takes me a while to clock why. It's the same color scheme as Fairhaven. Dark wood, light blue details and plush beige. The back of each seat is an emblazoned C, complete with the curved embellishments I've seen so many times on the wrought-iron gates.

I wait until we've taken off before I mention it, running my finger along the wood of the table. "This plane looks like Fairhaven."

"I had it designed that way." West's voice is low, his hand around a glass of scotch.

"James built it?"

"He did. Same as ours." Rafe rolls his neck, his legs stretched out into the aisle. He says it so easily. *Ours.* But he's in charge of where the Montclair plane goes and when. Has been for years. Dad never looped either of us into the important decisions, and then he passed unexpectedly, and now... Rafe has continued the practice.

When my brother leaves to go chat with the pilots, I watch his retreating back. As soon as he's gone, I lean toward West.

He's already looking at me.

"West!" I put my hand against my neck, covered by the fabric. "Why did you do that?"

"I didn't mark you on purpose." He reaches over, and I hold still as he folds down the fabric. His eyes are focused on the bruise. "I was a little... distracted."

"I can't wear a turtleneck on the beach." The rough pad of his finger strokes along my neck. "But I brought makeup."

"Smart." His thumb strokes my skin one more time before he lets the fabric slide back up. "I should say I'm sorry. I *should* be sorry."

"You're not?"

"No. I like my mark on you." He leans back in his chair. The distracted air he had earlier, when he chatted with my brother, is gone. His full focus is on me now.

"Asshole," I half-whisper. Rafe is still gone, so I lean forward again. "You know what? I've been thinking of something to ask you."

"What's that?"

"Your first time," I say. "Was it with someone special? Were you in love?"

His hand stills over the armrest. He doesn't glance behind him, but I can tell he wants to. "Nora..."

"Considering it's so important for me, I mean. That must mean that you had a good experience too?"

"I know what you're getting at," he says, "and you're doing a great job at practice arguing, but this is *not* the best time for it."

"I'm not arguing. Just asked you a simple question."

"It was fine," he says, "but I wasn't in love and neither was she."

"Different rules for you and different rules for me?"

His jaw works. "*Yes.* And that doesn't mean I don't—"

The curtain parts and Rafe walks out with a bottle. "Look at this!" he says to me. He holds up the bottle. "Found West's supply. He stocks the 2006 vintage."

It's produced by one of the champagne companies Maison Valmont owns.

"Of course I do," West says. He looks the picture of ease again. Long legs stretched out, face blank. "Because I know how much you prefer the 2005."

Rafe chuckles. "So it's just to piss me off, is it?"

"Everything in my life is designed to piss you off," West says smoothly.

Rafe grins at me. "Should we show him how a European drinks?"

"You're both just as American as you are Swiss or French," West says. "And I'll win."

"This is how the entire trip will be, isn't it?" I ask. "You two are bad enough, but add in James and, god, Alex…"

Rafe grins. "If you want to stay by the pool for the whole trip, I'll understand."

I accept the glass he hands me. "Maybe I'll join in."

The villa overlooks the ocean.

It's giant and bright, and it's equipped with staff that are waiting for us on arrival. The villa manager shows us around, and I get a room on the second floor with bright white linens and French doors that open up to a balcony and the ocean. It's breathtaking. Surrounded by the greenery and the sun, I breathe deeply.

There is no way the stalker followed me here.

For a few days, at least, he isn't completely aware of my movements.

Alex is already there. He's sitting out on the patio, and I grin when I see him.

"Alex!"

He lifts me up and spins me around. "Little Montclair!"

"You've been drinking," I say with a laugh, my hands braced against his shoulders.

"Yes," he says. "It's a lost weekend. It's a rule." He sets me down, still smiling widely. Under the bright sun, his auburn hair looks more reddish than brown, and his Scottish accent makes me smile.

I've always liked Alex.

"This is the first time we've had family members along on one of these trips," he says, and hands me a glass. "Your view of Rafe is going to change drastically over the next few days. I can't wait."

"Don't give her any ideas!" Rafe calls from inside the house.

I laugh and look from Alex over to where West is standing. He's watching us, arms crossed over his chest. "I know I'm crashing your trip, but I'm excited."

"Good." He lets go of me and reaches for the bottle of whiskey he's nursing. "We're doing adventure poker this trip. I have it all set up."

"Adventure poker?"

Rafe walks out behind me, holding a large bottle of water. "She's not playing," he says.

"That's for Nora to decide, don't you think?" West says.

I give my brother a triumphant expression.

He sighs. "You came here to be safe, not do whatever

idiotic thing Alex has planned for us to risk our lives this time."

"I'm right here," Alex says. "And also, thank you. I aimed for spectacularly idiotic this time."

West runs a hand along his jaw. "What are we playing for this time?"

"Rights to decide on the locations for next year's trips."

He whistles. "Damn. There's no way James will agree to that."

Alex waves a hand. "He never agrees to anything these days."

"Well, with that as the prize, I want to win." I look from Rafe to West with a smile. "Are you ready to go to Siberia four times in a row?"

"You're not playing," Rafe says again.

I narrow my eyes at him. My brother loves to flex his muscles, but over the years, it's become almost second nature. When his tone doesn't vary regardless of whether he's talking to me or one of his employees. To our mom, younger siblings or to his assistant.

I jump off the edge of the table. "You're that scared of losing?" I ask him.

It's false bravado.

But Rafe turns to look at me, mild surprise in his eyes. "You don't know what the game is."

"I'm not sitting in the house the whole time we're here," I say. "I've had enough of doing that for a lifetime." I look over at West and find him looking steadily at me.

There's a burn of something in his eyes. A look I've come to crave. *That's my girl*, I hear.

"What is adventure poker?" I ask.

"Something we came up with over a decade ago," West says. "It's ill-advised, reckless, and, at times, illegal. Over the course of the days, we have to do things to earn chips. On the final night, we play poker with the chips we've earned."

"We've done some stupid shite," Alex agrees. "Remember when you bungee-jumped naked, Rafe?"

My brother puts a hand over his face with a groan.

I just stare at him. "You did what?"

"Thanks for sharing that with the group," Rafe mutters. "Yes. Thank god there are no photos."

"Well, I wouldn't say there aren't," Alex says in a drawling, accented voice. "Maybe I have a safe somewhere, just ready to—"

"I'd kill you," Rafe says.

"You're welcome to try."

"What kind of challenges are on the table for this trip?" I ask.

"Oh, nothing too wild," Alex says. "Just zip-lining, diving, racing horses on the beach. White water rafting. The usual."

I look from Alex to Rafe, and from Rafe to West. "I'm in."

CHAPTER 40
NORA

The next day is wilder than I could ever have imagined. Costa Rica is hot, and the guys set a relentless pace. The afternoon includes zip-lining in a humid, beautifully green jungle. I've never done it before, and the instructor zips me up, but sweat is beading on my forehead.

Must be the heat.

I tug on the straps a final time and watch as James goes, then Alex and Rafe. Finally it's just West and me left on the platform. The instructor has left, too, reassured that West knows what he's doing.

"How are you doing?" he asks me. His own gear is strapped on tight, and he's in a beige linen shirt, sleeves rolled up and the top three buttons undone to show the dusting of dark hair there.

"Good. I think. Heights aren't my favorite thing, but I'm excited."

His lips curve. "Are you telling yourself that, or are you telling me?"

"Both." I look over at the other platform. I can only barely make out the other guys through the leaves, and we're hidden up here. "We're alone."

"Yes."

"Thank god," I murmur and pull the edge of my tank top up to wipe my forehead. It comes almost all the way up, exposing my stomach… and the sports bra I'm wearing. "It's so hot."

"Nora…"

I lower the top again. "What?"

His eyes are on my chest, his jaw tight. "It's your turn to go."

"Do you want to get rid of me?" I take a step closer and put a hand on his chest. His eyes flicker down to my lips. "They can't see us here."

"I know they can't." He lowers his head and brushes his lips once over mine in a quick kiss. "But don't think I don't know what you're doing."

"And what am I doing?"

"You're flirting."

"I'm learning to ask for what I want. And what I want right now…" I rise on my tiptoes and press my lips to the edge of his jaw. I move it down an inch, and then another, until I'm kissing his neck. "Is to know if you like this as much as I did."

West groans, his skin vibrating beneath my lips. "That's not a question."

"It's not?" I put a hand on his chest and slide it down… all the way until I can grip the belt of his pants. "I want to know what you like."

"Our lessons are about you."

"They're about sex, aren't they? Except we're not having sex."

"That's right. We're doing… everything else." His hand finds my chin, and he pulls my face up. "You're trying to make me budge."

"Is it working?"

He brushes his lips over mine with tantalizing slowness. "You tell me," he murmurs and shifts his hips forward.

My hand brushes over the distinct hardness. "Whoops."

He tips my head back and bends to kiss my neck again. I had to use makeup to cover up his hickey. "Damn, you smell good."

"I meant what I said. I'm hot," I say. My eyes flutter closed at the feeling of his lips there. It makes my head too thick to think.

"You sure as fuck are," he mutters. "That's always been the problem."

"Calloway!" a voice bellows. "Are you coming today, or what?"

West groans against my neck and takes a step back. He leans against the trunk of the tree and reaches down to palm himself through his pants. "You go first," he says.

"I'm sorry."

His eyes narrow. "You're not the least bit sorry."

I smile. "No. I'm not."

"Go. You've done enough damage here," he says, but he doesn't look sorry either.

The rest of the day is a flurry of activity. The afternoon finishes with white water rafting, and by the time we're down at the bottom, I'm smiling from ear to ear. It felt like skiing, but far less controlled.

West was in the back of the boat with the oars. Sailor that he is. He collected an extra chip for that alone. By the end of the day, we've all won a fair amount of them. Alex is in the lead, which James says is nothing out of the ordinary. "He's the one with the least care for his own life," he says.

We're sitting at a bar a block from the villa. The chairs and tables are on the sand, with rolling waves only a few feet away. I slide my feet out of my shoes and bury them in the sand.

It's been years since I hung out with my brother's friends like this.

James is still the most silent one. When he speaks, he does it cuttingly. Just how I remember him. His Englishness is a stark contrast to Alex's Scottish brass.

West sits opposite me. He's wearing a dark navy shirt, two top buttons undone, sleeves rolled up. His long legs are spread out, and he's drinking from a glass of rum.

And his attention often drifts to me. Especially when I cross my legs in the short dress or take a sip of my drink. Like his eyes can't help but wander over, even as his expression remains neutral.

I've never felt this kind of power before. To know that I'm wanted and to revel in it. When my brother leaves to use the restroom, I deliberately swipe my hair over to expose the mark West left.

His gaze zeroes in on me immediately. His eyes narrow with warning. I didn't cover the mark up with makeup tonight.

I lift a shoulder in a shrug and cross my legs again. I'm not wearing any underwear, but West doesn't know that. Yet.

His jaw tightens.

"Nora," Alex says. He's sitting to my right, a long arm draped along the back of his chair. "How are you finding the trip so far? Living up to expectations?"

"You know, I think I understand the point of a Lost Weekend now. It makes you feel alive. Is that why you guys do it?"

Alex nods. "Nothing makes you forget a board room as quickly as jumping off a cliff."

James scoffs. Even in this heat, he's in a crisp white shirt. "Some of us don't need to jump off cliffs to feel alive."

"No," Alex retorts with a crooked smile. "Some of us just never do, huh?"

"I'm plenty alive. And you haven't been in a boardroom long enough to complain about it," James says. "You're neglecting your company."

Alex shakes his auburn head. "It runs itself. I'm more interested in Nora. How are things going with the stalker?"

James lowers his glass. "Alex."

"Are we not supposed to talk about that?"

My gaze flickers over to West, but he's just watching me. There's a steadiness there that brings me back to myself. "It's okay," I say. "We can talk about it. There's not a ton of updates, to be honest. But we're hoping he does something stupid now that I'm away. Pretending to date West has been good. Seems to have shaken him lose a bit from his old patterns."

"Nora is safe," West says. "We're closing the noose, but it's been a longer process than we would have liked."

"This guy is a professional," James says. "I don't like that."

"Me neither. I've been looking into it," West says. I know he has been. He has his team searching for patterns based on lists of names both Rafe and I have given him. Every shoot I've done in the past year, itemized and submitted.

"What is it like to pretend to date West?" Alex looks at me with a grin. "Tell me it's terrible, please."

"You really want to know?"

"Oh, yes."

"Give us ammunition," James says.

I look over at West. He meets my gaze with one of his own, and there's dry amusement there. "It's been... a real learning experience."

James looks at me. "What have you *learned*?"

"Just how annoying he can be," Alex suggests. "That he claims to *hate* being in charge but somehow always ends up there. He loves doing his duty. Whatever it might be. I think it's his kink."

"You having any kind of knowledge about his *kinks* is disturbing," James says.

"Neither of you know my kinks," West answers calmly. He's still looking at me, and I hear him in my mind, whispering sweet, filthy praise. "And you weren't the person asked. Nora was."

"Well…" I reach up and rub my neck. "He is surprisingly good at pretending. Playing to a crowd when he wants to. But he's also stubborn. Unfailingly honest. Argumentative."

"All true," James says.

"Have you discovered his doll collection yet?" Alex asks.

I glance at him. The large Scotsman is looking at me with too-bright, too-innocent eyes. "No."

"He can be shy about it, but it's something to behold."

West groans. "Not this again."

"His middle name is Maude, too."

"No, it's not."

"Has been since our first year at Belmont. We had him re-baptized. Didn't we, James?"

James lifts his glass. "To Weston Maude Calloway Junior, the greatest of his line."

I laugh and meet West's exasperated gaze. Adrenaline is still flowing in my veins from the day, and from my second margarita of the night. "I didn't know that! Would have been great to know when your sister quizzed us about middle names at family dinner."

He shakes his head, but his lips are curved.

"I love that you're pretending in front of his family too," Alex says. "You're really doing him a solid there, you know."

"Keeping his mother from throwing beautiful women at him?" I cross my legs again. The dress rides up another inch, and West's eyes drop. "Yes, I'm doing him *such* a favor."

James looks from West to me, his gray eyes narrowing.

"Well, you're helping him buy time," Alex says.

"Buy time?"

West leans forward. "We should order more drinks."

"That we should." Rafe says. He appears behind West and claps him on the shoulder. West tenses. Like the touch hurt. "The next round is on me."

"I'll come with you." I stand to join him and make sure to bring my phone with me.

Rafe orders another round and leans against the bar. "You're doing good," he says. "Keeping up."

"Keeping up? I plan on winning the poker game."

His grin widens. "You remember how to play?"

"Of course. You and James taught me one holiday, remember?" I ask. James spent a few holidays with us during the boarding school days. He would rotate, sometimes at ours, sometimes at West's.

"That was years ago."

"I've still got it," I say.

His gaze drops to my neck. "You're hurt."

Shit. I've forgotten to push my hair back. "Just a burn."

He frowns. "A burn?"

"Yeah, from the shoot the other week," I say with a little shrug. "They curled my hair and came too close."

"Morons," he mutters. "You okay?"

I roll my eyes at him. The lie came easily, but my heart is beating hard. "Yes. I'll survive this grave indignity against my person."

Rafe's eyebrows lift. "You're in a good mood tonight. You have been this whole trip."

"I'm having fun."

"I can tell. There's something… different about you. You seem happier."

"Maybe I am. Going to New York was a good decision." I shake my head. "Even if Mom still asks me almost daily when I'm coming back to France. She can't seem to accept it."

"We'll all feel better when you're closer to home again." He hands the bartender a large bill. "Coming?"

I shake my head. "I'm going to order something extra for me."

And I'm going to text West that I forgot my underwear.

CHAPTER 41
WEST

Rafe returns, but Nora stays at the bar. She chats with one of the bartenders. He's attractive. Smiles at her a bit too widely.

She's in a short dress that ends only halfway down her thighs, leaving her long legs bare. She crossed and uncrossed them earlier, knowing I was watching.

She's playing her own kind of game, and I have no doubt it's payback for what she said on the flight here. *Was your first time romantic?*

"You listening?" James asks.

I drag my gaze away. "Yeah."

He looks at me for a second too long. "Then what did I ask you?"

"If I'll let you win tomorrow. And the answer is no."

"The day I *ask* you if you'll let me win is the day I've lost my mind," James says. "I *told* you that you're going to lose. It was a statement. Not a question."

"Right." I glance back at Nora. She laughs a little and smiles at the bartender. Like she's *flirting.*

"Have you solved the estate issue yet?" Rafe asks.

"Let the man relax for one night," Alex protests, "before you remind him that he's losing his ancestral home."

"Easy for you to say when you hate yours," Rafe tells Alex. He turns to me. "Have you figured it out?"

"No. But I'm not losing it."

"That," James drawls, "is not an answer."

"My lawyers called me early this morning. The last option we're working on is likely too high risk."

"Contesting the trust?" Rafe asks.

"Yes. There's a possibility we could make a stronger case by making it a public lawsuit."

"*Public*?" James shakes his head. "Don't do that."

"It's not ideal," I admit. None of us like our private business aired in front of an audience. "But it might work. There's a clear argument that the trust violates modern-day principles of equal rights and fairness. Amber can't even inherit the estate with the trust's complicated rules, for fuck's sake."

"She must be furious," Alex says.

"She is. As is her right."

"What happens if you lose a public lawsuit?"

I shrug and take a deep sip of my drink. No one says anything for a few seconds.

"Well. Shit," Alex says.

"Yeah. That's about it," I say. "I have the Maverick to thank for a lot, but I want to punch him for this. The lawsuit might work, yeah, but it's too risky to do before I'm married. Once that's settled, we have years to work on a permanent change to the trust."

James drapes an arm along the back of his chair, his expression sharp. So much of him has always been sharp. A sword ready to stab. "Our ancestors knew how to fuck us over," he says. "I have one of the oldest remaining estates in England, and I'm required to preserve it by historic preservation law, even if costs me a fortune to do so."

"That's not a problem," I tell him. "You have several."

The look he gives me is withering. "I'm sorry," he says. "I

thought we were complaining about things that have simple solutions. Or are you the only one allowed to do that?"

Alex laughs, and Rafe shakes his head with a smile.

"Having to get married is a simple solution?"

"Not easy. Simple." James lifts a wide shoulder in a shrug. "There are thousands of women who would take any deal you offered them."

"I have a prenup ready, and I'll offer cash. Live apart, courthouse wedding. But you know none of us are fit for a true marriage." I look over at Nora again. She's sitting on the barstool now, one of her bare legs extended and her toes pointed. She's smiling widely. It looks real. And devastating. My hand tightens around my glass. "We're all too fucked up to make it last."

"You're a bad drunk tonight," Alex says.

"Tell me I'm wrong," I say, my gaze shifting to him. He loves a laugh, and he loves a dare, but we all know how messed up he was all those years ago. How messed up he still is. "Will you ever get married? With your family history?"

The smile doesn't slide off his face, but it hardens. "Yes. Definitely a bad drunk."

"He's scared he's going to lose tomorrow," Rafe offers.

James ignores them both and turns to me with steel-gray eyes. "Offer her money, have her on your arm sometimes, get your estate. Live separate lives. Handle the trust quietly and thoroughly, and if you don't want children, leave it all to Amber's. Divorce."

My phone buzzes in my pocket. I look over at Nora right away and see her sliding her own back into her bag. Her gaze lingers on me for a moment before she keeps chatting with the bartender.

Something dark snakes up my spine and grips my chest with a cold hand.

"You make it sound so simple," I tell James.

"Because it is," he argues. "I'll never understand you sometimes."

"Not all of us can shut off our emotions," I snap.

"No, clearly not," he says with cold precision. "Fight the trust or give into it. I don't care either way."

Rafe sighs. "It's too early in the night for a fight."

"And it's not even a fun one," Alex protests. "Not like the weekend we had in Ibiza."

All three of us groan, and Alex's smile widens. "What? That was epic. How much damage did we do to that yacht?"

"Of course *you* don't know, because I'm the one who wrote the check for it," I mutter and shake my head. "You have no respect for boats."

"I think," Rafe says, "that West just insulted you in the worst way he knows how."

We were younger then, and the Lost Weekends were far more damaging. All of us had fewer responsibilities.

I reach for my phone and pull it up. And there it is. A text from Nora.

NORA

I'm practicing what you taught me.

I type a quick response.

WEST

I can see that.

Her response comes only a few seconds later, still from where she is over at the bar. There's a glass in front of her with something pink in it.

NORA

And guess what? I just realized I forgot to wear underwear tonight.

My gaze snaps up to where she's nodding at something the bartender is saying. The dark, jealous feeling threatening to drag me down tightens its grip. He's stayed too long to chat with her when surely there's work to be done.

My eyes drop to the length of those legs and the short hemline. A memory of how she sounded in my ear when she came floods me. How her body arched on the pool table. Her legs bent for me with her pussy so prettily displayed.

And now she's here, with all these people, all these men who can't look away from her, and she's *bare*?

Her eyes meet mine and her smile falters. I watch as she says something to the bartender and jumps off the chair with that hemline riding dangerously, tantalizingly, *devastatingly* high. Grabs her drink... and walks our way.

Alex pulls out her chair. She smiles and sets down her fruity drink. "I'll be right back," she announces.

Then she disappears inside the bar.

The guards aren't as close by tonight, and I see Rafe rise to follow her. I shake my head at him.

"I've got it," I tell him.

The grateful nod he sends me is searing. If only he knew the real reason I get up and follow her into the darkness of the bar.

CHAPTER 42
NORA

Inside, the bar is pretty dark and half empty. Most guests are sitting outside by the waves and open ocean. I wind through empty tables toward the restrooms. I'm nearly there when I hear the footsteps behind me, but I don't turn.

He catches me around the waist a second later and pulls us into the nearest bathroom.

He took the bait.

I tuck my body into the curve of his. "Hi."

"You're playing a dangerous game." He drags his mouth down my cheek, down to my neck. I tip my head back to give him better access. "And not a very subtle one."

"Subtle enough," I say. "You're the only one I'm playing with."

"The *only* one? You were flirting."

I turn in his grip. "Yes. I was really trying to be present and just enjoy the moment." I grin at him. "He was attractive."

West's eyes are dark. "The poor guy won't be able to sleep tonight."

"All we did was talk for a bit."

"Don't underestimate yourself." West dips his head and brushes his lips over mine. "And you did it in front of me."

"Yes. You see…" I grip the fabric of his shirt. "The guy I'm pretending to date told me that he won't take my virginity. So I'll have to find someone who will."

He closes his eyes on a groan. "You're punishing me."

"No. I'm practicing arguing, just like you told me to. Do you like it?"

"No." His hands slide up my ribcage, and his thumb brushes the underside of my breast. "But you've been incredible today. You didn't bat an eye at the challenges."

"They were a lot," I admit.

"Yes. Rafe was terrified for you. I had to tell him that you could handle it."

"You did?"

"Yes." West kisses me again, hot and insistent. His thumb moves higher and brushes the sensitive, taut nipple through the fabric. "You're hard here."

"Guess we both have that problem around each other."

He groans, and his hands slide down to grip my waist. He lifts me up and puts me on the edge of the counter. "That's it. Sit there for me, pretty girl." He grips my knees and spreads them to make himself fit between, but he doesn't look down.

He just looks at me.

"Teasing me is a bad idea."

"Not with my goal," I say.

His eyes flash. The hands on my thighs curve and tighten. We're both thinking of the same thing. *Losing my virginity.*

On my thigh, his hand slides higher up. "Were you telling the truth out there?" he asks. "Did you really go without your panties in front of all of those people?"

"I was covered," I protest. "Perfectly decent."

"There's nothing *decent* about how you make me feel," he mutters. His eyes darken, and he slides the hand on my inner thigh higher. An inch, and then another. "What will I find, trouble? Were you bare out there for hours? Only feet away from me..." His fingers brush higher. Another inch... and then he's stroking across my folds.

West groans like I've wounded him. "You weren't lying."

"I would never lie to you," I say in a teasing voice. His fingers feel like fire against my bare skin. I've never gone without panties in public before, and for the last few hours I've felt it, keenly, just how exposed I've been.

With no one around knowing.

West rests his free hand on the wall behind me, like he can no longer stand without help. "You were sitting out there bare like this?"

"You really thought I was lying?"

"I hoped," he mutters, and his fingers stroke against me. Up and down, faint, exploring touches that make me shiver. He brushes over my clit, and my breath catches.

"This is what you wanted, isn't it?" he asks. "You wanted to push me into doing this."

"Yes," I breathe.

West's fingers disappear, but only to pull my skirt up. He lifts it slowly, his eyes fixed on mine. Only when the fabric is bunched up by my waist does he look down.

"Look at that. My perfect girl." His fingers move between my lips. "You're already a bit wet, too. Did you get excited out there? Knowing you were sitting out there bare?"

I nod. He touches me reverently, expertly, his eyes on every single one of his movements. "Of course you were," he murmurs. "And you're being so good, letting me look." When he brushes over my clit again and I mewl at the sensation, he makes a soft shushing sound. "You have to be quiet, sweetheart. Can you do that for me?"

My hand in his hair turns into a vise. "Yes."

He circles my clit with steady pressure, and my breath speeds up. His lips are on mine then, kissing me with bruising intensity. "This is what you wanted all day, for me to break?"

"You want me," I whisper. "True or false."

"More than I can handle," he says. "More than I should."

He makes a quick drumming motion over my clit, and the sudden rhythm makes me gasp. His fingers stroke down, teasing my entrance. "Push me away," he says.

I shake my head.

"Nora," he murmurs. "We can't get caught in here, and right now, I'm really fucking close to ignoring that fact and staying in here until you've come at least twice. The others would notice."

"I'm tired of pushing you away." I scoot forward on the counter and moan when his finger slides against my entrance. "I want to practice the opposite. Use your fingers."

"Fuck," he mutters. His finger pushes inside me, and there's that faint pressure again from the other day. My breath catches, and he pauses. His thumb returns to my clit and presses steadily downward.

"Oh," I murmur and slide my hands down to grip his shoulders. "Oh, that's…"

"You're doing so good." His breath is hot against mine. "Tell me how that feels."

"Strange. Good. I like—oh!—when you do that."

He kisses me again, and his finger slowly pumps in rhythm with the motion of his thumb.

"You can take another one for me," he says. I nod against his lips, and the burn sharpens when he slides another finger in. "That's it. You're doing so good, sweetheart."

I breathe deeply, and the stretch turns into pleasure, sweet and heady. "I packed the vibrator. The big one," I say. "You said you won't… oh my god… you won't help me have sex… But can you help prepare me for it?"

His fingers pause inside me, his thumb stilling on my clit.

Every single muscle in his body is locked tight. Like I've punched him.

"West?"

"I've never argued with anyone like you," he says, and his fingers curl inside me. "You know just how to twist the knife, don't you?"

"I'm not trying to… oh!" A surprised sound escapes me, because his fingers are doing something new, that curved, stroking motion, and I slide my hands down his back.

West winces.

I immediately pull my hands away. "What's wrong?"

"Nothing," he says. He bends to kiss my neck, and his finger keeps moving inside me. "Keep your hands locked around my neck."

"You're hurt," I say. The way he winced earlier tonight, too…. "What happened?"

"Nothing."

"It's not nothing." I reach down and grab his wrist between my legs. It's firm beneath my grip, but I manage to still it. "Have you gotten it checked out?"

"It's fine. Knocked into one of the rock walls while river rafting." West's dark eyes search mine. His pupils are blown out wide, and he looks like pain is the only thing he can feel. "There's nothing I want more right now than to make you come and forget about anyone else. That bartender, your future—"

I push at his chest, and he pulls out of me with a frown. The sudden lack of his fingers is startling. "Let me look at it."

"No," he says.

"What do you mean no?"

"If you get injured, you lose the challenge," he says. "You lose the chip. I'm fine. It'll heal."

I jump off the dresser. "That's ridiculous."

"Those are the rules."

"Well, I don't accept." I'm still on edge, but I'm annoyed

OLIVIA HAYLE

now too. "If you won't let me fix you up, then you don't get to make me come."

His jaw works as he looks at me. But I just stare right back at him. I'm not intimidated by West Calloway's stares anymore. There's high color on his cheeks, and his hair is mussed from my hands. The top button of his shirt has come undone, too. If he walked back out like this, there'd be little doubt that something had happened to him.

Back out. To the others... including my brother.

We've been gone for too long already.

I pull my dress down, and his eyes track the movement. "I'm going back out there. I'm going to drink a few more drinks, maybe chat with Thiago a bit more."

"Don't say his name," West says.

"Why? Are you jealous?" I give him a sweet smile. "I'm only doing what you've taught me. What you've told me to do."

"You'll have to go out first." He reaches down and palms himself through his pants. "Second time today. My balls are gonna be fucking aching."

"You know there's someone here willing to fix that for you. As soon as you let me look at your injury." I open the door. "It's up to you, Calloway."

"Go," he mutters and motions for the door. "And well done, trouble."

CHAPTER 43
WEST

The darkness around the villa is complete. It swallows it up whole and sets off the blue lighting in the pool outside. The air is humid and thick with the scent of greenery and ocean.

It's a beautiful country. And I can't help but resent the other guys, men I consider family, for being here when it could just be Nora and me. For constantly standing in the way. Rafe handed me a beer earlier, and I had to bite out a *thank you*.

There's a pool table in the villa, and we've been playing since we got back from the bar. Nora joined in for some of it, winning two straight games before declaring she's going for a late-night swim. Alex dipped off to join her, and I've been watching as the two of them swim outside beneath a starry sky.

She looks happy and light, far away from the stalker and the worries of New York. I want to join them, but I can't take off my damn shirt without showing off where some rock grazed me and lose a point.

Rafe and James want to keep playing pool. So I stay and watch her through the windows. She wears nothing but a bikini and a smile.

My entire body aches from the day I've had. From touching her and not getting to *keep* touching her. She was so damn fine against my fingers. Soft, and sensitive, and getting wetter with each circle of my finger. Her face was so expressive too, those long eye-lashed eyes locked on me when I touched her. Pushed a finger inside and heard her sweet gasp.

If you won't be the one to take my virginity, I'll have to find someone who will.

"West." Across the pool table, Rafe is leaning against his cue. "What's wrong with you?"

"Nothing." I refocus on the table. Shit. It's my turn.

"You're out of it."

I line up my shot and pocket the ball in the far-right corner. "Even out of it, I can still beat you."

James is leaning against the wall behind Rafe, a cigar in his right hand. He long ago stopped smoking. Cigars are reserved for trips like this. "He's thinking about how he'll be a husband in less than three months."

"How long is your mother's list of potential new Mrs. Calloways?" Rafe chimes in.

I walk past them both and turn to face the table. I could aim for the far left one… and hit a bank shot. "I won't marry someone my mother chooses."

"No grand wedding," James drawls. "What a disappointment."

I line up the shot and hit it. The ball rolls perfectly into the second pocket, and I straighten. "Let's not talk too much about it around Nora."

"Why not?" Rafe walks past me and reaches for his own glass of whiskey. It's MacKenzie '64, the best vintage from Alex's family brand. Smoky and amber-colored.

Yes, why not?

"She doesn't know. I don't want her to think there's a time limit," I say. "On staying at Fairhaven, being under my protection."

Both James and Rafe look at me. One gaze steely gray and amused, another green and narrowed. "If it came to that, she'd be back under mine," Rafe says.

"I know. Just don't want her to worry, that's all." It's a thin excuse. I walk around the table, looking for a new angle.

I shouldn't have said something.

Shouldn't have agreed to this damn trip at all.

The sliding doors to the terrace open. Alex walks in with a towel slung over his neck. Nora walks in after him. She's wearing an oversized shirt, the sleeves just a bit too long. It falls right below her ass. In her left hand is a jumble of green fabric.

She's wearing Alex's shirt.

She took off her wet bathing suit, and now she's in Alex's shirt.

My hand turns into a death-grip on the pool cue. She smiles at him, her hair wet down her side, a big, beautiful smile. An authentic smile. She's not acting or people-pleasing.

And she's naked underneath that shirt.

His shirt.

"You were right," James says in his British drawl. "He is out of it."

I focus back on the ball and pull my cue back. I hit it too hard, and it misses by a wide margin. Out of the corner of my eye, I catch Nora disappearing up the stairs without a second glance back at any of us.

"What a shame"—Rafe grabs his own cue—"that I didn't bet on this game."

"You haven't won yet."

"No. But I'm close enough." He walks around the table, analyzing angles. "And look, if you don't want your mom to pick a woman out, do it yourself." Rafe looks over with a shrug. "It could even be fun. Host auditions."

I drain the last of my whiskey. It does nothing to stop the

burn down my spine. Alex walks up to us, still wet from the pool, and I have to look away from him.

"What are you playing for?" he asks.

"A gentleman's honor," James says.

Alex chuckles. "How terrible, then, because none of us have any." His Scottish accent is always stronger when he's been drinking.

"Speak for yourself," Rafe says, lining up his shot. The ball rolls smoothly into the pocket. "I'll have you know my honor is intact."

"Is that what you tell all the girls?" James drawls, taking a drag of his cigar.

"Don't be jealous," Rafe tells him. "I'm sure you could still have fun. If you tried really, really hard."

Alex grabs a cue and leans against the wall, watching us play. I can feel his eyes on me, and it takes everything I have not to look back at him. To not tell him to put on a fucking shirt. "James doesn't do fun," he says with a wide grin. "It's not noble."

"Shut up," James says. He has never liked when any of us bring up his title, which is why none of us will ever stop.

For all of his manners, he bites.

"Did I hit a nerve? I apologize, your grace."

"Now, now, children." Rafe lines up another shot, his dark hair falling over his forehead. "Do play nice."

I lose the game.

"Don't take it too hard," Rafe tells me afterward. He slaps me on my good shoulder. "You're a victor in so many other ways."

I push him away, and his grin widens. "Patronize me one more time."

I watch the others play a game before I call it. *I'm tired,* and all that, and ignore the insults they throw my way. My bedroom is at the far end, and Nora's is on the other side. Just like back home.

On opposite sides of a corridor that always seems to be too long.

I make sure my bedroom lights are off and the door closed before walking over to hers. I knock twice.

She opens the door, and she's still in that fucking shirt. Her wet hair is in a low ponytail, and she smells like shampoo and soap. "West?"

"The deal you offered me earlier." I step inside and close her door behind me. "I'll take it."

Nora pulls me into her room, into the bathroom. "*Finally,*" she says, and pushes me toward the edge of her bathtub. "Sit."

"You're annoyed with me." I look at the shirt she's wearing. The hemline kisses the tops of her thighs. Just like earlier today, she's probably bare beneath it.

Her brother is downstairs. I might have to marry to save my estate. She just wants us to practice for when she goes forth and dates men she actually likes.

But none of that matters, because here I can pretend she's mine.

"You're hurt." Nora undoes the buttons of my shirt. "It happened hours ago, and you've just been drinking and relaxing like you're fine."

"It's just a scratch."

"It's not. Look at this! You bled through the shirt. Good thing it was navy, or you'd have lost your precious chip. That rule, by the way, is the most idiotic thing I've ever heard."

"It's supposed to stop us from getting hurt. Alex was very good at taking things to the extreme." I pause for a moment. "It was James's idea. Not the worst one he's ever had."

She pushes the fabric off my shoulders. "I want this off."

"When did you become a nurse?"

"When I found myself surrounded by idiots," she says. "You can't go on and on about my safety when you ignore your own like this."

Her hands on my shoulders feel good. There's a pattern of freckles on her left thigh, like a constellation of stars. I want to trace them with my lips. "That's different," I say.

"No, it's not."

"Your safety and mine aren't the same."

"And why not? This needs disinfecting… And maybe stitches. But I'm not good enough for that."

"You know how to sew."

"Yes. With fabric. Not… God." She reaches for something out of a cabinet, and I watch her long, bare legs. Wonder what they would feel like wrapped around my waist. "Here's disinfectant and some gauze. You will sit perfectly still."

My lip curves. "You're bossy. I like it."

She returns between my legs, and this time, I can't help but grip her hips. She feels good beneath my hands. Firm curves, a steady thing to hold.

"I hope this stings," she tells me. There's something sharp against my shoulder, and I grit my teeth.

It smells like chlorine.

My hands grip the fabric on her hip. "What are you wearing?"

"A shirt."

"I can see that. But it's Alex's shirt."

"Yes. He lent it to me, but maybe I should go downstairs and give it back." She leans back a little. "He said it was okay. Do you think he minded?"

"If he minded?" I reach for the hem. "I don't give a fuck about him. I mind."

She dabs at my shoulder. It stings like a motherfucker, but it's nothing like the thread of jealousy that has my chest tight. Thinking about her with someone else, her with the bartender, her with Alex, her with future nameless men who won't appreciate her the right way.

"I'm going to put some gauze on it and use some of the

medical tape. But you need to get it looked at when we get back home."

I pull the hem upward. "I will. If you take off this shirt."

"You're impossible." She stretches her hands up and lets me pull it clean off her body. *Fuck.* She's not naked beneath it, but almost. Nothing but a pair of navy blue panties. They're lace, and they have that little pearl at the front elastic. Just like the ones she modeled.

I toss the shirt away. "Don't wear his shirt."

Nora runs a hand along the edge of my jaw. "If I didn't know better, I'd say you're jealous. And I'd say you were jealous earlier too."

"Maybe I am." I lean forward to brush my mouth over her ribcage. Between her perfect tits. "Maybe I don't like the idea of you using our lessons with someone else."

She bandages my shoulder as I kiss her, tease her nipple with my teeth, slide my hand down to tease the seam of her pussy through her panties.

"Not fair," she says. Her breathing has sped up. "I'm trying to concentrate."

"I was promised a reward for letting you patch me up."

"You'll get there quicker if you let me work," she says, and there's logic to it, but she's growing damp through her panties and there's no way I'll stop. "There. You're all done."

"Thank you."

"I'm still annoyed with you," she says. "But I also want my part of the deal, and that means an orgasm."

That makes my lip curve. "That's my girl. Ask for what you want."

"I want you to make me come using the vibrator I packed." She tilts her head a little, and her cheeks are a beautiful warm pink. "It would be good for me to know that I can handle something that big before I…" She takes a deep breath. "Well. Before I have sex with a man for the first time."

CHAPTER 44
NORA

I can tell that I'm pushing him, that I'm beating against whatever barriers he's erected between us. My brother. My virginity. Both of them seem to matter more to him than they do to me, and there's a part of me that wants to backtrack, wants to swallow the words.

But the bigger part of me is exhilarated. He's repeatedly told me to be myself, to express my wants with him. And it feels too good to stop.

"You brought it?" he says.

I nod. "It's fully charged, too."

He groans against my chest and spends another few minutes sucking my nipples and touching me through my underwear, making my knees feel weak. He takes his time. And finally he leans back, inspecting my reddened nipples and the damp spot in my underwear, nodding like he's pleased at what he sees.

"Perfect," he mutters and pulls me into my bedroom. I sit on the edge of the bed. A new set of nerves creeps up, but it's the good kind, the ones I've come to crave around him.

"You've pushed me hard today. Did you think about that when you took off your bikini out there with Alex?" he asks.

"Yes," I confess. "He didn't see anything. I had his shirt on."

"But you knew I'd see it when you came back in."

I stretch back on the bed. The only scrap of fabric on my entire body is between my thighs, and he's watching me like he's hungry.

"I did," I breathe. "And you noticed."

West runs his hands over my thighs, still standing by the end of the bed. "My brave, sweet girl. Even when you knew what might happen. That I'd come find you, aching."

"Are you aching?"

"I'm past aching."

"I've never teased anyone before." I stretch up, raise my arms over my head. "It feels good to be wanted. Not scary. Just… good."

His hands slide down and push my legs apart. "I do want you, sweetheart. Do you know how hard it's been to focus since you showed me how bare you were out there?" West stretches out on top of me on the bed, his body on mine, and kisses me.

I moan into his mouth. He's never been on top of me like this. No one has. There's a delightful heaviness to it, to him, and I grip his hips with my thighs on instinct.

His skin is hot against my chest. The hair there tickles against my breasts, and I kiss him back. But he doesn't stay there. He moves down past my lips, to my neck. It's so hard to focus with him there. He knows it, too, and the brush of his stubble only heightens the sensations rushing through me. A steady warmth pulses down my chest, my stomach, pooling between my legs.

I tilt my hips up against him, and he groans against my neck.

"And now you want me to fuck you with a vibrator," he says. He lifts up on an arm. "That's it, isn't it? You want me to help stretch you out. Make you come with something big inside you."

I nod quickly, needily. He's the most frustrating man I've ever met. I hate that he can make me feel this way, and I think I might cry with gratitude that he can. I've never felt this way before. Never *wanted* this way before.

It's the most addicting thing I've ever experienced.

"I feel like all you and I have ever done is pretend." I slide my hand into his hair and breathe hard as he kisses his way down my body. "In front of others. With each other. Now we have to pretend in front of the guys that we're not... that this isn't... that the lessons aren't happening. Maybe that's why I teased you today. I couldn't pretend well enough."

West pauses, lips on my sternum. "You don't pretend with me." His voice is hoarse. "That's the one thing you don't do, trouble. You're real with me when we're alone."

My hand grasps for purchase against the sheet. I find none. "That was hard, in the beginning. Now... I think it's too easy."

"Fuck. Do you know what hearing that does to me?" He grips the edges of my panties, and there's no hesitation as he pulls them down my legs. "Touch yourself while I get the vibrator. Can you do that for me?"

I nod and reach down to find the soft skin between my legs. Embarrassment wars with the primal, almost painful need inside me. "Yes."

"Good girl."

"It's in my bag. Beneath the... sketchbook."

He returns with the purple silk bag and sets it beside me on the bed. My hand stills, and he makes a soft, tsking sound. "Keep going," he orders and pulls out the curved black vibrator. "That's it."

"I didn't pack lube."

"We don't need it," he says. "You get beautifully wet on your own." He sits on his knees by the edge of the bed. I can see his face between my thighs, above my bare pussy and my moving hand.

"From here on out, before we leave the house, I'll have to pull up your dress and make sure you're not bare under there."

My chest feels hot, my breath coming fast. I don't think I'll ever get enough of this feeling. Of slowly, comfortably losing control around him, because I know he's there to catch me.

"Or what?"

"Or you'll get punished." He bends down and presses hot kisses to my thighs, to my hipbone, to my clit.

I was hot earlier.

Now I feel like I'm starting to smolder, a low fire simmering deep in my stomach. I lift my left leg and brace the foot against his shoulder.

"This doesn't feel like punishment." My voice doesn't sound like it belongs to me. Low, and lazy, and confident.

His mouth closes around my clit, his tongue flicking back and forth, and a gasp escapes me. That's when I feel the thickness of his finger sliding inside me.

"This isn't punishment." His voice is hoarse. "But next time there will be. Would you like that, trouble? I've praised you. I've taught you. I can punish you, too."

"Yes." My breath is coming fast.

It's still such a different sensation, his thick finger moving inside me. We both watch as he slowly adds a second to the first. "You're tight," he mutters. "We'll go slow."

"I'm not fragile."

"I know you're not." He bends back down and presses another kiss to my clit. Between his tongue and his slowly working fingers, he gets both inside me and starts a slow, pumping tempo.

My hips rise up to meet the movement.

He chuckles around my clit, and I nearly come right then and there. He lifts his lips and keeps pumping his fingers.

"*Are you jealous?* she asks." There's a low groan in the back of his throat. "You know I want to fuck you. That's never been the problem. You're so good and so sweet. I'd give my right arm to feel you come around my cock. To tell you just how good you take me."

My feet curl over the edge of the bed, my knees bent and spread for him. "*Please.*"

He pulls his fingers out of me.

I lift up on my elbows. "What are you doing?"

"I'm doing what you asked me to," he says, and reaches for the vibrator. It looks big from this angle, and my knees fall together. This felt like such a great idea a few hours ago.

"The only person," he says darkly, "I should help prepare you for is me."

He kisses my legs apart again and runs the silicone of the vibrator along my folds. Coating it, I realize. His eyes are nearly black. "Remember to talk to me, sweetheart. Will you be good for me and tell me if it gets to be too much?"

"Yes," I breathe.

"Good." His other hand slides up, coming to grip my hipbone. Grounding me and reminding me that he's here. That we're doing this together. My spread knees, his warm hands, the pounding of my heart.

"Breathe," he murmurs. There's a heavy pressure against my entrance, and he pushes it inside, just an inch. The stretch burns. I take another deep breath and feel his thumb smoothing circles over my hipbone. "That's it. Relax."

His hand moves down, finds my clit. I take another long breath, and the burn starts to fade. "That's okay."

"Yeah?"

"Mhm. You're bigger than that vibrator, though."

He groans. It's a guttural sound, half buried in his throat. "Yes. But it's good practice. Can you do that for me, sweet girl? Can you practice?"

"Yes," I breathe. "I can do that."

He pushes it inside another inch, and I've never felt quite this full before. There's something shifting inside me, and the burn is there, but it's growing fainter, and his thumb moves back to my clit. "That's it. You can take all of that."

Something shifts, and he turns on the vibrations. It's a low setting, but it reverberates inside me, makes the slick intrusion easier. A second later, he's bent his head to press open-mouthed kisses to my clit.

It's all too much and not enough, and is this the way it's meant to feel? Why haven't I been able to do all of this before? I think of the years I wasted not feeling like this, not having West in charge of my pleasure.

"That's... I..."

"I know," he says, and there's another faint push inside me. "It's all the way in now. You're doing so good, baby. Seeing your pussy spread like this..."

He keeps it buried deep inside me and returns to licking my clit. I feel stretched and overstimulated, and the vibrations are deep, deep inside me, setting off a trembling in my lower stomach.

It would scare me if I hadn't experienced this before.

It takes a few more minutes before my breath catches and my knees lock together. The orgasm starts deep inside me this time. It's not a faint fluttering thing, but a deep tidal wave of feeling. I try to curl up. I can't handle it, my mouth parts on a half-shout—

His hand is there the next instant, a warm press against my lip. "Shh, sweetheart. Fuck. That's it. Breathe..."

My eyes widen, locked on his only inches away from my face. "Whoops," I mumble against his hand. I hadn't realized I was making noise.

"It's criminal to tell you to be quiet when you come so beautifully. But we can't have anyone else in this house hearing."

"I'm sorry."

OLIVIA HAYLE

"Don't apologize. Never for that." He bends to press his forehead against my shoulder and chuckles against my skin. "Never apologize to me for anything."

I pull him up, tug at him until he comes to rest beside me on the bed. I feel like a wrung-out rag, sun-drunk, happy, sweaty and warm. He runs a hand up and down my spine.

"I like this, too," I murmur against his neck. "I love it when you hold me."

He reaches for something, and then a soft sheet settles over me. Over us. His arm returns its movements along my back. "I won't leave until you fall asleep," he says against my hair. "You're safe here too, sweetheart."

Sleep claims me fast.

CHAPTER 45
NORA

The next evening is our last one. It's what the entire Lost Weekend has built to, and it hangs in the humid air, the scent of jasmine and anticipation. A poker table has been set up on the terrace outside the villa.

I have played poker before, but it was a good while ago, so I read up on the rules earlier today by the pool. The chips I've won during the days here are in my bag. A jangle of black and red plastic, and I slot them through my fingers.

Alex is already sitting at the poker table. One leg bent over the other, his hands braced against his shin. He still plays a lot of sports, and you can tell in the muscles bunched beneath his shirt. He's the heir to a whiskey empire that practically runs itself. Too much money and too little sense.

He grins when he sees me. "You made it."

"Of course." I hold up my stack of chips. "Please tell me you guys will trash talk. I've been practicing insults in my room for the past half hour."

He laughs. "That's the spirit, lass. Come. Sit next to me. Calloway will be here soon. Our dear duke just went to get some more liquor. Your brother, I don't know. Probably working on that deal he's trying to close."

"He does love to work," I say.

"They all do. It's their one failing."

I sit next to Alex. "I've heard you guys can get pretty intense during these games."

He nods to the pool behind us. "Someone's going to get tossed in there tonight."

"Really?"

"Yes."

"How do you know?"

"Because I'll be the one doing the tossing," he says.

I roll my eyes. "God, I walked into that one."

"You did, and I thank you for it." He looks past me, and his grin widens. "Look at that. He finally tore himself away from ruling his empire."

Rafe joins us. He's holding a drink in one hand, and in the other, he's got a small box. He sits to my right. "You sure you remember how to play?"

"Yes. You're the one who taught me, so if I'm bad, you know whose fault it is."

Rafe lifts an eyebrow. "I like the attitude." He nods at Alex. "We've got over a decade of seeing through each other's bluffs. No one knows yours. Use that to your advantage."

"If you coach me too well, I might win," I tell him. "Do you really want me in charge of where your next lost weekends will be?"

Rafe runs a hand through his dark hair. "You can try. And don't go head-to-head with Alex in recklessness. He'll win every time."

"I'm sitting right here," Alex says. "And thank you."

"That wasn't a compliment."

"Sure it was."

"Are you giving your sister tips on how to win?" West asks. He's appeared opposite me, hand gripping the back of a chair. The gravity shifts beneath my feet, and I straighten up in my seat.

He slept in this morning. He cursed when we woke up, kissed my forehead, and slipped out my door as quietly as possible.

"Or he's ensuring I lose," I say lightly. "I can't be sure yet."

"I'd never. Family over everything," Rafe says, but he's wearing a crooked grin that tells me he's full of it.

"Where's James?"

"He's tending his dukedom," Rafe says.

"Shut up," comes a tired, cultured voice. James takes the seat between Rafe and West and puts a bag on the table with a clink. "Let's get this over with."

"The enthusiasm," Alex says. "It's heartwarming to see, really. You love us so much."

"I put up with you all," James says, "because I must."

West glances from person to person at the table before looking at me. "There's a buy-in. It's not our earned chips, though."

"It's much better," Rafe says. "You buy into the game in one of two ways. Wager a one-of-a-kind object of high value... or share a secret. Something the others will want to hear."

James tips the pouch and out falls a thin diamond necklace. It settles snakelike on the table. "Heirloom. It's priceless, et cetera and so forth."

"No secrets for us this time?"

"No." James crosses his arms over his chest. He's gotten a tan during our days here, his skin not as pale as his hair. "I enjoy the fallout from yours far more."

I stare at the diamonds in the center of the table. That's worth... I can't even fathom. And an heirloom? Was he joking? If the buy-rate is *either* something that priceless or a secret, the secret must be good.

"You guys are sadists," I say. "Or masochists. I can't decide."

"Alex's the masochist, James's the sadist," Rafe says. "I'm also buying out of the secret this time. Here."

He offers up an Artemis watch from an old collection, and I stare at it. How many of those do we have left? It's one of the originals, from when our grandfather started the small Swiss clock shop. Before it became a giant and that giant was turned into an empire.

Alex drums his fingers against the table and looks around at us all. "Right. My turn, then, and I'm going to preface it with... I'm sorry."

"Here we go," James says. "If either of you gets so angry that we don't finish the game, I'll stop servicing your planes for a full year."

Alex looks over at West with a single shrug of his wide shoulders. "Sorry, mate. So, Vivienne's last party? The Paradise Lost themed one that only Calloway could attend? He took Nora as his date, and I've heard that they looked real cozy next to the poker table."

"Alex," I whisper.

His blue gaze slides to mine, and there's a real apology there. "Sorry, lass. There are no secrets here, I'm afraid. And I do very much want to win."

West is staring at my brother with a steady, unfazed expression on his face. Like we haven't done anything wrong. Like my heart isn't pounding out of my chest.

"You took her," Rafe says in a low voice, "to one of *Viv's* parties?"

James groans. "And that's why you should have brought a physical item, Alex."

"I forgot."

"My cousin was there, and I wanted to send a signal," West says evenly. "She was safe the entire time."

"It was just a party," I tell Rafe. "It was fun."

He keeps looking at West. "Looked cozy?"

"You wanted us to fake date." His voice is cool and

controlled. Like we might as well have been talking about the weather. He reaches out and grabs his chips. Stacks them with one large hand, deft fingers shifting. "So we pretended to date. You know who goes to those parties, Rafe. People talk."

"That's what we wanted. For people to talk," I remind my brother. My heart is still in my throat, and the threat of a confrontation hanging in the air tastes sour. Maybe I haven't gotten as used to arguing as I thought.

Rafe sighs. "It was a risk."

"Marginally," West says. "Nora can speak for herself too. She just told you she had fun at the party."

"I did, and the stalker is my problem too. I don't want to avoid parties just because of some asshole," I say. My tone is placating. "Let's play."

My brother hesitates only a second before nodding. "Fine. Just two more buy-ins. Calloway?"

West's gaze meets mine for a second before he looks back out at the ocean. He could say anything. So could I, when it's my turn next. Unless he takes that secret we share first and spills it to this table and lets the crumbs fall where they may.

"The Paradise Lost party," he says, "was at the Whitman house."

Alex groans. "Fucking hell. That's a bit on the nose."

"You didn't tell us earlier because you wanted to save it for a buy-in," James says.

West's gaze slides to him. "Yes."

He nods, a faint look of amusement on his bored features. "I respect it."

"Was Hadrian there?"

"I didn't see him. But he was invited." West's jaw works once. "The place was half empty and trashed."

"Fuck," Alex repeats.

I look around the table and clear my voice. "He used to be your friend, right? When you were all at boarding school."

"Once upon a time, yes," West said.

There are unspoken secrets between them, tightening and pulsating in the air. I wonder at the four friends who are more like brothers, and the fifth one who fell away all those years ago.

It's James who finally speaks. "He's irrelevant tonight. Nora, you're next."

My gaze flickers up to West again and then over to where Alex is grinning. "The secret doesn't have to be about me. Does it?"

"Sure doesn't," he confirms.

I meet West's gaze. He's watching me beneath those thick eyebrows, one scarred, one whole. Then I move on and look at my brother. "When Rafe was nine—"

"Oh no," he groans.

"Oh *yes*," Alex says.

"—he lost at Monopoly to one of our cousins and cried for six hours straight. He had to be carried upstairs and threw a fit in his room. What did you destroy? Books, right? Ripped out every page."

"Yes," he mutters.

"*Six* hours?" James asks.

"I'm committed to making money. What can I say?" Rafe sends me a dark glare, and it doesn't make me wilt. Doesn't make me feel guilt.

I smile at him in triumph. "Whoops."

Alex holds up his hands. "Look, mate, is that what happens every time you lose one of these games? Is that why you disappear for six hours?"

"Six hours," West repeats, "of crying?"

"Thank you very much for sharing that with the group," Rafe tells me in a pained voice. "I appreciate it so much."

"I do." Alex reaches out to pat me on the shoulder. "You're playing with us every time from now on."

My cheeks warm. "I could have done worse, Rafe."

He mutters something unintelligible and starts dealing out

the cards. Across the table, West's eyes are on me. There's a smile in them, and I don't need to hear him speak to see the praise he's sending my way. *Well done.* Heat spreads down my chest, pools in my stomach.

I lift my cards and keep them close to my chest. The others do the same. Alex groans, and James tells him to shut up and stop bluffing.

And so the game begins.

CHAPTER 46
WEST

"I can't believe you won," Rafe says.

Nora doesn't look bothered by her brother's incredulity or that it's the third time he's said it. She just keeps rolling her luggage through the airport and shrugs. "I'm going to send you guys on the worst trips. I already have a few ideas."

"This might be a good time to remind you that I'm your favorite," Alex says. He's about to head along with James and Rafe on Rafe's plane back to Europe. They'll stop in London before he flies back to Paris.

And he's *not* her favorite.

But I don't say anything. Swallow the annoyance that's been buzzing inside me this whole trip—at having to fake *not* being with her and pretend that she's still my best friend's little sister and nothing more.

That she hasn't upended my world.

James puts a hand on my arm when we're in the hangar, waiting to board. Nods toward the array of drinks and snacks in the private lounge.

I walk with him. "Yeah?"

"I saw you." He makes himself a gin and tonic with cold precision. "Coming out of her room yesterday morning."

My teeth grind together. "James…"

"We've done a lot of idiotic things together," he says. "But of all the things…?"

"I know." A glance over my shoulder shows Alex, Rafe and Nora chatting half a room away.

"This is going to end badly."

"I know that."

"That's why she doesn't know you need to be married?" He lifts the glass to his lips. He's as put together as always, if not for the circles under his eyes. The man never sleeps.

"I'm handling it."

"You're not, though," he says calmly. He glances over at Rafe and then back at me. "Is she in love with you?"

"No. She wants relationship practice, and she wants true love one day. A real relationship. *Not* a marriage of convenience." I pour myself a knuckle's worth of scotch. It's too early, and we were up too late, and I want to get far away from this conversation.

James looks at me, his steel-gray eyes seeing more than I want him to. "I hope you're right," he says. "For all of our sakes."

We join the others and head down to the tarmac. The planes are parked next to one another. James's aviation manufacturer is one of Britain's oldest and finest, and he oversaw the building of both of ours.

Nora and I say goodbye to the others and board my plane. She looks tired and tan and gives me a happy smile after she settles into her seat.

"I can't wait to go home," she says.

Home.

She means my home. She means Fairhaven, and damn if it's not an arrow straight through me.

"You did really well this trip."

"I did, didn't I?" She buckles her seat belt. "I can't believe I won."

"I can."

She turns to me, resting her head against the headrest. There's something relaxed about her, but her eyes are determined.

"What are you thinking about?" I ask her.

"After we get home," she says, "I want to go out in public again. Maybe make out the way we did at the Fashion Institute and see if he texts me again."

"You do?" I reach over and find her hand. Thread her fingers through mine. "I would never ask you to play bait."

"I know. But I want to end this, once and for all." She looks down at my fingers, curved around hers. "Let's set a trap."

CHAPTER 47

NORA

"Are you scared?"

I look up at West. "No."

A smile tugs at his lips at my quick response. He looks out at the people around us, the food stands, the chaos. We're on a pier an hour west of King's Point for a sailing regatta.

"You can tell me," he says. "I won't hold it against you."

I'm a little annoyed at how easily he's read me. "I know you won't," I say, "but I'm not scared. I'm… tense."

"Tense," he repeats.

"Yes." It's weird to know that he might be here, looking, watching us even now. It's unsettling, even if this was the point. West even made sure his attendance here was announced beforehand.

His hand slides down my arm, coming to rest at my elbow. "It's okay. You're safe."

I look over West's shoulder and briefly meet Sam's eye. He's wearing a blue cap today with the name of a yacht club on it, dressed in a T-shirt and a pair of frayed jeans. In one hand, he's holding a beer.

Just a casual attendee.

The curly ends of his hair cover the earpiece he's wearing.

He meets my gaze for a millisecond before turning back to chat with another undercover guard.

I shift closer to West. "I know. Still, it feels…"

The last time we were in public together, my phone lit up. We're hoping the same thing happens today. That West and I can provoke the stalker to reach out if he's watching us in person.

"It feels like what?" he says. "Tell me."

"Is this a lesson too?" I ask, striving to make my tone light. "In sharing our feelings?"

"I'm not sure I'm the best at teaching that one," he says.

"I have a great therapist I could recommend. Dr. Zeina Fares. She mainly practices in French, though."

West's face doesn't change. It's easy, when he looks like that, to see the man I once thought I knew. Arrogant, a bit cold, gruff. But there's amusement in the liquid of his honeyed eyes. "Could I ask her about you?"

"No. Told you—privileged information."

"What I wouldn't give to hear your conversations."

I shake my head a little. "I'm sure it would be endlessly amusing, but—"

"Not amusing," he cuts in. "Enlightening."

"I'm an open book," I say.

West lifts his scarred eyebrow. "*You're* an open book?"

"Compared to you, I am." My gaze slips past him to the boats passing beyond the pier on the roaring waves to mine. They've already rounded the farthest edge of the course. "You used to compete in these. I saw the trophies. In the library."

"Yes." The answer comes easily, steadily. "Did you like sailing the other week?"

"You know I did." Behind us, outside the VIP section, someone walks by with a giant grip of balloons. "Do you think he's watching now?"

West's eyes darken. "I hope so. And if he is watching…" He tilts my head back and brushes away a tendril of my hair.

His eyes are bottomless on mine. Inscrutable. "He'll see that you're mine."

I slide my hands up his broad chest and over the slightly rough linen of his shirt. It's a warm spring day, and there's laughter in the air, shouts to the sailing boats passing. A strong wind from the ocean and the hot sun. "Is this when I look at you like I'm deeply in love again?"

"Try," he says. He's so much more than I once thought he was. More of *himself*, more dimensions, more intrigue. But he still swallows all my attention when he's around. Consumes it.

Looking at him like I'm in love might be the easiest thing in the world.

"Look at that pretty smile," West says. "I'm going to kiss you now."

I dip my head in the smallest of nods.

"It's going to look possessive," he warns.

"Isn't that the point?" I press up, my lips inches from his.

His eyes flash, and then he presses his lips against mine. It's a hot, claiming kiss. It's the kind of kiss he's given me in private, a little open-mouthed, warm, dizzying. I hold on to his neck and feel the world shift beneath me when his tongue brushes against mine.

His hands slide down my body and come to rest right above the curve of my ass. An inch too low to be entirely decent. He's pulled me flush against him, like I really am his. Like he's feeling possessive.

Like all the people around us don't matter.

Or maybe they *do*, and it's a statement to them all. Here we are, and look how well we match. See how much we want each other.

I nip at his lower lip, and West groans into my mouth. "You're such a good fake girlfriend."

"I am?"

"The best fake girlfriend I've ever had." His gaze dips to my mouth again. "Your lips look rosy now."

I feel light. Like one of the sailing boats out at sea, bobbing across the waves. Someone knocks West on the shoulder, and he levels them with a stare. "Yes?"

"Sorry to interrupt, but Terry from the sailing association wants to talk to you. Something about the prize ceremony. He saw that you were here, and…" Madison shrugs. She takes a step forward, and her voice lowers. "Michael suggested we see what happens if Nora is alone. Maybe the stalker will text her then."

West looks down at me. "I'm not leaving—"

"Go," I tell him. "Sam is right here, and I know I'm being watched by all the guards. It's fine. Let's see if it works."

West kisses my forehead. "Fine. But I'm not happy about it."

"Noted," I tell him with a smile. I put my hand on his chest. "Now go."

He walks toward the prize podium. Madison disappears back into the VIP crowd around me, and I take a sip of my champagne.

Breathe in. Breathe out.

I want to find this bastard.

I want it to be over with, and I want my life to return to normal. To begin again. To stop being scared—

A hand grabs my upper arm, and I'm tugged backward around the edge of the tent. I shove my elbow back like West has taught me, connecting with someone's soft body. There's a low, muffled groan.

I turn, my knee already halfway up.

"Shit. Stop, stop…"

My knee pauses an inch from Dave's groin. West's cousin. The man we pretended in front of at the Paradise Lost party.

Last time I saw him, he was in a cigar-smoke filled room,

playing poker for stakes higher than I could imagine. Now he's standing in front of me under the blazing sun.

"What?" I ask.

He can't be the stalker. That's impossible. It has to be.

"I just wanted to talk to you." His hands are pressed against the side of his stomach. "Shit, you reacted fast."

"Talk to me? Why would you—"

Sam is there in the next instant, standing behind my shoulder, an arm out and pressed against Dave's chest. "Step back."

"It's fine. It's all fine," I say quickly. "Why would you want to talk to me?"

Dave's eyes dart from my guard to me. "Because it's near impossible to get you alone. I wanted to make you an offer."

"An offer?"

"Yes. We don't have much time." He glances at Sam again. "Clearly you know about the marriage clause for Fairhaven. You're dating my cousin."

I give him a small smile to hide the turmoil inside. "I'm dating West, yeah."

"And you're Raphaël's little sister."

"I am, yes. Do you know him?" My question is polite, but I can't help the hint of tenseness that seeps through. I don't like this man. Don't like how he pulled me back here.

"I haven't had the pleasure." Dave looks over at the crowd, like he's waiting for West to appear at any moment. "You're clearly getting ready to marry him before his thirtieth. I'm sure you think you're being compensated fairly and think you're doing him a favor. But think about what you're agreeing to," he says hurriedly. "A life tied to a Calloway isn't a happy one."

I don't let my face change from the neutral mask I'm wearing. I have a lot of practice in being kind and polite, and right now, I wield it like a sword. I glance down at his left hand. "I believe *you're* married."

"Yes," he says, "I am. Listen, we don't have much time. If Weston told you that you could get a divorce in a few years, he's probably lying. The trust is hard to break through. Tell me what he's paying you, and I promise to double it if you leave him."

"Double what he's paying me," I repeat.

Sweat beads on his forehead. "I'll triple it if you wait to pull out of the wedding until the week before his birthday. String him along."

Several things click into place at once, and it takes me a moment to find the words. To let the anger come, but when it does, it burns. "I'm not with him for money."

Dave laughs. It's a short and hard sound. "Yes, yes, of course you're not. Look, if you would rather have this conversation somewhere less public, I'm available." He presses a business card into my hand. "Just think on it."

There's always been such a weird insistence on marriage: West's mother, people's comments. *Marriage clause for Fairhaven.*

"Thank you," I say, "but I don't need saving, and I don't want your money."

Dave's eyes widen, as if he's realizing I might be a fool. "He can't give you love. Surely you must know that. Whatever he's promised you, it'll never turn into something real."

"And what would you know of that?" I ask him. My voice is still kind, but it drips with insincerity. "Are you the person who shares his bed every night?"

I've never spoken like that to anyone before.

Anyone who's not West.

Dave shakes his head slowly, and there's an incredulous look on his face. "I can't believe—"

"Can't believe what?" West's voice is arctic despite the spring warmth. He pushes himself into the narrow space between Sam and me, and his arm wraps around my waist, strong and steadying. "What can you not believe, Dave?"

His cousin is a few inches shorter and looks up at West with narrowed eyes. All pretense of civility wipes off his face. "Not competing today?"

"Had better things to do," West says. "You're not bothering my girlfriend, are you?"

"Just saying hello. Seeing as she'll become family and all that." Dave's smile is a razor. "Have fun."

"You too," West says in a voice that makes it clear he means *fuck off*. Dave gives me another look and then heads off toward the parking lot, away from the ocean.

West looks at me. His eyes are narrowed, arm tight around me. "Are you okay?"

"Yes. No texts. No calls." I tilt my head. "But I think I just learned something very interesting."

His lips thin. "What did he tell you?"

CHAPTER 48
NORA

"He offered me money to not marry you," I say.

West's face turns carefully blank. "Not here," he says, and takes my hand in his. He looks at the tables around us and the people chatting, drinking. Laughing.

He grabs a chair and turns it around so it faces the ocean. Away from the others around us. He sinks onto the chair and pulls me closer.

"You want me to sit in your lap again."

"Yes. We're good at it."

"I'm annoyed with you."

"I know you are. I can tell." He holds out his arms to me. "Can you be annoyed with me and let me hold you?"

I hesitate for another second before sitting on his lap in front of all these people, under a bright spring sun. I drape my arm around his shoulders and sit sideways so I can still see his face. We came here to play bait for the stalker, and we'll keep doing that.

"So you're in the market for a wife."

His expression doesn't change, but his eyes slide to mine, whiskey-colored and cautious. "No. I am not."

"Oh? I could have sworn I heard something about a

marriage clause, Fairhaven and you turning thirty." I tilt my head. "Your cousin offered me triple what you're allegedly paying me to not go through with it. Let me guess. He gets the house if you don't?"

West blows out a breath. "Of course he did."

"Is it true?" I slide my hand into his hair and look at him like I'm deeply, deeply in love. "You can lose Fairhaven."

"It's true."

"Oh." The word is simple and short, but it's like a puzzle piece finally completing an image. And then there's the hurt. "Why wouldn't you tell me that?"

He doesn't look away from me, but his eyes narrow. "Because I didn't want to complicate things."

"Complicate things," I repeat slowly. It doesn't add up. None of it adds up. Why would he want his mother to *stop* setting him up with women if he needed marriage? Why would he agree to pretend to date me?

It doesn't make sense.

I tilt my head. "Are people watching us right now?"

"I wouldn't know. I'm only watching you," he says.

"And if the stalker is watching… if we want him to lose control and make a mistake… then I should look at you like we have the hottest sex known to man every single night."

West's eyes are a brighter shade than usual beneath the sun. They're also cautious. He can hear the tone in my voice. "Where are you going with this?"

"You've been showing me off to your family. Your friends. At your party, in town, out at restaurants. We've been photographed together and written about. All of that to send a message to the stalker… but doesn't that make it *harder* for you to find a wife?"

His hand on my thigh tightens. "I don't want to find a wife that way."

"But you need one. And your family knows." Irritation

flares in my chest. "Your mom being so insistent, setting you up with women. That's why, isn't it?"

"Yes."

"Why don't you want her help? Don't you want to keep Fairhaven?"

"Yes. My lawyers have been working on a solution." His jaw works, and there's nothing but grim acceptance on his face.

"When did you find out about it?"

"Two years ago. After my father died."

"And you haven't found a solution yet," I whisper.

"No. We've tried, but the trust is... ironclad." He's stone beneath me, sharp and still, like he's not enjoying this conversation. But he's here. He's answering my questions. "We have a prenup drafted. If there's no other way, I planned to marry. But it would only be a legal marriage. And I won't give my mother the giant society wedding she craves."

Jealousy rips through me, like the sailing boats through the salty waves. "Would she live at Fairhaven?"

"No. It would be a sheet of paper, not a real relationship." His eyes are on mine. "You're angry."

"Yes," I say. "Funny, isn't it? You're the one who taught me how to be angry. Maybe you regret that now."

"No. I will always welcome your fire, Nora. Burn me with it when I deserve it."

I take a deep breath. "We're arguing for real this time."

"It would seem so, trouble."

"Why wouldn't you tell me?"

"Because I was handling it."

I trace the edge of his jaw, the role I'm meant to play slipping from my mind. "What kind of trust is this, even? Is it legal?"

"Unfortunately," he says. "I have to be married by thirty or the estate goes to the next married male Calloway heir." He takes a deep breath. "Which is Dave."

I blink at him. "That's *barbaric*."

"Yes. It's archaic, an offense to my sister and, quite frankly, an offense to the entire family. Dad thought he had changed the trust, or so Mom says. It was meant to ensure Fairhaven isn't split apart. Divided up by an ever-growing pool of descendants. It can only be passed down to one Calloway—and one that is married and set to produce heirs of their own."

"Dave," I murmur. "He was at that party…"

"Yes. You've seen him gamble." West's eyes glitter with irritation. "He would gamble away the estate on the day his name appeared on the deed. Sell it to the highest bidder."

"West," I say. "*Why* didn't you tell me?"

West sighs, his expression unreadable. "Because I was handling it. I'm still handling it."

"That's not a real answer. If you want my honesty, I want yours."

He takes a deep breath. "I didn't want you to worry. The clause doesn't mean our lessons have to stop, and I didn't want you to think that you'd only be under my protection until a certain date. If the stalker hasn't been caught by then…" He pauses, his voice dropping. "You would have been welcome with me forever."

"Forever?" I echo. "Even if you don't want one now, you'll want a real wife one day."

He leans his head back against the chair. "No. I won't."

It hurts. It shouldn't, but it does, the insistence that he doesn't want the kind of relationship that I do. The real kind of love that I've always wanted to experience one day. The kind of love that's been growing inside me, for *him*, now feels like it might choke me.

"I guess we both have our deadlines, then," I say.

His expression darkens. "It's not the same thing."

"Isn't it?" I counter. "You have to be married before you

turn thirty. I don't want to be a virgin after I turn twenty-five. We have a few months left."

His jaw tightens. "Those two are not comparable."

I shrug, like this is nothing at all, like my heart isn't aching. "No, it's true. Yours is much more serious."

"I should have told you." West's free hand tilts my head back to meet his gaze. "I never wanted you to think that this was a possibility."

"But it is," I tell him. "You're not the kind of man who loses."

"Nora," he says.

"It won't be one of the women your mother wants you to marry," I guess. "It won't be a big wedding. Maybe it'll be an assistant of yours, someone you work with. Someone you pay. A quid-pro-quo agreement. But you won't lose Fairhaven."

"Nothing has to change," he tells me. "*Nothing.* Do you hear me? You and I, nothing has to change."

"Everything changes," I say. "It's the only certainty in life."

His fingers dig into my waist, tighten until I can feel the pads of them. "I won't be controlled. Not by my mother, and not by a trust written by a man who's been dead for almost a century."

"And yet," I say, tracing my nail along the scruff at his jaw, "you *are* in the market for a wife, and that's entirely his doing."

West's teeth grind together like he hates that fact. I bet he does.

I've never felt this way before. The anger, the want, the frustration. It all coalesces around *him*. And Fairhaven. He can't lose it. Of course he can't.

I don't want to lose it, either.

"Sir." It's Madison again. She nods at West and then at me.

"Sorry to interrupt. But we apprehended someone taking pictures of you two. Michael is interrogating him now."

West's face hardens. "Take me to him."

RAFE, WEST AND NORA

WEST

We just caught someone photographing
Nora. He's one of several hired to cover her,
or so he says. He works for an undercover
security agency.

NORA

Guess who hired them.

RAFE

What the fuck? How did you make him talk?

WEST

The guy's a hired gun. All you have to do is
pay him more.

NORA

Ben Wilde hired them. Wilde, who you're
negotiating with!!

RAFE

Send over all the information you've got.

WEST

Don't share it with your team.

RAFE

I won't.

NORA

They never wanted to stalk me. It's like you said, as a joke. They wanted to bother you. Knock you off your game. The Wilde's hated Dad for decades, Rafe. They always said they'd never sell out. And now you have them cornered.

RAFE

The mole in my office. Probably someone Ben Wilde paid, too. Fuck.

WEST

Maybe they wanted you to fly to New York in a panic. Maybe they just wanted you off your game.

RAFE

Whatever it is, the Wilde's will pay.

WEST

I can't wait.

CHAPTER 49
NORA

"You're still mad at me."

His words aren't an accusation. They're just a statement of fact, coming from where he stands at the base of my bed. It's been a long day. Longer still with all the information that's come out, and I *am* still angry.

But I'm also relieved and aching and frustrated and a mess of emotions. I'm everything all at once. Before him, I would have hid that deep down. Would have painted on a smile whatever the cost.

"Yes," I say, because I'm not that person anymore.

"Do you still want me to sleep here?" He looks tense. A dark outline against the bedside light.

"Yes," I say again and flip the covers open.

His shoulders sink, like he's relieved, like he was expecting the opposite. He undoes the buttons of his shirt while I lie on my side, watching him.

"You're annoyed," he says, "and I get it. I'm used to it. That was our status quo. Before."

"Before," I repeat. He steps out of his jeans, and it's all long muscles and tan skin. He had the gash on his shoulder

OLIVIA HAYLE

checked out, and it's covered in gauze now. Far more professionally done than I managed in Costa Rica.

He gets into bed on the side that's somehow become his.

I reach out and brush my fingers along his cheek. His skin is dry and a bit rough to the touch. He hasn't shaved today, and I love the feeling against my palm.

His eyes close. I repeat the movement, trace up to his temple and to the scar in his eyebrow. "Your father thought he fixed the trust?"

"Yes." West's voice is tired, resigned, but he doesn't shy away from my touch. "He and my mother married when they were in their mid-twenties."

"I'm sorry you lost him. My father passed a few years ago, too."

West's whiskey eyes open. "I know. I'm sorry."

"Do you miss yours?"

"I think I hate him a little more with each year that passes. But yes. I still miss him."

The raw honesty in the statement makes me smile. "I know the feeling," I murmur. "What was he like?"

"He was godlike when I was a child." West shakes his head a little. "Then he was a tyrant. Neither he nor my mother was made to be a parent. They weren't made to be married to each other, either."

"Your mother hasn't mentioned him to me," I murmur. "In our conversations."

"My parents didn't exactly have what I'd call a successful marriage," he says.

"What was it like?" I asked.

"Well, when I was small, I thought they were in love. I suppose they were, in their own sort of way. It was all-consuming. Toxic. I was twelve when I discovered the first affair, thirteen when I told them about it. They shipped me off to Belmont shortly after."

My fingers still on his cheek. "They did *what*?"

"I caught my dad out on the tennis court. So I went to my mom. Turns out she already knew." He chuckles again, but it's not a particularly happy sound. "She'd had affairs of her own, and she'd *just* made up with my dad. It was inconvenient to have me around. I saw too much."

"West... that's awful."

"Yeah," he says, lifting one shoulder in a shrug. "I suppose. But that was their marriage, and neither of them ended it because that wasn't possible, either. Calloways don't divorce," he says, his tone wry. "Outwardly, they were great at it—the perfect, sparkling couple. I remember one of their anniversary parties. My mom went up and gave a beautiful speech to my dad. People were entranced. There were barbs threaded throughout that speech, of course. That was the way they used to play."

"That sounds terrible," I say. And relatable. I was young when my parents divorced, but I remember the fights too.

"During that speech, she wore a brand-new diamond necklace that her lover at the time bought her."

"Oh my god," I say.

He shakes his head a little. "It is what it is. But I never want to end up in that situation. To see someone turn resentful, angry—trapped."

"You won't." I brush my hand over his jawline. He's always been handsome. I knew that from the start, and now it's so painful to me, just how much I love looking at him. Touching him. "For what it's worth, I think you'd be a good husband."

His eyes darken. "You do?"

"I've gotten to know you during these months, you know."

West's hands slide in under the camisole I'm wearing, brushing over the bare skin of my low back. "You didn't like me for years. I've grown on you, then?"

383

I run my finger over his eyebrow. The scar there smooth after so many years. "Maybe."

"Maybe, she says," he mutters. "You're harsh."

"You like it when I'm harsh."

"I do."

I smile a little. "I think you might be the only person who does."

"No," he says. "Stand up for yourself more, and you'll see that people won't mind nearly as much as you think they will."

I dig my teeth into my lower lip. "Do you remember a Christmas party a few years back? When I asked…"

West's eyebrows pull low. "By the fireplace?"

"Yes. I wasn't sure if you remembered."

His thumb sweeps back and forth over my skin. "I remember."

"Well, I liked you before then. I'd been drinking that night, and I figured…" I shrug a little. Embarrassment makes my cheeks tinge. "Anyway. You weren't interested."

"Nora," he mutters. His eyes are narrowed.

But I have to keep going, or I won't share any of this. And now that I've started talking about the past, I want it all out. "Half a year later, you were at a party my father threw at the Lake Como house. All of you were. I was upstairs, on the balcony facing the lake… taking a breather. And you were downstairs. Talking to Alex."

West's jaw tightens. "Go on."

"I overheard your conversation," I say. "He said I looked beautiful that night. Asked if you knew if I was single."

"I remember." His eyebrows are drawn low. "What did I say in response?"

I wet my lips. "If you remember, why should I say it?"

"Tell me," he says. "And tell me how angry you've been at me for it."

"You said that I was pretty enough, but boring. That I was... the last person you'd date."

West's eyes close. He's still as a statue, only inches from me. "Yes. I said all of that."

"I hated you for it," I whisper. It was the final nail in the coffin of my stupid crush. And now I want to hurt him with it, too, because he's getting married, and he didn't tell me. Even if it's just a business transaction. Even if he and I can never be, because of my brother and their stupid pact.

West's eyes open, and this time they're blazing. "Good. I never meant for you to hear those words."

"So we've both changed our minds about each other, haven't we? I'm not the least bit bland."

"I didn't mean a word of it."

I roll my eyes. "Right. And why would you have said that—"

"Because I wanted him to stay away from you."

My heart is in my throat. "Why? You didn't talk to me. Barely looked at me."

"You're my best friend's younger sister," he says. There's agony in that tone. "You were then. You still are. There was no looking. There was no talking. You were forbidden. Alex knew that, but he was—still is—reckless." West's jaw works. "He wasn't good enough for you."

"You were jealous," I breathe. "Even then."

"Yes. I was."

The confession makes my stomach tighten. "Oh."

"You were never meant to overhear it. It was a lie." His right hand finds the curve of my waist beneath the cover, settles where he usually keeps it. "Don't tell me you believed it, trouble."

"I did," I admit.

He tsks. "Not you. Confident, bubbly, sparkling. Wide smiles to everyone, long legs, shiny hair. It hurt to look at you." His eyes track the movement of his hand sliding down my neck, settling over my collarbone. "Did you really think I didn't like you?"

"I used to. But not anymore."

"Thank god."

"It's what made me feel comfortable arguing with you in the beginning," I tell him honestly. My anger is seeping out. Replaced with frustration, and warmth, and the confession. He didn't mean it.

I wish things were simpler. That this little bubble here with him would never end, never stop, never burst.

"Then I'm grateful for it," he says, and pulls me against his chest, "if it let me see the real you."

CHAPTER 50
WEST

I want every night to be like this.

Nora, sitting opposite me in the orangery, eating dinner, with her hair undone and a true smile on her face. Telling me about her final design and how nervous she is about the fashion show next week.

What would it be like? If she were the one I married? If Rafe wasn't an issue, if I could make her love me... If she wore my ring. If this was dinner every night.

She's excited about the Spring Ball tomorrow, the famous Calloway party, and Rafe showing up. I'm not, but her excitement is enough to make it all worth it.

"The cat?" she tells me, drawing up her knees after dinner. "I'm going to keep him."

"Keep it, are you?"

"Well. On your behalf." Her cheeks are rosy. "I bought him a collar, and I'm trying to think of a name. He belongs here. At Fairhaven. Don't protest, because you're starting to like him too."

I tap my fingers against the table. "I am?"

"Yes, you are. You're charmed, despite yourself." She tilts her head a little and looks at me. She's the one who should stay. Move in here permanently. There's a fierceness in her tonight.

"I'm still a bit annoyed with you for keeping that secret, you know."

"Mhm."

"Despite that… I still enjoy being around you."

My fingers still. "Is that a first for you?"

"Yes." She cocks her head. Her eyes are narrow, and dancing, and beautiful. The whole reason she's here, that she's living with me, that we're dating… it's falling away. Crumbling.

She pushes back her chair and walks around the table to me. I open my arms, but she doesn't sit in my lap. She reaches for my hand instead. "Come with me. I want to try something."

That's how I find myself being pushed into one of the armchairs in the library, the door shut behind us, with Nora kissing her way down the column of my throat. She's told me to keep my hands on the armrests, and I dig my fingers in to keep from touching her.

"I want to try," she says, unbuttoning my shirt, sliding down my body, "what a real girlfriend would do. We just had dinner together. It was a date."

"Nora…"

She drops to her knees in front of me. The rush of want that floods me takes all the air with it, and I harden so fast it makes my head spin.

She reaches for the buckle of my belt. "I know we don't have much time left now. We know who the stalker is, you're heading for a loveless deal of a marriage, and I have my own deadline."

No, I think. That's not where I'm heading. That's not where *she's* heading, but I can't say that, so I grit my teeth to keep the words locked inside. "Let me make you feel good instead," I tell her.

It's not right, none of this is, but then her hand reaches inside, and *fuck*, it's good. Her touching me like that. I've been aching for weeks, with no release other than my own right hand, and feeling her fingers…

"You are bigger than that vibrator. I was right." She sounds delighted, and I can't look away from her pretty face so close to my cock. Nora leans forward and licks a tentative stripe along the underside of my head.

"You want to do this?" I ask her. My hands are tight along the edges of the armchair.

She nods. There's nothing hesitant in her fiery expression. "Show me how you like it."

It's blasphemy, it's pain, it's salvation. But I reach down and cup her face and tap my thumb against her lower lip. "Open up… that's it. Suck on the head. Yes. Like that."

Her pretty lips spread wide, her mouth hot and warm. And maybe she does want to learn how to do this. "Grip me here at the same time."

Nora wraps her hand around my base, and she starts bobbing her head gently up and down. It's soft and not as hard as I need it, and it's the best torture I've ever experienced.

She asked for this. She wants to learn.

"You're doing so good. Can you take me deeper?" My hand is on the side of her cheek, and it's obscene, feeling it hollow out when she bobs farther down. "That's it. That's my girl."

And who am I kidding? I'm taking advantage of her here. I'm the one dancing right along the edge, and it's with someone who's never given head before. How is someone so inexperienced making this so fucking unforgettable?

Nora flicks her tongue along the underside of my head, and I groan. My hand slides back to grip her hair, and fuck, I have to be gentle, have to be good…

"Do that again. Just like that…." She does, and if her

mouth feels this good around my cock, how good would it be to be inside her? To introduce her to the real thing, to be her first, to come with her fluttering around me.

Nora speeds up. Her green eyes are locked on mine with triumph, excitement and a hint of something fierce. She's learning, and she's making a point, and she's taking what she wants.

Her other hand digs down into the fabric, grips my balls tight. I hiss, but I stroke her cheek to tell her to keep going. "Look at you." It's all I can say for another long minute. "Taking me so damn well."

I coax her through it, praise turning low and hoarse. I'm hovering on the edge. Have been for so long around her that it doesn't take much to send me tumbling.

I shouldn't be enjoying this, shouldn't want her the way I do every single fucking day, but I do.

Rafe can never find out that I let his little sister do this.

Because I'm letting her suck me off, and it's proof that I'm wrong for her. What kind of sick bastard would let his best friend's virgin sister do this? When she's under my protection; asked me for help with sex; is angry at me for keeping a secret.

I want her to do this every single day for the rest of my life. But I don't deserve her doing just that.

"I'm going to come if you keep doing that." My fingers flex in her hair.

She takes me deeper, and the wet, hot suctioning of her mouth is the center of the universe. Pleasure races down my spine, and she's not stopping, looking at me with those eyes.

Her eyes close on a slow blink, and then she moves her hand in time with her mouth, her tongue, her lips. I should warn her again, but then she flicks her tongue, and *fucking hell*. My hips lift once off the armchair before I can lock my muscles down.

I come with a loud groan.

Fingers in her hair, shudders racking through my body. Not looking away for a second as she drains me. Not even blinking, and when it's done, she kisses the crown and sits back on her knees with a small smile.

Her lips are rosy, cheeks red. Waiting, and when I realize what she's waiting for, my spent cock twitches against my stomach.

"You did so well, sweetheart. Swallowing it all like a good girl." My shirt is open, legs splayed. *Destroyed*. "You've made me very happy."

Nora smiles. Pleasure dances in her eyes. "I've wanted to try that for days."

"Yeah? To see if you could wreck me?"

"Yes." She leans forward and rests her hands on my thighs. Her hair is undone around her shoulders, glossy in the dim lighting of the library. "Is this how you'll treat your wife?"

My eyes narrow. "What?"

"Will you call her your good girl too, when she pleases you?" She cocks her head a little. "Will you fuck her the way you won't fuck me?"

"No."

She sits up straighter, and she strokes a single finger along the length of my cock where it rests against my stomach. "Why not? You won't lose Fairhaven. You've been preparing me for a future guy." Her fingers tap against the sensitive head, and I grit my teeth. "Why can't I talk about your future wife?"

"I don't want a wife." *Unless it's you.* I grip her wrist and tug her up instead. She settles on either side of my knees. "And I don't want to talk about your *future* men."

"So you want us to pretend instead. Like we used to." She tilts her head again, and her fingers find the scar in my eyebrow. "You're a hypocrite, Calloway."

My eyes narrow. "How so?"

"You act like you don't believe in relationships, but you're telling me to wait to have sex with someone I care about. With someone who truly matters. That's a very romantic notion for someone who claims they don't believe in love."

I find the curve of her waist and grip her tight like it will keep her from ever leaving. She's killing me, slicing through me word for word. "Yes. I still stand by it."

"So you don't believe in love for yourself, but you believe in it for me?"

My breath is ragged. "I want more for you than I want for me."

It's a lie. Maybe the first I've ever told her, because fuck if I don't want it all with her.

Her, or no one.

She smiles. It's a small, ravenous expression that speaks of victory, and I harden again beneath her. Could take her just like this, in this armchair, if I wasn't held back by the guilt.

"Thanks for the date," she says, and she slips off my lap. "It was very… informative."

CHAPTER 51
WEST

My sister looks distraught.

She's sitting on the edge of the counter in the kitchen, chewing on one of Melissa's bread rolls. "It's annoying," she says. "You think he's different, and then he just turns out to *not* be, you know?"

Nora nods. "Yeah. I know what you mean."

"Who is he?" I ask.

"I'm not telling you," Amber says. "You're not allowed to be overprotective."

"He's someone you're dating?"

"Just for a short time." She rolls her eyes. "He was playing hot and cold, and I hate it when they do that."

I cross my arms over my chest. My sister has always been bold, sometimes wild. She dates. She's strong and has no problem standing up for herself, and here she is, heartbroken and back at Fairhaven.

She dropped by last night and took one of the guest rooms. She stayed up late with Nora, watching a movie. I joined them for a while, until I felt like I might combust from sitting so close to Nora and pretending like we were nothing but friends.

Amber turns to Nora. "Okay, you have to figure out a name now."

"But it's so hard," Nora says. "I have a few ideas, but…" She trails off and grabs her sketchbook. "It's not like he's mine to name, you know?"

"Of course he is," Amber says.

She looks at me. "I think he technically belongs to West, since he moved into Fairhaven."

"You name him," I say. "He likes you the best. What are your options?"

"I'm thinking something literary. Because we found him in the library, and that's still his favorite room." Nora takes a few steps toward the doorway. "I'll keep thinking. Gotta go work."

"See you later," Amber says.

Nora leaves the kitchen and disappears up the steps to the atelier to make more design pieces.

Amber grabs another cup of coffee. "I'll head out later too," she says. "I have a meeting in town."

"You sure you won't tell me his name?" I ask.

"No, I'm very, very sure."

I narrow my eyes at her, and she just shrugs a little and reaches for a freshly baked muffin. It strikes me that this might be Nora after all of this is over—if she sets up dates with assholes who don't really listen to her, don't care about her. She might revert back to some of the people-pleasing.

My grip tightens around the coffee cup.

Amber sets her half-eaten muffin down. Lemon poppy-seed has always been her favorite. "You know, you two are being ridiculous."

My gaze returns to her. "What?"

"I'm not blind," she says. "You two are not pretending around each other. This might have started out as a fake arrangement, but it's pretty real now, isn't it?"

I can't talk about this with Amber. I can't talk about this with anyone.

But I find that the confession comes out of me anyway, low and anguished. "Yes."

Amber sighs. "Then why are you holding back? Why don't the two of you just—"

"It's complicated."

"It's not," she argues. "Dating is really hard. I know, because I'm actively doing it." She crosses her arms over her chest. "If you actually find someone you like, and they like you—which you two obviously do; I can see it—then just go for it."

"It's not that simple," I say.

"Of course it is. You're probably gonna have to marry someone. Why not her? Get your head out of your ass."

"Because marrying me wouldn't be good for her," I snap. "It would be great for me, yes, but it's not what she wants or what she needs."

Amber shakes her head again. "You've always been very good at deciding what other people need. But sometimes that's up to them to decide." She lifts her hands up again. "All I'm saying is, if you like her? Don't give up the fight so easily."

I just look at her. She makes it sound so easy.

"And now," Amber says, "I'm going to take the longest shower known to man. I'm not gonna bother your not-so-fake girlfriend, because I know she's on a deadline. But after all this is over, she and I are going to become really good friends," she tells me. "Whether or not you're still in the picture."

I hold up my hands. "You should. She's amazing."

"Have you told her that?"

"Yes, I have."

Amber lifts an eyebrow. "Then sort out whatever simple little obstacles are in your way and make her happy. Make *yourself* happy. I'd much rather you marry her than lock your-self into a business arrangement of a marriage."

I shove my hands into my pockets. It's not that easy. I know that. But she's right about one thing. Dating is hard. Amber is used to it. She's able to stand up for herself, and she *still* finds it hard. She still came over here last night, sad and upset.

The idea of Nora losing her virginity to someone else has felt harder and harder with each passing day. That some guy might hurt her the way Amber's been hurt.

"I hear you," I say. Just like I heard Nora the other night. She knows what she wants.

I might not be good enough for her, but at least I'd never hurt her. I can't say the same for who she might find after me. Someone who doesn't know her body like I do, someone who can't make it as good for her as I can.

Someone who doesn't love her.

CHAPTER 52
NORA

The apple orchard is in full bloom.

It's a warm, sunny spring day, and I have to take advantage of it. I race to finish my work for the day so I can spend the afternoon outside sketching new designs. Sunlight falls dappled through the branches. They've exploded in the past week with white flowers that speak of the coming summer.

I'm lying on a large picnic blanket I found in one of the estate's many cupboards. Pink flowers dot the fresh grass, and I think maybe *this* is my happy place.

I draw a curved line with my pencil, the sweep of a bow down the back of a ballgown. A single petal falls and lands next to the shape.

Of all the places in the world for my heart to feel at peace, it has to be Fairhaven. West's home. What I first saw as a prison has become a refuge.

Summer must be gorgeous here.

But I can't stay here. Maybe I can stay in New York, though, after the fashion show. Now that we know who the stalker is, there should be more freedom. Fewer guards. Ben Wilde is invited to the Spring Ball on Saturday, and we're planning to confront him then.

And after that…

It all ends.

I sketch a flowing train and pause to look up at the deep blue ocean that stretches out in front of me. A few white sails dot the distance. I want to swim in it before I leave.

I want so many things.

It's like all the years of trying to fit into what others want from me have built up a dam, and now that dam has burst, and I'm an endless swirl of needs. Of desires and wants and thoughts and ideas. Maybe this is how it feels to live life for me.

To be my true self.

A shadow falls over my sketchbook. I look up and find West standing beside the picnic blanket. I've been so lost in my thoughts that I didn't hear his steps in the soft spring grass.

"Hey." I shade my eyes. He's in a pair of dark pants, a white shirt. "Come to do your work out here?"

"I just got a call that you're looking into getting back into your apartment. The one in town."

I push up to sitting. "Yeah."

"Why?"

I pat the space next to me on the large blanket.

He sits down, long legs taking up the rest of the blanket. "You're leaving Fairhaven?"

"Not now, no. But eventually I am."

"Why?"

"Why? You know why. We know who the stalker is. We're handling him at your ball… and I won't need your protection anymore. You don't really need me to keep your mom's matchmaking at bay, either. You'll have a wife by September."

His eyebrows draw together. "You can live here for as long as you want to."

"You don't really mean that."

"I do." His jaw works. "The other night. In the library. What you told me…"

A blush races up my cheeks. I was frustrated and angry, and I wanted to prove a point. It had felt powerful, to wreck him the way he's been wrecking me. "Yeah?"

"You were right," he says. "About all of it. You were right. I've been a hypocrite. And I'm jealous at the thought of any man but me touching you." He reaches out and slides a finger under the strap of my dress. "I imagine you with someone else… and it feels like I'm dying. Like I can't breathe. I thought it would fade, but it hasn't, trouble. It's going stronger every single day."

"Why have you been holding back, then?"

"Holding back," he mutters. "It doesn't feel like I have. I never want you to regret it if you sleep with me. I couldn't fucking bear it if you did."

"I won't." My voice is fierce. "Don't talk like that, like I don't know my own mind. You *taught* me to be clear about what I want. Trust me when I do."

"I'd try to make it good for you." His eyes shift back to mine. "So good."

"I know."

"I want you every minute of the day." His fingers smooth down to the valley of my breasts. "The idea of never having you…"

"Then have me." I arch my back, and he groans, eyes on the spot between my breasts.

His mouth finds mine. It's hot and warm, and he kisses me with heady urgency. His free hand is on my bare knee, sliding up, and up, and up. My dress follows his touch, and then he's brushing his thumb over the damp front of my panties.

I thread my fingers through his hair. Somewhere close by, a bird sings. It sounds triumphant.

"I can't take it anymore," he says. His mouth is hot against my neck. "I've tried to be honorable, but I can't. I *can't.*"

"I don't want you to be."

He lifts up on one arm. In the sunlight, his eyes look brighter than ever. A warm amber. We both watch as he strokes long fingers over my panties, my knees parted for him. "You need to tell me, if you don't want this."

I smile against his lips. "I've been telling you that I do for weeks. Can you please just fuck me?"

He groans, and I laugh a little against his lips at the tortured sound. "It's all I've ever wanted. Here, then." He grips my panties. "Up, sweetheart."

I lift my hips, and he slides my underwear down my legs. West's hand returns, circling my clit, eyes between my bent thighs. He always looks at me like that. Eyes trained like my pussy is the best thing he's ever seen.

I burn with a hunger that he's awakened and stoked. I stretch out in the sunlight, in my summer dress, and let West touch me like I'm a goddess.

He slides a finger inside me, and a bumblebee ambles past my half-closed eyes. I'm breathing heavily. That used to be something I thought about, used to be an insecurity when we started this, but he blazes away all those thoughts.

"You're so fucking sweet. And you're tight. Even with our practice."

He settles between my legs, and then he's going down on me again, and I've gotten so used to this now, the way he uses his tongue like I'm the sweetest thing he's ever had. "I want to be inside you so bad," he says against my skin. "It's all I think about. It's what I *dream* about."

"West," I whisper. He's flicking his tongue back and forth, and it's so *fast,* how he's learned just what I like and what I need. I stretch out my left arm, find the fresh spring grass. "Don't stop."

He doesn't stop, doesn't relent, and the orgasm shudders

through me. Slow at first and then quick toward the end, my knees bent, feet braced against the picnic blanket.

I feel sun-drunk and heavy and aching. West finds the buttons on my sundress, and he undoes them, one by one, spreading the fabric out around me.

He looks like he's transfixed. Eyes roaming, like he doesn't know where to settle them. I'll never get enough of it.

The way he wants me, the way it makes me feel.

The way I ache and the way he's the only one I want to fill me.

"You told me you're not afraid of this. But I am." His hand goes into his back pocket, and he pulls out a foil packet. Has he been carrying that around all this time? "I'm terrified that if I have you once, sweetheart, I'm never going to stop craving this. Craving you. And whatever you've started here with these lessons… I won't be able to stop. Consequences be damned. I'll keep you."

The words are everything I've ever wanted to hear. I can't think around them. *Keep me.*

"Maybe I started out as your teacher, but you hold all the power now," he says.

"You brought a condom?" I reach for the buckle of his belt. We're outside. But we're on his property, beneath his apple trees, with the ocean glittering behind the trunks. There's nowhere else I want to do this.

He watches me pull his belt clean out of the loops. "I've been carrying one around since you first asked me to help you."

"You have?"

"I knew it was only a matter of time before I caved." His hand slides under my chin, tilts my face up. "I can't have you regret this. Regret any of it. As much as it would kill me not to be your first, not to be inside you, it would damn me to hell to be something you later regret."

"I won't regret this." I work his zipper down. "You have to trust me."

He's already hard, granite in my hand, and he groans at my touch. I run my thumb over his damp head.

"I want my first time to be without a condom. I'm on birth control. Have been for years, and, well… you know I haven't been with anyone else."

In the weeks since the first lesson, since he asked me all those questions, I've thought about it. Touched myself to the thought of it.

"Fucking hell." West takes a deep breath, like he's collecting himself. "Do you remember what I told you? All those weeks ago?"

"To always put a man through his paces."

"That's right." His hips tilt forward, and his cock twitches in my hand. Eager, hard. Big. There's no way it'll all fit, and I can't wait to try. "What else did I say?"

"To ask for proof before I let a man come inside me," I say. "Well, Calloway? Where's your proof?"

"I had my yearly health check-up two months before you came to New York. Haven't been with anyone but you since," he says. "I can show you the paperwork."

"That's awesome."

He tuts and strokes a reverent finger down the length of my pussy. "You should look at the paperwork. Men will say anything, do anything to get the privilege of being inside you."

"Except you."

"Especially me," he mutters. He kisses me, his body braced above mine. The linen of his shirt is just a bit scratchy against my bare stomach, and the slide of his erection against my inner thigh is everything. I'm wet. I can feel it, embarrassingly, disastrously, dripping down my leg. "This shouldn't hurt. We've practiced, warmed you up. If it does hurt, even a little, you tell me."

"I'll tell you."

"Good girl." West slides a strong arm beneath me, and then he's rolling us over. He settles me over him.

"I don't know how to be on top," I say, like there's *any* position I'm good at. I've never tried a single one. But I thought he would be the one to handle it.

"I know, sweetheart. But you control the pace this way." He reaches down and grips himself. He looks so big from this angle, and even though I've craved it, wanted it, a tendril of nerves snakes through me.

West drags the thick head along my folds, and we both stop breathing. Watch him do it, coating himself, and it's several agonizing seconds before he notches himself at my entrance.

I brace my hands against his chest, feel the burn in my thighs. "That's it," he grinds out, hand gripping the base of his cock. "Sink down on me."

It's impossible at first. A puzzle piece that won't fit. His head is broader than the vibrator, and it won't work. We've tried so hard, and it won't work. But then he changes the angle slightly, and something suddenly gives.

I slide down an inch.

The stretch burns faintly, like the toy, like his fingers.

"You're doing so well. Breathe for me." His praise sends a rush of heat through me, and I push down another inch. And then another. The stretch grows almost uncomfortable, but I—

West's hands turn into an iron grip on my hips. "Slow down, baby." He looks at where we're joined. He drags his wet thumb over my clit in hard circles. "Be a good girl and just breathe for me. Can you do that?"

My knees grind down into the blanket, my fingers relaxing the grip on his linen shirt. And I slide down another inch. And then another, until I can feel the metal of his zipper against the curve of my ass.

"That's it... Look at that. You're taking all of me."

I draw another shaky breath. The fullness inside is strange, all-consuming, thought-ending. I feel stretched full. It's not entirely comfortable, but it's not bad, either, and there's a low ache pooling in my stomach.

He brushes over my clit again. "Look at your pretty pussy," he mutters, "stretched around me. How does it feel?"

"I feel full," I say.

"Keep breathing."

I stay still, feeling, settling. Under the bright spring sunshine, I can see every taut line of his body beneath mine. How his muscles tense and how his eyes are locked on my body. It's a kind of power I've never known.

I think of the woman I saw at the Paradise Lost party, who was riding her partner on the chaise. Her confident hips, her bouncing breasts. How he watched her with adoration.

West is looking at me like that.

I'm sitting perfectly still, and he's still looking at me like that.

"Faster," I say, and West's thumb speeds up against my clit. The stretching burn turns into nothingness, and then into sweetness. I rise onto my knees and sink back down again.

"Oh." I do it again and again. His hands grip my hips, helping my rhythm. I brace my hands against his chest, and the petal of an apple blossom dances past me. It lands in his brown hair. "West, we're having sex."

A glorious smile spreads over his face. "Yes, we are. And you're doing so well."

I tilt my hips a little, and it's not easy, the burn in my thighs from riding him like this. Of all the positions I've fantasized about, it's never been this. Never *like* this. It was some alternate version of me, some future perfect vision of me, who was never awkward, never unsure. But here I am, having sex, and it's still just me. And it's West. And it's us.

It's so much better for it.

He talks me through it, returns his wet thumb to my clit

until I'm overwhelmed and too hot and every nerve ending is on edge. "West," I beg, sliding back down to take him in to the hilt. "I want… can you…"

"I can." He sits up and wraps his arms around my waist. "Hold on. Okay?" He turns us over on the picnic blanket, still inside me. The angle is different now. The sunlight falls through the blossoms and turns his brown hair alight. Gilding him above him.

My knees fall open, and he's there, between them, inside me. He thrusts slowly, and I didn't know it would feel like that. That I'd feel him so deep inside. Maybe I whisper the words against him, because he pauses, forehead against my neck.

"What's wrong?"

"Nothing." His voice is strained. "Just can't end too soon."

"Why—oh."

"Yes. *Oh.* You feel too good."

"I'm sorry?" It comes out half whispered, and West groans into my skin. "That was a joke. I'm not really sorry."

"Neither am I," he mutters, and starts to move again, hands braced on either side of me. I look from him down between our bodies, at where he's disappearing inside me.

Oh.

West's movements are methodical, precise, but he's holding on by a thread. He grips my knee and pulls it up to his hips. "Wrap your legs around me, sweetheart. Yes. Just like that… So good."

I want him to feel as undone as I do. Like he's made me feel over, and over, and over again. With his fingers and toys and tongue. "Don't hold back." I run my nails along his back. "I want it all."

There's a brief second where I can tell that he teeters on the edge, and then he falls, his hips speeding up. He mutters dirty things into my skin, about how good I feel, how he's never going to last, how he *knew* I was going to be perfect.

I soak it all up like sunlight.

There's something so honest about it, about being consumed by his want. He was right. This is about trust. It's always been about trust.

Everything we've been doing has led us here.

He groans that he's not going to last and I tell him I don't want him to, and then his hips stutter against mine, and he's fracturing.

He groans like his soul is tearing in two.

I was full before. Now I feel like I'm overflowing, and he's a heavy weight on top of me, warm and big and *everywhere*.

I squeeze my eyes tight, like it will keep the moment from ending.

We lie there for a long time. He might be my new favorite blanket.

"That was…" He pushes up on an elbow, and there's wonder on his expression. "Fuck. I went hard there at the end. I'm sorry."

"Don't be. I wanted you to." I brush back hair that falls over his forehead and smile at him, and somehow, I feel shy and perfectly at ease at the same time.

His own lips curve. "Yeah?"

"Mhm."

He shifts to his side and pulls out of me. I wince at the sudden emptiness, and he catches it, like he catches everything. "Are you sore?" He looks between my legs, and I laugh, pushing my knees together.

"West," I protest.

His hand is there, brushing my thighs apart. "Lie still and let me look."

"It's embarrassing."

"No, it's not. I'm the one who left a mark there."

I let him spread my legs apart, and for a few long moments he just watches me, a serious expression on his face.

And then he groans. He falls forward, head against my knee, like a tree felled.

"What's wrong?"

"Nothing's wrong," he mumbles. "Everything's right. *Too* right."

"What does that mean?"

"It means I'm dangerously obsessed with you." He reaches for the edge of the blanket and checks that it's clean before folding it up and using it to gently wipe between my legs. I'm swollen and a bit sore, and he gives me an apologetic look. "Hope you didn't like this blanket."

"It'll survive a wash."

"You didn't bleed." There's something deeply pleased about his voice, and I think of his mouth on me, of my orgasms, his fingers stretching me out.

His words are like a warm, tight grip around my heart. *I'm dangerously obsessed with you.* And *don't move out* and *I've dreamed about this* and maybe, maybe…

"This should have happened in a bed," he says. He zips himself up, and then he's fitting my panties back around my ankles, pulling them up my legs.

"Probably," I say. "I think I saw one of your gardeners over there."

West's hands stop at my hips. "*What*? They're fired."

I laugh and reach to push against his chest. "I'm joking."

"Don't." But his voice has no bite, and one by one, he does up the buttons of my sundress. Afterward, he stretches out beside me and pulls me against him, and I ask if he has to work or if he can stay.

"Yes," he says, and I know he means both. "So? What did you think?"

"About having sex?"

"Mhm."

"It was okay," I say, and he groans into my hair.

"*Nora.*"

I giggle and sling my leg over his. "You once told me you didn't have a fragile ego!"

"I lied."

"I suspected." I kiss the skin exposed by the open V of his button-down. "I liked it. A lot, a lot."

He wraps his arms around me. His heart is beating steadily beneath my ear, and he's warm, too, and above us, the blossoms fall gently in the breeze.

He was wrong, before. But he was also right. Because in the end, I did do it with someone I love.

WEST & JAMES

WEST

I know you won't want to talk about it. But I'm drowning, man.

JAMES

So it's not just a casual thing?

WEST

I don't think it ever was. Not for me. And there's no way it can work out.

JAMES

I'm sorry. I know it doesn't help. Never does. But for what it's worth…

WEST

Appreciate it. Getting my will in order too. Rafe is going to murder me if this ever comes out.

JAMES

He might.

WEST

This would never happen to you.

JAMES

No. It wouldn't. What will you do about getting married?

WEST

I can't if it's not to her.

JAMES

Would she marry you?

WEST

No. Even if she would, I could never ask that of her.

JAMES

So you'll lose Fairhaven.

WEST

I don't see another way.

CHAPTER 53
WEST

She consumes me.

Her taste, her touch, her smiles. It's all I think about in the days leading up to the Calloway Spring Ball and Rafe's arrival. The party itself is a yearly tradition, has been for almost a century. A necessary evil.

A place to see and be seen.

Nora sleeps in my bed now. The cat even jumped up to join her one night, nose in her face, and I woke up to her giggling beside me at his whiskered sniffing. Darcy, she decided, after the hero of *Pride and Prejudice*.

He was just as hard to charm, she told me, with a cat purring beside her. *Proud and loyal. And he's a library cat!*

Fairhaven becomes a hub of activity again, preparations for the ball filling all rooms on the bottom floor, and all I can think is that I can't let Nora go.

After Rafe comes and we solve this whole thing with Wilde, clear the threat against her, I'll ask her about it. If she'll stay. If she'll go on another date.

A real one this time.

The night of the party, I go to find her before the guests arrive. She's not in her rooms. She's not in her atelier on the top floor, either, or downstairs alongside the bustling preparations. I find her in the conservatory instead.

She's flanked by two large palm trees, looking out over the ocean. Her hair is dark down her back and she's in a glittering pink dress that flows down to kiss the marble floor.

She's fluid even while standing still, like she's just stepped out of the Atlantic and walked up my lawn. A mermaid, a mirage, a glittering illusion. Like she might disappear just as easily.

"Hi," I say. It's not *you kill me*, but it's close.

She turns. The dress hugs her tight before it drapes out past her knees. The fabric shimmers and sparkles in the dim lighting. Like she's dripping in it, caressed by it. "Hey," she says, and runs her hands down her hips. "What do you think? It's my showstopper dress for the fashion show. I wanted to give it a trial run."

I let my eyes linger over her bare arms and the silky hair that kisses her shoulders. "You know pink's my favorite color."

A matching flush races up her cheeks, and she laughs a little. "I don't know what to say when you tell me things like that."

"You don't have to say anything. It's the truth." I reach into the pocket of my suit jacket and grab the velvet box. "You're going to win that Fashion Showcase."

"Maybe, maybe not. But I'll be in front of the judges, and that's a win." Her eyes warm, looking me over. "You don't look too bad either. I love you in a suit."

I tilt her chin up and smooth my thumb over her full lower lip. "We have to fake it one more time. Can you do that for me?"

"Act deeply in love with you?" Her eyes are warm and teasing. "Yes, West. I can do that."

"I had something made for you." I open the box I'm holding. Inside is a delicate tennis bracelet studded with diamonds. She lifts it out with careful fingers. "Look on the inside."

She turns it over, and then her breath catches. "*Be a good girl and get angry*," she reads. "You had it engraved?"

"If you ever need a reminder. If I'm not around to tell you to stand up for yourself."

"West, this is…" She holds out her wrist. "Put it on me."

I fasten it and let my fingers linger over her soft skin. She's not wearing any rings, her nails painted pink, short, oval. I stroke my thumb over her knuckles. *Stay*, I think. *Stay with me.*

Don't go out into the wide world. Don't use your newfound skills on dating, on strange men, on relationships. The words are there on the tip of my tongue.

"Is Wilde coming tonight?" she asks.

I turn her hand, thread her fingers through mine. "He's invited. He's never gotten an invite before, and from what I've heard, he likes… being seen. But I don't know if he'll be brave enough to show."

She blinks a few times. "I'm not sure if I want to see him. To think that he has made my life hell for the last few months… and only to get to Rafe?"

I pull her closer, and she flows into me like water, her hands pressing against my chest. Holding her has become the easiest thing in the world. The most natural thing. "You don't have to confront him if you don't want to. But you should get the option."

"Rafe would hate it if I did," she says. Her fingers play with the bow tie at my neck, straightening it.

"He's allowed to hate it. He's not important here. You are." I kiss her forehead. "But you don't have to meet Wilde if you don't want to. We'll handle it for you."

CHAPTER 54
NORA

The Calloway Spring Ball has left Fairhaven transformed. There are hundreds of people here, mingling through the large rooms on the first floor and outside on the terrace overlooking the gardens and ocean.

It feels like the house has come alive.

Like the old and the modern blend, parties held here decade after decade, generation after generation.

My very first night at Fairhaven had been a fundraising party. I was frustrated then, scared and angry. I remember what that felt like, but it's like a faded memory, chipped and torn.

Now this place feels like home.

I join Amber and Cordelia on the terrace. It's a rare moment to catch West's mother alone, it seems, for she is always being pulled in different directions by guests.

"The Winthrops are here?" Amber asks. "I thought they were on the no-no list."

Cordelia lifts one shoulder in a shrug. "They were. But a decade is time enough to reflect on what they did."

"Which was what, exactly?" Amber says.

"I can't remember," Cordelia says. She puts a hand on my

shoulder, and the smile she gives me is a true one. "I really am so grateful that West has found you."

She asked me just half an hour ago if we were serious. And now I know why. She wants to see her son married so this, *all of this*, this magical place that's been in the same family for over a century, doesn't fall into ruin.

Faking it never bothered me before. It was full of lessons and exercises, and that made me feel safe. Safe to explore and to push boundaries with him, because there were no consequences. It was all a game.

But all games eventually come to an end.

"Me too." I'm giving her hope, but it's false hope.

"Have you seen your brother yet?" she asks. "I haven't seen Raphaël in over a year. It would be lovely to say hello."

"He had business in town earlier, but he's coming tonight."

"Is everything… set?" Amber asks carefully. They both know about the stalker, and it seems they've been informed about tonight too. There are guards everywhere. I've already seen Amos. He's a few feet away, doing his best to blend in with the red brick wall. Madison is stationed right alongside the edge of the terrace.

"He's on the guest list, but no one knows if he'll show," I say with a shrug.

"The asshole," Amber says.

"Amber," Cordelia chides, like her daughter isn't twenty-seven.

"You were thinking it."

There's a brief pause. "Yes, I was. I know Wilde and his brand well. They've been a success story. A local one. But I'm never buying another pair of Mather & Wilde loafers."

"I'll burn mine," Amber says, "in solidarity."

"Well, that's just wasteful," Cordelia says, and looks back out at the crowd.

I smile at both of them. My own mother was far more

dramatic when I told her that we had confirmation about who had hired an entire team to scare me. *You're going to kill me, you kids. One of these days*, she said, like it was either Rafe's fault or mine that the whole thing had happened.

Cordelia is pulled away, a queen surveying her kingdom. As soon as she's out of earshot, Amber looks at me over the rim of her champagne glass. Her strawberry blonde hair is piled high tonight. "How are things with you and my brother?"

I laugh a little. "Well…"

"That good? He's smiling more, you know." She tilts her glass to mine. "You're really good for him."

"We aren't… nothing is… it's complicated."

She shrugs. "I know all about complicated. Sometimes complicated is fun, until it's not. Can you simplify things?"

"Maybe. I would like that," I admit, and look back out at the beautifully clad people in the gardens. It's a warm spring night, and the sky is painted a beautiful pink by the approaching sunset. "I'm building up the courage to have a conversation."

"I know the feeling," she says.

"Speaking of…" I take a step closer. "I've been meaning to ask you, that night, at the Paradise Lost party. You were there. Right?"

Amber looks at me for a long moment. Her eyes, so like her brother's, are framed by dark lashes that contrast her fiery hair. "My brother can't find out."

"I won't tell him. I promise," I say. "But that was risky."

"I know. I didn't think he'd come." She takes a deep breath, and I remember what he told me, that it was *her* his former friend had once gotten involved with. That it was his house the party was at.

"Did you have fun?" she asks, and I recognize a deflection tactic when I see one.

"I did. That party was… exhilarating."

"Yeah, they tend to be," she says. "At least before they go completely off the rails. Oh, and here he is. Your brother."

Raphaël steps between us, tall and dark. He bends to kiss Amber on the cheek with the familiarity of someone who's basically family. "Amber. This party is beautiful, and so are you."

"And you say that to everyone," she says. "Hello, Rafe."

Rafe nudges me. "Hey."

"Hi."

"How are you holding up?"

I raise my glass of champagne. "I'm fantastic, thanks for asking. How are you? How were the meetings in town?"

"Met with my American legal team."

My hand tightens around the delicate glass. "You're still planning on taking over their company? The Wilde's?"

"Yes." His voice is smooth, but there's steel beneath it. "And after it's mine, I'm going to strip every Wilde from the board, the leadership, and positions of power. Before I tear their company apart and bury the brand."

"But they still have a significant stake. Right? Someone still has to sell to you."

"They will."

"Even after you confront Ben Wilde?"

"Yes." He says it like a vow. My brother has been single-minded for the last few years, focused on growing Maison Valmont bigger and stronger than our father left it. Wilde is one of the few companies that have resisted decades of Valmont's expansion in the luxury space.

Of course he won't give it up.

Even after this.

"Not everyone at that company is involved in stalking me," I tell him. "Some of them are normal people."

Rafe lifts an eyebrow. "Are you asking me to show them mercy?"

"I know better than that." And really, I shouldn't be

surprised that what *I* think regarding this situation doesn't matter, despite it being *me* Wilde targeted to get Rafe off balance.

His eyes fall to my wrist. "You bought something new?"

I look down at my bracelet, with its engraved words resting against my skin. I've never gotten angry at Rafe. Even when he's made decisions about my life.

"Yes," I say. "It's new."

"It's pretty." He looks back out over the crowd. "Now let's see if Wilde shows…"

"He won't." The words are West's. His hand comes to rest at the small of my back, and his shoulder brushes mine, and it's like I can take a full breath again. Like order is restored. "He's been spotted at a restaurant in the city."

"Maybe he knows he's been caught," I say.

Rafe shakes his head. "Not likely."

"He might," West agrees, like my brother hasn't spoken. His eyes drop to my bracelet. "If one of his hired guns has turned on him. Or he doesn't want to overplay his hand. As my girlfriend, he knows you'll be here."

My lips curve. "You think he can't face me?"

"I think he might struggle to, yes."

Rafe looks between us and at West's arm around my waist. There are people everywhere. Eyes that follow, eyes that track. It's all a façade. My brother knows that.

And yet, when Amber puts a hand on his arm and asks him if he doesn't think West and I make a beautiful couple, his answer is tense. "Yes," he says, eyes on West's arm. "They do."

Invitations to the party are coveted, and now that they're here, everyone wants to talk to West. "Don't leave me," he mutters in my ear between polite conversations. "I might die if you do."

I laugh. "Are you addicted to me?"

"Yes. Dangerously so." His hand finds mine and locks our fingers together.

"Good thing I'm still your fake girlfriend in public, then," I say. "Would your mom have invited a dozen single women otherwise?"

West pulls me closer, like he's about to press his lips to my temple like he usually does. But he stops himself at the last minute. We're only supposed to be pretending, and my brother is here. "Yeah, don't look *too* in love with me, Calloway."

"I'm trying my best," he says, and something flutters in my chest. *We need to talk,* I think. *I need to tell him how I feel.*

There's another low, incessant ringing from my bag. I open it, and what I see doesn't surprise me.

West mutters, "Again?"

"It's her sixth call in the last hour. Maybe I should just answer it," I say. "When Mom gets something in her head like this, she's not gonna stop."

"You've already texted her and said you're unavailable."

"Yes, but you know how she gets."

He looks over his shoulder at the guests standing only a short distance away. Two of them have already tried to get our attention twice. "Okay," he says. "Come. Let's end this."

He takes my hand and pulls me into the house, down through the east wing. He finds the door to the library and pulls it open. The large room is dark and quiet, and we pause just inside the door.

"Answer it this time," West says, "and tell her off."

I look down at my phone. "I'm not sure if I can do that."

"You can," he says. "We've been practicing. Of course you can. I'm right here."

I take a deep breath and answer the phone. Mom's frantic voice is on the other end. "*Finally*," she says. "I was getting so worried."

"There was no need to worry," I tell her, my gaze on West. "I texted you just twenty minutes ago that I was perfectly fine."

"Yes, but Rafe told me that he was handling the man who hired those guys to intimidate you, maybe tonight? And you might be there too?"

There are birds chirping in the background. It's no surprise she's already awake. She's in her new phase of getting up really early and going for long walks. I wonder how long it'll last.

"He isn't going to show," I say. "Even if he did, I'm surrounded by security. Rafe shouldn't've... I'm fine, Mom. I'm fine."

She sighs on the other end. It's one of those resigned, dramatic sighs I've heard my entire life. It means I've done something wrong. It means she's about to lay her emotions on me.

It's my job to fix them. My job is to please her.

"I feel like we never talk anymore, Nora. We used to talk almost daily, and now..." Another sigh. Shorter this time. "With you being off in America... how long will you be there? I didn't even know about tonight until my son told me."

"At least until the Fashion Showcase," I say, and meet West's whiskey eyes.

"I liked it so much when you were in Paris. London was okay too, but—"

"Mom," I say, exhaling. "We have a six-hour time difference. It's not huge."

"It's significant," she says. "I can feel it, physically feel how far you are from me." She sighs again. "I'm out here on my walk, and I thought it would be nice to talk to my daughter. Is that so wrong?"

West's hand finds my waist again. His face is uncompromising. "You have a life," he mouths.

I keep my voice light. "It's lovely that you want to talk to me, Mom, but I can't always chat when it suits you. As I said in my text, I'm not available right now."

"I know," she says, "but I figured I'd keep trying anyway."

In front of me, West's face tightens. Of course he can hear. My mom speaks loudly.

"Boundaries," he says. And this time, he's not bothering to keep his voice low.

She's going to get upset.

But maybe that's not the end of the world.

Maybe I can live with being uncomfortable for a moment if it grants me long-term peace.

"Calling me eight times in a row doesn't increase the chance that I'll pick up. If it's an emergency, that's different. But this wasn't an emergency," I say.

"Nora." She imbues my name with enough censure that it would have caused me to reverse course years ago. Like I'm twelve again, telling her about the movie I want to watch. The sport I want to try. The girl being mean to me at school. *Nora,* she'd say, and I'd know it was time to stop talking.

West is steady, and I lean into his touch like I can steal some of that confidence. "I mean it. I won't be able to talk all the time, and that's okay. I still love you. We're still close. I'm at a party that I really want to go back to. Enjoy your walk, okay? Next time I'll call you."

There's the briefest of pauses on the other end. No sigh this time. Just my mother's brisk voice. "Noted. Have fun."

"You too."

I hang up. The silence is deafening, broken only by my quick exhale. "Oh my god."

"You did so well." West leans in closer, brushing his lips at my temple like he's been dying to for the past hour. "How did that feel?"

"Not as hard as I thought it would. Terrifying. Exhilarating." It's such a small thing in the grand scheme. I've modeled in lingerie, walked catwalks, presented my designs to my peers at fashion school. And yet, this cuts me to the core.

"Standing up to your family is going to change everything for you." His lips move down to my cheek. Hot, quick kisses that tell me just how proud he is of me for it.

I grip his lapels, and surprised laughter bubbles out of me. "I don't think I've ever said no to her like that before."

"My brave, beautiful girl." He kisses me fully then, lips against mine, and I melt into the warmth of it. The approval he gives me. Maybe I'm exchanging one form of people-pleasing for another, and maybe I shouldn't crave his compliments as much as I do, but maybe I don't care about *should*s anymore. Maybe my own opinion is the only one that matters.

And with him, I'm allowed to just be me.

"Not a pretty little liar anymore, am I?" I smile and step out of his arms. Our hands are still connected. "I'm going to leave first. Come find me."

"Always, trouble."

CHAPTER 55
WEST

The door shuts behind her, and I can't wait. I'm already walking to open it again. "What," a low, furious voice behind me says, "was *that*?"

Someone is sitting in the armchair in the corner, by the pool table. Half hidden in shadows. I hadn't seen him, hadn't thought anyone would be in here.

This room is off-limits for the ball. But of course he would know his way around. "Rafe?"

He walks past the pool table and into the dim light of the room. "You're…" He shakes his head. "The two of you? It's not fake?"

I spread my arms out, hands wide. "I didn't want you to find out like that."

"No? How did you want me to find out?" He reaches up to undo the bow tie at his neck. "Were you two planning to sit me down and tell me you're a couple and ask me to be happy for you?"

I can't say yes. I can't say anything, and my hands fist at my sides.

"Exactly," Rafe spits. "I know you won't do relationships,

and she was under your protection. I asked you for a favor, and this is how you repay me? How you repay *her*?"

"I'm not playing with her."

"The fuck you're not." The anger pours off him in waves and out through the library. "Is this about the estate? Is my sister your backup plan?"

"Fucking hell, no. Absolutely not."

"You're too strategic not to have thought about it." Rafe takes a step closer. "Get her to like you, trust you... then tell her you needed a favor in case your lawyers can't solve it. She'll help you keep Fairhaven *and* your reputation."

"Rafe, that was never the plan. Never."

"You forget that I know you." He turns from me, his shoulders heaving. "How long?"

"Don't—"

"How long?" he grits out.

"When we started pretending in public, we also started... in private."

No sisters is one of the oldest rules we have. It was one of the first things we said, sitting in the common room at Belmont Academy, looking around and realizing the five of us could be the brothers none of us ever had. We've lost Hadrian, but the four of us have stayed true.

Until now. Here I am, over a decade later, and I've fractured it.

The punch comes faster than I can dodge. I wouldn't if I could. He has every right to it. His fist hits me across the cheekbone, and pain blooms. He's always been a damn good fighter. Polished by day and unbound by night, if he still frequents the rings.

"How could you?" His voice is ragged. "You took her in, you promised to keep her safe... She's far too good for you."

"I know that," I tell him. All too well.

"When I found out you brought her to one of Viv's poker

games, I wondered if you'd lost your mind. Now I know you have."

I narrow my eyes at him. "She's her own person. You treat her like something delicate, something to look after. And she is, for fuck's sake, of course she is. But she's also strong, and fierce, and you didn't even make sure she knew basic self-defense! She was being stalked for *months* before she came here to me, and you hadn't taught her how to protect herself."

"Because she will never have to." He shoves me, hands against my chest. "That's what we're for. That's what the security teams are for. I will *always* protect her."

"But what about how she feels? Don't you think she'd sleep better at night knowing she has skills of her own? She's been terrified, and she's been too scared to tell you."

Rafe shakes his head. "I don't want to hear how well you *think* you know my sister. Don't mention her sleeping habits again."

"Then punch me again," I say. "We've fought before. Give me your worst."

His shoulders rise. "You don't know her better than me, and you don't know what you're asking for, West."

"Sure I don't." I lift my chin, giving him my uninjured side. "You and your mother have put so much pressure on her to be perfect all the time that she doesn't even let herself be real around either of you."

The punch lands hard, and I take a step back from the pressure. "Do not talk about her," he tells me. There's nothing of the Raphaël he presents as in front of me now. His bow tie is undone, and there's glittering rage in his green eyes. "She is not yours."

"She's not yours, either. She's hers." I shove him away. "Ask *her* what she wants."

"Right, because she's been the one to set the tone between you, has she? I do know her. She doesn't date. She's not interested in relationships, and you have plenty of experience."

"You have no idea," I tell him, "what you're talking about."

"And I don't want to." He walks to the drink cart and grabs the crystal decanter of whiskey by its neck. He raises it toward me, a finger pointed. "Don't call me. Don't call her. Stay the fuck away from my family."

"I can't promise that," I tell him. "It's up to her, man."

The look of betrayed anger on his face sears me to the core. But I won't lie to him anymore. He isn't the arbiter of Nora's fate, and neither am I.

Only she is.

CHAPTER 56
NORA

He doesn't come to find me.

I walk through the rooms of Fairhaven to find him. Past dancing couples in the grand room, the champagne tower in the conservatory, and the busy terrace. He's nowhere to be seen.

Because he doesn't want to be seen.

Maybe... I slip out of my heels to walk barefoot on dewy spring grass down through the gardens to the boathouse.

That's where I find him. Standing past the boathouse, he's silhouetted against the darkness, only a faint outline visible against the green light at the end of the dock. It's windier out here, the sound of waves softly beating against rock and pillar.

"West?" I ask. He turns, and the light reflects on the glass in his left hand. I can't make out his expression. Can't see his face properly. "What are you doing out here?"

"Thinking." He reaches for me, and I let him pull me in. He's warm despite the late-night winds. Somehow he always is.

"My brother left. I saw him get into a car." I search the

edge of West's jaw. He won't meet my eyes. "I thought he was staying here."

"Change of plans."

"He's not going after Ben Wilde, is he?"

"He better not be. Not without me." He's tense beneath my hands, and he's holding me like I'm a lifeline. A buoy.

"Are you okay?"

It takes him a long moment to answer, his lips by my hair. "Yes," he finally says. "I might be the only one who's okay in all of this."

"What happened?"

"Rafe knows about us."

My hands find the lapels of his tuxedo jacket. Grip them tight. "How? I thought we were careful…"

"He was in the library, in the corner. He saw us. Your mom calling… when I kissed you."

I blink up at West. Rafe knows. Rafe *knows.* "What does he know? Did you tell him… all of it?"

"That I deflowered his little sister on my back lawn?" West lifts his drink to his lips, and he knocks back over half. "No. I spared him the details."

"Give me some of that." I take the cold glass from his hands and lift it to my lips.

He watches me take a long sip. It burns, and I fight to hide the grimace. It's only when I blink a few times and focus on him again that I see the darkened bruise starting to spread under his eye.

"*What?*"

"It's nothing. It's—careful, trouble," he warns, but I'm already brushing my fingers over the bruise on his cheek. "Rafe *hit* you?"

"I let him," West says. "It was his right."

"Bullshit. That's *bullshit.*" I let my hand drop. "Why are you not putting ice on it?"

"I don't know if you've noticed, but my house is filled

with guests. I would rather not let anyone see me like this and start rumors."

I take his glass from him, and he doesn't flinch when I slowly lift it up and press it to the skin beneath his eye. It's not ice, but it's cold, and it's something. "I don't like having to patch you up."

"You don't have to. But for the record, *I* like it." His hands slide down, fit the span of my waist.

I give him a withering look. "Tell me you didn't goad him into it."

"Into hitting me? Your brother has a temper of his own."

"Yes, I know that. But I also know that you seem to love feeling guilty about this, when getting involved with you was *my* decision."

"Getting involved," he repeats. Out here in the darkness, he's achingly familiar and like a stranger, all at once. "Is that what we are, trouble? *Involved*?"

I focus on the way the light reflects off the crystal tumbler. "I would say so. Wouldn't you?"

"Yes," he says, and it's the best word I've ever heard. He's shown me over and over again that he wants me. He's never made me doubt it, not once, and that's why I feel brave enough to find the next words.

"Your mother asked me if we were serious again today." I cup my free hand to the side of his neck and feel the warm skin, the sharp stubble. "And I asked Amber about the marriage clause when I couldn't find you. She said your mother has a short list of women you can marry if we don't work out."

West has gone very still beneath my hands. "Doesn't surprise me."

"They're women in your circle. Probably some that you already know, through family connections or… or… college." I tap my finger against his neck, and if it wasn't for the night, he'd be able to see my heated skin. "You'll marry one of them, or a woman you find on your own, to keep Fairhaven."

His jaw works. I can feel it beneath the glass I'm pressing to his cheek. "You sound so sure," he says. "Is that what you want me to do?"

"You can't lose Fairhaven." This place, it's magic. And it needs to be protected.

"And that doesn't make you jealous?" He's watching me carefully. I'm safe on this dock, with water below our feet, but it would still be so easy to drown in him.

"Marry me," I say.

His breathing stops.

I haven't seen him shocked often. But he's shocked now, his eyes searching mine. He swallows hard and parts his lips. But no sound comes out.

"Marry me," I repeat, and lower the tumbler from his swelling bruise. "Why not? It would solve everything."

He takes a deep breath, like it takes effort to pull himself back together. "Your brother would—"

"He knows now. The pact, whatever thing you guys promised… it's done. You *did* deflower me in your backyard." I take a step forward, like this will be easier if my words have to travel through less space. "It's the obvious solution, West. We're already pretending to date in front of your family, friends, the entire world. I love… living here. Nothing would have to change. Marry *me*."

He's breathing fast and shallow, the muscles in his shoulders tense beneath my hands. "You don't mean that."

"I do. It would help you, wouldn't it?" I try to smile, but it comes out a bit crooked. He's reacting strongly, and I know him well enough to know that he's not used to it. He's not good at it. He's used to being in control, and right now he isn't.

Maybe he's never considered it before. Marrying me. Maybe he just needs some time.

"We could keep going with the... well. We can have more sex. You told me there's still so much to try. I want to try that. With you."

He rests his forehead against mine. The wind catches on my hair, and his hand slides up, fingers threading through it. "Your brother would never speak to me again."

"Leave him to me."

"You'd marry me?" His voice is hot and half broken. "You'd *marry* me."

"Yes. You'd get to keep the estate." I smile against his lips. *See how much I want this?* "But I want the cat. He's mine."

"You can have him. He doesn't like me anyway." West slides his hands down. "Hold on to me."

He lifts me up. The dock creaks under his quick steps into the salty darkness of the boathouse.

"I can walk," I protest. But I'm smiling widely, too, because he's cracking open, all of his want pouring out of him. I can feel it in his hands, his hot mouth against my temple.

He doesn't think it's a bad idea. He doesn't think it's a bad idea at all.

"You've been in heels all night," West says, and sets me down on a large coil of rope. "And I need you."

CHAPTER 57
WEST

She's offering me everything I've ever wanted.

I spend the night after the party reveling in it. Gauging myself in the pleasure of us, of her, of her thighs on either side of my face and her body stretched out in my bed. How unreal she feels around me and the nails she rakes down my back. And then her pleased smile after she comes and the soft sound of her breathing as she falls asleep in my arms.

But I wake up to the knowledge that I'm the one benefiting here. To a throbbing bruise beneath my eye and Fairhaven in post-party disarray.

Nora is still asleep, curled on her side, dark hair across the pillow that's become hers. I can't see her wake up. Can't handle the guilt that kept me awake for most of the night as I held her.

She's too good for me. Too good for all of this.

Rafe told me not to contact him and to stay away from his family. I didn't heed the second command, and in the car on the way to Calloway Holdings, I go against the first.

> Be angry at me. Don't be angry at your sister. She's innocent in all of this.

He won't respond. But it has to be said.

She values her relationship with her brother. She always has, and I'll be damned if I'm the reason it breaks down.

Maybe our friendship is over. More than a decade of having him as my own brother… Fuck.

But as long as it's not her. Whatever happens, she can't be the one who pays the price. I won't stand for it.

I use the gym at the office, sit in on meetings that have more than a few of my senior executives looking at me sideways. Coming in unannounced always has them nervous, and here I am, sitting silent, angry, and with a black eye.

Early in the afternoon, I walk into the jeweler. Unease makes it hard to focus on the diamonds under the counter. Harder still when the smarmy well-dressed woman assisting me asks me who the lucky woman is.

Lucky.

I'm the one who's lucky, and too much of a bastard to let Nora go. She offered marriage because it's what I need, not because she's ready for it. She hasn't even been in a relationship before.

Over and over again, she's said that she wants to learn how to date, to let guys in, to be in a relationship. To stop being afraid and one day find true love. Getting shackled to me wasn't on her list of goals.

But I've seen just how kind she is.

Kind enough to offer to marry a man she likes, a man she trusts, just to make his life easier. Kind enough to tell herself she might even like it. Might even be a nice, neat solution.

And I'm enough of a bastard to have accepted it when she offered because I want her that badly. Because I'm willing to have her, even without her love, even knowing that she offered just to do me a favor.

I tuck the pear-shaped engagement ring into my back pocket, but I don't give it to her when I see her that evening. I can't bring myself to.

Every time I see her, every time I hold her, it's torture. Knowing that she doesn't feel like I do.

Alex sends me a delivery a day later. It's a giant box of magnum condoms, along with a note that makes it clear he's spoken to Rafe.

I'm too young to become an uncle again. Magnum was generous of me, which I want noted. Happy for you. You took a risk with this. I approve. Burn this note after reading, though, and don't tell Rafe. I'm playing both sides here. You get it.

I do get it.

This could blow up so much more than just my relationship with Rafe. It could destroy the group.

The diamond ring stays in my pocket. And it burns. I feel like I'm drowning in the want of it. Of her beside me. Of the promise of a forever with her.

Of more nights, more days, of her sketching on the lawn and gripping my hand on flights and the small moments, us at dinner, her teasing, her smiles.

I want it so fucking much, and she's doing me a *favor.* I know her well enough to know that she puts other people's needs ahead of her own as easily as breathing. It's what she's always done. And I never wanted her to do it for me.

The guilt is acidic. It hurts.

At least there are things I can do for her. Things that need handling, and Ben Wilde is high on that list.

Rafe wanted to handle him quietly. That was never my strategy.

He's going to hate me for this, too, but he already hates me. What's one more reason if it's one that will keep Nora safe? Wilde needs to know that he's done playing this game.

That we're going to come after him with everything we've got and it's not going to be pretty.

My team has gotten intel that he's throwing a party in the Hamptons, so I spend the afternoon driving the surrounding streets. Scoping out the place. Scoring an invite shouldn't be difficult, but I don't want any trace of my name on the list.

I'm driving up a curved tree-lined street when my phone rings. It's not Nora. It's not Rafe.

I sigh but hit answer. "Hello, Mom."

She tells me about the thank-you cards she's been signing all morning from the Spring Ball and how the bartender wasn't up to par. I do my best to make it seem like I give a single fuck.

"Is there something I can help you with?" I ask.

"Can't I just call to chat with my son?" she asks. "But yes, there is. Nora. You've been dating for a while now, and you're only three months out from your thirtieth birthday."

"I'm aware."

"Have you asked her to marry you yet? I have a caterer on hold for the weekend before your birthday. I booked them over a year ago; they do fantastic roasted lamb."

I close my eyes. "Mom."

"Have the two of you discussed it? I may not live at Fairhaven anymore, but that doesn't mean I don't want it to remain yours. To be passed down to your kids. It can't be torn apart." She takes a deep breath. "I don't understand this, Weston. You've known about this for two years. What do you have against marriage?"

That makes me laugh. "What do I have against *marriage*?"

"Yes. Your father and I were together for almost three decades, and we had a wonderful time together."

There are days when I can nod at my mother's cultured delusions. Days where I play along with the narrative she prefers over the truth. Today is not one of those days. "You hated each other," I say. "*Wonderful* time? How many affairs did you have? How many affairs did Dad have? I could never keep count."

There's silence on the other end, and then her low, furious voice. "West."

"I suppose that was the point, though, with sending me off to Belmont. If I wasn't around, I couldn't keep track." My voice is cold. "What do I have against marriage? *Everything*."

"Your father and I loved each other."

"That's not what love looks like," I say, thinking of Nora sleeping in bed this morning. Of the furious, painful need inside me to protect her. Even from herself and her own people-pleasing.

Which should also mean from me.

"You don't know everything," she says.

"No, I suppose I don't. But from where I stand, can you blame me for not wanting a marriage like yours?" My words are cruel, but they're also true, and right now I don't have it in myself to be restrained.

"Why do you think your father and I married? He was just as much a subject to the clause of the trust as you were. But he decided to do it right, consider a lot of candidates. We arranged it all nicely." Her voice is far more aloof now. "Nora is a beautiful girl. You will make a lovely couple, and she clearly adores you. It's a great start."

My hand tightens around my phone. "That was all fake."

There's complete silence on the other end.

"We pretended. She was pretending every time you saw her."

My mother laughs. It shocks me enough that I have no response. "That girl is head over heels, West, and if you can't see that, then I can't help you," she says. "And the fact that you're hemming and hawing over the simplest, most strategic course of action tells me that maybe you are too."

"If I marry her, it will be for my own good," I tell my mother. "Not for hers."

"Marriage is compromise. Your father and I may have had our moments, but we understood that from day one." Her voice hardens. "The question is, do you?"

CHAPTER 58
NORA

West hasn't been himself since the night of the Spring Ball.

He's busy, and so am I, working from early in the morning until late to perfect the pieces for the Fashion Showcase. It's only days away. West used to be around, though. Popping by with a cup of tea for me or texting to suggest we grab dinner.

But now he's not around at all; not at the estate. Not in his office, not in the library. And when I see him, it's brief interactions, short conversations with a heaviness in his eyes.

He's here. He's holding me. His lips brush over my temple, and his kisses are still hot and hungry, but his whiskey eyes have shuttered.

Yesterday, I woke up to him sliding into my bed and turned toward his warmth instinctively. *Didn't mean to wake you,* he'd murmured into my hair, and pulled me to drape over him. He once told me he slept better if we were connected somehow. A hand on my waist, a leg intertwined.

None of that has changed. He still wants me, I know that, deep in my bones. Even if he hasn't brought up the marriage thing once since I said it.

"Where were you?" I asked.

"Worked late. Trying to map out Wilde's movements." He

sighed in what sounded like relief when I pressed close to him. "God, you feel good."

"Mmm." I was sleepy and annoyed at his absence, but too glad that he was back to protest. I fell asleep again, warm and happy and determined to talk more properly the next day, only to find him gone again when I woke.

So I stick to my usual routine. Go for a run with Sam and Madison, eat breakfast in the kitchen, perfect hems and stitches and folds.

Ignore my brother's calls.

He's called every day since the party. Twice the day after, three times yesterday. But on the third day, he sends me a text I can't ignore.

If you don't talk to me, I'm coming to pick you up this afternoon.

He answers on the first ring.

"Nora?"

"Yeah. Hey."

"Finally," he says. "Are you okay?"

"Yes, of course I am. Though West still has a black eye." My voice is calm, but I can't help myself. "Courtesy of *you*, I heard."

He switches over to French. It wouldn't surprise me if he's at work and doesn't want people to hear. "I'm getting you out of that house."

"No, you're not."

"Nora, I can't have you stay there."

"It's not your decision."

Rafe keeps going as if he hasn't heard me. "I'll send one of the drivers to pick you up by three p.m. You can stay in the New York apartment. His security team is good, but I can find one just as good. You won't have to worry about a thing."

"Rafe," I say, "you won't do anything."

There's a brief pause on the other end. "What?"

"I'm fine where I am. I don't need you to come save me because I'm not in need of saving." I play with the bracelet on my right wrist. I haven't taken it off since he gave it to me. *Be a good girl and get angry.*

"Nora," he says, his voice tight, like he's trying to rein in his temper. "I don't know what he's told you, but I don't want you to be taken advantage of."

"What makes you think I've been taken advantage of?" I ask. "You haven't asked me once how I feel about this. About West or dating him. You're just making demands. West hasn't done anything I didn't want."

"He hasn't told you about needing to be married to keep the estate."

"I know about that."

"Then you know he's going to marry someone else in a matter of months? Are you okay with that?" His voice sharpens. "Or he might be planning to ask you."

"He's your best friend, Rafe. He's not trying to trick me. If anything, he didn't *want* this to happen *because* of you. Do you know how big of an obstacle you have been? And I don't even understand why, because it's so stupid. You two are friends."

"He's strategic. He looks ahead, and he—"

"I asked *him* to marry me," I say.

There's total silence on the other end. One heartbeat, two... "What did he say?"

I don't want to share that with my brother. Not when we haven't spoken about it since it happened, not when uncertainty makes it hard to think. "We're working on it," I say instead.

Rafe takes a deep breath. "He said it's been going on for over a month. In Costa Rica, you two pretended to be... nothing but friends."

"Yes." My pulse is high. I don't like having this conversation. But I'm not going to run from it either. "Because he was scared of your reaction. And so was I."

Rafe's voice turns low. "I asked him to look after you. I trusted him, and he—"

"Did what? Made me happy?" I squeeze my eyes shut. "The only reason you're reacting like this is because you still see me as your little sister who needs protection. Not someone capable of making her own decisions. And you've felt this way about me for years. For as long as I can remember. After we lost Etienne, and you went to Belmont... It changed. We changed."

"That's not true."

"It's not?"

"You're my responsibility, Nora." Rafe's voice is tight. "Wilde wanted to target *me,* but he used you to do it. Do you know how angry that makes me? You were only made to feel afraid because of me."

"I'm not angry at you for that," I say.

"Well, I am. Enough for the both of us," he says. "And now West and you? *Marrying* him? You've been under so much stress these last months, and with your fashion show, too, and the stalker..."

I blink a few times and find that my vision shimmers. I always get teary-eyed when I'm angry, and I hate it. Traitorous tears. "Remember when you said the Fashion Showcase was silly?" I pause, swallowing the lump forming in my throat. "But I want to do this without your help. Because I'm genuinely good at it. Because I have talent and skill, and not because of our family resources."

"I've always thought you had skill."

The admission hits me harder than I expect. My throat tightens, and I say, "It's never felt like that."

"It hasn't?"

"Dad never allowed mistakes. Mom never allowed any

but her own. And you—you never made *any*. It made it so hard to try new things. To be okay with failure. To be okay with not living up to the person you all wanted me to be."

"Nora," my brother mutters on the other end. "You've never said any of this before. None of it is true."

I look up at the beautiful spring sky. "I like West. I like him a lot. Whatever happens, I won't regret it. Not a single thing that's happened between us. And you can either treat me like an adult and trust me when I say that... or you can ignore what I think so you can keep being mad at West because he broke the rule you all made back at Belmont."

"He told you about that? About... Amber?"

"Yes. Well, some of it. Rafe, you *punched* the man I'm dating instead of talking to me."

"He's my oldest friend." His voice sounds tired all of a sudden, and so much older than his twenty-nine. "I trusted him, and he hid this from me."

"I was the one who came on to him first," I say.

"*Sure*. He always watched you too closely," Rafe mutters.

There's nothing to say to that. I take a deep breath. "I don't like feeling like I'm disappointing you, but I'm not going to back down here. It's my life, and I can't live it on other people's terms."

He's quiet for a few long seconds. "So you don't want me to come pick you up?"

I laugh a little. "No, I'm fine where I am."

"Fairhaven is a beautiful house."

"It really is," I say. "And don't let this ruin your and West's relationship, okay? No one is in the wrong here."

"Maybe," he says, and I know it's the best I'm going to get.

"I'll talk to you later. Bye, Rafe."

"Bye," he says softly, and I hang up the phone.

It takes me a long time to relax after that. I sit by the ocean, next to the boathouse, and watch as the waves come in. A single sailing boat passes out on the open water, and I breathe in deep. Let the air fill me up. The clouds are rolling in, heavy and dark, and there's rain in the air. There's a spring storm coming in, and I breathe it all in.

I'm not the person I was when I came here.

And I'm not going to wait for West to open up to me. Not going to sit pretty in a corner and give him sweet smiles. I turn my bracelet around, feel the engraving against my skin.

I don't doubt that he wants me. That this is more than a convenient solution, that there's something real here. I see it, and I feel it, and I've never been more sure of anything.

But I'm going to have to force him to admit that. I'm going to have to get a bit angry. And I'm going to use the skills he's helped me hone.

When I call Amber, she answers on the fifth ring. "Have you recovered from the hangover from the party? Because I swear to god, it's taken me three full days."

"Just in time for another one," I say. "Want to go out tonight? I feel like dancing."

"Absolutely, I do. Let me guess. My brother?"

"He's frustrating me at the moment."

"He does that sometimes." I can hear the smile in her voice. "I'll come pick you up. Are we bringing your guards?"

"Yes."

"Be there at eight."

CHAPTER 59
WEST

I push open the double doors to Fairhaven. The rain has just begun. Warm, heavy droplets, but it's only going to get worse. It's a classic spring shower.

I need a change of clothes, and then I'm heading back to where Ben Wilde is having his party. Nora has said she doesn't want to confront him, and I don't want her anywhere near him, so it works perfectly for me.

Can't wait to see his smug face—

High, feminine laughter echoes from the sitting room. The click of heels follows, and my sister walks into the entryway. Nora follows close by, the two of them smiling.

Amber pauses when she sees me. "Uh-oh," she says, and looks down at her glass of wine. "This is absolutely *not* one of your fine vintages. I promise."

I can't look away from Nora. She's done something to darken her eyelids, making her eyes look luminous. Her hair is swept back messily and she's in a short skirt that leaves her legs mostly bare. Her top has long, draped sleeves, but there's a stripe of skin visible along her midriff.

"Where are you going?"

"Out," Amber says.

"To drink and dance." Nora's eyes land on mine, and she shrugs once. "Maybe flirt a bit. Who knows?"

"Flirt," I say.

"Yes, flirt." She tucks a bag under her arm. "We're bringing Sam and Amos too. I might even be able to get Amos to drink tonight."

"No, you won't. He won't."

She shrugs. "I won't tell if he doesn't."

I cross my arms over my chest. "What are you doing?"

"I think this is my cue." My sister gives Nora a wide smile and mouths *good luck* at me before stepping toward the front door. "I'll wait outside!"

The door shuts behind her, and it's just the two of us left in the large hallway. "What am I doing? I'm having fun," Nora says. "I'm going out. Want to come?"

"I can't."

Her lips thin. "I'm not surprised. You've been avoiding me for days."

"I haven't been avoiding you," I say. It's a fucking lie, but it's also the truth, because she's all I think about. I can't avoid her even if I wanted to.

And I don't.

She pulls a black card out of her bag. "Remember when you told me to spend more of your money?" She rises to press her lips to my cheek. "Thanks for tonight. Amber and I are going to buy the entire bar a round of drinks."

Before she can dip back down, I grip her waist. My fingers brush over the bare skin of her lower back. "I know what you're doing."

"Do you?"

"You're arguing with me."

There's a flash of fire in her eyes. "Yes. I am."

"What are you angry about?"

"You disappearing from me. Not *talking* to me." She brushes something off my shoulder. "If you want me to wear your ring, Calloway, you have to *propose.* And you have to actually be here."

I grip her left hand, run my thumb over the knuckle. *Stay here,* I want to say. But if I tell her what I want, what I *truly* want, I risk driving her away.

Or worse… see that lovely fake smile on her face when she's trying so hard to be nice. It would kill me if she ever aimed it at me.

"Go, then," I tell her. "As long as you know who you're coming home to."

"That depends." She walks toward the door, her heels clicking against the marble. "Will you be here when I come back?"

Always, I think. "Yes."

"See you later, then." She slips out the door, and I stand there for a long few minutes, fists clenching at my sides.

Jealousy and anger burn beneath my shirt, and I pull the first two buttons undone. At least there's something I can do for her tonight.

A situation that needs solving.

It takes less than an hour to drive back to Wilde's party. I park a ten-minute walk away. The party barely has any security at all. Just a single security guard by the door and a widely smiling man with a clipboard to check off guests.

The house behind it is empty. It's for sale, from what I saw earlier, and I walk through their garden to get to the garden of the event space. I shrug out of the jacket I threw on for the rain and hide it behind the fence. Sneak through the hedge…

And then I'm in.

No one notices me walking through the garden in the rain. There's no one on the terrace, anyway, despite it being covered. I move along the outside of the house, finding the back door. I pass by a waiter and turn the corner to find… there it is. The spiral staircase.

I've done my research on the venue.

The second floor is deserted. I find a small overlook cast in shadow, and beneath it the grand ballroom is on full, glittering display. Wilde didn't skimp on the invite list. He's turning sixty, and there's an open bar and a band playing.

I lean against the wall. A shadow moves beside me, and it shouldn't surprise me that he's here.

We think the same way.

"Found your way here?" Rafe's voice is low. Neither of us wants to be seen up here.

"For the same reason you did."

"I doubt that." He looks down at the mass of people below. I recognize a few of them. Others are strangers to me, but they're still here. At a party he's thrown, a man willing to terrify a young woman for the hope of *maybe* throwing the Montclairs off their game. They're all guilty by association.

I cross my arms over my chest. "You've been considering how to play your hand. Admit it."

Rafe blends into the wall. "I don't need to admit anything to you."

"You were thinking, just for a moment, how to spin this to your advantage." My hand tightens at my side. "Use it as a bargaining chip."

"You would too."

"Not when Nora is concerned."

"We've worked years on this deal." There is anger beneath his usually controlled voice. "That company will be mine. Sooner or later. And it won't be with that asshole at the helm. I want more than just a single night of embarrassment for him."

"We agree on that."

"I don't want him to ever work again."

"I don't want him to draw breath." My voice is flat, harsh. It's the ugly truth, and it's not something I will act on, but fuck if the anger I'm feeling doesn't make me see red. "But I will settle for ruining him."

He made Nora cry. He made her fear sleeping alone; he made her change where she lived, her habits, her *life*.

Don't have to wait long. He comes walking through the room, a smile on his face. Ben Wilde is in a dark navy suit and purple pocket-square, with his graying hair slicked back. He clasps hands, nods, takes pictures.

He still thinks it's his night.

Rafe and I have known each other for over a decade. He might hate me, but I know what he's thinking. Can hear it in the silence between us. "You came for her tonight."

"Yes. I want a shot at him."

"I want to talk to him." He's controlled again. He's pulled the dark threads back inside, like he's so good at. "Let him know I'm watching. I want him looking over his shoulder for months, not sure when the blow will come."

"Too mild."

"It's not your situation to handle."

I turn to him, and the anger that I've kept at bay boils to the surface. "She's spent months terrified and too afraid to talk to anyone about it, and I want him to pay. It's all for her."

Rafe's green eyes slide to mine. "And you think I don't? She's my little sister. My flesh and blood."

"I know that. Just like she's my…"

"Your what?" His lips thin. "Tell me, West. What is she to you? You've always made your stance on relationships crystal clear."

"She's everything," I say. "And you know how I *felt* about relationships. Not how I feel now."

"Is that what you are, then? A couple?"

My gaze tracks Wilde beneath us as he half hugs, half slaps another man on the back. The self-congratulation hanging in the air feels suffocating. Dark and oily. "We need to get him alone."

"You didn't answer me."

I turn to Rafe, and he's right there, eyes barely visible in the dim lighting. "I'm here to scare Wilde badly enough that he or any of his hired men won't set foot in the same *city* as Nora again. Will you help me? Because I'm not going to be subtle."

The offer hangs between us, stretches taut. I know I'm overstepping, but I can't step aside, not when she's involved. Not when I know she wants this handled too.

Rafe gives a tight nod. "Bribe the staff?"

"Yes. I'll do it. You're too recognizable."

"So are you."

"Yes, but you're the one who shouldn't be seen here." I glance back down and toward the open door to the far right. "There's a wine cellar at this venue. Looked private from the pictures."

"I saw it too. I'll make sure it's clear."

"Meet you there."

Ten minutes later, I've slipped one of the waiters a wad of bills to tell Wilde that there's a surprise waiting for him in the wine cellar. *If he asks, tell him it's organized by his wife.*

No one sees me when I walk down the flight of stairs to find Rafe already there. He's sitting by the barrel table in the middle of the cellar, surrounded by rows and rows of stacked bottles.

He's opened one and set three glasses on the table. "Figured we'd welcome our guest."

"Is there arsenic in his glass?"

"I was all out," he says. His voice is tight and calm, but there's murder in his eyes. It only takes a few minutes before heavy steps sound outside the door. I wait beside it, and as soon as Wilde wanders into the room, I close the door behind him.

He stops in the middle of the cellar.

"Good evening," Rafe says. He pushes a glass of red wine in Wilde's direction. "Let's have a birthday toast."

Ben is standing stock-still. Slowly, like a sudden movement might set Rafe off, he looks around the room. He clocks me and quickly looks back at the glass he's being offered. "What's the meaning of this?"

"It's a party." I don't try to hide the distaste in my voice. "Our invitations were lost in the mail, I'm guessing."

He takes a step forward, accepting the glass. It's a stilted movement. "Gentlemen…"

"Explain yourself," Rafe demands. His voice is almost friendly.

Almost.

"I don't know what you mean," Wilde says. "If you're here about our negotiations, that's for our lawyers to handle."

"Lawyers." Rafe takes a long sip of his wine and stretches his legs out. "Did you hear that, West?"

"I did, yes."

"As if there's anything legal about what you've been doing."

"I'm not doing—"

"You hired great people, Wilde. I'll give you that. But our people are better. And everyone leaves a trace." I walk around him, stopping a few feet away. "Nora Montclair."

He looks between us, but his face whitens. "I don't know—"

"Don't embarrass yourself with lies."

"Family is off-limits. Always has been, always will be." Rafe's voice is steel. "What was the plan? Split my attention, throw me off my game? Make this deal so time-consuming that I walked away?"

Wilde's face hardens. "We've never wanted to sell to Valmont. To you. This is business, gentlemen. You both know that. It was… a strategic move."

This smug son of a bitch. The anger that flows through me then is cold as ice, but it's a calculated move when I push him up against the barrels. "You threatened an innocent woman for a business deal." I use my forearm to keep him there and revel in the way his eyes widen. "She's had to look over her shoulder for *months* because of you. But for you? It'll be the rest of your life. I'm going to come for everything you have."

"It's business, Calloway," he wheezes. "The girl was never harmed. It was all just… pretend."

"No," I tell him. "Someone will be harmed."

And then I punch him.

We exit the party the same way I entered it. The rain has picked up. It's fresh and warm, and my fist aches. "Damn, that felt good."

"It did." Rafe glances sideways at me. "Did you have to punch him, though? Now we've left evidence."

"He won't do shit."

"You haven't punched anyone in over a decade."

"No. We can't all be you." I glance at him. Rafe doesn't often talk about it, the fighting he used to do at night. The underground rings where he'd work out his guilt and frustration. We'd all tried to get him to stop.

I don't know if he has.

"That was years ago," he says, so easily that I can't tell if he's lying or not. We're on a leafy side street, but we might as well be back at Belmont. The years have fallen away, suit jackets turning into uniforms, racing from the headmaster's residence with a stolen trophy in hand. "Fuck."

"You swearing? It's a bad night."

"It's a *good* night. It's a really fucking good night." He grins at me, and I grin back at him. "Nora will hate that you punched him."

"No she won't," I say. "She'll say that she does, but she'll secretly be thrilled."

"I hate that you know that."

"I know you do."

"She told me you spoke of marriage. So you're getting what you want in the end." His voice isn't judgmental, but it is resigned. "And you'll be my brother-in-law."

"She offered." Somewhere in the distance, a dog barks. The rain picks up, and it's seeping through the fabric of my jacket, slicking my hair to my head. "For what it's worth, I didn't want it to be your little sister. The woman I fell in love with. I tried very hard to make it not be her. For you."

A car passes us. It's the only one out in this weather.

"In love?" he asks.

I confess it to the night. "Yes. Love."

He blows out a breath and curses in French. I catch enough of it to get the gist.

"Yeah. I know."

"But she doesn't know?"

"She doesn't." I run a hand over my face. "So I can't let her marry me to do me a favor. I'll only marry her if she wants it as much as I do."

CHAPTER 60
NORA

It's only midnight when Amber and I get home. She wanders off in the direction of one of the guest rooms, yawning hugely and telling me, "We should do that again."

We found a bar nearby that had good music, people our age, beer and wine and not a fancy cocktail in sight. We danced and talked and were approached by two groups of guys. I talked to a few of them, and I didn't get too nervous.

But I don't want a single one of them.

And I don't want to go to sleep—not in his bed, not in my own. I'm too wound up, too irritated, too drunk and too angry at West. He swept into my life, gave me all these lessons, made me feel special, made me fall in love with him. And now? This silent, brooding act reminds me exactly of why he frustrated me so much years ago. His walls are back up, and I don't know how to bring them down again.

He's told me he doesn't like marriage, but ours wouldn't be like that. Doesn't he realize that? Unless… he's worried about being shackled to me. Maybe he likes me now, but he's never actually said it. Not quite like that.

Neither of us has.

That's how I find myself upstairs in the studio at nearly

one a.m., the lights on, while Darcy lies sprawled out on an old futon, watching me steam silk.

The fashion show is in two days. I've gone over everything, *everything*, but I'm too restless to relax.

The white corset dress might not be strong enough. It might need more flair, more color, or a better fit. I might not win. It might be a disaster.

And now he's out somewhere, and I don't even know where. I've never cared about a man like this before. For a long time I wasn't sure that I even could.

At least I have experience now. If I have to, I can find that strength with someone else. I'll have to do what I did tonight over and over—chat with men, desperately trying to find a sliver of interest to compete with the roaring feelings I have for West.

It'll be great. Fantastic. Wonderful.

That's when I hear the creak of a door and two sharp knocks.

The cat's ears perk up, and I glance toward the half-open studio door. "Hello?"

The door opens fully, and there's West. He's in the same clothes he wore when he left, but they're wet now. His jacket is discarded, and the sleeves of his shirt are rolled up to his forearms. His eyebrows are drawn low.

"There you are," he says.

My grip on the steamer tightens. "You were looking for me?"

"Yes," he says. "First in my bed, then in yours. But you weren't there."

"I'm not ready for sleep," I say. My voice doesn't waver. "Where have you been?"

"Out," he says.

"That's wonderfully descriptive."

He takes a step forward, and I watch as the cat's tail twitches in irritation.

"Rafe and I confronted Ben Wilde," he says. "You'll be left alone now."

"Oh… you went together?"

"It wasn't planned that way. But yes." His eyes move over the dresses and outfits I have hung on the rack, the two dress forms. "I told him that he's not allowed to be angry with you."

"Rafe?"

"Yes. If he needs to be angry at anyone, it should be me, not you. I can't ruin your relationship with your brother."

I turn the steamer off and set it down. "If anyone's going to be responsible for the breakdown in my relationship with my brother, it's going to be me," I say, "and my own actions."

West's jaw tightens. "I can't take things from you, Nora. I can't handle that—you making sacrifices."

"You don't take things from me," I say, "except these last few days. You've been… you've been like a different version of yourself, ever since we agreed to…" I can't say the word. It was something beautiful back then, an exciting idea—the prospect of being his wife.

Now it feels dirty, tainted by his reaction and by how he feels about marriage. Outside the windows, another bolt of lightning flashes over the ocean.

"I'm sorry." His voice is rough. "It wasn't fair of me. I've been struggling with all of it, and… Sweetheart. I can't let you marry me."

I look away to blink back the tears that threaten to choke me. "All right." My voice sounds thin. "It was just a suggestion. If you don't want to, you don't have to."

"Nora," he says.

I'm already up and out of the chair. "We can pretend we never spoke about it. It's fine. You'll find someone else, someone better suited, and I'll just move out. Thanks for taking care of the stalker." My arms wrap around my chest. "I appreciate that."

His face is pained, like he's the one being hurt. "No, it's not like that."

"Then what is it like?" I ask. "You've barely spoken to me the last few days. I thought we were—I thought..." My voice chokes up. "Damn you."

"Yes. Damn me." His hands are tense at his sides, like he wants to reach for me but can't bring himself to. "That's why I can't let you agree to this. Not when you'd be giving up so much."

"Giving up so much?"

"When you offered to marry me..." he says, illuminated by another sharp twinge of lightning outside the window. The thunder follows like clockwork. "Fuck, Nora, when you said you'd be my wife, I got it all. Do you realize that?"

The air between us feels charged. Electric. I take a step back, and my calves brush against the low futon I've been using to drape fabric over.

"I got every last thing I could ever ask for, and I've hated myself for agreeing." He takes a deep breath. "You offered because it would help me. You're kind and loyal and beautifully pragmatic, and I bet you think it's a great solution. Maybe you even tell yourself that it's what you want. But Nora, I'm the one who benefits. I'm the one who sacrifices nothing and gains everything. I get you *and* Fairhaven."

"West," I say. I sink backward into the futon. Above us, the roof of the manor patters with rain. "That's not true."

"It is. I've seen it, how you bend and smile and placate, and it would *kill* me to do that to you. That's what we've been trying to work against. And I can't..." He takes a ragged breath. "I cannot be the one you shackle yourself to and then start to resent. It doesn't matter how much I want it. I can't let you. Not when I know you're only marrying me to do me a favor."

It's hard to breathe. I shake my head, faster this time. "You didn't tell me all of this. You just pulled away from me. You left me all alone in this."

"I know." He sinks to his knees, bracing his hands on either side of me. "I'm sorry. I've been fighting with myself every day. Because I'm selfish, trouble. So damn selfish."

I blink away tears. "So you're pulling away to *help* me?"

"Nora." His voice is agonized. "You deserve more."

"More? But we… We used to talk before this. We used to… it felt like… was I imagining it, West?" My voice shakes. "You and me? That it felt like so much more than just…?"

"No. You haven't imagined anything. Nothing about this has been fake. Not for me." His face is level with mine. "I want you more than I've wanted anything. I want you here, forever. I want you as my wife. That's why, selfishly, it took me days to tell you this, because you've given me exactly what I want. You." He shakes his head slowly. "But I can't handle the thought of you marrying me just to help me out—that you're thinking of what I need and not what you want."

He bends forward and rests his forehead in my lap. It's a genuflection and an apology, his hands turning into fists beside my legs. One of them is bruised over the knuckles. Has he been fighting again? "I'm sorry for everything. Fuck, Nora, I…"

I run my hand over his hair. This is familiar, even when it feels like my insides are breaking. Shattering like the electricity outside the windows, breaking into a thousand tiny pieces.

Breaking open.

"What are you telling me?" I ask him. "That you want to marry me, but you can't, because it's not actually what I want?"

West pushes back up. There's fire in his eyes. "You can't marry me to make me happy. It has to be to make *you* happy."

"To make me happy," I repeat.

"Yes." He takes a ragged breath. "I love you. I know that

wasn't on your list of things to practice, but here it is. I love you. And it's torn me apart, knowing that all the practicing we were doing was for someone else. Someone in your future." His hands slide closer, gripping the outside of my thighs, like he can't resist. "I want to be your future. But I won't let you tie yourself to me unless you know what marriage would mean. Unless you know exactly how *not* fake I want it to be."

"You love me," I whisper.

"So much that it's breaking my heart, trouble." He smiles a little, but it's a pained expression. "And if you don't want this… then we don't get married. I can be your boyfriend. We can keep practicing dating if you want that. I'll be anything you want, I'll be your friend, as long as I can be in your life."

I can't look at him, but I can't look away. Can't think around the roaring in my head.

He loves me.

He wants me.

And he waited to tell me all of this.

I grip the collar of his rain-soaked shirt. "West," I tell him. "Why don't you trust me?"

His eyes widen. "I do. I trust you more than anyone."

"But you don't trust me to know what I want," I say. "I told you that I wanted to marry you."

"Yes. But not because it's what you craved." His hands slide up, come to grip my waist. His usual handhold. "I wanted to talk to you. I wanted to tell you all of this. But I was fucking terrified, sweetheart, that I'd see you use your techniques on me. I never want you to humor me."

"When have I ever humored you?" I hold up my right hand, and the bracelet still around my wrist. "You're the one person I can get angry with who won't walk away. You told me that."

"It's still true."

"Then I am angry with you."

"Good," he says. "That's good."

"You love me?" Something hot tracks down my cheek, and of course, I always cry when I'm frustrated or overwhelmed. Why would this be any different? "You want to marry me?"

"More than anything."

"Tell me. Tell me all the things you want," I order. He hesitates, glancing out the windows to the stormy night beyond. "It won't influence my answer. Trust me to be honest."

He looks back at me. "What I want, Nora," he says, his voice raw, "is for you to stay here forever. For you to be mine. For there to be no more faking between us—not ever. I want you on my arm. I want you wearing my ring. More than anything, I want you happy. I want to see you designing. I want to hear you say no a thousand more times. I want to make you come, and I want to watch you smile and laugh. I want to watch you charm everyone we meet. I want you in my bed. I want you in my office. I want you by my side." The words hang in the air, making it hard to breathe. "It's terrifying, I know. It terrified me. Marriage has always been something to be avoided. I've seen the way my parents did it, the punishments, the secrets, the games... if you give someone the key, they will wreck you. But you already have the key, sweetheart. And you're welcome to wreck me as long as it means you'll stay."

He shakes his head, his voice dropping. "I'm scared of what you'll say now because... you love making people happy." He pauses, closing his eyes for a moment before opening them again. They're glazed. "But I still want your honesty, now more than ever. Even if it destroys me."

The crack inside me feels wide open, a gaping chasm, and the only way through is to dive in. To give him the same honesty that he's given me.

"I'll be honest. And you have to trust me when I tell you what I want this time, okay? You're the one who helped teach me how to do it." I take a deep breath. "For years, I've wanted love. I wanted to *want* someone, but it never happened. I kept everyone at arm's length." My hand around his collar softens, slides up to his neck. "And now you tell me you love me."

"I do," he says, "but you don't have to say it back unless you mean it."

"So little faith you have in me." But I'm smiling a little, another tear rolling down my cheek. His eyes track it. "West, do you know why I suggested we marry?"

He doesn't seem to be breathing. He's still on his knees, arms braced on either side of me.

"Because I didn't want this to end. Because I didn't want to leave you," I say. "You've made me feel safe and wanted and supported. You made it effortless for me to be myself with you. You've made it so easy to love you. Every step of the way, you've made me feel more things than I ever thought I could. I love you too. Of course I do."

There's no reaction in him. Nothing apart from the quick uptick in his pulse, pounding beneath my fingers on his neck.

"West," I murmur.

His eyes are incredulous. "You love me?"

"Yes." I smile at him, a bit shy. "This is what it feels like, right? Like I've been given an extra dose of energy, of self-confidence, of happiness. Like I can't focus, can't think when you're not around. Like you're my favorite person in the world. The person I can be myself with."

"I think so." He's smiling now, and rain continues to pour down outside, but in here, it's blazing summer. "That's how it feels for me. Like you've become the center of my universe."

"You haven't…?"

"Before you? No."

"I guess you can't teach me this, then." My nails scrape gently over the back of his neck, his hair tickling my fingers. "We'll have to figure it out together."

He leans in and kisses me. It's soft and warm, and the crack that yawned open inside me fills up with him.

"As long as you want me, I'm yours." He kisses my cheek, my nose. Rests his forehead against mine. "We don't need to get married. I'll be your boyfriend."

"You can't lose Fairhaven."

"Don't marry me because you think there's a sword over my head. The estate doesn't matter. I'll lose it before I lose you." His hands tighten around my waist. "I won't let you go."

"I won't *let* you lose it," I tell him. "I won't let you lose anything. We're a team, you and me. We love each other." My voice falters at the end, at the words being put out into the universe. At a truth so recently acknowledged being spoken aloud.

"Things should happen at your pace. When you're comfortable," he says. "If we do this… you'd marry me at the end of the summer."

"Yeah. I've done the math." My lips widen into a smile. "I'd do anything for you, West."

He shakes his head slowly. "But I'd never ask you to do a damn thing for me."

"I know. That's why I would."

"Be selfish, Nora. Please."

I tighten my hands behind his neck. "But I am, West. This is crazy and wild, and I want it. Trust me to make my own decisions. That's what I want, in every area of my life. Including this one. I want to be your wife."

"You mean that." His low voice vibrates with emotion, and his hands pull me forward, off the futon and into his waiting grip. I land in his lap, legs on either side of his kneeling form. "You really mean that."

"I really, really do."

"I don't deserve you, my brave, pretty girl." He presses kisses to my temple, my cheek, and something feels like it

461

bursts inside me with warmth. "But I'll always try to. I promise that."

"I promise to be honest with you. And to get angry at you when I need to."

"That's my girl." He kisses me slowly, sweetly. Heat runs through my veins and drowns out the sound of the storm raging around us.

I lift my lips from his and press a finger to them when he tries to close the distance again. "But Calloway, you still have to propose."

Beneath my finger, his mouth spreads into a wide grin. "Oh, I will."

CHAPTER 61
WEST

The storm passes during the night, sweeps past the house and moves farther inland, but I don't notice until it's nearly dawn. Nora's running her fingers over my bare back, lying half beneath me, bodies languid and heavy with near-sleep and pleasure.

She woke me up by burrowing into me, and one thing led to the other until I was inside her with her toy tucked against her clit.

"That rain," she murmurs, "probably destroyed the last of the apple blossoms."

"Mhm."

Her fingers move over my skin like I'm her cat. "It's almost morning."

"Doesn't matter. We're not leaving this bed."

Her voice is sleepy. "You probably have work to do too."

"I'll cancel it."

"All of it?"

I smile into her shoulder. "For you? Of course."

She laughs a little. "You're going to spoil me."

"Good." I shift closer, press my lips down to her warm neck. We've barely moved since we had sex, not even to clean up the mess between us. "I know you've got a big day, though."

"Yeah. I've given the collection everything I have, and now I just have to hope it'll be enough."

"It will be."

"You don't know that."

"I do. Your best will always be good enough."

I kiss her collarbone, and she relaxes under my touch, her nails raking lightly down my back.

"I'm excited but nervous," she says. "For a long time, those two emotions didn't belong together in my mind. But they do now. I think you taught me that too. Because you always made me both at the same time."

She constantly disarms me.

I lift my head to respond, but a soft pounce on the bed makes us both turn. A low, whiskered face and yellow eyes stalk our way. Darcy was annoyed with me for stealing her away from her atelier earlier, but he followed us into her room with a raised tail and a cautious look at me.

Now he pads across her comforter without paying me any mind.

"Good morning," she says with the same loving voice she just used on me. "Want to join?"

"I'm not into threesomes," I mutter against her neck.

"What?"

"Nothing."

The cat flops down beside Nora's free hand and starts to purr. She's got one hand on me and another stroking down the cat's back. I recognize defeat when I see it and turn onto my back beside her.

"The fashion show," I ask. "Can I be there beside you?"

Her gaze slides to mine. "Do you want to be?"

"Of course I do. It's been in my calendar for weeks."

A smile spreads across her face. "Thank you."

I help Nora to the fashion show, carrying garment bags to the car. She's in a sleeveless black dress that fits her like a glove, with her hair up in a ponytail. Her expression is tight. It's no-nonsense, focused, ambitious.

I love it.

She's a force when she's in her element. There's no people-pleasing backstage at the venue, her hands capable and her voice smooth and in control. She helps models don the looks she's crafted and fixes a last-minute hem.

When a zipper catches, she turns to me. "You have strong hands. Can you help me?"

I take the skirt from her. "I'll fix it."

"Be careful," she warns me, and I can't resist a smile.

"You know I'm good with my hands."

She rolls her eyes. "Thanks."

"Anything for you, trouble."

When it's almost time, her models stand in a tight row backstage. Nora smiles at them all. It's an encouraging, kind, beautiful smile, and she shines amid all this busyness. She knows exactly what it's like to be in their shoes.

"Thank you," she tells them. "I appreciate each and every one of you. Have fun out there."

I move closer, lean against the wall behind her. There's a large black curtain that separates our area from the runway. The designers can't come outside; it's one of the few ironclad rules today.

Everything has to be anonymous.

The whispers are hushed, and silence settles over the room, and through the curtain, the presenter's voice comes muffled but audible.

Contestant number six! Applause rings out, and Nora gives

a nod to the first model, a redhead in an asymmetrical dress that falls to the floor. I'm no fashion expert, but even I can recognize Nora's skill.

One after another, the models walk out.

On the monitor, we can see what the audience sees. Her clothes on the models, walking in front of a fully packed audience and a row of judges. Nora leans against me. I wrap my arms around her waist, her back to my front, and feel the tension slowly bleed out of her.

"Oh my god," she says. "I did it."

"You did it."

"Look at that one," she says when the final model walks in a long flowing skirt and asymmetrical top. "I love the way that fabric looks. It was so hard to work with, though."

I kiss her hair. "You've done so well."

"Yes I have, haven't I?"

My arms tighten around her waist. "Are you praising yourself?"

She looks up. "Does that mean I've finally aced that lesson?"

"Yes. Straight A's across the board."

She laughs a little. "Thank you for being here."

"Nowhere else I'd be today, trouble."

Applause rains down outside the black curtain, and on the screen, we see the models start to make their way back up the long, curved catwalk and toward us. That's when Nora leans in suddenly. "Oh my god."

"What?"

She points at the small monitor, to someone sitting in the front row right beside the judges. The pixels obscure his identity, but we both know him well enough to make him out.

Rafe is in the audience.

He's going to cause a media stir. *The young Maison Valmont CEO is here, scoping out his latest acquisition…*

"I didn't know he was coming," I say.

"Me neither." Nora takes another deep breath and steps away from me to welcome the models back. I help where I can and get out of the way when it's needed. And soon, her things are back in the garment bags.

We end up in the designers' waiting area outside, and I hand Nora a bottle of water. "Drink." She looks at me for a second before obeying. "You've been on your feet for hours."

"I'm exhausted," she admits, "but I'm too keyed-up to relax."

"Of course you are."

"How are you so calm in all of this?"

I grin. "Because I have complete faith in you. Come here."

She walks into me like I'm a wall, arms at her sides, her face into my chest. I chuckle and hold her tight. "You're going to sleep for twelve straight hours after today."

"Twenty-four," she says, and finally reaches up to wrap her arms around my neck. "I did it."

"You did it."

Her eyes glow, and there are other people in this room, but I kiss her like none of them exist.

"Ugh," a voice says beside us. Annoying and annoyingly familiar. "I know I just came around to the idea of you two, but do I have to *see* it?"

I lift my head and give Rafe a stare. But I don't step away from Nora. "Too soon?"

"Too soon," he says.

Nora looks over at her brother. "Well," she says, "that's *too* bad."

And then she kisses me again.

I'm laughing when she finally steps back. Rafe has turned his back to us, arms crossed over his chest. He's rigid, but there's no anger in him. That much is clear.

It feels like a giant fucking relief.

"We're done now," Nora announces.

Rafe turns, his dark eyebrows pulled low. He got more of

their father. Darker hair, more olive skin. Still, the similarities are there. They have the same green eyes.

"You came today," she says.

He nods. *"Bon travail."*

"You don't know which one was mine."

"No. I don't. But I still know you did really well."

Nora lifts her chin. "Which one was your favorite?"

"Does it matter?"

"Yes, I think it does. I want your honest answer," she says. *"T'inquiète."*

I've heard them talk this way before. Their constant switching back and forth between their two mother tongues, and damn it, I'm going to have to do this for the rest of my life now. I studied Latin at Belmont when it should have been French.

"Number six," he says. "But I have been paying attention, you know. I recognize your work."

Nora's breath catches. "You have?"

"Of course I have." He runs a hand through his hair and glances at me. There's reluctant acceptance in that look. "I'm sorry I didn't make that clear to you. I'm sorry I didn't make you feel... like you could... be honest with me. Or like you had to be strong all the time."

Nora glances over her shoulder at me. Maybe I didn't mention all the accusations I hurled at Rafe in the library that night. Sometimes the truth hurts.

"I'm really proud of you," he says. Rafe's voice turns hoarse. "And *je suis vraiment désolé.*"

"For what?"

"Tout." He runs a hand through his hair. "Wilde wouldn't have targeted you if it wasn't for me. If I ever made you feel like you were a burden to me, or like you couldn't be scared..."

"It's okay," she says.

"No. It's really not."

Nora takes a step closer to her brother, her hand on his arm. Another volley of quick French is fired off, and I catch only hints. Rafe nods twice during her words, but his face is drawn tight.

"Yes," he says when she's done. "You're right."

"I know I am."

His lips tug. "You're more confident these days."

"I've worked on it," she says, and hugs him. He looks over her shoulder at me with an expression I can read all too well. A bit embarrassed, a bit grateful.

"Does this mean I've lost you to the other side of the Atlantic?" he asks her.

I'm not the one asked, but I nod regardless. *She's mine now.*

Rafe rolls his eyes.

Nora laughs and takes a step back out of her brother's arms. She says something again in rapid French, and his gaze softens. There's something about trust in that sentence, I think. Something about family too.

Behind them, the door to the waiting room opens. Someone with a headset and a clipboard calls out for our attention.

Nora and Rafe don't hear her.

I put a hand on their shoulders. "Hey. This heartwarming reunion will have to wait a bit."

The attendant clears his throat and tells us that the judges are done convening. There's a result.

Contestant number six should get ready to go out on stage.

GROUP CHAT

ALEX

You guys have made up now, right?

JAMES

Finally. Can we use the group chat again?

ALEX

James and I were just a few days away from flying over and knocking some sense into the both of you.

RAFE

It took me less than a week to get over it. I think that's very fair of me, all things considered. You'd both react the same way if it was your sister.

ALEX

Only child, lad. Same for the duke.

JAMES

...

Is West not responding because he's too busy?

ALEX

Busy doing what, I wonder?

RAFE

DO NOT CONTINUE THAT LINE OF CONVERSATION.

WEST

I was very busy, in fact. Returning a ring that wasn't quite right and getting my grandmother's resized.

RAFE

Will I be the best man?

ALEX

That's unfair. He can be the best man on the bride's side. This is my only shot!

RAFE

So you've given up on me or James getting married, then.

ALEX

We've all given up on James.

JAMES

Fair.

WEST

Fight it out amongst yourselves.

CHAPTER 62
WEST

I lean against the banister of the main staircase and wait for Nora to come down. Darcy's sprawled in a sunspot on the marble floor, tail flicking, yellow eyes locked on mine like he's trying to outstare me.

I don't blink.

Neither does he.

"Are you two having a staring contest?" Nora asks, coming down the stairs.

"No," I reply, still watching the cat. "We're reaching an understanding."

"You can't be competitive with a cat."

"Watch me." He hasn't been my biggest fan, and I don't blame him.

Nora is infinitely preferable.

But the other day, he spent an hour sleeping beside my desk while I worked, and that was progress.

Nora reaches me, and I immediately lose the staring contest. *Damn.* Her brown hair is loose around her face, now brushed with the sun and freckles from the first week of summer.

She's in a long-sleeved shirt and a skirt that's shorter than she usually wears, leaving her long legs on full display. Sunlight clings to her skin, hugs her.

"Hello, gorgeous."

She smiles. "Like it?"

"I like you." I look at the pendant resting around her neck —the one I gave her on one of our first dates.

A necklace. A bracelet. And I can't wait to give her a ring, too.

"You're so damn pretty."

"It's pretty short. This skirt." She tilts her head and smiles. "I have a surprise for you. A challenge, really."

She's enjoying this—teasing me, pushing me. God, I love that look on her face. "A challenge?"

"Yes. You once told me that if I did this again, there'd be consequences."

It takes me a second. "You're not."

"I am." She takes a step back, her eyes alight. "Ready to go?"

"Absolutely not." I bend and lift her up over my shoulder, a hand on her ass over the skirt. Nora shrieks, but it turns into a pealing, half-huffed breath of laughter that makes my stomach tighten.

I walk into the conservatory. She hangs off my shoulder, hands gripping my shirt.

"I'm going to check," I warn her.

There's a small room adjacent to the conservatory once used for planting. No windows and total privacy. I kick the door shut and set her down.

She grins. Her top is askew now, revealing a sliver of her taut stomach. "What's my punishment?"

"I have to investigate the crime first." I nod to the skirt. "Lift up for me, sweetheart."

Nora's hands grip the fabric obediently, and she pulls it up the smooth roundness of her thighs.

Up past her hips.

I groan. She's beautifully, painfully bare. No panties in sight. And fuck, her pussy is so perfect. "Look at you. All pink and pretty."

"I didn't want panty lines to ruin my outfit." She cocks her head. "No one would have known."

"A gust of wind, and they'd all see what's mine." My erection pushes against my zipper. I don't think it'll ever stop responding this way around her, ever stop wanting her. "Turn around. Hold on to the counter."

There's excitement in her eyes, and she turns, bunching the skirt at her waist and holding on to the table as instructed.

The globes of her ass are a lovely cream color. I run my hands over her skin and hear her faint exhale. "Remember how I told you I'd punish you if this happened again?"

"I do." She arches her back. "We spoke about getting a bit rough."

"Mhm. I told you I don't like pain. But I do like..." I smooth my hand over the curve of her ass. "Light spanking. Want to try that?"

She nods, and I brush my hand down between her legs to touch her. Her folds are soft, and delicate, and already a bit damp. "Talk to me, trouble."

"Yes. I do."

"And can I trust you to be a good girl and tell me if it gets to be too much?"

"Of course." She looks over her shoulder, and there's bright color on her cheeks. "Don't focus so much on my orgasm this time. I want you... I want..."

"Say it."

"I want to feel a bit used," she says, her voice half shy and half excited. "Like you just can't stop yourself."

I nod back toward the counter. "Hold on."

She does, breathing fast. It's all a game of exploration with her. Last week she showed up in bed one night, freshly showered with her hair in a braid, bringing a card game she'd bought.

Eighty positions for curious couples.

I laughed, and she looked affronted. *I want to try them all,* she said, and I laughed again and told her that I was always, *always* game, but that over half of those would require some serious stretching beforehand.

She's a delight, my little overachiever.

Curious and hungry, now that she's learning to express what she truly wants. Her true self is the greatest gift I've ever been given.

"You wanted this. Knowing I'd find out." I rub circles against her clit with quick, rough movements. "But you knew I wouldn't like it. So I won't let you come first."

She nods quickly, and her head bows. It's a change of pace. I always focus on her pleasure first. It's been the guiding principle, every single time we've had sex, that my face starts between her thighs.

But she wanted something different this time.

I pull my zipper down. I step closer and fit myself between her upper thighs. I nudge her legs tightly closed, locking me in against her warm pussy. "That's it," I tell her.

I smooth a hand over her right cheek, and then I lift my hand and spank her.

She gasps.

I pull my hips back and thrust against her, between her thighs. "That's it. Stay still for me."

I do it again. I'm not slapping her hard, but it jiggles the fullness of her ass and sends lovely color blooming over her skin.

And against my cock, I feel her growing wetter.

"I'm going to check every time now," I say, and thrust between her thighs again. "Before you leave the house, I'm going to have to bring you in here and have you pull up your dress to show me."

She nods and gasps when I spank her left cheek. We've had sex more than a dozen times by now. I've been inside her side by side, holding her into the cradle of my body, early one morning while she whispered that she loved me. She's ridden me again, brave and beautiful above me, and I've made her shatter beneath me.

But we've never fucked from behind like this. Not standing up.

She's wet against my cock, and I finally notch myself at her hot entrance. I grip her hip with my other hand and push in an inch.

"This is what'll happen, sweetheart, if you do this again." I hold her still and slide in slowly to the hilt. Groan out a low-pitched *fuck*. "You're too damn pretty to walk around bare. I'll fuck you if you do."

She looks over her shoulder, and she's glorious. "Is that meant to deter me?"

Her heat makes it hard to think. It's always been that way, from the very first time, being inside her. It strips me down to the basest instincts.

I spank her again. Buried inside her, I can feel the faint vibrations, and control spins out of my grasp. Holding her hips for leverage, I start thrusting.

The ring I have for her, my grandmother's, lies in the pocket of my pants. I'm going to give it to her later this evening, at dinner.

Ask her for real.

She's mine.

With every stroke inside her, I tell her how good she is, how perfect she feels, how well she's taking it. Her muscles flutter around me. She's never come from penetration alone, but she's close.

Her phone rings.

It echoes from somewhere around her waist, where her skirt is bunched up. From a pocket?

I pause, hands on the handholds of her hips. She fumbles with the folded fabric. I lean forward, still buried deep inside, and look over her shoulder.

We both see the name flashing over the screen.

It's her modeling agent.

Nora blows out a breath. Her thumb moves to end the call.

"Don't," I say. "Answer her."

She pauses. "What?"

"Tell her you're done modeling. For good." Nora spoke to Rafe about it a few days ago, when he was still in New York. She's gearing up to tell her mother.

This is a good start.

"I can't. We're... you're..."

"You can do anything."

She laughs, quick and breathless, and lifts the phone to her ear. "Hello?"

Every muscle in my body aches to keep moving. I grit my teeth and stay still. She's so hot and tight around me.

"Next month? I'm not sure..." Nora says. I roll my hips, and her breath catches. "No, I am sure. I'm not available."

There's a beat of silence when her agent responds, and I use the time to reach around her body to find her clit. I press down in hard circles.

She reaches up, braces her free hand against the wall. "No, I'm done with modeling. I'm not available. Ever."

I don't stop touching her. Buried this deep, I can feel every tremor of her muscles. "I'm changing careers... yes, exactly. Yes. I've spoken about it with Valmont. Thank you... oh!... yes. Thank you."

I kiss her warm neck. She's doing so well.

"You too. Bye." She clicks off the phone and immediately gasps. "Shit. West..."

"That's my girl. How did that feel?"

"Good. Great. Don't stop." She's breathing hard, and I don't stop. I start moving my hips instead, fucking her slowly while I touch her. It doesn't take long. She was on the edge before, and now her orgasm barrels through her.

She braces her hands on the counter and moans my name. Lightning strikes down my spine, and I come with a groan, one hand on her pulsing clit and the other holding her hip tight.

Afterward I hold her tight, still locked inside her, and tell her how proud I am of her. I run my hands over her body, soothing, loving. Smooth the globes of her ass. When I pull out of her, we both realize that the whole no-panties thing has another downside.

I watch the mark I've left between her legs while I dig into the pocket of my pants for a tissue. I sent her the paperwork for my clean bill of health the day after we had sex for the first time.

"I'm never going to tire of that," I tell her, and bend to gently wipe at her swollen pussy. "Never knew it was my thing, but with you, sweetheart…"

She runs a hand over my hair. "You like coming inside me?"

At her saying those words… "Like it? No. That's too small a word." I kiss her thigh and reluctantly pull her skirt back down. "I adore it. I love it almost as much as I love you. I want to—"

The sound of the doorbell rings out. It's loud enough to echo through the bottom floor, connected to the front door of Fairhaven. Few people use it. Most people who move around the house have keys.

"What's that?"

Ernest will handle the delivery. It was meant to arrive while we were out, a surprise for when we got back. But now that it's here, and we're already delayed…

"Come. Let's go see."

There's a large box in the hallway of Fairhaven. Nora releases my hand and approaches it cautiously. "What is it?"

"Open it," I tell her.

She looks at me with a small smile. Her hair is wild now, and there's beautiful color in her cheeks. "You're making me nervous." But she opens the box and reaches inside.

Then she pauses.

"*No.*"

"Yes."

"You bid on it?"

"I did," I say. "Your evening was ruined. But I still wanted you to have it."

She lifts up the green dress she so admired at the Fashion Institute. It's wrapped in protective plastic. "Oh my god. This must have cost a fortune."

"It's a good thing I have one, then."

A smile spreads across Nora's face. "I can't believe this. This... West... I..."

"The upstairs atelier? That's your workspace now. Permanently." I shove my hands into my pockets and feel the velvet box. The ring I bought while drowning in guilt wasn't right. This one is. "If you need more space, I have enough rooms. Have more. Have all of them."

She clutches the dress to her chest. There's something glittering in her eyes. Is she...?

I take a step closer. "Nora?"

She swallows hard. "I don't know what to say."

"In a good way?"

She nods and carefully folds the dress back into the box it came in. And maybe this is the moment. Here, at home.

"I was going to do this later. At dinner. But you know I don't like big public spectacles." I go down on a knee in front of her and hold up the velvet box.

I open the lid.

Nora's green eyes widen, and I never thought I'd do this. Would never have done this if it wasn't her. "West," she breathes.

"Will you marry me, trouble?"

She blinks quickly, and a tear slips down her cheek. "Yes. Please."

"*Please*," I say, and reach for her left hand. My grandmother's diamond slides on perfectly. I had it resized, measured her finger while she slept in my arms. "I'm the one who should say please."

She shakes her head. "No. I love you. I think… I want…"

Her words die off, and I get up to pull her close. "What do you want, trouble? Tell me, and I'll give it to you. Whatever it is."

A laugh escapes her. She kisses me, her mouth still in a smile. "Oh, West. I think I've gotten everything I want now."

"That's what you were going to say?"

"Yes." She kisses me again, pushes up and against me. "You don't have to give me anything else. You've already given me everything."

EPILOGUE
NORA

The best part about getting married at your own house is not having to go anywhere afterward. Most of the guests have left, sleeping up in Fairhaven's guest rooms or over in a nearby hotel.

Only our closest friends are still here. Sitting on the terrace with us, surrounded by the remnants of the party.

Of our wedding party.

Ernest and I chose some of the late-blooming August roses from the garden for my bouquet. The August heat was tempered by cool winds from the ocean, and down by the water's edge, West and I said our vows.

It wasn't a giant wedding.

It wasn't a small one either.

It was the perfect size. Our friends and family, both biological and chosen. A wonderful band and caterers that were, like West's mother assured me, truly the best.

My mother and West's were seated near each other for the dinner. Over the past months, they've found a tentative kind of friendship; one is tightly controlled, and one is not controlled at all. But they both enjoy the finer things in life and meddling in their children's lives, and maybe that's something to bond over.

The day is over, and the new one hasn't quite begun yet. West's beside me on the sectional, the bow tie of his tux undone. He has an arm around me and a lazy smile on his lips.

My husband.

And somehow, he has a plate with his second serving of wedding cake. I have no idea where he found the space. Or the cake.

Across from us are the few brave souls still awake. Amber and Rafe. Alex and James. There's a half-empty bottle of champagne on the table, and Amber's slipped out of her heels. She hides a yawn with her hand.

It's been a long day. A long week.

"Nora, tell the others," Alex says, "what you did."

He won the spot for best man. James did too, and Rafe. They all stood up there as groomsmen, with West insisting that he had no favorites.

"You're going to have to be more specific," I say, and reach over to take West's fork out of his hand. He watches with a smile while I take a bite out of this cake.

"West hates when you eat off his plate," Alex says.

"I do hate it," West says, and takes back the fork I hand him, "when it's anyone but my wife."

I smile at the word, and he smiles at me.

Rafe reaches for the bottle of champagne. "You two…"

"It's their wedding day. Well. Night," Amber says. "They're allowed to be sappy."

"I don't know what it says, that you're choosing to spend that night with us, by the way," James says.

West ignores them all. He polishes off the final piece of cake and then reaches for my legs, pulling them up and onto his lap.

His left hand rests on my thigh. Gold wedding band on his ring finger.

"Tell them," he says, and there's pride in his voice. "What you did."

I smile at our friends. "I sent Ben Wilde an invitation to the wedding."

There's a variety of shocked gasps around the circle. I wanted him to know that I knew. Even if I never confronted him.

Rafe leans forward. "You did what?"

"Brilliant, wasn't it?" West asks.

"He'd never show up. But I wanted him to feel…" I shrug a little. "Awful."

Amber laughs. "You're ice cold. I love it."

"I want him to know that I know."

"Kill him with kindness," West says. There's pride in his eyes. At first, when I sat down weeks ago, and in a beautiful, slanting calligraphy, wrote an invite to a man I don't like, he thought I was out of my mind. "You're better than me."

"While I hate Ben Wilde," Alex says, and gestures over at me and West on the couch opposite him, "he's sort of responsible for this happening."

Rafe groans. "No. We're not thanking that bastard for a single thing."

"That's not what I'm saying, and you've had too much to drink." Alex reaches over and grabs the bottle. "Leave some for me."

"You've all had too much." James is sitting on the far left, and there's a cigar in his left hand. He nods over at Alex. "Billiards?"

"Thought you'd never ask." He stands and stretches with a groan. "We have to get some kind of competition in before Nora over here sends us on a silent meditation retreat for the next Lost Weekend."

I pretend to shush him. "That was a secret!"

My brother groans. "Don't do that to me. Please."

"Please do, Nora," James says. He leaves his cigar to die on the tray and pulls Alex into the house. Amber rises with a yawn and joins them inside.

West smooths a hand over my ankle. His fingers are warm, finding the skin beneath the hem of my white dress.

"You're not playing?" he asks Rafe. The two of them have settled into a new kind of friendship over the past few months. It took him a while, my brother, to fully accept this new reality.

Me speaking out. West dating me.

The two of us... getting married.

"No. I should go to bed," he says. "But I'm not sure what kind of reception I'll get." Rafe is sprawled out, his head against the headrest. His dark hair is mussed, and like West, he's long since undone his bow tie.

He's turning something over on his own ring finger.

Because West and I aren't the only ones who got married this summer.

GROUP CHAT

FROM EARLIER THAT SUMMER

WEST

Update us, Rafe

ALEX

Yeah, it's been a few days. How hostile is your takeover?

RAFE

Hostile. Mather & Wilde hate it.

WEST

Good.

Is it yours yet?

RAFE

Almost. There was a snag, but I'm handling it.

JAMES

Pay them more.

RAFE

I've tried. This is personal for them, and money didn't sway them. It's fine. I'll get to destroy Ben Wilde's legacy soon enough.

JAMES

Salt the earth. I approve.

ALEX

What's the snag?

RAFE

The Wildes are cornered and they know it

I'll marry Ben's niece to get the last of the shares, and then the brand is mine.

JAMES

Fuck

WEST

Relationships aren't that bad, you know

ALEX

Is she pretty?

WEST

Of course that's what draws you into this conversation.

RAFE

Haven't met her yet. But it doesn't matter if she's the prettiest woman on earth. She's a Wilde.

JAMES

She'll hate you, as soon as you start driving that brand into the ground

RAFE

Let her. The feeling's mutual.

THE SERIES CONTINUES

The Billionaire Games continues with Rafe's book. He's a man on a mission… but unfortunately for him, so is his new wife.

One villa. One summer. One marriage built on hate.

Coming fall of 2025

DELETED SCENE

WEST

This is a deleted spicy scene from The Faking Game…

I wake up to movement beside me, and to Nora turning in the bed. "No," she mutters. The voice is half-muffled. "West…"

The sheet is half twisted around her nude body, the long lines of her limbs curved. The hint of a hard, pebbled nipple through her camisole.

She looks like she's in pain.

"Nora." I reach for her, and find her skin almost feverish to the touch. "Sweetheart, you're dreaming."

Her eyes rove beneath her closed eyelids. Long lashes dance over the tops of her cheeks. "West," she murmurs again.

I pull her tight against me. "Wake up."

She stiffens in my arms for a second before softening into my grip. Her eyes blink open.

I brush her hair back. "You were dreaming."

"A dream." Her hands tighten around the edge of the comforter. "Yes… I dreamt that we were actually…"

"You dreamt about us?"

"Yes." She closes her eyes and takes a shuddering breath. "You were inside me."

My hand stops on her shoulder. "You dreamed we were having sex." It's not a question. It's a statement, my voice hoarse.

She curves inward in my arms, like she wants to get closer. "I've never felt like this before," she says. "I've never burned like this. I didn't know that I could want like this."

"What did you dream about, sweet girl?"

"I dreamt... that you were on top of me. And we were getting closer, and I tried to make myself come, but I couldn't." She takes a deep breath, and the fingers clutching the fabric soften. "I didn't finish. You didn't either."

"Were you close?" I brush my lips over her temple, and find her skin just as hot there.

"Yes. I'm still close." She buries her face against my neck. "I want..."

"Tell me." I push away the thin covers to fit her more firmly into my arms. There's a coiled energy in her, one I've rarely experienced before.

She's here because she wants safety. Because she doesn't want to sleep alone.

But I still grip her thigh and pull her leg up over my hip. Nora sighs, her hips rolling against my leg. "I want you."

"We can't have sex," I tell her.

"I want to try." Her voice is stronger now, her heat pressing against my thigh and fuck, but she's scorching. Wet through her thong. "I want to know what it would feel like. With you. Even if we can't."

I close my eyes, and my hands on her lithe body tighten. She's too sweet when I hold her like this. When she begs like this. I have a very thin control over my sanity, on remembering why I can't, why we can't.

"Come here," I tell her, and pull her on top of me. I spread her thighs a little so she can straddle me comfortably and pull away the last of the sheet that covered us. "There. Stay right there."

Her palms land flat on my chest, her dark hair falling forward. "West?"

She's sitting right on my cock. I'm half-hard, growing more by the second. "We've never been in this position before."

I grip her bare hips. They're the perfect handhold, her skin criminally soft under my fingers. "Want to know what it would feel like?" I press her down, her hotness against my erection. It sends a flash of heat through me. "Grind on me, trouble, and find out."

She takes a shuddering breath and rolls her hips. She takes three tries before she lets out a low moan. "Oh," she says. "Oh…"

She's using me to gain friction against her clit with every shift of her hips. It's enough to set my teeth on edge. It's terrible. It's incredible. It's torture, and I never want to end.

Her pussy is so fucking close.

Only a thin piece of cotton fabric separates us.

She dreamt of me. Of us.

Of me being inside of her.

It's enough to make my vision darken at the corners, and my fingers tighten on her hips.

She sets an undulating rhythm. "Does that feel good?" I ask.

"Yes." Nora's hands are hot against my chest, her breath still coming fast. "I'm close."

"That's my girl, using me to make yourself come," I tell her. "You're riding me so good. Do you know how fucking pretty you are right now?"

She shudders again, and her eyes flit closed. "I can't handle it when you say those things," she murmurs. Her thighs clench around my hips. "But don't stop."

"So pretty. So perfect," I tell her. "And so soaked. You're

so good for me, getting so soaked every time we play like this."

"I can't help it," she admits, like it's a sin.

A confession.

"You shouldn't."

Her hips speed up, and so does her breathing, growing labored in the dim bedroom. Her waist moves with hypnotizing swells. The fabric is shimmery, and my hands slide it up, thumbs brushing over her ribs. "I want…"

"Tell me," I insist, and buck my hips up to get more of the friction.

I think I might die from it, the heat, the soaked fabric, the way my cock is trapped against her.

"I want you on top of me," she says. Her tits bounce with every roll of her hips, her nipples poking against the fabric. "I want to know what it's like."

I grit my teeth. It takes everything to hold back, to hear her ask and not give it to her, and I don't have everything anymore. She's chipped away at all of it. My control. My loyalties. My sanity. And when she says it like that, looks at me like that…

There's nothing I love more than Nora asking for what she wants.

I sit up and grip her waist. "Hold on to me."

Her arms lock around my neck, and I turn us over on the bed, fitting myself against her body. Her skin is so damn soft it should be a crime. She opens for me so beautifully.

It's like coming home.

I push my hips more firmly against hers. "That's it, sweetheart. Spread your thighs wider for me." I reach down and help push them up, notch them at my hips.

"I like this." She lifts her head up to kiss me again. Her lips are warm and hot. I grind against her, and she gasps into my mouth. "Oh. Oh."

I do it again, and then another time, listening to her

gasping breaths every time I brush against her clit. "That's how it would be like."

Her hands slide up to my neck. "Do that again. Please."

I reach down between us. "Let me make it better, sweetheart." Her thong is soaked. I tug it to the side, and slick my cock against her heat. "I'm not pushing inside," I tell her, my left arm trembling from the pressure.

I lose years of my life, not entering her then and there. Instead I make sure I'm coated, and press my length against her slit. I pull my hips back slowly, and when I push forward again, the fit works perfectly.

My cock slides between her lips and nudges at her clit.

Nora gasps. "Again," she says. "Do that again."

I thrust against her, and the release of pressure from that alone is immense. To not have to hold my hips back. I groan at the heat of her, the softness of her, and lower my forehead against hers. "Feel that?"

Her hands turn into claws on my shoulders. "Yes."

"That's how it would feel," I murmur, continuing to thrust against her. "If your dream was real."

Her knees tighten around my hips, and she kisses my neck. My shoulder. Anywhere she can reach, with a striving arch like she can fuse us even closer. "Don't stop."

I quicken the pace. The urge to reach down, to fit myself to her, to push inside, is almost unbearable. It claws at the base of my spine.

My lips brush her temple. This is about her, and her experiences. She had told me she wanted to practice. "You're so wet for me," I tell her. "That's why this works, pretty girl." Her breathing is quick in my ear, and with every slow thrust of my hips, with every brush over her clit, it catches. "You don't have to be quiet now. There's no one to hear us."

She smiles against my cheek. "Thank God."

I grind my hips closer to hers, tighten the space my cock has to move. It increases the pressure on us both. On my next thrust, she moans against my shoulder. "West," she says. "Oh my God. I think… I think…"

"I've got you." I keep up the rhythm, my own spine pounding with impending release. For weeks I've dreamed of this. Thought of it when I jerked off in the shower and at night bed. Nora beneath me, her body gripping me tight. "Fuck, I want you so much."

Her heavy breathing is a symphony. "I want you to come too," she says on a broken exhale.

"I will, sweetheart. I always will with you." My hips speed up, pushing against her. She's slick and warm and *so close.* I grind down against her clit and watch her expression. The fluttering of her dark eyelashes, the brown hair sticking to her temple. The parted, rosy lips.

It feels sacred to make her feel this good. To be the first one who ever has.

"I'm close." She arches, her nipples brushing against my chest. "Oh my god, West…"

My name on her lips undoes me. Rearranges the universe, and it's a foregone conclusion now, that one day I'll be inside her. I'll give anything to have this happen again. To make her shiver and moan like this over and over again.

I'd sign over the fucking estate to get to keep her.

Her fingers turn into claws on my shoulders, nails digging in like I once told her I liked, and the knees that have opened wide to let me between them tighten at my hips.

I keep moving through her orgasm and watch as it takes her. I tell her how pretty she is and how good she's doing and then it's all over for me, too.

Fire rips through me. I shudder against her, hips stuttering, and spill all over her stomach and her pretty camisole with a loud groan. The world disappears and my head goes blank.

There's only her and this and the consuming heat that tears me apart,

Afterwards, she's breathing as hard as me. It takes me longer than it should to realize I'm crushing her.

I lift my head from the crook of neck.

She looks beautifully, disastrously wrecked.

"Hey," she whispers, and the smile on her lips makes the room brighter. I smile back before I see the silvery tears seeping out the corners of her eyes.

I shift my weight onto one arm and brush them away. "Hey. You okay?"

"Yes." She blinks a few times, and the smile stays on. It's a genuine one. "I don't know why I'm... I was... that was intense."

"It was for me, too." I bend down and kiss at the salt. "It's okay to cry, sweetheart."

"They're good tears."

"I know." I kiss over the bridge of her nose, over to her other eye. Over her damp skin and her softness. "You did so well."

"I wanted you so much." There's wonder in her voice, and pride, too. "I doubted, for so long... that this would ever happen to me. I thought there was something wrong with me. Like I couldn't feel the *desire* my friends did."

"There's not a single thing wrong with you." I kiss the edge of her swollen lips. "My perfect girl. You were just afraid before."

She nods. "Yes. It drowned everything out." Her legs relax around me, slide down to hook behind my knees. She's warm beneath me. And sticky. Our bodies are stuck together.

I sit back on my knees and study the devastation before me. Her lips are rosy, her face tear-streaked and happy, her left nipple ruby-red where it peeks up above the lace of her camisole. My come is all over her stomach. Between her splayed thighs she's swollen and beautifully, stunningly pink.

Pretty as a fucking painting.

"Stay right here," I murmur. "Can you do that for me? Don't move."

"Yes," she says, smile widening, like she can see just how much she affects me.

I leave her only long enough to wet a towel with some warm water. She watches while I clean her up, her cheeks as rosy as the rest of her. "Is this normal, too?"

"Is what normal, trouble?" There's a dark, depraved part of me that wants to keep her like this. Sticky and covered in me. But I gently wipe over her skin, and only when she's free of me do I use the towel on my own chest.

"What you're doing now."

"Cleaning you up?" I toss the towel away and turn her on her side, so I can tuck her into the curve of my body. "It was my mess."

"It was nice." She takes my hand and guides it up to her breast, and I can *feel* her contended sigh. The coiled energy, the striving, the brazenness she'd awoken with is gone. The fire sated. "Thank you."

"Nora, remember how I told you that you never have to apologize to me?"

"Mhm. I remember."

"Well, you never have to thank me, either."

ACKNOWLEDGEMENTS

The word acknowledgements has the word *know* in it, which feels ironic, because I know very few things for certain. And the more books I set out to write, the more I discover I have left to learn.

But I am sure of three major things.

That West and Nora were always meant to be part of my own journey.

That I keep putting poker in my books despite not knowing how to play it. I've finally decided to rectify this, and I've ordered a set of poker chips. Step one accomplished (let's see if I actually learn how to use them).

And thirdly, I know that books aren't created in a vacuum.

That's never been more true than with this book. West and Nora went through a lot before they ended up here, in their own happily-ever-after.

There are so many brilliant, kind, smart and VERY patient people who've had to listen to me ramble about this book for more months than I want to think about.

Nora mentions her therapist in this book a few times (because therapy is incredible). I have to say thank you to my own therapist, who has taught me many useful things, including a tool that made its way into this book.

Thank you to Becca Syme and Becca Mysoor for author coaching and story coaching, respectively. Thank you to my author friends who have listened and advised and helped when this book challenged me. You make this job infinitely more fun.

Thank you to the amazing dev editors who helped me make sense of Nora and West's tangled web. Andie, Jen and Heidi; thank you for letting me borrow your brain.

The alpha readers: Sarah and Catherine. This book is so much stronger because of you. Thank you!

The beta readers: Nikki, Conner, Emily, Laura, Valentina and Sarah, who helped me refine the story further. I am beyond grateful for taking up your time.

Thank you Beth, for doing a fantastic job copy-editing this book and making it flow. You're fantastic.

Chloe Quinn drew West and Nora on the cover, and I couldn't be more grateful for the opportunity to work with her. She captured the characters and Fairhaven perfectly!

Nora's story is the culmination of work I've spent years on; long before I started writing her story, and long before I became a writer. Bringing her struggles and concerns to the page and creating a dream hero to match her nuanced personality has been one of the best experiences of my writing career. And one of the hardest.

If you connected with Nora, even in a tiny way, I'll consider that a great honor. Speaking your piece and staying true to you, even in the face of others displeasure, is hard. It's terrifying.

And it can be incredibly rewarding.

BOOKS BY OLIVIA

The Billionaire Games

The Faking Game
West and Nora

Rafe's Book
Coming in 2025

Book Three
Coming in 2026

Book Four
Coming in 2026

The Connovan Chronicles

Best Enemies Forever
Gabriel and Connie

The Perfect Mistake
Alec and Isabel

BOOKS BY OLIVIA

One Wrong Move
Nate and Harper

The New York Billionaire Series

Think Outside the Boss
Tristan and Freddie

Saved by the Boss
Anthony and Summer

Say Yes to the Boss
Victor and Cecilia

A Ticking Time Boss
Carter and Audrey

Suite on the Boss
Isaac and Sophia

12 Days of Bossmas
Christmas anthology

The Seattle Billionaire Series

Billion Dollar Enemy
Cole and Skye

Billion Dollar Beast
Nick and Blair

Billion Dollar Catch
Ethan and Bella

Billion Dollar Fiancé

BOOKS BY OLIVIA

Liam and Maddie

Brothers of Paradise Series

Dark Eyed Devil
Lily and Hayden

Ice Cold Boss
Faye and Henry

Red Hot Rebel
Ivy and Rhys

Small Town Hero
Jamie and Parker

Standalones

Between the Lines
Aiden and Charlotte

How to Honeymoon Alone
Phillip and Eden

Arrogant Boss
Julian and Emily

Look But Don't Touch
Grant and Ada

The Billionaire Scrooge Next Door
Adam and Holly

ABOUT OLIVIA

Olivia is a hopeless romantic who loves billionaires heroes, despite never having met one. So she took matters into her own hands and creates them on the page instead. Stern, charming, cold or brooding, so far she's never met a (fictional) billionaire she didn't like.

She picked up the pen in 2019, and she hasn't put it down since. With over two million books sold, Olivia writes fast-paced, swoon-worthy stories filled with banter and spice. Join the heroes as they meet, clash with, or stumble into the ambitious heroines that make them fall, and fall hard.

Join her newsletter for updates and bonus content.
www.oliviahayle.com.
Connect with Olivia

facebook.com/authoroliviahayle

instagram.com/oliviahayle

goodreads.com/oliviahayle

amazon.com/author/oliviahayle

bookbub.com/profile/olivia-hayle